The MX Book
of
New Sherlock Holmes Stories

Part XVI:
Whatever Remains . . .
Must Be the Truth
(1881-1890)

THE MX BOOK OF NEW
SHERLOCK HOLMES
STORIES

PART XVI
WHATEVER REMAINS . . .
MUST BE THE TRUTH
(1881-1890)

SOUTHAMPTON
STREET

359

EDITED
By
David
Marcum

OFFICES

TRADITIONAL HOLMES
ADVENTURES
COMPILED FOR THE
BENEFIT OF THE
RESTORATION OF
UNDERSHAW

First edition published in 2019
© Copyright 2019

ISBN Hardback 978-1-78705-502-5
ISBN Paperback 978-1-78705-503-2
AUK ePub ISBN 978-1-78705-504-9
AUK PDF ISBN 978-1-78705-505-6

Published in the UK by
MX Publishing
335 Princess Park Manor, Royal Drive,
London, N11 3GX
www.mxpublishing.co.uk

David Marcum can be reached at:
thepapersofsherlockholmes@gmail.com

Cover design by Brian Belanger
www.belangerbooks.com and *www.redbubble.com/people/zhahadun*

CONTENTS

Foreateds

Adventures

(Continued on the next page . . . .)

The following can be found in the companion volumes
The MX Book of New Sherlock Holmes Stories
Whatever Remains . . . Must Be the Truth

Part XVII – (1891-1898)

and
Part XVIII – (1899-1925)

(Continued on the next page . . . .)

**These additional Sherlock Holmes adventures
can be found in the previous volumes of**
The MX Book of New Sherlock Holmes Stories

(Continued on the next page . . . .)

PART III: 1896-1929

PART IV – 2016 Annual

(Continued on the next page . . . .)

PART V – Christmas Adventures

(Continued on the next page . . . .)

PART VI – 2017 Annual

(Continued on the next page . . . .)

(Continued on the next page . . . .)

Part IX – 2018 Annual (1879-1895)

(Continued on the next page . . . .)

Part X – 2018 Annual (1896-1916)

Part XI: Some Untold Cases (1880-1891)

(Continued on the next page . . . .)

The Adventure of the Silver Skull – Hugh Ashton
The Pimlico Poisoner – Matthew Simmonds
The Grosvenor Square Furniture Van – David Ruffle
The Adventure of the Paradol Chamber – Paul W. Nash
The Bishopgate Jewel Case – Mike Hogan
The Singular Tragedy of the Atkinson Brothers of Trincomalee – Craig Stephen Copland
Colonel Warburton's Madness – Gayle Lange Puhl
The Adventure at Bellingbeck Park – Deanna Baran
The Giant Rat of Sumatra – Leslie Charteris and Denis Green
        Introduction by Ian Dickerson
The Vatican Cameos – Kevin P. Thornton
The Case of the Gila Monster – Stephen Herczeg
The Bogus Laundry Affair – Robert Perret
Inspector Lestrade and the Molesey Mystery – M.A. Wilson and Richard Dean Starr

Part XII: Some Untold Cases (1894-1902)

Foreword – Lyndsay Faye
Foreword – Roger Johnson
Foreword – Melissa Grigsby
Foreword – Steve Emecz
Foreword – David Marcum
It's Always Time (*A Poem*) – "Anon."
The Shanghaied Surgeon – C.H. Dye
The Trusted Advisor – David Marcum
A Shame Harder Than Death – Thomas Fortenberry
The Adventure of the Smith-Mortimer Succession – Daniel D. Victor
A Repulsive Story and a Terrible Death – Nik Morton
The Adventure of the Dishonourable Discharge – Craig Janacek
The Adventure of the Admirable Patriot – S. Subramanian
The Abernetty Transactions – Jim French
Dr. Agar and the Dinosaur – Robert Stapleton
The Giant Rat of Sumatra – Nick Cardillo
The Adventure of the Black Plague – Paul D. Gilbert
Vigor, the Hammersmith Wonder – Mike Hogan
A Correspondence Concerning Mr. James Phillimore – Derrick Belanger
The Curious Case of the Two Coptic Patriarchs – John Linwood Grant
The Conk-Singleton Forgery Case – Mark Mower
Another Case of Identity – Jane Rubino
The Adventure of the Exalted Victim – Arthur Hall

PART XIII: 2019 Annual (1881-1890)

Foreword – Will Thomas
Foreword – Roger Johnson
Foreword – Melissa Grigsby
Foreword – Steve Emecz
Foreword – David Marcum
Inscrutable (*A Poem*) – Jacquelynn Morris

(Continued on the next page . . . .)

The Folly of Age – Derrick Belanger
The Fashionably-Dressed Girl – Mark Mower
The Odour of Neroli – Brenda Seabrook
The Coffee House Girl – David Marcum
The Mystery of the Green Room – Robert Stapleton
The Case of the Enthusiastic Amateur – S.F. Bennett
The Adventure of the Missing Cousin – Edwin A. Enstrom
The Roses of Highclough House – M.J.H. Simmonds
The Shackled Man – Andrew Bryant
The Yellow Star of Cairo – Tim Gambrell
The Adventure of the Winterhall Monster – Tracy Revels
The Grosvenor Square Furniture Van – Hugh Ashton
The Voyage of *Albion's Thistle* – Sean M. Wright
Bootless in Chippenham – Marino C. Alvarez
The Clerkenwell Shadow – Paul Hiscock
The Adventure of the Worried Banker – Arthur Hall
The Recovery of the Ashes – Kevin P. Thornton
The Mystery of the Patient Fisherman – Jim French
Sherlock Holmes in Bedlam – David Friend
The Adventure of the Ambulatory Cadaver – Shane Simmons
The Dutch Impostors – Peter Coe Verbica
The Missing Adam Tiler – Mark Wardecker

PART XIV: 2019 Annual (1891 -1897)

Foreword – Will Thomas
Foreword – Roger Johnson
Foreword – Melissa Grigsby
Foreword – Steve Emecz
Foreword – David Marcum
Skein of Tales (*A Poem*) – Jacquelynn Morris
The Adventure of the Royal Albert Hall – Charles Veley and Anna Elliott
The Tower of Fear – Mark Sohn
The Carroun Document – David Marcum
The Threadneedle Street Murder – S. Subramanian
The Collegiate Leprechaun – Roger Riccard
A Malversation of Mummies – Marcia Wilson
The Adventure of the Silent Witness – Tracy J. Revels
The Second Whitechapel Murderer – Arthur Hall
The Adventure of the Jeweled Falcon – GC Rosenquist
The Adventure of the Crossbow – Edwin A. Enstrom
The Adventure of the Delusional Wife – Jayantika Ganguly
Child's Play – C.H. Dye
The Lancelot Connection – Matthew Booth
The Adventure of the Modern Guy Fawkes – Stephen Herczeg
Mr. Clever, Baker Street – Geri Schear
The Adventure of the Scarlet Rosebud – Liz Hedgecock

(Continued on the next page . . . .)

PART XV: 2019 Annual (1898-1917)

The following contributions appear in the companion volumes:
The MX Book of New Sherlock Holmes Stories
Whatever Remains . . . Must Be the Truth
Part XVII – (1891-1898)
Part XVIII – (1899-1925)

Editor's Introduction:
"Whatever Remains . . . ."
by David Marcum

People like mysteries. We read books about them. We watch films and television shows about them. We look for them in real life. The daily unfolding of the news – *What's the real story? What is the truth behind these events that I'm following? What will happen next? What will tomorrow bring?* – is just another form of mystery.

Some people claim that they don't like mystery stories, instead preferring other genres. But consider for instance how often a mystery figures in a science-fiction story. I've been a *Star Trek* fan since I was two or three years old in the late 1960's and saw an Original Series episode on television, and I can say for sure that many – if not most – *Star Trek* television episodes or films have strong elements of mystery somewhere within the story, and in most cases the characters serve as detectives, leading us from the unknown puzzle at the beginning of the story to the solution at the end, working step-by-step and clue-by-clue to find out what happened, or to identify a hidden villain. *Is that harmless old actor really Kodos the Executioner? How exactly does Edith Keeler die? Why does God need a starship?*

To extend the Sci-Fi theme a bit: I don't like *Star Wars*, although I guess that one way or another I've seen just about all of it, so I'm certainly aware of the mysterious elements throughout the story. *What did the hints imply about Luke's father, before the answer was provided? What exactly was the emperor up to before all was revealed? Who are Rey's parents?* It's all a mystery, cloaked in space battles and pseudo-religion Force-chatter and light-sabre fights. In *Dune*, which I do like, mysteries abound as the story unfolds, with questions that must be answered, followed by more questions. These stories may not be a typical "mystery story" – a murder or a jewel theft, with a ratiocinating detective or a lonely private eye making his way down the mean streets, but they are mysteries none-the-less.

Look at other genres: Romance books and films? Who is the tall dark stranger, and how can his background be discovered by the heroine, layer-by-layer, using detective-like methods? The Dirk Pitt books by Clive Cussler, along with books about Pitt's associates "co-authored" by others, are most definitely mysteries, although clothed in incredible world-shaking plots. (I've lost track of the Sherlockian references that

1

continually pop up in the adventures of Pitt and his friends.) The original James Bond books, before Bond became so currently complicated and far from his origins, were each labelled as *A James Bond Mystery*. Stephen King, known for his supernaturally-tinged masterpieces, writes stories that are full of mysteries, and sometimes with actual detectives, showing just how much influence that the early mystery writers like John D. MacDonald had on him. Television shows like *Lost* or *Dallas* or *How I Met Your Mother* respectively asked questions like *What is the Island?* or *Who shot J.R.?* or *Who is the mother?* None of these were specifically mysteries, and they are draped in all sorts of other trappings – time-shifting castaways, oil-baron shenanigans, or a typical sit-com group's antics – but the plot points that drive the shows are no different than what would be found in a mystery story. It's the same for stories that are nominally for kids like *Gravity Falls* or *A Series of Unfortunate Events* ask *What's Grunkle Stan's story?* and *What's up with that ankle tattoo and the VFD?*

And liking mysteries is just a step away from pondering greater unknowns. It's a human trait, as shown in cultures around the world. No matter what place, and no matter what era, we find stories of ghosts, and monsters, and questions raised about the nature of death, and whether there is more going on all around us than can ever perceived. It was that way thousands of years ago, when mankind squatted in caves around fires, waiting for the dangerous night outside to pass, and it's that way right now, as we hide in our fragile constructs of civilization and wires and thin walls and fool ourselves into believing that we've pushed back the night. (Look around. We haven't. The night is here.)

The Victorian Era, with its rapid strides in scientific knowledge, brought science crashing up against superstition and religion and spiritualism. Scientists had been gaining an understanding of the workings of the universe, and our little speck of it, for decades – chemistry, physics, astronomy, and so on – but the means for spreading that knowledge and educating the ignorant was very limited. Many people still lived much as their ancestors had a hundred years before, or longer, close to the land and nature, and uninterested in explanations about weather patterns or how atoms and molecules interacted. It was much easier to rely on superstitious explanations for natural phenomena, in the same way that the ancient Greeks and Romans had created their gods to explain the sun and moon and lightning. In daylight, all might be rational and modern, but when the sun went down, it was much easier to believe that *there was something out there* . . . .

The Victorians were gradually becoming educated, but the skin of knowledge was still thin, which allowed such things as the fascination with death and the spiritualism crazes of the late 1800's to take such a strong hold, even luring in those who wouldn't be thought to be so gullible – Dr. Watson's *first* Literary Agent, Sir Arthur Conan Doyle, for example. It's common knowledge how he ruined his reputation during his later years by going over so whole-heartedly to the spiritualists. Additionally, he was shamed for his avid and naïve support of the Cottingley Fairies hoax. It can be taken as a fact that Mr. Sherlock Holmes, indirectly associated with Sir Arthur by way of Dr. John H. Watson's writings, was not happy that his reputation might be linked to such foolishness. Fortunately, there is ample evidence that Holmes forsook neither his beliefs nor his dignity.

Many people brought cases to Holmes throughout his career that seemed to have hints of the supernatural or the impossible about them. A few of these were published by way of the Literary Agent: "The Creeping Man" begins with the story of a girl's father who is seemingly changing into some sort of beast. "The Sussex Vampire" finds a woman accused of sucking the blood from her own baby. "The Adventure of Wisteria Lodge" has voodoo intruding into the supposedly modern English countryside. And of course there is *The Hound of the Baskervilles*, in which a curse from centuries past seems to have reawakened, killing a respected Dartmoor resident and threatening to destroy his heir as well.

These tales are part of the pitifully few sixty adventures that make up the The Canon. It contains references to many other "Untold Cases", some of which have seemingly impossible aspects – a giant rat and a remarkable worm and a ship that vanishes into the mist. We can be sure that Holmes handled each of these with his customary excellence, and that any sort of supernatural explanation that might have been encountered along the way was debunked. For Holmes, the world was big enough, and there was no need for him to serve as a substitute Van Helsing.

Holmes's stated his rule, with minor variations, for getting to the bottom of seemingly impossible situations several times within The Canon:

- "How often have I said to you that when you have eliminated the impossible whatever remains, however improbable, must be the truth." (*The Sign of the Four*)
- "It is an old maxim of mine that when you have excluded the impossible, whatever remains, however improbable, must be the truth." ("The Beryl Coronet")
- "We must fall back upon the old axiom that when all other contingencies fail, whatever remains, however improbable, must be the truth. ("The Bruce-Partington Plans")

- "That process . . . starts upon the supposition that when you have eliminated all which is impossible, then whatever remains, however improbable, must be the truth." ("The Blanched Soldier")
- "That is the case as it appears to the police, and improbable as it is, all other explanations are more improbable still." ("Silver Blaze")

Thus, the first part of the process is actually *eliminating the impossible*. And to a man with a scientific and logical mind such as Sherlock Holmes, this means that the baseline is established that *"No ghosts need apply."* So Holmes explains to Watson at the beginning of "The Sussex Vampire", asking, *". . . are we to give serious attention to such things? This agency stands flat-footed upon the ground, and there it must remain. The world is big enough for us."*

If Holmes were to start every investigation with all possibilities as available options, including those beyond our human understanding, he would be finished before he even started. Imagine Holmes saying, *"This man may have been murdered – or he may have been possessed by a demon, overwhelming the limits of his body and simply causing him to expire. I'll sent you my bill."* Think of the time wasted if Holmes were an occult detective, with nothing considered impossible, all possibilities on the table, and virtually nothing that could be eliminated in order to establish whatever truth remains. The Literary Agent, Sir Arthur Conan Doyle, was willing to accept ridiculous claims about spiritualism and fairies and all sorts of nonsense. Not so for Sherlock Holmes – and thank goodness.

That's not to say that Holmes was closed-minded. There were many intelligent men in the Victorian and Edwardian eras who mistakenly believed that all that *could* be discovered *had* been discovered – but Holmes wasn't one of them. There is an apocryphal tale where Charles H. Duell, the Commissioner of U.S. patent office in 1899, stated that *"everything that can be invented has been invented."* In *A Study in Scarlet*, while discussing crime, Holmes himself paraphrased *Ecclesiastes* 1:9 when he told Watson, *"There is nothing new under the sun. It has all been done before."* And yet, with a curious scientific mind and an exceptional intelligence, Holmes would have certainly realized that there *was* more to be discovered, and that things are always going on around us that are beyond what we can necessarily perceive or understand – invisible forces and patterns of interaction on a grand scale beyond our comprehension. In relation to his own work, Holmes explained:

" . . . life is infinitely stranger than anything which the mind of man could invent. We would not dare to conceive the things which are really mere commonplaces of existence. If we could fly out of that window hand in hand, hover over this great city, gently remove the roofs, and peep in at the queer things which are going on, the strange coincidences, the plannings, the cross-purposes, the wonderful chains of events, working through generations, and leading to the most outrè *results, it would make all fiction with its conventionalities and foreseen conclusions most stale and unprofitable."*

Thus, in spite of his statements that *"[t]here is nothing new under the sun"* or *"the world is big enough"*, Sherlock Holmes would have been open-minded enough to realize that – with our limited perspectives – the impossible isn't always easily eliminated when identifying the truthful improbable.

Sometime in late 2016, when these MX anthologies were showing signs of continued and increasing success, it was time to determine what the theme would be for the Fall 2017 collection. When I had the idea for a new Holmes anthology in early 2015, it was originally planned to be a single book of a dozen or so new Holmes adventures, probably published as a paperback. By the fall of that year, it had grown to three massive simultaneous hardcovers with sixty-three new adventures, the largest collection of its kind ever – until we surpassed that in the spring of 2019 with sixty-six stories, and a total of nearly four-hundred.

Initially, in 2015, I thought that it would be a one-time event. But then people wanted to know when the *next* book would appear, and authors – both those in the original collection and others who hadn't been – wanted to contribute more stories. So of course the original plan was amended, and it became an ongoing series.

It was announced that a fourth volume would be published in the Spring of 2016, *Part IV: 2016 Annual* – with the word *"Annual"* confidently assuming that it would be a yearly event. But there was such great interest by participating authors that I realized a Fall collection in that same year was necessary, beginning a pattern of two collections per year that has continued to the present – an *"Annual"* in the spring and a themed set in the autumn. And so I announced and began to receive stories for *Part V: Christmas Adventures*, published later in 2016.

These types of books have to be planned with plenty of advance notice for authors to actually write the stories. So halfway through 2016, the book for the following Spring, *Part XVI: 2017 Annual*, was announced, and very soon it was necessary to figure out what the Fall 2017 collection's theme would be.

That came to me while I was mowing my yard, where I do some of my best thinking. We have 2/3's of an acre, and I still have a push-mower, so that's good for a couple of hours of intense perspiration and pondering. And on that day, I had only been mowing for five or ten minutes when the idea of *Eliminate the Impossible* popped into my mind.

That title, *Eliminate the Impossible*, had been used before by Alistair Duncan for an MX book in 2010, something of a catch-all examination of Holmes in both page and screen. (In fact, this was the first Sherlockian title published by MX, and look what that led to!) This new anthology, however, would feature stories wherein Holmes's cases initially seemed to have supernatural or impossible aspects, but would absolutely have to have rational explanations – "*No ghosts need apply.*" And yet, after the rational solution was explained and the case resolved, it would be acceptable if there was perhaps a hint that something more was going on beyond Our Heroes' understanding. I explained by paraphrasing Hamlet when soliciting stories from the various authors: "*There are more things in heaven and earth, [Watson], Than are dreamt of in your philosophy.*" For instance, after the culprit is revealed, and Holmes and Watson could be departing, the investigation complete. Watson might look back and see . . . *something impossible.*

> "*Holmes,*" (he might say.) "*Do you see it?*"
> "*It is nothing, Watson,*" (would be Holmes's reply.)
> "*Mist. A mere trick of the light.*"
> "*But still . . . .*"

And so the rational ending would be preserved, but the idea that there are more things in heaven and earth would be possible as well.

When I had the idea for the theme of the first MX collection of this sort, 2017's *Eliminate the Impossible*, I wasn't sure how it would go. I received a bit of sarcastic push-back from one person who referred to this as a "Scooby Doo book". I was disappointed at his reaction, and I'm glad to report that the success of both simultaneous volumes of *Eliminate the Impossible* proved that his assessment was incorrect.

Still, a few people were surprised that I would encourage a book of this sort. They shouldn't have been. I make it very clear that I'm a strict Holmesian traditionalist. I want to read more and more Canonical-type stories about Holmes and Watson – and nothing whatsoever never ever in any form about "*Sherlock and John*"! – with no parodies or anachronisms

6

or non-heroic behaviours. That's what I collect, read, chronologicize, write, and edit, and also what encourage in others as well. There have been many times when I've started reading a new Holmes story, only to realize that, no matter how authentic the first part is, the end has veered off into one-hundred-percent no-coming-back supernatural territory – Holmes is battling a real monster, or facing a full-fledged vampire or wolfman, or perhaps a brain-eating fungus from another planet. There is a misguided belief that, just because someone wishes it to be so, Holmes can be plugged in anywhere like Doctor Who, or that he's is interchangeable with Abraham Van Helsing – and he most definitely is not.

As someone who has collected, read, and chronologicized literally thousands of Canonical Holmes adventures for almost forty-five years – and that certainly passed quickly! – I'm dismayed when this happens. As I make notes for each story to be listed in the massive overall Canon and Pastiche chronology that I've constructed over the last quarter-century, I generally indicate when a story has included "incorrect" statements or segments, and I include notes identifying those parts that were really and truly written by Watson, as compared with paragraphs or pages or chapters that were clearly composed and added by some later editor who has taken Watson's notes and either changed parts, or stuck in completely fictional middles and endings to fulfil his or her own agenda. Sometimes the story goes so far off into the weeds that even pulled-out pieces of it can't be judged as authentically Watsonian, and the whole thing is lost.

But the stories of *Eliminate the Impossible* – and now this collection as well – are fully traditional in the best Canonical way.

The idea of a story where Holmes and Watson were presented with circumstances that initially seemed supernatural but ended up having a rational solution was not new, and I can claim no originality for thinking of it. Before those volumes in the ongoing MX series appeared in late 2017 – *Eliminate the Impossible Part VII (1880-1891)* and *Part VIII (1892-1905)* – there were many other tales of that type. In my foreword to *Eliminate the Impossible,* I listed a number of them, and since then there have been more. As I explained then, there are far too many stories of that type to catalogue in this essay . . . but here are some of them for friends of Mr. Holmes to locate.

First, I have to recommend the stories in *Eliminate the Impossible,* Parts VII and VIII of this ongoing anthology series. They are some of the finest Sherlockian adventures to be found, and *Publishers Weekly* wrote of the two volumes: "*Sherlockians eager for faithful-to-the-canon plots and characters will be delighted*" and "*The imagination of the contributors in coming up with variations on the volume's theme is matched by their ingenious resolutions.*" Other MX anthologies in this series also have stories along these lines, although they are mixed in with more general Canonical adventures, in the way that "The Sussex Vampire" and "The Creeping Man" were included with Holmes's other non-*outrè* investigations.

While assembling the three-volume set that immediately preceded this current collection, the *Spring 2019 Annual*, containing general Canonical tales in *Part XIII: (1881-1890)*, *Part XIV (1891-1897)*, and *Part XV (1898-1917)*, I received a number of stories that could have just as easily fit into this current collection. I considered whether I should contact the contributors and see if they wished to hold those stories for publication in this Fall 2019 collection, *Whatever Remains . . . Must Be the Truth* (Parts XVI, XVII, and XVIII), but in the end decided to go ahead and use them in Parts XIII, XIV, and XV instead. And I'm glad that I did, because the inclusion of those narratives in the Spring 2019 books made for a really excellent set of adventures.

Among the many other places that one can find Holmes stories – some full-on supernatural and some that fit my own requirements – are *The Irregular Casebook of Sherlock Holmes* by Ron Weighell (2000), *Ghosts in Baker Street* (2006), the Lovecraftian-themed *Shadows Over Baker Street* (2003), and the ongoing *Gaslight* series edited by Charles Prepolec and J.R. Campbell. These titles include, *Gaslight Grimoire* (2008), *Gaslight Grotesque* (2009), *Gaslight Arcanum* (2011), and most recently *Gaslight Gothic* (2018). John Linwood Grant is editing a forthcoming book in which Holmes will team with noted occult detectives, such as Thomas Carnacki, or tangentially with Alton Peake, an occult investigator of my own invention who has appeared in some of my Holmes narratives, although always off-screen.

Holmes battled the supposedly supernatural in countless old radio shows, including "The Limping Ghost" (September 1945), "The Stuttering Ghost" (October 1946), "The Bleeding Chandelier" (June 1948), "The Haunting of Sherlock Holmes" (May 1946), and "The Uddington Witch" (October 1948). An especially good radio episode with supernatural overtones was "The Haunted Bagpipes" by Edith Meiser, (February 1947), later presented in comic form as illustrated by Frank Giacoia, and then again adapted for print by Carla Coupe in *Sherlock Holmes Mystery Magazine* (Vol. 2, No. 1, 2011)

And of course, one mustn't forget the six truly amazing radio episodes of John Taylor's *The Uncovered Casebook of Sherlock Holmes* (1993), and then published soon after as a very fine companion book. Then there's George Mann's audio drama "The Reification of Hans Gerber" (2011), later novelized as part of *Sherlock Holmes: The Will of the Dead* (2013).

In addition to numerous radio broadcasts, there were similar "impossible" films with Holmes facing something with other-worldly overtones, including *The Scarlet Claw* (1944) and *Sherlock Holmes* (2009). Television episodes have tackled this type of story. The old 1950's television show *Sherlock Holmes* with Ronald Howard had "The Belligerent Ghost", "The Haunted Gainsborough", and "The Laughing Mummy". The show was rebooted in 1980 with Geoffrey Whitehead as Holmes, and had an episode called "The Other Ghost".

In 2002, Matt Frewer starred as Holmes in the supernatural-feeling *The Case of the Whitechapel Vampire*. Nearly a decade earlier, Jeremy Brett performed in a pastiche that was loosely tied to "The Sussex Vampire" entitled *The Last Vampyre* (1993). The supernatural elements were greatly played up in that film, although it had a rational ending. Brett's performance was extremely painful to watch, as at that point he had foisted his own personal illnesses – both mental and physical – so heavily onto his portrayal of Holmes and there was really nothing of Holmes left, but other aspects of the film were tolerable, if one looks past the acting and accepts that this was a separate story entirely from "The Sussex Vampire".

Brett's tenure as Holmes limped to an end the following year, and since that time, except for a few stand-alone films – three more Matt Frewer adaptations, a curiously odd and unpleasant version of *The Hound of the Baskervilles* (2002) starring Richard Roxburgh, a mild effort starring Jonathan Pryce called *Sherlock Holmes and the Baker Street Irregulars* (2007), and Rupert Everett's emotionless Holmes in *The Case of the Silk Stocking* (2007) – there have been no other versions of Sherlock Holmes on television whatsoever. (It's hoped that Holmes will return to television sooner rather than later, since it's been a very long time since 1994, when the last Holmes series was on television – not counting a few Russian efforts – and it's sure that when he does, a few seemingly supernatural stories will certainly be included as part of the line-up.)

In print, there are many other examples of this type of story. From the massive list of similarly themed fan-fictions, one might choose "The Mottled Eyes", "The Case of the Vengeful Ghost", "The Japanese Ghost", "The Adventure of the Grasping Ghost", "Sherlock Holmes and the Seven Ghosts", "The Adventure of the Haunting Bride", "The Problem of the Phantom Prowler", *That Whiter Host*, or "The Vampire's Kiss". There are countless novels, such as the six short works by Kel Richards, or Val Andrews' *The Longacre Vampire*, or *Draco, Draconis* by Spencer Brett and David Dorian. One shouldn't ignore the narratives brought to us by Sam Siciliano, narrated by Holmes's annoying cousin Dr. Henry Vernier, all featuring supposedly supernatural encounters. Check out Bonnie

MacBird's second Holmes adventure, *Unquiet Spirits*, and David Wilson's *Sherlock Holmes and the Case of the Edinburgh Haunting*. Then there are several by David Stuart Davies, including *The Devil's Promise*, *The Shadow of the Rat*, and *The Scroll of the Dead*. One can read Carol Buggé's *The Haunting of Torre Abbey* and Randall Collins' *The Case of the Philosopher's Ring*, and the different sequels to *The Hound*, including Rick Boyer's most amazing *The Giant Rat of Sumatra*, Teresa Collard's *The Baskerville Inheritance*, and Kelvin Jones' *The Baskerville Papers*.

Holmes has battled Count Dracula in too many encounters to list, but in almost every one of them, he finds himself ridiculously facing a real undead Transylvanian vampire who can change into a bat. Often, Holmes is simply inserted into the Van Helsing role within the plot of the original *Dracula* story. Although I own each of these, I've always ignored them, as the *real* historical Holmes would never encounter an *imaginary* creature such as this. The one exception so far that I've enjoyed and been able to finish has been Mark Latham's remarkable *A Betrayal in Blood*– finally, a Holmes-Dracula encounter that I can highly recommend.

A list of this sort is really too long to compile, and this shouldn't be taken as anywhere close to the last word. There are numerous supposedly impossible circumstances or supernatural encounters of one sort or another contained in many Holmes collections, tucked in with the more "normal" cases, and these are but a few of them:

- "The Deptford Horror", *The Exploits of Sherlock Holmes* – Adrian Conan Doyle and John Dickson Carr
- "The Shadows on the Lawn", *The New Adventures of Sherlock Holmes* – Barry Jones
- "The Adventure of the Talking Ghost", *Alias Simon Hawkes* – Philip J. Carraher
- "Lord Garnett's Skulls", *The MX Book of New Sherlock Holmes Stories – Part II: 1890-1895* – J.R. Campbell
- "The Bramley Court Devil", *The Adventures of the Second Mrs. Watson* – Michael Mallory
- "The Ghost of Gordon Square", *The Chemical Adventures of Sherlock Holmes* – Thomas G. Waddell and Thomas R. Rybolt
- "The Ghost of Christmas Past", *The Strand Magazine* No. 23 – David Stuart Davies
- "The Mystery at Kerritt's Rood" *Sherlock Holmes: Tangled Skeins* – David Marcum

- "The Devil of the Deverills", *Sherlock Holmes: Before Baker Street* – S.F. Bennett
- "The Case of the Devil's Voice", *The Curious Adventures of Sherlock Holmes in Japan* – Dale Furutani
- "The Adventure of the Haunted Hotel", *The Untold Adventures of Sherlock Holmes* – Luke Benjamen Kuhns
- "The Death Fetch", *The Game is Afoot* – Darrell Schweitzer
- "The Yellow Star of Cairo", *The MX Book of New Sherlock Holmes Stories – Part XIII: 2019 Annual (1881-1890)* – Tim Gambrell
- "The Adventure of the Devil's Father", *The Great Detective: His Further Adventures* – Morris Hershman
- "The Horned God", *The MX Book of New Sherlock Holmes Stories – Part X: 2018 Annual (1896-1916)* – Kelvin Jones
- "The Dowser's Discovery", *The Strand Magazine* No. 58 – David Marcum
- "The Phantom Gunhorse", *Sherlock Holmes: The Soldier's Daughter* – Malcolm Knott
- "The Adventure of the Winterhall Monster", *The MX Book of New Sherlock Holmes Stories – Part XIII: 2019 Annual (1881-1890)* – Tracy Revels
- "The Case of Hodgson's Ghost", *The Oriental Casebook of Sherlock Holmes* – Ted Riccardi
- "The Case of the Haunted Chateau", *The MX Book of New Sherlock Holmes Stories – Part XV: 2019 Annual (1898-1917)* – Leslie Charteris and Denis Green
- "A Ballad of the White Plague", *The Confidential Casebook of Sherlock Holmes* – P.C. Hodgel
- "The Adventure of the Dark Tower", *The MX Book of New Sherlock Holmes Stories – Part III: 1896-1929* – Peter K. Andersson
- "The Adventure of the Field Theorems", *Sherlock Holmes In Orbit* – Vonda N. McIntyre
- "The Adventure of Urquhart Manse", *The MX Book of New Sherlock Holmes Stories – Part I: 1881-1889* – Will Thomas
- "The Haunting of Sutton House", *The Papers of Sherlock Holmes Vol. I* – David Marcum
- "The Stolen Relic", *The MX Book of New Sherlock Holmes Stories – Part V: Christmas Adventures* – David Marcum

- "The Chamber of Sorrow Mystery", *The Outstanding Mysteries of Sherlock Holmes* – Gerard Kelly
- The Case of the Vampire's Mark", *Murder in Baker Street* – Bill Crider
- "The Case of the Phantom Chambermaid", *The Execution of Sherlock Holmes* – Donald Thomas
- "The Ululation of Wolves", *The MX Book of New Sherlock Holmes Stories – Part I: 1881-1889* – Steve Mountain
- "The Night in the Elizabethan Concert Hall in the Very Heart of London" *Traveling With Sherlock Holmes and Dr. Watson* – Herman Anthony Litzinger
- "The Adventure of the Phantom Coachman", *The MX Book of New Sherlock Holmes Stories – Part IV: 2016 Annual* – Arthur Hall
- "The Strange Case of the Voodoo Priestess", *Sherlock Holmes: The Hidden Years* – Carole Buggé
- "A Dormitory Haunting", *The Associates of Sherlock Holmes* – Jaine Fenn
- "The Night In The Burial Vault Under The Sanitarium At Soames Meadow", *Traveling With Sherlock Holmes and Dr. Watson* – Herman Anthony Litzinger
- "The Witch of Greenwich", *My Sherlock Holmes* – Gerald Dole
- "The Adventure of Jackthorn Circle", *Sherlock Holmes: Mysteries of the Victorian Era* – Rock DiLisio
- "The Phantom of the Barbary Coast", *Sherlock Holmes in Orbit* – Frank M. Robinson
- "Sherlock Holmes, Dragon Slayer", *Resurrected Holmes* – Darrell Schweitzer
- "The Adventure of the Towne Manor Haunting", *Sherlock Holmes, Consulting Detective: Volume III* – Andrew Salmon
- "The Mysterious Mr. Rim", *The MX Book of New Sherlock Holmes Stories – Part XV: 2019 Annual (1898-1917)* – Maurice Barkley
- "The Haunted House", *The Singular Adventures of Mr. Sherlock Holmes* – Alan Stockwell,
- "The Dorset Witch", *Sherlock Holmes: The Soldier's Daughter* – Malcolm Knott

12

- "The Devil's Painting", *The MX Book of New Sherlock Holmes Stories – Part XV: 2019 Annual (1898-1917)* – Kelvin I. Jones
- "The Adventure of the Phantom Coachman", *The MX Book of New Sherlock Holmes Stories – Part IV: 2016 Annual* – Arthur Hall

In the spring of 2018, it was time once again to start planning for the 2019 MX anthologies, and again while I was mowing – in pretty much the same spot, so there must be something buried there that radiates some kind of beneficial mind-influencing waves – I had the idea for these current books. If *Eliminate the Impossible* had been so successful, why not do it again? And what else could it be called but a variation from the same Holmesian maxim?

The three companion volumes that make up *Whatever Remains . . . Must Be the Truth*, like those in *Eliminate the Impossible*, contain stories where Holmes faces ghosts and mythological creatures, impossible circumstances and curses, possessions and prophecies, Some begin with the impossible element defined from the beginning, while others progress for quite a while as "normal" cases before the twist is revealed. Some are overt encounters with supposed monsters or phantoms, while others are more subtle, pondering the nature of existence and the vast patterns around us that we cannot perceive. As with all Holmes adventures, this collection represents one of the great enjoyments of reading about The Great Detective – the reader never knows where each tale will lead. And while each of the adventures in these volumes is categorized by Holmes *eliminating* the impossible to obtain, however improbable, the truth, the various impossibilities contained within these covers are presented in an incredibly varied and exciting manner. I'm certain that you will enjoy all of them.

As always, I want to thank with all my heart my patient and wonderful wife of thirty-one years (as of this writing,) Rebecca, and our amazing son and my friend, Dan. I love you both, and you are everything to me!

Also, I can't ever express enough gratitude for all of the contributors who have donated their time and royalties to this ongoing project. I'm constantly amazed at the incredible stories that you send, and I'm so glad to have gotten to know all of you through this process. It's an undeniable fact that Sherlock Holmes authors are the *best* people!

The contributors of these stories have donated their royalties for this project to support the Stepping Stones School for special needs children, located at Undershaw, one of Sir Arthur Conan Doyle's former homes. As of this writing, these MX anthologies have raised over $50,000 for the school, and of even more importance, they have helped raise awareness about the school all over the world. These books are making a real difference to the school, and the participation of both contributors and purchasers is most appreciated.

Next is that group that exchanges emails with me when we have the time – and time is a valuable commodity these days! I don't get to write as often as I'd like, but I really enjoy catching up when we get the chance: Derrick Belanger, Bob Byrne, Mark Mower, Denis Smith, Tom Turley, Dan Victor, and Marcia Wilson.

A special shout-out to Tracy Revels, Arthur Hall, and Kelvin Jones, who joined me in writing multiple stories for these volumes. When the submission deadline was fast approaching, I wrote to Tracy, who had written one story at that time for this set, and asked if she'd be interested in writing others to appear in the companion volumes. She took it as a challenge and wrote two more amazing tales in just a week or so. Arthur consistently pulls great tales from The Tin Dispatch Box, and I'm glad that they end up here. And I was a fan of Kelvin's work back in the 1980's, so I'm very happy that he's a part of these books.

There is a group of special people who have stepped up and supported this and a number of other projects over and over again with a lot of contributions. They are the best and I can't express how valued they are: Larry Albert, Hugh Ashton, Derrick Belanger, Deanna Baran, S.F. Bennett, Nick Cardillo, Jayantika Ganguly, Paul Gilbert, Dick Gillman, Arthur Hall, Stephen Herczeg, Mike Hogan, Craig Janacek, Will Murray, Tracy Revels, Roger Riccard, Geri Schear, Robert Stapleton, Subbu Subramanian, Tim Symonds, Kevin Thornton, and Marcy Wilson.

I also want to thank the people who wrote forewords to the books:

- Kareem Abdul-Jabbar – Along with your fame as a sportsman, you are a necessary, noted, and effective voice for improving society. And on top of that, you're a Sherlockian too! Thank you for helping to round out our understanding of Mycroft Holmes, and for participating in these books as well!
- Roger Johnson – It seems like a lifetime ago when I sent a copy of my first book to Roger, because it really mattered to me that he review it. He had never heard of me, but he was most gracious, and we began to email one another. I've been incredibly fortunate to have since met him and his wonderful wife, Jean Upton, several times in person during my three Holmes Pilgrimages to England. Roger always takes time to answer my questions and to

14

participate in and promote various projects, and he and Jean were very gracious to host me for several days during part of my second Holmes Pilgrimage to England in 2015. In so many ways, Roger, I can't thank you enough, and I can't imagine these books without you.

- Steve Emecz is always positive, and he is always supportive of every idea that I pitch. It's been my great good fortune to cross your path – it changed my life, and let me play in this Sherlockian Sandbox in a way that would have never happened otherwise. Thank you for every opportunity!
- Brian Belanger – Just a few days before I wrote this, I received a series of new cover designs from Brian for a forthcoming three-volume set that I edited, *The Further Adventures of Sherlock Holmes – The Complete Jim French Imagination Theatre Scripts*. What Brian sent was typical – excellent, brilliant, and with a great understanding of what needed to be conveyed. He's very talented, and very willing to work to get it right, instead of simply knocking something out or insisting that it be *his* vision. I'm very glad that he's the cover designer for these and other projects that we assembled together.

And last but certainly *not* least, **Sir Arthur Conan Doyle**: Author, doctor, adventurer, and the Founder of the Sherlockian Feast. Present in spirit, and honored by all of us here.

As always, this collection has been a labor of love by both the participants and myself. As I've explained before, once again everyone did their sincerest best to produce an anthology that truly represents why Holmes and Watson have been so popular for so long. These are just more tiny threads woven into the ongoing Great Holmes Tapestry, continuing to grow and grow, for there can *never* be enough stories about the man whom Watson described as "*the best and wisest . . . whom I have ever known.*"

David Marcum
August 7th, 2019
The 167th Birthday of Dr. John H. Watson

Questions, comments, or story submissions
may be addressed to David Marcum at
thepapersofsherlockholmes@gmail.com

Sherlock, Mycroft, and Me
by Kareem Abdul-Jabbar

If you're reading this, there's nothing new that I can tell you about being passionate about Sherlock Holmes. You wouldn't have bought this book unless you shared that passion. It is a robust passion shared by hundreds of millions of fans around the world. There are over two-hundred-and-fifty international societies dedicated to the Holmes legacy. It is a testament to fans' loyalty that they persist in gobbling up new Holmes stories by literary interlopers such as myself, despite Sir Conan Doyle's own dismissive attitude toward Holmes, even to the point of killing him off in "The Final Problem". Explained Doyle: "*I have had such an overdose of him that I feel towards him as I do towards* paté de foie gras*, of which I once ate too much, so that the name of it gives me a sickly feeling to this day.*"

Fortunately, we don't share that feeling.

For eight years, Doyle fought against public outrage at Holmes' "death" and intense pressure to produce another story. And ever since he brought Holmes back, the character has become immortal. I am delighted to be one of the many authors who have contributed to his immortality through my three novels and graphic novel featuring Mycroft Holmes, Sherlock's smarter brother.

My love of the genre was inspired by watching Basil Rathbone and Nigel Bruce playing Holmes and Watson in the movies when I was a child. Later, when I was traveling so much as a professional basketball player, I read all the Holmes stories on the long plane flights. This in turn led me reading other mystery writers, which I continue to do today.

Why then did I choose to write about Mycroft rather than Sherlock? Part of the reason is that the stories barely mention Mycroft, except to say that he was smarter and less disciplined than Sherlock. This gave me leeway to create from practically nothing the character I wanted to write about. One of the things I like about mysteries is that they are, at their core, morality tales in which characters must grapple with choices of right and wrong. The best mystery writers offer layered detectives who struggle and who try to restore justice and order to the chaos created by murder. For me, that chaos was symbolic of the endemic injustice in society, so I wanted a detective who was willing to face those injustices head-on with courage and intelligence.

Sherlock is a bit of an anomaly in that he uses his remarkable abilities to quench his own intellectual thirst. If someone else benefits, that's just a happy byproduct. Mycroft, on the other hand, uses his abilities to further justice and to benefit society. Sherlock is more like the amoral Sam Spade in Hammett's *The Maltese Falcon*, whose motivation for solving the case is that it would be "bad for business" not to. Mycroft is more like Marlowe in Raymond Chandler's novels or Ross Macdonald's Lew Archer. They also doggedly pursue the truth, but they do so out of a commitment to justice. Although I am entertained by brilliant loners like Holmes and Spade, I admire characters like Mycroft and Marlowe who want to better their communities.

In both my novels and graphic novel, I write about the young Mycroft. Basically, it's a superhero origin story about how he came to hone his skills and why he chose to use them to make the world a better place for everyone. Maybe it's my own origin story: Honing my basketball skills and using my fame as a platform to better society. And when the basketball days were done, honing my writing skills to tell stories about a young genius who time and time again faces moral crossroads – and each time chooses the right path.

It's not just that he chooses the right path, but that he uses rational thinking to do so. We are in an Age of De-enlightenment, when politicians openly lie because they know their followers don't care about the truth. We have smart phones, the most powerful educational tool in the history of the human race, and we use it send photos of our food rather than fact-check our leaders who control our economic and social futures. The Holmes brothers represent logic, rational thinking, keen observation – all the tools people need to seize control of their lives and improve their communities and country. They represent us at our intellectual best and present a benchmark that we should all strive toward.

More important, they're entertaining and exciting.

We all have our personal reasons for loving the stories of Sherlock Holmes. Whatever yours are, Dear Reader, you need only to turn the page with giddy anticipation because on the other side, the game will be afoot.

Kareem Abdul-Jabbar
June 2019

All Supernatural or Preternatural Agencies are Ruled Out As a Matter of Course
by Roger Johnson

In his preface to the 1928 anthology *Best Detective Stories of the Year* (London: Faber & Faber), Mgr. Ronald A. Knox wrote:

> *I laid down long ago certain main rules, which I reproduce here with a certain amount of commentary; not all critics will be agreed as to their universality or as to their general importance, but I think most detective "fans" will recognize that these principles, or something like them, are necessary to the full enjoyment of a detective story. I say "the full enjoyment"; we cannot expect complete conformity from all writers, and indeed some of the stories selected in this very volume transgress the rules noticeably. Let them stand for what they are worth.*

The second rule – "All supernatural or preternatural agencies are ruled out as a matter of course" – seems obvious, though it had already been successfully broken by William Hope Hodgson in his tales of *Carnacki the Ghost-Finder*, who applies proper detective methods to determine whether a supposed haunting is genuine or not. [1] The rule would be broken again, of course, most notably, perhaps, by John Dickson Carr in some excellent short stories and an outstanding novel, *The Burning Court*.

Knox's commentary on this particular rule reads in full:

> *All supernatural or praeternatural agencies are ruled out as a matter of course. To solve a detective problem by such means would be like winning a race on the river by the use of a concealed motor-engine. And here I venture to think there is a limitation about Mr. Chesterton's Father Brown stories. He nearly always tries to put us off the scent by suggesting that the crime must have been done by magic; and we know that he is too good a sportsman to fall back upon such a solution. Consequently, although we seldom guess the answer*

18

to his riddles, we usually miss the thrill of having suspected the wrong person."

That dig at G.K. Chesterton's most famous contribution to the genre is rather curious. It suggests that the identification of the culprit is the only point of a detective story. Mgr. Knox may have believed it,[2] and the term "whodunnit" unfortunately perpetuates that blinkered idea, but it ignores character, atmosphere and two of the essential puzzles posed by Chesterton and solved by Father Brown. To the question of *"Who?"* we should add *"Why?"* and – most important in this context, though dismissed by Knox as mere riddles to be guessed – *"How?"*

Like Sherlock Holmes in at least three indisputable Canonical exploits, the little priest is faced with situations that appear to be impossible and therefore the work of unearthly powers. But he knows, and we know, that magic has no place here: A human, or at least a natural, agency is at work. Despite Knox's censure, we are not deprived of *"the thrill of having suspected the wrong person"*, *and* we have the additional excitement of trying to work out how the apparently impossible was achieved.

We know too that Sherlock Holmes was there before Father Brown. The tradition established by Arthur Conan Doyle in *The Hound of the Baskervilles*, "The Devil's Foot", and "The Sussex Vampire" lives and flourishes, as this collection proves!

Roger Johnson, BSI, ASH
Editor: *The Sherlock Holmes Journal*
August 2019

NOTES

1 – One of Carnacki's investigations, a very neat little detective story called "The Find", doesn't even hint at the supernatural.

2 – His own mystery novels are rarely read these days, unlike the Father Brown stories.

Stories, Stepping Stones,
and the Conan Doyle Legacy
by Steve Emecz

Undershaw
Circa 1900

The MX Book of New Sherlock Holmes Stories has now raised over $50,000 for Stepping Stones School for children with learning disabilities and is by far the largest Sherlock Holmes collection in the world - by several measures, stories, authors, pages and positive reviews from the critics. *Publishers Weekly* has been reviewing since Volume VI and we have had a record ten straight great reviews. Here are some of their best comments:

> *"This is more catnip for fans of stories faithful to Conan Doyle's originals"* (Part XIII)

> *"This is an essential volume for Sherlock Holmes fans"* (Part XI)

"The imagination of the contributors in coming up with variations on the volume's theme is matched by their ingenious resolutions" (Part VIII)

MX Publishing is a social enterprise – all the staff, including me, are volunteers with day jobs. The collection would not be possible without the creator and editor, David Marcum, who is rightly cited multiple times by *Publishers Weekly* and others as probably the most accomplished Sherlockian editor ever.

In addition to Stepping Stones School, our main program that we support is the Happy Life Children's Home in Kenya. My wife Sharon and I are on our way in December for our seventh Christmas in a row at Happy Life. It's a wonderful project that has saved the lives of over 600 babies. You can read all about the project in the second edition of the book *The Happy Life Story.*

Our support of both of these projects is possible through the publishing of Sherlock Holmes books, which we have now been doing for a decade.

You can find out more information
about the Stepping Stones School at:

www.steppingstones.org.uk

and Happy Life at:

www.happylifechildrenshomes.com

You can find out more about MX Publishing
and reach out to us through our website at:

www.mxpublishing.com

Steve Emecz
August 2019
Twitter: *@steveemecz*
LinkedIn: *https://www.linkedin.com/in/emecz/*

Undershaw
September 9, 2016
Grand Opening of the Stepping Stones School
(Photograph courtesy of Roger Johnson)

The Doyle Room at Stepping Stones, Undershaw
Partially funded through royalties from
The MX Book of New Sherlock Holmes Stories

Sherlock Holmes (1854-1957) was born in Yorkshire, England, on 6 January, 1854. In the mid-1870's, he moved to 24 Montague Street, London, where he established himself as the world's first Consulting Detective. After meeting Dr. John H. Watson in early 1881, he and Watson moved to rooms at 221b Baker Street, where his reputation as the world's greatest detective grew for several decades. He was presumed to have died battling noted criminal Professor James Moriarty on 4 May, 1891, but he returned to London on 5 April, 1894, resuming his consulting practice in Baker Street. Retiring to the Sussex coast near Beachy Head in October 1903, he continued to be associated in various private and government investigations while giving the impression of being a reclusive apiarist. He was very involved in the events encompassing World War I, and to a lesser degree those of World War II. He passed away peacefully upon the cliffs above his Sussex home on his 103rd birthday, 6 January, 1957.

Dr. John Hamish Watson (1852-1929) was born in Stranraer, Scotland on 7 August, 1852. In 1878, he took his Doctor of Medicine Degree from the University of London, and later joined the army as a surgeon. Wounded at the Battle of Maiwand in Afghanistan (27 July, 1880), he returned to London late that same year. On New Year's Day, 1881, he was introduced to Sherlock Holmes in the chemical laboratory at Barts. Agreeing to share rooms with Holmes in Baker Street, Watson became invaluable to Holmes's consulting detective practice. Watson was married and widowed three times, and from the late 1880's onward, in addition to his participation in Holmes's investigations and his medical practice, he chronicled Holmes's adventures, with the assistance of his literary agent, Sir Arthur Conan Doyle, in a series of popular narratives, most of which were first published in *The Strand* magazine. Watson's later years were spent preparing a vast number of his notes of Holmes's cases for future publication. Following a final important investigation with Holmes, Watson contracted pneumonia and passed away on 24 July, 1929.

Photos of Sherlock Holmes and Dr. John H. Watson courtesy of Roger Johnson

The MX Book
of
New Sherlock Holmes Stories

Part XVI:
Whatever Remains . . .
Must Be the Truth
(1881-1890)

The Hound of the Baskervilles
retold by Josh Pachter

"See here, Mr. Holmes," Dr. Mortimer said,
"Henry Baskerville's boat reaches England at five.
"Events at the Hall having come to a head,
"Reinforcements are needed to keep him alive."
"Let Watson go with you," the Master replied,
"Of his wisdom and fortitude you can be sure.
"Come here, my dear fellow." He pulled me aside.
"Keep Henry in sight and stay clear of the moor."

Henry encountered and started to court
One Stapleton's sister, mysterious Beryl,
Leading to dinner, cigars, glass of port,
Merripit shrouded and Henry in peril.
Explanation? A mastiff in phosphorous fire.
Stapleton perished alone in the mire.

The Wylington Lake Monster
by Derrick Belanger

"Ah, Watson, I do believe you were correct." Holmes said as we stood overlooking the majestic lake of Wylington. "Some peace and tranquility away from Baker Street will do us both good."

I had finally convinced my friend, with some additional coaxing from Mrs. Hudson, our landlady, to take a week-long sojourn on the invite of my friend, Russell Jones. He was a former soldier that I had saved on the battlefield, sewing up a bad wound which, if left untreated, would have surely led to him bleeding to death.

Soon after we moved into our rooms in Baker Street, Jones had written to me, thanking me for saving his life. We struck up a friendship via letters. He told me of his life as the captain of a one-hundred-foot steamer which he used to give tours of the glacial lake. Wylington had become a destination for sight-seers from around the globe, and Jones made a respectable income from his employer.

"*I would love to have you and that detective chap you've written so fondly about come here for a visit,*" Jones wrote. "*I have a guest house overlooking the sea which you are welcome to use.*" I shared the invitation with Holmes, but he scoffed and told me he had much better things to do with his time than watch sailing vessels. I would bridge the subject of the invitation over the course of several months, but Holmes always dismissed me.

"It will be good for you." I assured him. "Nothing like mountain air and a cool breeze to invigorate the senses."

"Watson, my senses are quite sharp and need the complexity of thwarting a criminal enterprise more so than the sounds of nature."

But Mrs. Hudson wholeheartedly agreed with me and tried, in her own way, to get Holmes to take Jones up on his offer. "I certainly wouldn't turn down a nice holiday in the North, Mr. Holmes," she'd scold with a wag of her finger and click of her tongue, to which Holmes would read *The Times* and harrumph.

So it was a complete surprise to me when one morning Holmes, while sipping tea and reading over a manuscript on developments in the combustion engine, declared, "Watson, I think we should take your friend up on his offer."

"What friend? Which offer?" I asked, baffled for I really did not know who or what Holmes was talking about.

33

"That Jones fellow. The Lancastrian."

"Jones," I said, my eyebrows raised in surprise.

"He offered to put us up for a time in his cottage. I think you should wire him, and let him know we shall be there tomorrow evening."

"Tomorrow?" I said stunned. Then my eyes creased and I dryly added, "You've a client."

"Yes," Holmes answered without looking up from his papers. "A woman." He took a sip from his tea. "Says that her husband was killed by an eachy."

"An *Eeky*?"

Holmes choked on his tea at my gross mispronunciation. "No, no. *Eachy*. *EE*-chee. A water spirit. Looks like a man but is tall, slimy, and grotesque. Seems to be a harbinger of death."

"You can't be serious," I said. I was still getting used to Holmes's quirks.

For the first time in our conversation, Holmes glanced up from his newspaper. I thought he'd let out one of his odd silent laughs or have a mirthful look about him. Instead my friend's grey eyes were steel, his lips thin. "I am deadly serious, Watson. While I don't adhere to a belief in mythical beings, I do believe there is something to the woman's claim about her husband being killed."

My cheeks flushed in anger and I was going to berate my friend with how illogical he sounded, but as I tried to find the right words, my tongue kept tripping over syllables, and I finally deflated and muttered. "If I wire Jones, should I tell him we are investigating a lake monster."

"You should," Holmes replied. "After all, it was Jones's idea to have the client write to me."

We arrived at dusk, and Jones, my Lancastrian friend, was there to greet us at the station. He was a scruffy man, his beard a wild blonde mane, his hair matted and shaggy. His eyes crinkled as he gave a toothy grin upon seeing us. He walked with a slight limp from a fall from a horse. It was the fall that led to his early discharge from the service after only a few months in Afghanistan. His leg had been badly broken in several places, and it never healed quite properly.

"Watson, my man! I would recognize you anywhere!" Jones bellowed. He came up to me as quickly as he could and gave me a hard slap on the back. "Still got that twinkle in your eye, aye, the one the ladies always adored. And this must be the astounding Mr. Sherlock Holmes!" Jones made a move to embrace my friend, but Holmes quickly countered by shoving his hand forward, firmly grabbing Jones's, and giving a stiff shake.

34

"I am indeed, Mr. Jones," Holmes said matter-of-factly. "Thank you for kindly inviting us to stay with you, and also for referring Mrs. Vermilion and her unusual case."

"Nothing unusual about it," Jones said sharply, almost as though he was insulted by Holmes's words. "Around these parts, folks know much more than you city folk. We don't dismiss that which isn't in a book. Woman saw an eachy, and then her husband died. Nothing unnatural about it."

"Yet Mrs. Vermilion believes her husband met his end by foul means," Holmes said, "and you suggested that she contact us."

"Well," Jones said grabbing one of my suitcases, "it sounds like you could use the money." Holmes gave me a glare that could kill a bird in mid-flight. Jones told us to follow him. We moved along the crowded station, making our way to Jones's dog-cart. "I didn't say that her husband wasn't murdered," Jones explained as we maneuvered our way through the crowd. "Seeing an eachy means death's coming. It doesn't mean a natural or unnatural death, just a death. Personally, I think there's something to Margaret's story. And I figured if anyone can solve it, from what Watson says, it's you Mr. Holmes. Johnny-boy Watson was always a good judge of character." He turned to me and gave me another pat on the back. "I'm happy to call you my friend."

We reached Jones's cart, a well-worn carriage with chipped paint and splintering door. Holmes loaded the luggage in and Jones carefully climbed up and took the reins. I was surprised to see Jones acting as driver. "You drive your own cart?" I inquired.

"Of course, Johnny-boy. I can't trust anyone else. I have to be in control. Just like steering a ship. I can't abide a different captain besides myself. Now climb on in so we can get going."

The ride to the cottage was slow and bumpy. Along the way, I talked with Holmes a bit more about the legend of the eachy and about the case. "You said the creature has been spotted in this area before."

"Yes. Throughout history, there have been sightings of a strange tall being, anywhere from seven to nine feet tall. It is scaly, like a fish, with dark set black eyes that seem to be all pupil. The creature is slimy and appears grotesque with its *ichthyian* features. According to legend, if one sees an eachy, then death shall follow."

"But in the case of Mrs. Vermilion, she is still alive," I countered.

"Yes, Watson, but her husband is not. Shortly after her sighting, her husband died, drowned in the lake. He and their son were out in a row boat, fishing. From what Mrs. Vermilion wrote to me, they were anchored when they felt something below them rock the boat. Mr. Vermilion stood

35

up to look over the side when the boat was again shaken. He lost his balance and fell into the water. Somehow, he became tangled in the anchor and drowned."

"How horrible," I said, shaken by such a tragic death.

"Yes, it is an odd accident, and the reason that I agreed to investigate the matter."

"You don't think that the death was caused by this eachy thing – that it dragged the man down into the water?" This was a category of detection so unlike my friend's consulting work done in the comfort of 221b. I couldn't tell where his mind was going in connecting the pieces.

"Not at all, Watson, but I believe we are being led to believe that is what occurred. In all the legends of the Eachy that I've uncovered, the creature is a harbinger of death, but it is never death's agent. We shall start the day tomorrow meeting with Mrs. Vermilion at her tavern in the village."

"The woman owns a tavern!" I was taken aback that a lady would indulge in such a venture.

"My dear Watson, she runs the business, but technically her son is the proprietor. He has been away at school but should be returning soon. He will take over the business when he is of age. Give Mrs. Vermilion credit that she has been able to keep her business profitable after the death of her husband. Many women wouldn't be able to handle such a task."

We arrived at Jones's cottage soon after ending our discussion. He had a good-sized piece of land, with several acres on the south end of the lake, looking at the hills to the north. The views were breathtaking, particularly with the setting sun striking the water, allowing shades of greens and blues to sparkle.

I told Jones I was impressed that he had such a beautiful location, and he replied that it was land that had been in the family for many generations. There were three cottages on the property, overlooking the lake, and his home, a farmhouse with a stone fence, was set back several yards from the cottages, but atop a hill so that it still had a beautiful view of the serene lake and mountains to the north.

Jones explained that he rented the cottages to the tourists who visited Wylington. With his view of the water, his location was in demand. "You and your friend timed it well," he told me. "When you wrote to me, I had a Dutch couple ask about renting this cottage. I turned them away as I wanted to save it for you. Otherwise, you'd have to share a room in the farm."

Holmes and I thanked my friend for his kindness. We brought our bags in, started a fire, and then Jones wished us a good night. Our cottage was a three-room abode made up of a sitting room and two bedrooms. There was a nice-sized wooden table with four chairs beside the fireplace. Holmes and I sat reading that evening for an hour or so before turning in.

The next morning, I was awakened by the sun's light hitting directly upon my eyes. I sat up and realized that I'd slept in. I felt a bit groggy and took a minute to stretch before opening my door.

The sitting room was empty. I called to Holmes in case he was in his chamber, but there was no answer. I then saw a note resting on the center of the table next to a very fine set of binoculars. I held them to my eyes and peered out the window. It took a moment or two to adjust the lenses so that the view wasn't blurry. I stared out at the lake and was surprised at the detail of my vision. It must have magnified the view eightfold, for I could clearly see two young men in bathing suits moving along on a sailboat.

"Remarkable," I heard myself say aloud. Then, remembering the note on the table, I turned and grabbed it. I assumed the note was from Holmes telling me his whereabouts, but it was actually from Jones. It read:

Johnny-boy,

> *Looks like the sandman has given you an extra dose of his powder. Your superiors wouldn't take too kindly to your sleeping in, but that's what a holiday is for. Mr. Holmes and the other guests are dining at the farm. When you're ready, please join them, and Bernice, my cook and housekeeper, will make you a hearty breakfast.*
>
> *Also, I left you a pair of my binoculars. Careful with them, as they are expensive. I thought you might like to look around the property with them. There are some nesting red-breasted mergansers on the first island you will see out in the lake. It's fun to see the little ones waddling in the water.*
>
> *I am off to work. I hope you have a restful day, and I shall see you this evening.*

Your friend,

Jonesy

I smiled at my friend's kindness and decided that I was in no haste to breakfast. I dressed, and then stepped outside with the binoculars to see if I could spy the mergansers that Jones had mentioned being at the closer island.

The grasses were short and barely brushed against my ankle as I walked out of the cottage. I took a moment to focus the binoculars on the island. I saw some mallards resting on the shore and several geese in the water. I started shifting around the island when I heard a strange undulating sound much closer to me. I observed a man just off the shore in the water near me. There was something unusual about his shape, and so I used the binoculars to see who it was. I nearly dropped them, such was my surprise, when I saw a green-colored humanoid with clawed hands and a bulbous head. Strange giant black eyes were protruding from its head. I gave a cry and then ran as fast as I could along the shore toward the creature. The beast must have heard me, as it quickly made its way out into the water. By the time I reached where it had been, the creature was gone.

I looked for tracks, for any evidence, but there was none. The creature hadn't left the water.

"Ho, Watson!" I heard shouted behind me. I turned to see a small band of people running towards me with Holmes in the lead. The group apparently consisted of all of the guests. They had heard my startled shout and assumed that I needed help. I looked out towards the water and then down to the shore where the sole set of prints were my own. I wondered how I could muster the nerve to tell Holmes that I, myself, had seen a mythical creature – for, the only thing it could have been was an eachy.

For the next half-hour, I was bombarded by questions from Holmes. Where precisely did I see the creature? How tall was it? How did it move? Did it make any sounds? In what direction did it swim? *How* did it swim? Was anyone else nearby?

I answered as best I could. I really didn't know the height of the creature nor its weight. I described its slimy skin and bulbous eyes, and its odd call I overheard.

Holmes kept peppering me with questions, and the only thing that finally stopped him was our appointment to see Mrs. Vermilion. Even then, he talked to me about what I saw for most of the ride to her tavern.

"I can't wait to arrive at the pub," I grumbled as we jostled back and forth in the carriage that Jones had sent for us. "This bumpy ride will end. Your infernal questions will end. And I'll be able to eat some decent food!"

When Holmes and the other guests had reached me at the lakeside, I told them what I had seen. One woman in the group threw up her hands in fright, gave a scream, and dashed off. That woman was Bernice, Jones's housekeeper. The others had been as intrigued as Holmes, though being tourists they thought seeing a lake monster was just another exciting part to their visit, no different than spotting a gull with unusual coloring.

Without the cook, my breakfast consisted of a crusty scone and lukewarm water for tea. I needed real food in me.

Holmes was quiet after my outburst. He sat with his palms on his knees, deep in thought, running my descriptions of the eachy over and over in his mind. What he made of them, I did not know. At last we arrived at The Vermilion Tavern, a rundown building on the outskirts of the village. The paint on the sign over the entryway was chipped and faded, making it legible but unwelcoming. There was a man sleeping on the front porch by the entryway. When Holmes and I left the carriage and entered the establishment, I got a good look at the fellow, ragged and unshaven, and even from a slight distance, I could smell the whisky about him.

We entered the dimly lit establishment and found it to have more customers than I had expected at that hour of the day, all of them nursing whisky, beer, or rum, and looking sullen and destitute. This was a place where people with troubles came to get drunk, to try and forget their position in the world. It was a perfect business for the proprietor.

The barkeep called to us, "What'll it be?"

"We have an appointment with Mrs. Vermilion," Holmes answered. He then looked at me, inviting me to place an order. I didn't. Even with my stomach empty, the tavern was so unappealing to me that I had lost my appetite. I planned on getting a nice lunch by the lake when we were done.

Before long, Mrs. Vermilion stepped out from a room in the back and greeted us. "Mr. Holmes," she said to my friend.

"And I am Dr. Watson, Mr. Holmes's associate," I explained to the woman.

"Of course," she said matter-of-factly. "You're Jonesy's friend." I was taken aback to hear a woman refer to my friend by his army nickname. I was definitely in the country, away from the courteous norms of civilization.

Mrs. Vermilion invited us to sit at a booth. I noted that it was the nicest in the room. Its cushions were intact, and the table didn't have many letters carved into it. I surmised that this table was saved for meetings such as this one.

Mrs. Vermilion looked as worn as her tavern. I could tell that she had been beautiful at one time. In the dim light her features were striking – tall, statuesque, with skin that was at one time fair, and soft eyes with thin brows. Now, there was a harshness to the woman, her skin lined with stress and her eyes sunken in. Streaks of white and grey flowed over what parts of her hair were still black. Her green eyes still sparkled, but they were held by the crinkles and creases of a difficult life.

"Madame, could you please tell me why you sent for me a year after the death of your husband," Holmes began.

"It was Jonesy's idea. I can see you are surprised by my calling him that, Dr. Watson," she said to me. "You see, I was his governess when he was younger. I'm twelve years his senior. We've always been friends and remained close. When he told me about reconnecting with you, Dr. Watson, he also spoke of you, Mr. Holmes. I've always felt uneasy about my husband's death, and he thought that perhaps you could look into the matter when you visited."

"I see," said Holmes. He leaned forward slightly and looked directly into the lady's eyes. "I would like to hear your story from the beginning. Can you tell me about your marriage to Mr. Vermilion."

It was now Mrs. Vermilion's turn to be taken aback. "Why, it was no better or worse than anyone else's. Tom and I had good times and bad times. He owned this tavern and this is where we met. He courted me, and after a few months, we were married. Like most, we fought hard when we disagreed, but he never laid a hand on me. We had Phillip later in our marriage. We didn't think we could have children, but then fifteen years ago we were blessed with my boy. He's really the reason that I wrote to you."

"Your son?" I asked, surprised.

"Yes. He has just arrived back from school. I fear something terrible may happen to him, like the others."

"Others?" Holmes and I said together. We both gave a look of concern to each other.

"I thought you wanted me to investigate the death of your husband," Holmes said, saying it almost like a question.

"There's Tom. But then there's also Anthony and Randall," Mrs. Vermilion said in a quick stream of words. She said this with concern, but there was a coldness to her as well. I noticed that as she talked about her marriage, she spoke in a factual manner showing no signs of sadness.

"Perhaps you should start with your husband. Why do you suspect his death may not have been an accident?"

"That goes to my seeing that eachy," she said. "I was paying a visit to Jonesy, helping him out. He hadn't been back from the war for too long, and his housekeeper, before Bernice, had run off with some man. I had just finished sweeping the cottages when I heard a strange call from the lake."

My ears perked up at Mrs. Vermilion's statement, and the color drained from my face, for I knew what she was about to say.

"I thought that it might be Jonesy, out for a swim," Mrs. Vermilion continued. "So, I walked toward the water to say hello. When I got close enough, I saw that it was no man in the water – at least no human man. It

40

was a slimy man, like those mermen you read about in folk tales, but this one had legs, not a fish tail. I froze when I saw it, and once it noticed me, it quickly dashed away into the lake.

"It must have been ten minutes after it left that I mustered up the courage to go down to the lake to see if what I saw was real."

"And did you find anything?" I asked rather quickly, my nerves showing.

"I did not. The creature never left the water, so it left no tracks. I really wasn't sure what I had seen. Eventually, I made my way back up to the farmhouse and told Jonesy about it. He was taken aback, and we agreed that I had seen an eachy. It's supposedly a guardian of the lake, and if it is seen by humans, it's a warning of bad things to come. And that eachy truly was a sign of my life taking a turn for the worse."

When she said that last sentence, I shivered, fearing that I too might be cursed.

"Could you tell us about your husband's death," said Holmes. "You explained much of it in your letter to me."

"It is as I wrote to you. Tom and Phillip were out fishing on the lake just off of the Great Island."

"So they were near land?" I asked.

"Yes, but far enough out to be in the deeps. They were fishing, the boat shook, and somehow Tom fell overboard. He then got tangled in the anchor. But Mr. Holmes, that's what makes so little sense to me. What rocked the boat enough for my husband to fall in? And then how could he have gotten himself wrapped up in the anchor?"

"Did your husband take his work with him on his fishing trip?" Holmes asked tactfully.

"You mean, was he drunk?" Mrs. Vermilion countered. "I'm sure he had a flask of whisky with him. Most of the men in the village take a drink often. It's what keeps me in business. But I knew my husband, Mr. Holmes. He never drank to the point of putting Phillip in danger. He loved the lad and was always careful about the boy."

Holmes took in her words, paused for a moment and asked, "Did your husband have any enemies? Anyone who wished him harm?"

"Not a soul," answered Mrs. Vermilion directly, finding the question absurd. "Tom was a beloved soul. He catered to the needs of this community," she said with a wave of her hand, motioning to the customers around us. "Our whisky is cheap and does its job. People thank us for that."

"Any business rivals?" Holmes asked.

Mrs. Vermilion chuckled. "You've seen what's around here. We aren't stealing customers away from the establishments in the heart of the village. Sure, some of them have a similar patrons, but people down that way don't venture as much to this end of the village."

"Any debts?"

"No, none at all. In fact, we've always prospered."

I was a bit exasperated, for Mrs. Vermilion had given my friend nothing as to who would harm her husband. Holmes, though, gave a nod, as if he'd concluded a routine interview, and warmly said, "Thank you Mrs. Vermilion. I know it is difficult for you to discuss this subject. Could you also tell me of the other men you mentioned? Anthony and Randall?"

"Anthony was a good man. He was a butcher who was good friends with my husband. After Tom passed, Anthony helped me maintain the business, gave me advice, and so even though I didn't know much besides being a barmaid, I was able to keep this place from being sold off.

"My friendship with Anthony quickly turned to courtship. Things were moving along gradually when Anthony suddenly disappeared."

"Disappeared? He went missing?" Holmes enquired.

"Yes, one day, back in April, he came to see me at my house. We had a dinner engagement that evening, but he showed up in the middle of the afternoon banging on the door as though there was a fire. I asked him what was the matter, and he told me that he had to leave for a few days. It was very important. He was taking the train that afternoon and that he would explain everything when he got back. He apologized several times, and then said that he loved me and wouldn't leave unless he had to. He repeated that it was important. He asked me if I trusted him. I said that of course I did. He told me again that he loved me and that he'd return shortly. He never did."

"Can you describe him to me?"

"He was a big man, Anthony was. He had a big heart," she reminisced fondly. "Kept his hair close cropped. Wore a mustache."

"Can you tell me of his hobbies?"

"He liked to read and fish. He played cards with some men on Saturday nights."

"Thank you," said Holmes, almost interrupting her. "And what about Randall."

"Randall was the bartender here. He had been here for a good ten years. He was very nice, not much like you'd expect in a bartender. On his days off, he'd come by on occasion and help me with household chores – fixing broken steps, replacing a cracked sink. Then a few weeks ago, he disappeared as well."

Holmes frowned deeply. "Do you recall the last time that you saw Anthony?"

"Exact date, no. It was in April. The middle of the month. But not the exact date."

"How about Randall?"

"Sure. It was last month, end of June."

Holmes nodded his head. He bit his lower lip slightly, his eyes looking upward, deep in thought. Then he gave a quick shake of his head and stared back into Mrs. Vermilion's eyes. "Tell me why you are concerned about your son."

"Phillip is all I have left in the world, Mr. Holmes. It seems that because I am cursed, everyone I am close to dies or disappears. Phillip is away at school most of the year."

"Does he go to St. Anne's?" I asked, referring to the local school, wondering if Mrs. Vermilion could afford the tuition through a wealthy family member.

"No, I'm afraid I don't have the money to send Phillip there. I send him to St. Francis. You don't know it? I'm really not surprised. It is a small Anglican school near Scotland. It is a two-hour train ride from here. It keeps me close to Phillip, but it also provides safety for him by keeping his distance."

The way Mrs. Vermilion said the last part about distance caught my attention. There appeared to be some double meaning which I believe she did not raise consciously.

"My concern is that Phillip is now back home for six weeks. He stayed late for a brief summer term. The headmaster is quite impressed with him, and believes that he'll make a fine barrister someday. But he's home now, and I fear with everyone else disappearing around me, Phillip is sure to be next."

Holmes took in all of this information. He reassured Mrs. Vermilion that he would do all he could to help her. He concluded with, "Thank you. That will be all for now. We shall be in touch." Holmes and I stood from our seats and stepped out of the booth. Mrs. Vermilion followed. She called to Holmes, "Wait! Do you think . . . do you think someone killed my husband."

Holmes hesitated, and then turned and responded. "I can't say for certain. By the time I leave this village, I will know the answer, and so shall you. Good day." Holmes tipped his hat to her, and then he added. "I will say that you were wise to contact me."

We stepped out into the light of day. It was now late morning, and I was famished. I asked Holmes if he'd like to join me in getting a bite to eat.

"Not now, Watson. I need to do some research and see what resources this village has to offer. I shall probably be busy for most of the day."

"Would you like me to accompany you?' I asked, hoping that he would say no. Despite seeing the eachy that morning, I had enjoyed my quiet solitude and wanted some time to explore the area on my own. Holmes must have read my expression and known my desire.

"No, no. I plan on spending much of my time reading. Get yourself some food, and we shall meet back at the cottage this afternoon."

Holmes and I walked together into the village. As we took our stroll and he pointed out some interesting architecture, I had the strange feeling that we were being watched. I kept looking back over my shoulder, but no one stood out. Holmes didn't seem to notice anything as he went on about the shift in buildings over the last fifty years. When we entered the centre of the village, the establishments became more upscale, and when we came across a particularly nice looking cheese shoppe, I said my goodbyes and enjoyed a good luncheon.

I then spent the remainder of the day walking about the village and strolling by the lakeside. The beauty of the lake was breathtaking, and I enjoyed hearing the sounds of the steamers crossing from one village to another.

My mind kept returning to the creature that I had witnessed that morning. I found myself second-guessing what I had seen. Could there really be an unknown *ichthian homosapien* residing in the lake? Yet, I thought back to what Mrs. Vermilion saw and noted the similarities in our descriptions.

After enjoying the lake, I decided to go back and do some investigating of my own. I went to the more weathered parts of the village and found some old-timers who were willing to answer the questions that I had about the eachy. Many turned me away, or truly did not know what I was talking about. I did find a handful willing to converse (some needing a drink to help ply them), and discovered that recordings of eachy sightings went back for over one-hundred years. In some instances, the creature was described as a pale horse emerging from the water, while at other times it was a tentacled beast like a kraken, and then there were the times when the creature resembled the slimy man-fish that I had seen with my own eyes.

I spent a few hours going to different pubs and hearing these tales. When my mind and belly were full, my pocketbook lighter, and the afternoon late, I decided it was time to hail a cab and head back to Jones's. I wandered a bit longer, heading toward the centre of the village where cabs would be in abundance, thinking through all that I had heard. Most of the eachy sightings could easily be dismissed. The supposed aquatic horses could just be stray mares who had wandered into the lake, kicking up water as they ran, looking like they emerged from the sea. The kraken-like beast was most likely a misidentified group of eel, common in the lake, which writhing together near the surface would resemble a tentacled beast. The humanoid that I had seen though was harder to dismiss. I couldn't recall any creature that looked similar, nor how a human – even covered in mud – could be mistaken for such a beast.

At last, I came to several cabs and was about to hail one when a voice behind me called, "Hey, you there!"

I turned to see an imposing young man. He must have been six feet tall and burly, yet with a childish face, sporting a touch of fuzz upon his soft features.

"Why did you visit my Mama?" he asked, pronouncing "Mama" as *Muh-maw*.

"I beg your pardon?" I said to the lad, puzzled. I really didn't know what he was talking about, and suggested he had the wrong man.

"I know you. I've been watching you all day. Visiting Mama at the tavern, asking the drunks and vagrants about her." The boy sneered, and there was something strange about his look. It was brutish, almost territorial.

"I . . . ." Then I remembered. "You were watching when I left the tavern. Have you been following me all day?"

"So what if I have? You just stay away from Mama. You hear me?" He held up a clenched fist menacingly. "Now get out of here before I lay you out."

I did as he asked. I was perplexed by this strange lad. Why was he following me? When we were on the outskirts of the village, we passed by Vermilion's tavern and that's when I realised what should have been obvious to me all along: The boy was Phillip, Mrs. Vermilion's son.

When I returned to the cottage, I told Holmes about my experiences that day, explaining in detail my encounter with Phillip.

"I am not surprised by his behavior," my friend began to explain. "He has suffered through a traumatic incident, being the sole witness of his father's demise. As I'm sure you are aware, children who lose a parent can sometimes create an almost unnatural bond with the one that is living. That is also true of the surviving parent. Surely you noted Mrs. Vermilion's affection towards her son and her concern over his life."

Holmes did have a point. There were a number of journal articles written on the matter, but the research was in its infancy.

"I agree with you, but there was something odd in this boy's demeanor. He was possessive of his mother and jealous of our conversation with her. He threatened to strike me."

"Well, I'm sure that I shall soon speak with the lad myself. If he is as possessive as you claim, either we shall find him sometime tomorrow, or he will surely find us."

I nodded my head in agreement and asked Holmes of his progress that day. He made a face of disgust. "There are few libraries in the area. We are isolated. I spent most of my time wiring to my scholarly acquaintances in London, Manchester, and a few in Cumbria. I have to use my outside resources to make progress. After my attempts at research, I returned to Vermilion's. I wanted to speak to some of the regulars about the Vermilion marriage, and about anyone who might wish Mr. Vermilion harm."

"Any luck there?" I asked.

"Perhaps," Holmes said with a fade to his voice. His eyes moved to stare out the window for a moment. "Mrs. Vermillion was honest about being well-loved in the community. No one I spoke with today had a grudge against her husband, and no one could think of anyone who thought ill towards the man – "

"However . . . ." I interrupted, knowing there was more to the story.

"Ah," Holmes said giving off one of his odd silent chuckles. "You've known me but a few months and already recognize my style in discussing a case. There were several people quite smitten with Mrs. Vermilion. Anthony Boroughgard was Mr. Vermilion's closest friend. Some claimed that his friendship kept him in line when it came to Mrs. Vermilion. Some claimed that Mrs. Vermilion's feelings for Boroughgard were as strong as his were for her. Then there is Randall Stevens, the bartender. He also always had eyes for Mrs. Vermilion. Everyone says that he was respectable towards her, though, and never behaved in an unbecoming manner."

"But both of those men are also missing," I said, understanding the disappointment my friend felt in his research for the day. How could the prime suspects also be missing?

"I know, but missing does not mean deceased. There could be more to their involvement in the case. They could also be completely innocent. It is far too early in the investigation to begin theorizing. There is one more man who always eyed Mrs. Vermilion, a farmer by the name of Sizemore. He is a bit older than she is, married with five children. The customers with whom I spoke said that Mr. Sizemore comes in about twice a week in the late afternoon on Tuesdays and Thursdays, the days when Mrs. Vermilion works the bar."

"Surely you don't think a family man could be guilty of any crimes."

"Ah, you are new at this game, my friend. You would be surprised to learn just how many seemingly pious people have wicked hearts."

We heard an echoing bell from the farmhouse which ended our conversation. Dinner was served.

The food that evening was delightful. Jones had managed to talk his cook into returning, and she made a lovely lamb stew. Jones had me tell him about the eachy that I had seen that morning, and the other guests listened attentively. One was a Turkish fellow who had stayed at Jones's every summer for the last few years. The others were a young couple from Blackpool celebrating their second wedding anniversary.

When the other couples had retired, we stayed up with Jones, playing whist and drinking brandy. Holmes asked him about his time abroad during the war, and I asked if any of our fellow veterans had ever visited him. He said he was still in touch with "Sharp-eyed" Pete, noted for his excellent shooting skills, and had been visited once by Captain Brenner. Other than visits from those two, it was only me. We took some time to reminisce about the great and terrible things that we had witnessed in Afghanistan.

After some recounting, Jones said that he was tired and had to get ready for work in the morning. He invited us to take a tour of the lake, free of charge, on his steamboat. Holmes and I thanked him for his kindness and agreed that we'd be aboard in the late morning.

That night, I didn't sleep soundly. I kept having visions of the eachy, rising up from the lake, its slimy hands clutching at me, dragging me down into the darkness. At one point, I thought I heard a cry in the night. I awakened and looked out the window, but there was a thick fog, and I saw nothing outside but darkness.

Despite my tumultuous night, I rose early the next morning and joined Holmes for breakfast at the farmhouse. The young couple entered the dining area as we were finishing our tea and scones, but the Turkish man was nowhere to be seen. I was happy to note that I wasn't the only one who slept late on holiday.

Jones's steamer was a sight to behold. The pleasure boat was much smaller than the large ships which carried wagons across the lake. The ship was luxurious, with a covered seating area and a bar. Holmes sat in a cushioned seat, smoking his briar pipe, and reading over several messages that he had received from his contacts. We had stopped at the post office that morning before boarding the ship, where he collected a half-dozen telegrams and then sent off three more. It was odd seeing the man who often ventured out in disguises that made him look like a pirate or a priest using regular methods to conduct his business.

I walked back and forth between the two sides of the ship, sporting Jones's binoculars, looking across the lake, admiring the different waterfowl, hearing the steady putter of the engine, and smelling the crisp cool air. The aroma of the lake area was so much more pleasurable than the many putrid smells of London. I wandered over to the rear of the ship. There were a few people in seats, but no one was standing by me. I looked out on the water through the binoculars and gave a start, for there, again, was that water beast – the eachy.

This time its head emerged right in front of a small island. Its mouth opened in a sickly grin showing razor sharp fangs. Its eyes were much more expressive and sinister. I gave a cry and pointed out to the water. An older couple jumped up to see what the commotion was about. A woman in pearls squinted and said, "Oh, very nice." I looked back and saw a pair of swans resting on the island behind where I had seen the head of the eachy emerge.

I hurried back to Holmes to tell him what I had seen. He invited me to join him and, in a whisper, I related everything. "I believe that I have the answer to the eachy," he explained.

"The answer? You mean you know what it is."

"I think so." Holmes handed me a letter that he had received from an antiquarian in Cumbria, containing a news clipping from April. I read the headline, "*Body of Missing Inventor Discovered in Woods*". The article explained that Archibald Stuart, an inventor with several patents of aquatic diving equipment, was discovered buried in the woods on his estate. He had been missing since June. He was supposed to travel the Continent exhibiting his latest invention, an aquatic suit which allowed the diver to breathe underwater for sustained periods of ten minutes, but he had never arrived at his engagements, and so a search was made of his premises. Police were asking anyone with information about Mr. Stuart to please come forward.

When I read the last part, I dropped the letter and stared at Holmes. "So, you believe – "

" – that whomever killed Mr. Stuart took his suit and has used it to scare the citizens of Wylington," he answered coolly.

"But then I saw the man in the aquatic suit just now. He must be on that small island. Perhaps I can ask Jones to dock the boat and we can investigate. Surely that's where he is hiding."

"I'm sure that he was," Holmes answered calmly. "But we've now moved away from the island, Watson. To turn back would take time, and I believe that the man you saw also saw you notice him. He has probably taken a boat and is on the water, blending in with everyone else. I'm afraid our capturing the man will need to wait."

After our pleasurable cruise of the lake, Holmes and I left the boat and hailed a cab to take us to Vermilion's. Holmes wanted to make sure we'd arrive in time to speak with Mr. Sizemore.

We were fortunate to find the man sitting at the bar, giving Mrs. Vermilion a toothy grin as he nursed a beer. The man was much older than I expected, possibly in his sixties. He was a wiry fellow of average height, stooped, with leathery skin aged from the harsh work of a farming life.

Holmes asked if he would join us in a booth, to which the man brushed us off. "I've got no time for strangers," he groused.

Fortunately, Mrs. Vermilion, working as bartender, came to our rescue. "You'll make time," she told him, sharply. "It's important that you talk to these men."

Mr. Sizemore held up his hands in surrender. "All right, all right. You got me." Then, without missing a beat, he gave Holmes a deathly glare and whispered, "For ten minutes. When I'm done the round you're about to buy me."

Holmes acquiesced, and a few seconds later we were sitting at a private table with drinks in hand. "Now, gents," Sizemore started, "You've supplied me with a beer and Margaret says I should talk with you, and that she hired you to investigate Tom's death. Waste of time, if you ask me."

"So, you believe Mr. Vermilion's death was an accident?" I asked.

Here Mr. Sizemore's tone changed, and he looked over my shoulder to see if Mrs. Vermilion as watching us. "I didn't say that."

"I don't understand," I said to him.

Sizemore gritted his teeth and stared into his beer. "Mr. Sizemore," Holmes started sharply.

"Give me a second," Sizemore pleaded. "I don't like speaking ill of kin."

"Your kin?" asked Holmes.

"Naw. Margaret's kin, I mean." Here Sizemore paused, looking around the room again to make sure no one was listening. Satisfied that no one was, he continued. "I'm talking about Phillip. Something was never right with that boy. He's mighty possessive of his mother, and he always acted queer when he was with Tom."

"What do you mean by 'queer'?" I asked.

"Almost like he was jealous of his own father – like he wanted his mother all to himself."

"So you believe that Phillip murdered his father?" I blurted, aghast at the accusation.

"Whoa," called Sizemore defensively, as though I was a mare he was stopping in its tracks. "I never said that. Truth is, I don't know what

49

happened to Tom. Only one who does is Phillip, and I just think . . . ." He let out a long sigh. "I just think if there is someone who could have done Tom harm, it would be the only one who was with him when he died. Truth is, Tom died, then Anthony and Randall up and disappeared. Seems the only person jealous of all three was Phillip."

"And what about you?" asked Holmes.

"What do you mean, sir?"

"I mean we've heard that you also hold affections towards Mrs. Vermilion."

Sizemore stared at Holmes for a minute, wide-eyed and shaking. I thought he might shout at my friend or make a dash for the exit. Instead, the man burst out laughing. "Oh, that's a good one, Mr. Holmes."

"I've heard that you and Mrs. Vermilion . . . ." started Holmes.

"Flirt," answered Sizemore mirthfully. "Look at me gentlemen. I'm a married man a good twenty years older than Margaret. Of course I like flirting with her – makes me imagine I can still catch the attention of a woman at my age. Margaret knows it's a game. She plays along with me as she does with quite a few other old-timers. Makes us feel good and makes us spend our money here. But never, gentlemen, would I even think to dishonor my bond with my wife. Why, I'd be lost without my sweet Evelyn."

I found the man to be sincere, and I could tell from Holmes's expression that he did as well. I also thought to my own unsettling experience with Phillip. I wondered, could a boy kill his own father over his mother's affection? The thought chilled me to the core.

On the way back to our cottage, I asked Holmes his impression of Sizemore. "I concur with your assessment," he said. "Unless I learn some new information, I believe the man is not a murderer."

"It's too bad that Phillip didn't show himself today. I'm interested in your opinion of him."

Holmes gave a look of puzzlement. "Didn't show himself? Why, Watson, the boy followed our every step today. The only time he didn't accompany us was on the steamer."

"Why is he suspicious of us? Do you think Sizemore was on to something?"

"I don't know, but I intend to find out."

The next two days were rather uneventful for me. Holmes went into the village each day to send and receive messages, consult with Mrs. Vermilion, and also speak with other locals. I wondered if this would be one of the mysteries that Holmes never solved, or if he'd politely inform Mrs. Vermilion that her husband's death did appear to be an accident.

I spent my days on Jones's farm, walking the grounds, using a rifle that he'd left me for target practice, and using the loaned binoculars for birdwatching. Jones joined me when he returned from his job, and we took turns shooting at glass jars and decoys we'd put atop tree stumps.

"It has been nice having you around, Johnny-boy," Jones said after shattering an old milk bottle. "You should move here."

"It is beautiful on the lake," I agreed.

"You can live here with me," Jones said, seriously. "I have plenty of room." He handed me the rifle.

I loaded it and took aim at a decoy pheasant. "I have responsibilities in London."

"Bah!" Jones waved his hand as if the air was fouled by my statement. "You can always move here. We need a good doctor."

"I don't know," I said and took my shot. The pheasant fell from its perch. "This is a nice place to visit." I handed the gun back to Jones. "But I think the city is more my pace."

"At least consider my offer."

That evening I mentioned my conversation with Jones to Holmes. "You may need to look for another roommate," I joked. "He offered me free room and board."

"This is a pleasant community," Holmes said thoughtfully while enjoying his pipe as if he was seriously considering the offer. "I've enjoyed my time speaking with the locals. In some ways, I am saddened that my investigation is drawing to a close."

"You mean you've solved Mrs. Vermilion's case," I asked quite surprised.

"Not quite," he said. "Though I have made significant progress. Why, today I finally was able to interview Phillip."

"You did! What did that rapscallion have to say?"

"He is, as you said, a brutish fellow. While he has an intelligence, particularly at mathematics, and far beyond his years, his emotions are stunted, like that of a child much younger than his age.

"Phillip agreed to meet me at Vermilion's – well I should say his mother made him speak to me at Vermilion's. The young man stood out from the others in the pub, as he was well-dressed in a suit and necktie. He told me how upset he was that I was looking into the case of his father's death.

"'The fool fell overboard,' Phillip told me with a sneer. 'What else is there to investigate?'

"'You do not think it odd that your father, a man who lived his whole life on the lake, should make such a simple mistake as falling overboard?'

"'Father had been drinking that day. Anyone with a good amount of whisky in them can lose their balance.'

"'Your mother tells me that your father didn't drink to excess around you.'

"'That's just her making the sinner into a saint,' the lad said, rolling his eyes at his mother's ignorance. 'Mama can't admit to the truth. Father was drunk, fell overboard, and tangled himself in the anchor. That's all there is to it.'

"'What about your report that the boat rocked before your father fell into the water? Any idea what could have caused the boat to suddenly lurch?'

"'It wasn't so sudden,' the boy explained. 'We had some wind that day and encountered rough waters for a few minutes. The boat didn't capsize. I didn't fall in. No, you can't blame father's death on anything but himself.'"

I told Holmes that did make sense. If Mr. Vermilion were inebriated, it would explain how he lost his balance and became tangled in the anchor. Holmes told me that he agreed. He also pressed Phillip on his knowledge of the other missing men. "When I mentioned Anthony Boroughard to the young man, that is when his childish features truly came out. He acted like a schoolboy whose prized toy was taken away for not doing his chores.

"'That man just wanted to steal Mama away. Always looking for an opportunity, that one, pretending to be Father's friend just to steal Mama's affection. Well, it didn't work. He knew she didn't care for him, and so he went away. Same with that Randall Stevens.' Phillip pouted as he told me about these two, and he rocked back and forth slightly in his chair, hugging his body. I could tell that the thought of these two men greatly upset him, almost made him ill.

"'So you believe the two men left the village when they believed they couldn't win over your mother's heart?' I asked him.

"'Yes. They couldn't see that I was enough for Mama. With Father gone, she was content being a widow. I provided any affection she might need.'"

I told Holmes that was a shocking statement to come from a mother's son.

"Is it really, Watson? The boy has gone through a traumatic situation. He lost one parent and is now overprotective of the other. He sees the mother's suitors as competition for his affection."

"He strikes me as a bad seed, Holmes."

"Perhaps." Holmes looked grim for a moment, and then he asked if I'd like to smoke. In town that day, he had purchased some fine Cuban cigars. Of course I took him up on the offer.

We smoked for a while in silence, and then I asked Holmes where his investigation would go from here.

"It shall be concluded tomorrow," he explained. "Our time here has been enjoyable, Watson. I fear the weeks ahead shall not be."

"Why is that? If you will bring the case to a close, then you shall leave here with your pocketbook full after a pleasant time away."

Holmes looked sullen. I wasn't sure what was bothering him, but there was something about the case that he found unsettling. I pressed him, but he said all would be revealed the following evening. "I've told Jones that we shall be leaving in the morning. He was sad to hear of your coming departure, and I'm sure he shall keep you up late tonight talking. In the morning, our carriage shall stop at Vermilion's, where I shall inform Mrs. Vermilion that her husband's death was indeed an accident, and then collect my fee. We shall then go to the train station."

"From there?"

"From there, we shall take a different cab to a secluded house I have rented in the woods overlooking the lake. It is in that house that we shall capture our killer."

"I have my Webley at your disposal."

"Good, Watson, for I fear we may need it."

Jones behaved as Holmes expected, treating us both to a fine bottle of Merlot, and inviting us both to live on his property and move to Wylington. "Do either of you really want a life in that city?" Jones said to us somewhat in jest. "The more I read about it, the more it sounds like one of the nine circles."

Holmes agreed with that assessment. "That is the main reason my services are required there."

I thought of Holmes living in the country, away from his books and resources, away from the constant criminal activity. I wondered if he'd last more than a month in Wylington before going out of his mind.

We both thanked Jones for his hospitality and retired for the evening. That night my sleep was restless. I kept seeing the eachy, its dark bulbous eyes staring at me, its puffy lips parted to reveal its sharp, menacing fangs. "You aren't real!" I shouted at the fiend, to which it replied with dark and menacing laughter.

The station was bustling that morning, which made it easy for Holmes and me to disappear in the crowd without the driver or anyone noting that we didn't actually board a train to London. However, we didn't immediately go to the house in the woods. Holmes sent a few messages before deciding we could catch a ride to our evening residence.

"I needed to send word to the local constabulary," Holmes explained after we had boarded a dogcart.

"They will be there this evening?"

Holmes made a sour face. "No, they will not. If it was Lestrade, he'd be there. As much as I complain about the man, he is reliable. I have no relationship with the force in these parts. I let them know that I had information about the killer of Mr. Stuart, the inventor, and gave just enough details in my message to pique their interest. But I'm afraid that if they send a man to the house, he'll leave his carriage parked out front, alerting the killer, or will make a move before we get a confession. No, it is better for us to apprehend the man and then contact the police to arrest him."

I patted the Webley I kept holstered to my side. "We have all we need to capture the man. Can you tell me who it is?"

Holmes held his finger to his lips to indicate quiet. Then he whispered, "Not yet. There is always a chance . . . ." Then he shook his head and patted me on the knee. "Have faith, my friend. We shall apprehend the criminal tonight, and then you shall know all."

The "house" that Holmes had rented for the evening was actually a small castle from the sixteenth century overlooking the lake. The brickwork was old with vines and moss covering a good part of it. The interior consisted of a ground floor entry, sitting room, and kitchen. The first floor contained the bedrooms.

In the master bedroom, overlooking the lake, Holmes moved an armchair directly before the window. He then removed from his luggage an oversized shirt that he told me he had purchased the day before for this event. "This shall be my attire for the evening. When it comes time, I'll put on this shirt and sit by the window. Watson, I want you to stand in the closet, out of sight, with your Webley at the ready. I've sent the killer a letter which will most assuredly lure him here. For now, we shall enjoy our afternoon."

That we did. Holmes spent the time writing up some notes he had made about how best to use alcohol to ply the truth out of people. "You have to take into account the weight and height of the person," Holmes explained. "Too much alcohol in their blood will make them talk but not necessarily tell the truth." I walked the grounds, enjoying my view of the lake, wondering if I might spy the eachy again. All I saw were some geese and an occasional fish jumping out of the water.

After we enjoyed a smoke and ate sandwiches brought from the village, Holmes said that it was time to go upstairs. The sun was now setting in the sky. He lit a single candle on the mantel to give enough light so that someone from the road could look up and see the shape of a person in the window. Holmes pulled back the curtain and lifted the pane to let in the sounds from outside. He then sat in his chair, waiting. I took my place inside the closet. We stayed in our places for a long time, probably hours. The night had become quite dark, and the moon was obscured by clouds, so no lunar light helped illuminate the outside. As I stood in the closet, I began to wonder if the killer would make an appearance. Then, I saw Holmes sit up slightly, and I heard a rustling outside. The front door then creaked open and footsteps were heard climbing the steps, approaching us. The door to the room opened. Holmes remained in his seat. A man slowly entered the room, and I saw in the murky light that he clutched a dagger in his right hand.

Holmes jumped from his seat and the man started to charge but then stopped. I leapt from my hiding spot and called, "Stop!" The man turned to me and I nearly dropped my gun, for the figure that I saw before me was an impossibility. Standing in the light, wild-eyed, was *Jones*. His teeth were gritted, his features savage. His beard almost seemed to make a mane around his face. He was more primordial than human, a reversion to an extinct ancestor. I was waiting for him to pounce on me, to try and throttle me. I feared that I would need to shoot my friend.

Jones let out a guttural noise, then his face slackened and drooped, and his knife dropped to the ground. He stepped towards me, reached out a quivering hand. "Johnny-boy," he said, almost asking a question. "It's you. You didn't leave me."

"And it is I," my friend called, catching Jones's attention. He turned his head and stared at the detective as Holmes explained. "Surprised that I am not young Phillip, eh? The lad you came here to murder tonight."

"No! No!" Jones yelled at Holmes then he turned back to me and clutched my shirt, pleading with me. "You have to know, Johnny-boy – it isn't me! It's something *inside* me. Something that takes over. It is from the *lake*!"

Holmes walked to Jones and put his hand on his shoulder, pulling him back from me, prying him off. "The lake, Mr. Jones? Please explain." Holmes turned the chair from the window and offered it to Jones to sit. Holmes made sure that I kept my gun aimed at the man. Jones accepted the offer and sat in the chair. He held his face in his hands for a moment, and then looked up at us. "It started when I was a young lad. The lake . . . it *talked* to me. It told me to do the most vulgar things, starting with Margaret, my governess. I was able to keep the beast contained though, kept it deep within me . . . Then came the war. During that time, the creature surfaced. It controlled me, led me to slaughter dozens of people. I could feel the thing wanting me to kill more and more, to feed its hunger – not just enemy soldiers, but their women and children. Whole villages.

55

It happened just once. I was on a scouting mission with Scotts and Milton. We were ambushed. I don't remember what happened. One minute I was fighting alongside my friends, and the next I found myself miles away, drenched in blood, bodies of a family strewn all around me, their house in tatters. It was then that I threw myself from my horse."

I thought back to Jones's service to his country – how the superiors lamented his injury, and that we lost a great soldier who showed valor on the battlefield. I wondered what happened to Scotts and Milton who were reported as dead. Did enemy combatants kill them, or was it Jones in a manic fury?

"I came back to Wylington and resumed my life here, thinking I could keep the beast at bay again, but no. Now it had tasted blood and wanted more. It spoke to me, told me to do terrible things. I tried to resist it, but then it controlled me. First, it took my driver, and then my housekeeper. I wasn't sure what to do. Then I was visited by Captain Brenner, who stayed with me for a fortnight. When he was here, the creature seemed subdued. I can't explain it, but having a friend nearby gave me strength. So I wrote to others hoping they would come to me on a holiday. "Sharp-eyed" Pete came, and his visit kept the creature at bay, but then . . . *then the creature got its skin.*"

"You refer to Mr. Stuart's diving suit," Holmes explained.

"Yes, yes," Jones was shaking now, his fingers alternating from clutching at his beard to gesticulating wildly. "I read about Stuart in the news and saw a picture of his suit. The creature wanted it and told me it needed to have it. I went to sleep that night and awakened to find three days had passed. I discovered the suit in my cellar and also that I had made arrangements with my employer to be gone for a few days to visit a sick uncle that I'd invented.

"Then came Margaret's sighting of the eachy. I knew it was me and wanted to tell her, but I couldn't. That fiend was controlling me, controlling my actions. Then it visited me in the night, told me I could have Margaret, that I could do all the things to her that it had promised me in my youth. It just had to get rid of her husband, and then I could marry her.

"So, you killed Tom Vermilion," Holmes said.

"No!" Jones said, tears now streaming down his face. "*The creature did!* It used the oxygen tank, knocked Tom out of his boat, and wrapped the anchor around his neck. Then it killed several of my houseguests – they would just disappear in the middle of the night. They were out-of-towners who were often from other countries – foreigners, easy to say they just up and left and didn't say where they were going. My cellar . . . my cellar is full of their bodies."

"Why did you . . . ." I stopped myself to help my friend, "Why did the *creature*," I corrected, "kill Anthony?"

"Because he was on to us. He knew about the timing of Stuart's missing aquatic suit and Margaret seeing the eachy. Margaret told me about Anthony suddenly leaving, and the creature heard her, too. That night the beast killed Anthony. I have no memory of it. But the following night, the creature told me it had cornered Anthony and stabbed him to death. It did the same to Stevens, the bartender. It lured him out to the farm and gutted him, buried him in the cellar. The creature told me that I only had to kill Phillip and I'd have Margaret all to myself.

"But Phillip was away at school, kept under watch. The beast couldn't get him there, and so it waited, biding its time. Waiting for the perfect opportunity. It happened today when I received the letter. I'm assuming that you wrote it, Mr. Holmes."

Holmes nodded.

"Ah, that was a clever move, saying that Phillip suspected his father was murdered and wanted to meet me out here tonight. You brought the monster out. It is unstoppable now. Even your visiting me couldn't contain the beast, Johnny-boy. I thought that it could, but now that it has its skin, it taunted me by showing itself to you, and then it killed that Turkish fellow just to prove to me that I couldn't contain it anymore. There's nothing that I can do. Nothing that anyone can do!"

Jones then jumped from his seat, grabbed the chair, and threw it at Holmes and me. He gave a howl of despair, and then before we could stop him, he leapt from the window. We ran to see if he was still alive. The fall wasn't that far to the ground.

But Jones had gone down head first, like a diver. He lay on the ground, his neck snapped. The lake monster was dead.

Shortly thereafter, Holmes notified the local police. They were suspicious of Holmes and me when they collected Jones's body, but afterwards they had searched his house and discovered a dozen bodies they saw that we were telling the truth. Mrs. Vermilion thanked Holmes for solving the murders of her husband, her suitor, and her friend. "I can't believe Jonesy was capable of doing such horrible things. He was always so kind to me, so kind . . . ." she sobbed.

I had the same thought about my friend. How could he have such evil lurking inside him? What split his mind into two men, one good and the other evil? I later researched the occurrence in dual identity and saw that it was rare but not unknown. Most doctors and psychologists scoffed at the diagnosis and believed it to be false. It wasn't until a few years later, when Robert Louis Stevenson published his epic work, *The Strange Case of Dr.*

Jekyll and Mr. Hyde, that the science was taken seriously. I always thought it ironic that a work of fiction changed the medical world for the better.

After leaving Wylington, on the train ride back to London, I pressed Holmes on how he knew that Jones was the murderer. "When Margaret wrote to me about her case, I was suspicious of Jones, though not of him being Mr. Vermilion's killer. At first, I thought he just wanted you to visit him. Then, he had Mrs. Vermilion hire me to find her husband's killer. You remember it was Jones who suggested the idea to Mrs. Vermilion. I could see that he wanted you to visit him desperately, for if I visited, surely you would accompany me.

"Then came your sighting of the eachy. It was then I suspected Jones of seeking publicity. If it made the papers that a doctor and a detective from London saw the eachy, the sightings would be taken more seriously and could bring in more business to the village. But the eachy never appeared to me, and Jones never sought out the local press to capture your story. Then came the news of Mr. Stuart and his missing invention. The eachy had only been spotted by you and Mrs. Vermilion in the same spot by Jones's cottage, which led me to believe that Jones was behind the sightings. I surmised that Jones was behind the killings and was doing it to win the heart of Mrs. Vermilion. I admit, Watson, that I hadn't realized the full scope of Jones's delusions, his dual personality, nor the extent of his heinous crimes."

"There is, of course, one piece of the puzzle which doesn't quite fit," I said to Holmes.

"Ah, you refer to your second sighting of the eachy when we were on our boat ride. I've thought about that myself, and I have come to two conclusions."

"Which are . . . ?" I pressed.

"Holmes looked out the window at the passing countryside for a moment before answering, "The first is that you imagined the creature. You did say that the eachy looked quite different, it's features more pronounced, almost more lifelike. But then, after you shouted at seeing something, others saw only a few birds near the shore."

"I don't know Holmes, I have a hard time believing I imagined it. What is your second conclusion?"

"That you did indeed see an eachy."

"Really, Holmes," I grumbled. "Surely you jest at my expense."

He turned to me, showing me he was deadly serious. "Not at all, my good man. New species are being discovered every year. Why, I hear that a dwarf dolphin has been discovered in New Zealand, and a hairy man-beast is reported to have been sighted in the Congo. An *ichthyian* humanoid creature in a lake of this size is not an impossibility. The world

58

is a large place. Though it becomes smaller every day, I believe it has many wonders still to bestow upon us."

The *Juju* Men of Richmond
by Mark Sohn

Chapter I

I feel that enough time has passed that I may share one of the un-heralded adventures that involved my friend and colleague, Mr. Sherlock Holmes, and myself in the Year of our Lord 1882. As most of the protagonists and many of those with peripheral involvement have passed away or retired, perhaps those survivors of this extraordinary episode will forgive me for what I feel the public has every right to know. We live in an age of wonder, it seems, where every new month brings news of some great invention or development – passengers flying by airboats in America, the launch of the *Britannic* and *Aquitania* here. Yet as recently as a few years ago, Great Britain and Her Empire were imperilled by one of the most insidious plots ever conceived. This then, at last, is the story of what transpired . . . .

That early December in the year 1882 will be remembered by many as a wet, frozen one. The pavements were particularly treacherous with ice, and the juvenile gangs were out to "assist" hapless pedestrians who had gone over, robbing them of their valuables and fleeing, their progress all the easier for the spikes they had worn instead of nails. I had just returned from attending a breech birth in Marylebone and was alighting from the cab when just such a group of rapscallions fairly flew past me, clutching their spoils and hooting with laughter.

I looked to the pavement to see an elderly gentleman sprawled across the flags, red-faced with anger at the indignity to which he had been subjected. Seeing his plight, I offered my hand, and he was pulled to his feet with the additional aid of a passing drayman who had been on his way home. Stronger arms than mine hefted the portly frame as if it were a child's doll and, refusing thanks, the man handed the unfortunate gentleman his stick and was on his way while I was still brushing the snow and ice from the old man's Ulster.

A brisk southerly wind was blowing a cold rain along Baker Street and it was unbearably cold. I suggested a medicinal brandy, but the old fellow seemed keen to get on, thanking me for my assistance with a distracted air that spoke of purposefulness and a resolution to progress to his journey's end. It was only when we both went up to the door of 221b that I realised his destination was co-incident with my own.

There was no point in letting the poor fellow ring up, so I let us in with my key, and hats and overcoats were hung in the hall before I trudged those well-trodden stairs behind him to discover a hearty fire in the grate – and no Holmes. Finding our rooms empty, I rang down for the landlady and she provided us with sustenance in the form of the shortbread she had brought down from a recent familial visit to the land of her ancestors. She informed me Holmes hadn't been seen since the morning and showed herself out.

Taking my customary seat, I waved my guest to that customarily reserved for Holmes's clients and offered him a brandy, to which he acceded. Our visitor did not take tobacco, so only one cigar was lit and I felt myself ready to act in Holmes's stead until the detective himself were here.

"There, you see? Even beset by barbarians at the gate, we remain civilised. Pray tell me your name, sir, and your business with Sherlock Holmes." The gentleman leaned forward on his stick, which was somewhat unique, having a fringing of beads of some kind around it and an altogether African appearance, being shaped from some tropical hardwood with a chased-and-carved shaft and a knob in the form of what looked to be a monkey's skull.

"My name is easily given, Mr. Holmes. I am Silas Pym, and I came to see your colleague, Doctor Watson."

This was certainly unexpected and I was quite unprepared for it.

"Well, I am John Watson – Doctor that is – but why should you wish to see me? You do not appear ill."

"Indeed, I am the model of fortitudinous health, Doctor. However, it is not *me* who is the patient, so to speak." Pym's face was quite red from the brandy as he leaned forward in his chair.

"Are you, by any chance familiar with the Webb Anthropological Institute? I see you are not. The museum is a comparatively modest affair compared with the British, but it is held in high regard in academic circles." The name Webb seemed familiar, almost commonplace, but I couldn't recall it, much to my chagrin. My client – for indeed he had sought me out rather than Holmes – continued, explaining that the notable explorer and hunter Sir Tristram Webb had bequeathed his singular collection of finds and treasures to the Institute that now bore his name and to which he himself was Curator. At the mention of that valiant name, I felt ashamed not to have known it at once!

The exploits of Sir Tristram across three continents were known to every schoolboy in the Empire, from his triumphant conquest of the dark, untamable reaches of the *Rio Negro* to his expeditions to the Bambutoo pygmies of the Congo, there was hardly a corner of the Earth unknown to

61

this remarkable man. Indeed, it was said that to hold one's nerve in the face of a particularly vicious spin-bowler was to "Stand like Webb" after his cool-headed action in the Natal where he stood his ground against a murderous five-ton rhinoceros that had already killed five of his native bearers. With only two cartridges remaining, he brought the beast down just yards from the encampment where his wife was at that very moment giving birth to their son. With typical stoicism and humour, he gave the boy the middle name of Hornsworthy in honour of the creature.

Honoured though I was with such a visit, I had yet to discern any purpose for it.

"In what way may I be of assistance, Mr. Pym?" My question produced a most unusual reaction, as if the room itself were suddenly blanketed in fear. It cannot have been entirely my fancy that the fire itself seemed to shudder and shrink back from the grate, the air between myself and my petitioner rarefied and chill? When he spoke to answer, I could only stare in disbelief.

"Doctor, as improbable as this may sound, Sir Tristram Webb came back to the Institute in the small hours of this very morning."

"Improbable you say? How so?"

"Because I myself helped to bury him not three days since."

This was too much – surely the man was either demented or this was a ghastly joke, doubtless one of Holmes's own whimsies. It will be remembered that this was the man capable of such japery as placing a message in *The Times* simply stating "*To L. Flee at Once. All is discovered. Only Southampton safe.*" The chaos at the Southampton Docks when some two-hundred people with the correspondent initial clamoured to be allowed to board an already full ferry was widely reported at the time. However, I felt it my duty to enquire further and asked after Sir Tristram's current health. It was not, after all unknown for people to be buried alive. Only the last year, a famous case had emerged at St. Swithins. Fortunately, the woman in question had been rescued before the grave had been filled, though many others were, horrifically, not so fortunate.

"He is alive, then?"

"He is not." This plain answer roused my passion, by now I was determined this was a poor idea of humour.

"Then he must be dead, surely!" I rose to my feet preparatory to ejecting this specimen from my lodgings, but he merely shook his head.

"He is neither dead, nor is he alive, Doctor. That is why I sought you out." Rising to his own feet, he reached for his stick.

"I have the acquaint of a Lady to whom you and Mr. Holmes rendered invaluable service – I shall keep her name to myself as the matter was and remains delicate. I feel you alone of the medical profession would be sympathetic to such an impossible patient. If you would just come with me now to Richmond, you can examine Sir Tristram for yourself."

The ride was made eerie by the quiet. The hansom's wheels fell on snow hard with frost, and even the horses' hooves were largely silent as we progressed on our south-westerly course, passing by Kensington and below Shepherd's Bush, headed for the bridge at Hammersmith. My companion had relapsed into silence for most of the journey so I had plenty of time to consider the strangeness of the case that I was being asked to diagnose. Ordinarily, I would have smoked, but for some reason felt it inappropriate. I cannot say why to this day. The bridge passed below our wheels and I looked down on the Thames, not yet quite frozen, to see the usual traffic passing along London's great artery.

At length, we found ourselves skirting above the Great Park at Richmond, the pagoda at Kew visible for a time to the north of us. Finally, we entered the Mortlake Road and eventually drew into a massive villa to the south. I was determined, it must be understood, to remember precisely the details of our drive – perhaps even then I had suspected that Holmes's involvement might be foreseen in some way unknown to my conscious, rational mind.

The building itself was constructed in what I believe is known as the *Italianate* style, a signorial tower above a corniced roof. The gates were wide open and I caught a glimpse of large bronze discs on each bearing the name of the Institute. The lamplighter was at work as we pulled up outside an impressive bronze door. I caught my breath at the sight of intertwined dragons in relief and, as if he had expected such a reaction, Mr. Pym leaned closer and imparted the information that the doors had previously graced the Hidden Palace of Tibet. I had thought it a myth and said as much, but Pym merely smiled at my ignorance, ushering me inside.

The Webb Anthropological Institute was like no other building I have seen before or since. From the galleried marble hall, with its hanging tapestries and unrivalled collection of Italian weapons and armour, we walked through vast corridors literally lined with artefacts and curios from every corner of the globe. As it was near to closing time, there were few visitors other than myself. Warming to his role, Pym took delight in introducing me to Zulu spears and shields, Amazonian tribal masks, and Egyptian head-dresses. I must confess I found it all rather enchanting and had almost forgotten the grim purpose of my visit when, at length, we stopped at a locked door, above which a sign declared the rooms beyond to be *The Halls of Primitive Belief.*

63

Producing an over-sized key ring, Pym paused and turned to me, his expression sombre.

"Doctor, I would ask that you prepare yourself. Sir Tristram . . . well, he . . . ." Seeing the man lost for words, I laid a hand upon his shoulder.

"I have seen unusual cases before now. I have been in Afghanistan and saw something of the Zoroastrians there. Now, pray open this door and show me to my patient." How often have I regretted those foolish words since!

The chamber was large and mostly in darkness, the sole illumination coming from a lofty and distant skylight. As Pym went to light a lamp, I wondered why the gaslights were not in use. No doubt anticipating my curiosity, he answered it in a stage whisper that seemed rather melodramatic at the time.

"The light disturbs his eyes greatly – a few lamps are all that can be permitted." So saying, he handed me a lamp.

As my eyes adjusted to the sepulchral gloom, I was able to discern that the space in which we stood was arrayed with glass cases of varying proportion. Each contained an exhibit related to native superstitions from the inhabited continents. I could make out an aboriginal figure dressed in animal skins and carrying a pouch, a mannequin of a Mayan priest engaged in a blood sacrifice, and several more examples besides.

Clearly steeling himself as if expecting an ordeal of some type, Pym stepped forward into the void between the rows of cases, towards the ominous emptiness at the centre of the hall. I saw we were approaching what appeared to be a wall made of reed matting, surmounted by various human skulls and what seemed to be a crude altar, the backdrop for the most ghastly sight of my life.

"Good God!" I ejaculated. For there, seated on a rough wooden throne surmounted by garishly-coloured feathers which I took to be ostrich, was a man who was quite clearly dead . . . and yet he was breathing!

I went closer, raising my lamp to examine the hideous specimen. The eyes that stared at me were dull and quite opaque – yet they reacted to light. The skin was of a pallor associated with death, and *livor mortis* clearly displayed. The hands that were as claws clutching the arms of the throne were rigid, immobile, and yet I saw to my horror a faint, yet unmistakable pulse. With the aforementioned condition present, this was, medically speaking, quite impossible. Forgetting for the moment the repulsive condition of the man, I set my lamp down and reached out to take the pulse – for pulse there indeed was. The wrist that I chose was clammy and quite cold. Nothing in my medical career had prepared me for such as this abomination, yet my calling drove me to complete a basic examination.

A quick application of stethoscope showed there was no regular heartbeat, yet respiration was clearly audible, the chest rising and falling slightly with a sickening crepitation. Mystified, I attempted to examine the ocular nerve, yet was unable to do so to my satisfaction due to the corneal clouding present. I did think to draw off some blood, though by the time I reached the microscope I shared with Holmes, any attempt at examination would be rendered useless. In any case, my attempt to extract the vital fluid worked rather better than I had intended, a spray of dark, venous blood meeting the intrusion of the needle. I was able to fill a bottle with ease, though stemming the subsequent flow proved somewhat harder. In the end, a dressing applied under pressure seemed to do the trick, and I noted this as yet another example of the queerness of the whole thing.

Finally, I pronounced myself utterly at a loss to explain either the symptoms or the ailment that produced such startling and pronounced effects and turned to Silas Pym in failure.

"I am afraid this man is quite beyond my aid. He must be conveyed immediately to a hospital." The weathered old face creased into an expression of rueful regret.

"I am sorry, Doctor, but he cannot leave this room."

"And why is that, I should like to know?"

I can still hear his strident answer. "Because if he is removed from the immediate bounds of the altar, he will die!"

We sat in the Curator's office, a little cubby-hole of a place tucked away beneath the grand staircase that led to the gallery. The small cubicle was replete with bric-a-bracs and oddities and seemed in itself a microcosm of the building that surrounded it. Pym's curious statement could not be left unremarked, and I beseeched him to explain it. Curiously, he seemed unwilling to discuss his odd claim any further and I was left with the distinct impression that the man was frightened – though of what it was hard to say.

"Well, Doctor, I must thank you for your prompt attention. Please submit your bill and it will be settled promptly."

I had the feeling my presence had become extraneous, even tiresome, and stood to leave. I attempted to impose a sense of importance upon the man before my departure.

"I must insist Sir Tristram is either removed to a hospital at once or I shall be forced to report this to the proper authority."

"I assure you he is in good hands, Doctor. The family physician is in attendance and we are consulting with experts in tropical disease." Offering his hand, Pym got up to show me to the door where the hansom was waiting to return me. Clambering in, on a whim I directed the jarvey to take me to St. Bartholomew's Hospital in Smithfield.

Chapter II

My late return to Baker Street came as somewhat of a relief, especially when my weary step was met by the door to our lodgings being thrown open and I was hailed by Sherlock Holmes.

"Watson! The very man. Come in at once and warm yourself by the fire. Mrs. Hudson has made us some of her admirable cocoanut pastries and there are fish cakes on the warmer." Gratefully, I laid my bag on the chair by my desk and went to fill a plate. I had no sooner sat down when Holmes took up a twist and lit his disreputable and oily clay pipe, regarding the air between us with a forced aimlessness while I ate. My hunger proved resilient to the shock upon my system imposed by the atrocious condition of Sir Tristram, but even so I was taken aback when Holmes abruptly enquired as to my visit to Barts.

I had known Holmes for nearly two years then, and should have anticipated the question. I had not, and was unprepared for it.

"But Holmes, how can you place me at the hospital? I didn't see you there. Have you talked with Stamford today?"

"I have not. Really, Watson, it isn't too great a leap. If I explain, you're sure to think it commonplace."

"Please do so." I confess to being somewhat irked by Holmes's easy manner and determined to deflate him by finding some flaw in his reasoning.

Taking a languid pull at his clay, he stretched his arms out and settled himself back in his seat, one leg carelessly cocked over the other. "You returned from your midwifery at somewhat after twelve in the mid-day. Mrs. Hudson was clear on the hour as she herself brought up a supply of shortbread. She observed you in the company of a stout elder. This man sought you out after suffering some mishap – a fall perhaps. He is somewhat lacking in height, though not in girth, and walks with an exotic stick of tropical origin."

To admit that I was crestfallen would be an understatement. I was fairly aghast, dismayed even. Still, my natural obstinacy would not let me give in so easily.

"And how can you know this, Holmes?"

"The same way I know '*B*' and '*C*' follow '*A*', my good fellow. The marks on our carpet both here and downstairs show where his shoes and stick are in relation to each other. Such a short stride with so deep a tread!

The frequency of the indentations from the stick merely confirm my observation – and so, incidentally, did Mrs. Hudson." Again I persisted.

"And the mishap?"

"The glass on the table beside the chair I reserve for my clients – glass in the singular. You did not drink, therefore a medicinal drink, given to steady the nerve. The glass fairly reeks of cognac – the somewhat mediocre variety you insist on keeping. As for the stick, I found this – " He held aloft a small bead. " – on the rug. It is of native origin, though whether African or South American I have been unable to determine. As the man was unlikely to be wearing a necklace, it follows it adorned his stick."

Holmes really was uncanny in his method, but he had yet to explain his knowledge of my trip to my old hospital. Further, I felt his mania for observation of even the smallest object such as the incriminating bead bordered on obsession. I resolved one day to write a paper on the condition. Eschewing the pastries, I went to pour myself a glass of John Haig's fine whisky and went to the gasogene before selecting a cigar. With a look of expectancy, I resumed my chair.

"You asked how I placed you at Barts. It is simple: On returning, you placed your bag on the chair at your desk. Had your excursion been a satisfactory one, you would have put it to the side of the desk as is your habit. Therefore, you plan to continue with some sort of examination concerning the contents before you pronounce the case to be settled. If I were a physician faced with a problematic diagnosis, I would seek out the assistance of my *alma mater*." Holmes's aquiline features creased into a thin smile and I realised I was gaping.

"Yes, I can make out the platelets clearly. Hmm, interesting." Holmes was bent over the microscope examining a plate I had prepared at Barts earlier in the day, the blood from Sir Tristram upon the slide. I watched as he turned the wheel to better focus the instrument.

"I conducted a blood count using the Hayem Method and found it irregular."

Holmes looked up from his study. "How so?"

"The distribution of red and white cells was unusually biased towards the red – but that is not all I found. As you are aware, the microscopy at Barts is far superior to our own resource here."

"A parasite?"

"Precisely – the nature of it is yet to be determined. I sent young Matthews off to Greenwich with a sample. Their knowledge on the subject is unsurpassed." Setting aside the microscope with a muttered remark to himself, Holmes strode to his bookshelf and perused the contents, selected a volume on tropical diseases, and went to his desk.

I watched as my friend intently inspected the work, turning the pages furiously, making the oddest noises and comments until, with an exclamation, he stabbed at the book with a finger and turned expectantly. Looking at the page, I could see colour plates of microscopic samples showing parasites present in the blood. In fact, I had no great difficulty in identifying one as almost identical to the sample of Sir Tristram's blood under the more powerful lens of the microscope at Barts. The text below the plate set my own blood running cold. *Trypanosoma!*

Not much was known about the parasite in those days – Major-General Bruce had yet to enter the Army Medical School at Netley where I received my training prior to my service in Afghanistan. His discovery that the parasite caused sleeping sickness was some decades off, but I had heard rumours and exchanged stories with Army Surgeons who had travelled to Africa and knew of the chilling reputation the disease carried. First the fever, then the debilitating headache, and then the posterior cervical lymphatic swelling, the so-called Winterbottom's Sign. These symptoms would be distressing enough, but they were only the start, the herald of far, far worse things to come. The terrified sufferer would be plunged into a sleep filled with terror, confusion, and tremors, only to awake in a state of *mort-vivant* – the living death. Eyes wide open, the victim would be literally petrified, unable to call for or summon aid. Following this, the brain deteriorates, and the result is coma followed by a slow, agonizing death as, one by one, the bodily organs shut down, the vital ones last.

Shaken, I repaired to my chair for a pipe to steady myself. I confess my imagination was running rather wild after the events of the day. Noticing this, Holmes resumed his own customary perch and sat, eyes closed and fingers steepled in a position that resembled nothing so much as an Indian Buddha. After some minutes had passed in silence, he gave voice to his thoughts, eyes still firmly shut.

"I would not think the less of you, my dear Watson, if you enlisted my aid in this most bizarre and unlikely of cases." This kindness was touching, yet I could not find it in myself to accept.

"You cannot surely have anything to do with it? It is lunacy, the whole of it." At last those knowing eyes opened, fixing me with an intensity that spoke of the mind behind them.

"Ah, but Watson, life is infinitely stranger than anything which the mind of man could invent. Besides, the cases that come my way have been lacking in those interesting problems of logic and reasoning that this promises. Pray tell me more of this singular African patient of yours that uses hooves rather than feet."

It was my turn now to stare.

"Hooves? Holmes, you said *hooves* . . . ." A thin smile crept across his features at my shock.

"Really, Watson, you have wasted your talents – with all your training you did not see the obvious. That is *animal* blood – cow or pig I cannot say. It is infected with a parasite only found in certain parts of the Dark Continent, and clearly you have been duped in the most outrageous fashion by your nervous visitor." I bridled at my companion's nerve, but held my tongue. I was, after all in need of his assistance on the matter. Reaching for the Persian slipper in which he kept his tobacco, he thumbed a generous pinch into his cherry-wood. I sat and watched as he lit a twist of paper from the fire. This was the pipe he was wont to select in disputatious mood, and I was well aware of his capacity for obstinacy during such sessions.

Satisfied with the noisome cloud he was producing, Holmes warmed to his subject, pointing the stem abruptly in my direction.

"You travelled by cab with this man to examine a patient. I have already established the African connexion. You took blood, which we know to be a substitution of the most fraudulent kind. The question is, therefore, *why* such an elaborate charade? Does your client seek to persuade another he is suffering from a dreadful malaise? Now, if you would favour me with the details, we shall see what can be made of it."

Once more, Holmes assumed his sphinxlike immobility while I regaled him with the minutiae of my extraordinary expedition to Richmond. From Silas Pym's visit to the dreadful sight of Sir Tristram Webb's cadaverous figure, and Pym's inexplicable behaviour towards myself at the end of the visit. My report finished, I awaited a reply, but was disappointed when it came.

"Hmph. A fool's errand, indeed."

"Well? What do you make of it? Do you have any theories?"

"Several, but only three that fit the facts as you present them. Are you game for a burglary tonight?" This was most unexpected and I took a moment to reply in the affirmative.

Chapter III

The weather could not have been more perfect had Holmes chosen it himself. There was no moon, and the low clouds that roiled over London as we clattered through the streets that night seemed to conspire with us in our illicit and clandestine venture. Holmes sat quietly, with not even the glow of a pipe to illuminate his profile or thoughts. I had watched as he *accoutered* himself with the tools of the professional cracksman: Dark-lantern, putty, hand-drill, and his much-used roll of lock-picking tools. Finally, he wound a length of fine rope around his waist until he appeared to have gained a good fifteen pounds. He had about him a small wooden box, but when I ventured to inquire as to its contents, all he would say was it was a gift from an old friend. A rather odd smell emanated from his direction, but I refrained from commenting, as my own thoughts were on what lay ahead.

For my part, I had restrained myself to my service revolver and a rather contemptible Irish walking-stick known as a *shillelagh*. Made of smoke-seasoned blackthorn, this had been drilled for fifteen ounces of lead and was a present from Holmes, who himself had received it in part payment of a debt incurred in the ring from none other than "Gypsy" Joe Kelly. Hefting the stick and feeling the exquisite balance of the weapon in the hansom gave me a feeling of much-needed grit and determination. I confess that my nerve had been somewhat tested of late and I resolved not to show this to Holmes, so that I might aid him better in our endeavours.

Arriving at the Webb Institute, Holmes had alighted and paid the cabman before I had collected myself. The horse turned around and the cab was pulled away into the damp night, leaving us suddenly alone. I fought down a rising surge of dread and addressed my companion in crime.

"What do you make of it?" Evidently I had spoken too loudly, for he raised a finger in admonition, before drawing closer to reply.

"These are very deep waters. If my suspicions are founded, London itself may be on the brink." I said nothing, unable to formulate adequate response to such a statement. After a moment's examination of the padlock, Holmes beckoned me closer, indicating I follow him as he began striding along the high stone wall bounding the property.

It took some minutes before we found ourselves standing on a bare patch of earth to the rear aspect of the Institute. The only signs of life were some lights from the nearest houses, but they were comfortably distant for our purposes and, unravelling his novel waist-band, Holmes produced an ingenious device. It was a bar of steel some ten inches long, which unfolded to twice that, a pair of hooks springing into place as it opened. Affixing it to the rope, he took a piece of hessian from a pocket and quickly slipped it over the grapnel, which muffled the sound as he threw it over the wall. Pulling at the rope showed him there was no purchase to be had, so he "walked" it along the wall and tried again. At the third or fourth such attempt, the hooks evidently held, because he immediately pulled it taut and hissed at me to hold it so. No sooner had I applied tension to rope than Holmes was up and over the wall as if it were five rather than fifteen feet.

My own journey was not so smooth, I regret to say. Scrambling up, I heaved with all my strength and was over the top, my old shoulder wound causing me to gasp with the jolt of pain that surged through me. I was halfway down the other side when my boot slipped on damp stone and I fell, landing with a thump that fair winded me. I lay for a long moment, gasping for breath, the dulling pain from my shoulder beginning to recede when Holmes knelt over me.

"Can you continue?" I looked up to see those fine features creased with concern and vowed then and there not to fail this remarkable man. Nodding, I allowed him to help me up to the kneeling position in the wet grass.

Pointing, Holmes indicated the top windows, where a glimmer of light had passed. Soon enough, it appeared again, passing behind another casement. It seemed the place was not as abandoned as we were supposed to believe. Waiting for the light to pass, Holmes tapped me on the shoulder and we were away across the lawn, keeping to the edge so as not to expose ourselves more than needed. Looking across the lawn, my attention seized briefly upon two dark rectangles where some sort of excavation showed. Intending to mention it to Holmes, I realised he himself had not paused and hurried after his receding form.

After a nervous minute, we found ourselves in the comparative safety afforded by a large glasshouse. We had barely made the tenuous sanctuary when a lantern came around the farthest aspect of the building, accompanied by the barking and snarling of a large dog. Flattening himself against the glass, Holmes slipped back into the shadows and I followed suit. All at once the dog began snarling and, looking through the glass I was horrified to see it was a monstrous example of the mastiff breed. A shout from the dog's master alerted me to the fact that it had broken free and was charging over the grass towards the very structure behind which I was at that moment steeling myself to action, my stick clenched tightly in my fist. I had not, however, reckoned with Sherlock Holmes!

Suddenly, I was aware of a long tail flashing past my feet, a rag of some sort dragging behind. A small furry streak flashed across the lawn and in an instant, the mastiff had changed course and was loping along in pursuit of the smaller creature. I gave a start as Holmes placed a hand on my shoulder.

"It is a simple thing to attach a scented lure to the tail of a ferret – though I fear the cats of the district will have an evil time of it for a while. Now, we must move swiftly."

It was apparent from the racket coming from the darkness at the far end of the garden that the dog had failed to catch Holmes's ferret and the animal's keeper was berating the dog loudly for sending him on a fool's errand. A loud yelp was followed by a cry of pain as dog retaliated against man. We would have barely a minute before they resumed their nocturnal patrol and Holmes had not wasted it, escalating up the recesses in the stonework as if they had been a ladder placed there for that very purpose. I saw the lantern again and was about to call up when the rope dropped down to me.

Stick between teeth, I grasped the rope and hauled myself up, ignoring the pain from my old wound. After the most outrageous exertion, I found myself adjacent to a stonework balustrade and grabbed at it in vain. I could ascend no higher and was left dangling precariously, some height above the ground. From below, I could hear the panting of the dog and the glow from the lantern was evident from a quick glance downwards. I was sure to be discovered and resolved myself to such a fate as would be reserved for any common sneak thief. Just then, a strong hand reached down to grasp my wrist and I was aware of Holmes's enormous strength as his steel-like grip held me to prevent the inevitable fall.

Holding my breath, I waited for the dog to detect my unwelcome presence, a sudden snarl from what seemed uncomfortably close below confirming my worst fears. To my relief, however, the dog's keeper responded by yanking at its chain and roundly cursing the beast for its unreliability. The lantern glow passed and, after an agony of suspension, I was hauled up by Holmes, glad to get that stick out of my mouth at last.

The application of putty and a glass cutting tool saw us inside the door to the balcony in next to no time, and we stood silently for a while to allow our eyes to adjust to the dim light inside what seemed to be an unused bedroom. There were sheets covering the furniture, and I peeked under one to find an old dresser made of what appeared to be mahogany. Holmes, meanwhile had produced his dark-lantern and lit it, making sure the shutters were tightly shut first. A search of the room was deemed unnecessary and we shuffled forward silently towards the door. This proved to be locked, which gave Holmes an opportunity to exercise his legerdemain as he manipulated his lock-picks. With an un-nerving click, the lock succumbed after no more than thirty seconds and we found ourselves in a hallway leading to a gallery.

From deep within the building there came a muffled sound, which rose and fell in intonation as if it were beyond a door that had been rapidly opened and then closed again. I exchanged a glance with Holmes – we had both heard it: *Drums!* Moving forward to a pillar adjoining the gallery, Holmes bent down, then got on all fours and crawled to the edge like a Lascar *hicarra* spying on a Sikh encampment. From his vantage point, he could see down into the heart of the building, and he spent some minutes immobile as a tiger waiting to pounce on its prey, before gesturing for me to join him. Cursing my creaking bones, I prostrated myself and crept forward on my hands and knees as the drumming grew louder again.

Chapter IV

Looking down, I could see the marble floor below and where a wide arch led to the doorway through which I had gone earlier to make my piteous examination. Now the door itself stood open, but what was remarkable was the uncanny procession that was underway beneath our rather tenuous concealment. For there can be no other description than that of an African *juju* ceremony, with two rows of natives to either side of what was plainly a "witch doctor". This last was an extraordinary sight, his face hidden beneath an enormous mask fringed with long grass of some description. He carried in one hand a glass bottle from which he gave his acolytes a drink, the nature of which could only be guessed at. He spent the time in between offerings liberally haranguing the assemblage with the most extraordinary shrieking and altogether disported himself like a madman. The torches burning around the gallery only added to the effect of a war party.

I watched in a state of astonished stupefaction as the bizarre proceedings moved through to the chamber where the man who had been Sir Tristram was presumably still seated. I turned to Holmes to comment on the fact when I saw we had been discovered: More natives, two for each of us, stood as silent as statues. The warning cry I gave froze in my throat as I glimpsed their eyes – they were milky and clouded as with Sir Tristram's own, and at once a thrill of terror coursed through me. *They were zombies!* I had read of such in the accounts of the Haitian medical fraternity, but had rashly dismissed such things as childish fantasy. As one, they began breathing heavily, with laboured sighs that became a rhythmic chanting. I thought to draw my pistol, but these men were unarmed, so I raised my Irish stick instead as warning. Holmes stepped forward, opening the shutters on his lantern. There was no response to the brightness of the light, no ocular reflex whatsoever.

All at once there were more of the hellish creatures and we found ourselves surrounded. I lashed out with the shillelagh at once! Twice! To my dismay the blows had no effect, other than to open a vicious wound upon the jaw of the tribesman. We were trapped. The fingers that gripped my arms were as strong a bond as any chain, the force behind them quite inhuman. I was divested of stick and gun and I saw Holmes being relieved of his lantern and roll of tools.

We were herded – no other word will suffice – down the stairs and then pushed and shoved rudely before the sinister figure of the witch doctor, who stood at the doorway to the chamber. Our arrival was greeted in the most remarkable fashion, the whole tribal gathering hooting and hollering the same repetitive chant, punctuating these with the spears that several held. I demanded in no uncertain terms that we be freed, but Holmes seemed to content himself with a careful examination of the scene, as if committing it all to that extraordinary memory of his.

The masked fellow advanced and held out his bottle for Holmes to take a drink. Despite my shout of caution, he did so, before the bottle was proffered to me. I could smell the foulness of the contents from where I stood. Reluctant to imbibe such an uncertain potation, I pushed the offensive offering away at which the headman gave a shout and strong arms seized me. Struggle as I might, I had not the strength to refuse and the awful taste that burned through me spoke of its potency. I tasted a rude attempt at brandy, something gritty like sand or crushed shells perhaps, and a bitter aftertaste. Almost at once my mouth and lips were numbed and I feared we had been poisoned.

The next few hours were a procession of images and sounds the likes of which I had not experienced before and have not since. I had once looked through a child's kaleidoscope and the experience was not entirely dis-similar as I felt myself borne aloft by strong hands. I had a vague vision of Holmes being transported in like manner and then only terror as, my body rigid and immobile, I was laid into a crude coffin made of unfinished wood. I could hear sounds that could have been made only by animals, outlandish and unearthly moans and wails punctuated by the shrieks of what might have been exotic birds. Try as I might, I couldn't move a muscle, could not escape the unchallenging confines of the open coffin. Instead, I lay helpless, rivulets of sweat flowing freely from my forehead and body. So complete was my stupor that even a cry for help was beyond my capacity – indeed I was unable even to blink.

It was with a feeling of utmost dread that I realised that the lid was being placed on my coffin, and that the shockingly loud banging of nails would be the last thing I should hear. After a long pause, the coffin was heaved upwards in a jerking lurch and I was conscious of being borne aloft, of movement. Suddenly an image came through the madness to haunt me – and I was hard-put to retain any semblance of reason with the horror it evoked. The excavations in the lawn! They were *graves*!

Of all the horrors that assail the imagination of Man, there can be few as pronounced as the fear of being buried alive. Indeed, graveyards across the realm are fitted with bells for the unfortunate victims to ring to summon aid for that very purpose. The fate that awaited myself and, presumably Holmes, was too hideous, too frightful to contemplate. I could do nothing else, bound as I was by chemical paralysis. My mind, however, was relatively clear, despite the whirling shapes that I could still see even in my total darkness. I knew what was coming, even as I knew what the abrupt lowering of the coffin was a fore-token of the inevitable, the muffled thumps and scrapings that came from the sound of the earth being filled in over me. I can assure you, Dear Reader, that no man ever felt more lost than I that terrible night. Then came the silence.

There can be few phrases more apt than "the silence of the tomb". My grave was filled in – all I had to do was lie in it, as we all must one day. I pray that you will not be alive to experience it, because I do not recommend it. How long I lay there I cannot tell – certainly my watch was ticking in my pocket, but my limbs refused to aid me. How I yearned to strike a match! The thing that I did countless times every day without a second thought was as beyond my power as the moon is beyond my reach. Of course, the sceptical among you might well say that clearly I survived my ordeal to be able to recount it and they would be correct, but they are not present to see the trepidation that affects my hand as I write these words.

After some time had passed – it must have been minutes for me not to have suffocated – I became dimly aware of a distant scratching. Faint noises that indicated someone or something was digging. All at once there came a tremendous thump and a loud splintering as the lid of the coffin was forced from the nails holding it firm. I found myself looking up at a swirling mist in the form of a man, the actions of the drug rendering my eyes next to useless. The hands that reached down for me seemed unnaturally long and claw-like, but the voice that accompanied them was thankfully familiar. It was Holmes!

"My dear friend, I am so sorry that you have suffered this terrible thing. Please, forgive me when I explain – but for now, try and drink this." A vial of liquid was placed between my lips and a noxious solution poured into my throat, causing me to splutter and retch violently. Holmes forced me upright and, leaning close, asked if I felt able to stand. I could not even formulate a reply, let alone comply with his request, and I stared at my saviour in helpless fury. At last, however, I felt the numbness in my face lessen and found myself able to blink away the fog from my vision. With every ounce of my strength, I nodded and croaked what was meant to be a reply, but came out as an indistinct croak.

Some minutes passed before I was able to move my upper body, and at once I was overcome with a paroxysm of nausea, retching forcibly and heaving the liquid I had ingested out onto the freshly-dug earth.

"What – what the devil was that appalling muck, Holmes?"

"A solution of my own design, something that I have been working on at odd times for some time now. It is a mixture of atropine and a reagent composed of an anti-emetic and a sedative to counter the effects of the drug we were given."

"Good God!"

"Yes, it seems the anti-emetic did not work so well in you as my own dose." I was furious at Holmes's casual mention of taking such a dangerous cocktail and said so.

"You've ingested this concoction already? Don't you realise the danger?"

"Perfectly. However, this is neither the time nor the place for a discussion on medical ethics. We must get away from here before our resurrection has been discovered."

With Holmes bearing my weight, we made our way unsteadily towards the wall where we had originally entered the grounds. I was fervently hoping the mastiff and his keeper did not make themselves known, but need not have worried. There was, however, no way over. Even Holmes could not scale such a wall unaided and I was in no position to make an attempt. Propping me against the wall, he promised to return before dawn. I assured him I was fine and he clapped a hand on my shoulder before disappearing into the night. It was freezing and I was cheered to discover my flask still in my hip pocket. A pull of brandy revived me somewhat and I settled in for a bitter vigil.

Chapter V

Dawn broke across London with a brief yet fierce flurry of snow, though I was not there to see it. My dreams that night were haunted by *juju* men and burning torches, weird chants and terrible things. I awoke slowly to find myself in my own bed and the fire burning fiercely. I attempted to rise, but my head rebelled at the strain and I was compelled to regain the comfort of the pillow by a splitting headache. I had hardly issued a sound, yet I heard the sound of feet charging the stairs and Holmes burst into my quarters with a cry of triumph. The sound went through my brain like a needle and, seeing this, his noble features assumed an expression of concern.

"Watson, I have much to apologise for. I shall leave you to rest." I would have none of it, however and forced myself to rise. My watch showed the hour to be just shy of ten.

I found by holding the hand rail on the stairs I could just about negotiate passage down to the sitting room, where I found Holmes in a state of agitated ebullience. At once he sprang up and rang down for Mrs. Hudson.

"Watson! My dear, dear fellow. Please sit down at once. Mrs. Hudson has been quite inconsolable at your predicament – the scones are warming by the fire and a fresh pot will be with us in a jiffy." I found myself irritated by this show of concern and thumped over to the fire for my pipe. I took a glass of brandy from the carafe – Holmes refused to imbibe and I settled myself with a heavy sigh into the embrace of my chair, in no mood for any of it, yet furious at the way we had been treated the previous night.

Holmes proved to be quite the fusspot as he set about ensuring my comfort that day, shooing Mrs. Hudson away with a loud whisper about not disturbing the patient and making himself a nuisance with the tea until I was close to erupting. Indeed, the seed of suspicion was planted when Holmes insisted on buttering my scones and I had had enough.

"Holmes, really! I wish you'd come out with it instead of this nannying and fannying about!" No sooner than the words had left my mouth than I was seized with mortification for uttering them. I had insulted the man who had saved me. My attempt at apology, though, was barely launched when Holmes made a terrible confession.

Pacing the room before me, Holmes fairly wore a hole in the carpet in his agitation as he explained the events of last night. From the very moment I had mentioned my examination of Sir Tristram, he had suspected foul play. A keen student of both botany and chemistry, he had quickly gone to consult his text-books on African poisons whilst I had been dressing for our adventure. At once he saw that the whole thing was a lure, a trap set with the specific purpose of drawing him in and killing him. Before I reappeared armed for the purpose, he had taken a vial of his putrid antidote and secreted a second where it would not be found.

My own death was necessary only in order to seal my lips as to the little I knew of the affair. As he spoke, I knew Holmes had shielded me from the worst of it, leaving out the obvious fact that my own abilities as a physician were not sufficient to warrant such a visit as I had received from Pym. I was a mere general practitioner, not an expert in tropical disease. Why should anyone from Richmond travel across the river to seek such sparsely-qualified advice? I had failed to see this and my own inflated view of myself as a doctor had clouded my better judgement. I was a fool.

My anger at myself quickly subsided as I remained ignorant of several points.

"But why did you not give me this second dose if you suspected danger?" Holmes ceased his pacing and looked me directly in the eye, his own expression grim.

"Because it was untested. I could not risk your life on such unknown variables without good reason. At that stage, I was unsure that we were to become zombies." *Zombies!* The word itself was enough to induce a reaction of horror and revulsion.

I had read of the tribes of the Congo who worshipped the dead, of course, and whose *juju* men had been said to bring them back to life not to mention the Haitan *voodou* cult with their similar practices. The thought that Holmes and myself were to become such creatures was beyond the pale, to say the least. Taking a large sip of my brandy, I set the glass aside and filled a pipe as Holmes continued his bizarre elucidation.

"Have you ever heard of the iboga plant of central Africa?" My silence told him that I had not.

"It is a member of the genus *Tabernanthe,* a powerful hallucinatory and used in rituals among the tribes of the river Congo. Used with a paralytic, it renders the subject helpless to experience visions and the like." I nodded in a rather sardonic fashion. I had experienced the effects of this devilish weed only too recently for comfort.

"I have not thanked you for saving my life."

"And you have no need to do so. I merely secreted the grappling iron in my sleeve and used it as a tool to extricate myself – and then, of course, you."

"Then what took place afterwards? I vaguely recall you hoisting me over your shoulder and what seemed a long walk, but apart from that I know nothing."

"I went back in the same way as before. Pym's colourful friends were engrossed in a stupefying dance that they performed until they were in a state of trance. I was able to slip unobserved past them and examine Sir Tristram for myself."

I set down my pipe at this news.

"And?"

"He is quite dead."

"So my own examination showed, but he had a pulse – and respiration."

"Both were artifice. The blood came from a pump through tubes attached to the poor man's corpse from behind that screen. As soon as I saw it I suspected as much. The same for the breathing you observed: A mechanical bellows operated from behind the same inflated the lungs via tubes. A ghastly way to treat a gallant man's moral remains."

Holmes told me how he had then found himself trapped in the room when the witch doctor returned, followed by his acolytes. Using the remains of poor Sir Tristram to persuade the throng of his powers, the *juju* man performed an elaborate ritual in which several of the unholy congregation were anointed in blood and daubed with a white paint that would, he assured them, render them invisible. It did not.

"But surely, Holmes, these native superstitions are hardly fitting here in the beating heart of the Empire."

"Quite the contrary, I'm afraid. Unless I am mistaken, there goes the bell. Doubtless Lestrade has bungled it and has sent a carriage to fetch us. That is, if you are up to a ride out to Richmond."

No sooner had Holmes spoken than Mrs. Hudson bustled in in front of a red-faced young constable who stood at the threshold of our chambers in patent embarrassment. Mrs. Hudson upbraided the poor chap terribly about his helmet, which he removed, flushing even more in the process. Holmes intercepted her before she could set about mothering me and invited the lad to speak.

"Sir . . Sir . . ." He began. With a knowing look towards myself, Holmes threw out a hand impatiently.

"Out with it, Constable! Our attention is yours."

"Well, sir, it's the inspector. Lestrade that is. He wants you, you see. He said you've been of some help before. He's at Richmond, sir. At the Webb place."

"You have not told all of it, Holmes." My remark was made as we climbed up into the leather-and-walnut comfort of a rather plush "growler". Settling in opposite me, Holmes waited until the constable closed the door and clambered up to sit with the driver before answering.

"Oh, it is all fairly humdrum, I suppose. I waited for my chance to slip away unobserved. I knew you wouldn't last the hour in such bitter conditions and time was of the very essence." He reached into a pocket as he spoke. "As I waited, I spotted our possessions on a table, including this." Handing me my revolver, Holmes paused to produce a cigar case.

Accepting a *cohiba*, I cut and lit it. We both smoked in peace for a while before Holmes resumed his extraordinary narrative.

"Returning for you, I managed you as far as the shrubbery adjacent to the main gate, where I am ashamed to say I left you to the elements. I knew that the nearest police station was a wearying trudge, and a cab could not be found at that hour, so I made for the Royal Park Keeper's lodge. I found a keeper at the desk and, after no small difficulty, managed to persuade him to send a runner to telegraph the police at Scotland Yard. A jarvey was roused from his slumbers to take us back home. I curse myself for not remaining to nursemaid Lestrade! Ah, but here we are and there is no more time at our disposal to be wasted."

The scene at the Webb Institute could hardly have been more different. Where there had been open gates, there were now chains and padlock. Where only yesterday a bronze disc had declared this to be the same institution there was a rusted section of ironwork and I could see the windows had been boarded up. I had to assure myself this was the same place, so marked were the changes wrought upon the scene. A pair of constables were guarding the gates, and these waved us through to meet Lestrade coming down the steps.

"Ah, Mister Holmes, thank you for coming – and Doctor Watson into the bargain! I think we have solved it, but it is sometimes useful to have another opinion on matters like this."

"I venture to remark there *are* no other matters like this, Inspector. I take it Pym slipped through your fingers?" The only answer was an embarrassed silence, to which Holmes merely sighed and went inside. I had expected him to go straight to the large chamber, but instead followed in his wake as he strode to Pym's office, Lestrade's sallow expression one of concern as he struggled to keep pace. Clearly the place had been vacated in a hurry, as the room was in a state of total disarray. Holmes began a vigorous inspection, tearing at desk drawers and snatching papers down from the wall to which they had been carelessly affixed. He picked at the wastepaper basket, which had been subjected to fire, doubtless in an attempt to conceal some clue or other. I watched from the doorway, unwilling to intrude upon the scene. The inspector, it seemed, had no such inhibition.

"Mister Holmes, might I ask what you expect to find?" Holmes did not favour the official with so much as a sidelong glance.

"You might. Ah! What have we here!" Opening a drawer in a cabinet, Holmes had found a bottle of linseed oil.

Rummaging further, the detective retrieved a small unmarked bottle of liquid. Taking a cautious sniff at the contents, he reeled back, to my considerable alarm.

"Holmes! Be careful man!" In lieu of answer, he held it out for my inspection. The pungent fumes of what was unmistakably ammonia assaulted my olfactory sense and my eyes began to water uncontrollably. Holmes then went back to the desk and produced a sheaf of paper, which he smelled as if hoping to discover something. He rushed from the room, pushing past me rudely, and made for the public convenience, pausing at the Ladies' briefly before entering the Gentlemen's. Such modesty made me snort with laughter as there were, of course, no women present.

Following Holmes, I discovered him in the process of running all the taps and proceeding to dangle pieces of paper under them. I was about to inquire as to his state of mind when, with a gasp of triumph, he raised one sheet to the skylight and, without comment, dashed off again, leaving me to deal with the still-running taps and the sodden mess accumulated in the sinks beneath. I finally caught up with him in the great hall, where he was holding the sheet over a sconce, drying both sides with great delicacy as if afraid of burning or scorching the fragile object. At length he seemed satisfied, rolling the sheet into a tube and secreting it in an inside pocket before deigning to notice me.

"We may be too late. I suggest we return to Baker Street at once. Lestrade!"

The inspector hurried up, anxious to learn something from Holmes's singular endeavours.

"I shall require you tonight, with at least ten of your best men – rugger players if you can find them. The murderers we are after believe themselves to be invincible – they will not come quietly. Sir Tristram's remains can at least now be removed for proper burial." An expression of confusion marked Lestrade's face, but he nodded and went off to find a subordinate. I spotted a pair of constables at work piling up spears and suchlike, perhaps to use in evidence. Among this collection of weapons I espied my shillelagh and went to collect it, explaining that it was my property.

"Where do you think you might be going with that then, chummy?" Turning slowly, I realised I had not seen the burly sergeant of police who stood behind me, arms behind his back in regimental fashion and a sardonic gleam to his eye. Raising myself to my fullest height, I favoured the obstinate fellow with an icy glare.

"I am not your 'chummy', Sergeant, I am Doctor John Watson, and this is my shillelagh, thank you very much."

"Not a fitting instrument for a medical man, *Doctor*. What purpose have you for carrying such a weapon then?" Slapping the weighted end into my palm, I answered, "Anaesthetic," before taking my leave of the odious functionary. Leaving the Institute, we took the growler back to Baker Street as a cold wind began to blow icy flakes down across London.

Chapter VI

The lamplighters were busy early that evening. The lights of the Edgware Road were twinkling and sparkling invitingly. It would be easy to forget the events of the preceding day, to dismiss them as whimsy or fancy. To find such goings on in deepest Africa was one thing, but here, in London! I had to shake my head to assure myself it was happening and not some ludicrous dream. The familiar sight of Baker Street acted as a salve, however, and an anchor to the unreality of it all, and I was glad to regain our rooms. Whilst I contented myself with a quick wash and a change of clothes, Holmes launched himself into one of his examinations and, declaring it to be a three-pipe problem, banished me to my chamber to await results.

I'd had some medical volumes that had been delivered and, as yet, I hadn't had sufficient time to devote to them. Now seemed ideal, but I had barely started on a treatise on bone regeneration in the elderly when there was the most appalling racket from the sitting room. I ignored it as best I could, but after perhaps a half-hour I could stand it no longer and found Holmes seated Indian fashion on the carpet surrounded by all manner of books and papers.

"Really, Holmes, it will not do! Whatever are you up to?" Barely aware of my intrusion, he took a puff on his briar and waved distractedly at the paperwork strewn about. His manner was one of agitation, of despondency.

"I cannot crack it, Watson. I have failed!"

I poured a stiff brandy for us both as Holmes told me what he knew of the affair. The business with the paper at the Pimm Institute was necessary to reveal the contents of a hidden message.

"Have you heard of steganography?" I had not.

"It is a remarkable science, the art of covered writing. A message may be concealed – tattooed on the scalp of an agent, for instance, the hair is allowed to grow and obscure the message. There have been examples throughout antiquity – but surely none as fiendish in their intractability as the example on *that* paper." As he spoke, he jabbed the stem of his pipe towards the mantelpiece, where his jackknife now held the paper he had wetted. Where it had been blank, it now was covered with text, a poem of some kind. It seemed oddly familiar, yet I could not place it. I have reproduced it here:

> *Why seek ye in dust, forlorn,*
> *Ye heavenly tones, with soft enchanting?*
> *Go, greet pure-hearted men this holy morn!*
> *Your message well I hear, but faith to me is wanting.*
> *Wonder, its dearest child, of Faith is born,*
> *To yonder spheres I dare no more aspire,*
> *Whence the sweet tidings downward float.*
> *And yet, from childhood heard, the old, familiar note*
> *Calls back e'en now to life my warm desire.*
> *Ah! Once how sweetly fell on me the kiss*
> *Of heavenly love in the still Sabbath stealing!*
> *Prophetically rang the bells with solemn pealing,*
> *A prayer was then the ecstasy of bliss,*
> *A blessed and mysterious yearning*
> *Drew me to roam through meadows, woods, and skies,*
> *And, midst a thousand tear-drops burning*

I felt a world within me rise

That strain, oh, how it speaks youth's gleesome plays and
   feelings

Joys of spring-festivals long past

Remembrance holds me now, with childhood's fond
   appealings,

Back from the fatal step, the last.

Sound on, ye heavenly strains, that bliss restore me!

Tears gush, once more the spell of earth is o'er me.

"Good Lord! That's extraordinary. You uncovered it with the water, I suppose?"

"That is entirely ordinary, Watson. Do please try to focus on the problem, not the effects associated with unveiling it." Springing up, he went to the paper and removed the knife to hand me the paper for closer inspection.

"The method is German, the motive unclear. A mixture of linseed oil, ammonia, and purified water in the proper ratio will produce the ink, which dries to total invisibility. Often it is used in the margins of apparently innocent books carried by couriers for the Prussian Secret Service. We now may infer the nationality behind this outrageous scheme, but until we have the grasp of those words London – the entire Empire perhaps – remains at stake. It is too much!" Holmes seemed to physically reel from the challenge at hand and I feared for him when his hand rested on the mantel near the hated morocco leather case, but thankfully he turned away from the fireplace to sit again amidst his clutter.

"It does seem remarkable that such devilry can flourish right under the noses of a civilised society." The words had hardly left my lips when Holmes sat bolt upright. Clutching at my arm, his eyes took on an intensity that would, in another man be suggestive of madness.

"Watson, you have it! Devilry!" Holmes rose to throw himself upon his library.

"Devilry indeed! Really my dear fellow, you have that rare ability to focus intellect without the slightest inkling of having done so. A-ha!" Holding a weighty tome out for my benefit, Holmes seemed positively rejuvenated. Gone was the forlorn, weary figure of a moment ago. The book was a heavy one, leather bound with no title save that on the spine: *Goethe-Faust-1790.*

"Then this passage is from the book?"

"I'm certain of it. I haven't read Faust in years – and I only have the original of course. This paper contains a passage from the work translated into English. It only remains to decipher the message that is doubtless hidden within."

Holmes spent the next hour in solitary silence, but then the bell rang downstairs and, after a moment, the street Arab Wiggins came bounding in, pursued hotly by the landlady. Holmes shooed her away and closed the door, turning to find the boy making faces at her behind his back.

"If I were your father, my boy . . . ."

"You'd be dead drunk in a ditch somewhere, wouldn't yer?" I rose to berate the boy for this unmitigated cheek, but Holmes merely burst out laughing and ruffled the upstart's tousled hair.

"Right, let's have it." To me, he added that he had enlisted the services of the scruffy lout whilst I was in my room.

"The Baker Street Division of the detective force has been invaluable in the past, as you will recall from the Jefferson Hope business."

Wiggins indeed proved the truth of my friend's statement. The "Irregulars" had been dispatched across London with the aim of watching all the places livestock was to be found, kept, or sold. Instead of a report, however, the boy stood in mute defiance until Holmes produced a half-sovereign as if from thin air.

"I sent a yob to Smithfield to 'ave a Butcher's. I 'ad a cool round the yards myself, but I 'ad ter cut lucky when a blue-bottle seed me . . . ." Seeing my absolute mystification, Holmes politely translated that Wiggins had sent one of his lads to the Smithfield meat market in the square mile to have a look around. Wiggins himself checked the stock-yards, but was chased off by a constable.

"And what about the Metropolitan Market at Islington?"

"That's where it gets rum, Mister 'Olmes. I sends Balmy Benny and Legless Bill to the Sling, told 'em to step proper short-like, but they was kyboshed by a clockey, had to 'ave it away on their daisies – 'E gives 'em this proper bonneting after they bulled in to see these tea-pots with old Harry in them, all queer patter and bedlam. There was a queer gill with them too, afternoon-i-fied, 'e was. Anyway, they was touted halfway back to our drum, they 'ad to do a proper scoot an' all."

"His associates were told to move quickly, but were foiled and forced to make a run for it by a watchman who attacked them. They pretended to blunder in by mistake and saw some natives with the very devil in them. These men spoke in a foreign language and seemed mad. There was a strange man with them, well-dressed. They were followed when they left for home and had to run for it. Please describe this odd fellow to us, Wiggins." When the impudent little scruff fell silent again, a cheeky grin plastered on his lopsided features, Holmes produced another coin, this time a full sovereign, which he tossed into the air. Snatching the coin, Wiggins continued with a near-perfect description of Silas Pym.

Wiggins had left and Holmes called down for a cab, advising me to wear some warm, workmanlike clothing. I selected an Ulster and a cap, turning to find that Holmes had been replaced by the roughest market porter I had ever seen, his features partially obscured by luxuriant mutton chops and fierce eyebrows. He wore a leather jerkin and the most objectionable old bowler. Rough corduroy trousers and unpolished boots with a crude walking stick completed the disguise. All in all, not someone with whom I would normally associate! We both carried revolvers that night – the stakes were, Holmes assured me, too high to leave anything to chance. Mrs. Hudson called up that the cab was waiting, and we set off for Islington.

Although most people will have heard of the famous market at Smithfield, the Metropolitan Cattle Market, or, to most simply "The Caledonian", covered some thirty acres of North London. Bounded by a public house on each corner with an impressive central clock tower, the long rows of sheds seemed to stretch forever. The din was appalling. We alighted in the midst of chaotic scenes, the noise from hundreds of donkeys and goats adding to the terrified whinnying of the horses. Not for the first time, I began to question mankind's attitude to the animals with whom we share our planet. We had not even reached the market square proper and there was still perhaps five-hundred yards of public slaughter-houses ahead of us. Holmes had insisted we go this way, rather than take the cab to the building that the Irregulars had scouted.

After some time, we finally reached the private slaughter-houses, having passed the bullock pens, which were silent as no beef was sold here. At Holmes's suggestion, we ducked into the White Horse public house, so to be able to observe the building of interest from a discreet distance. I sought a seat with a view across the road whilst Holmes went to the bar. I had no luck, for the place was packed out, but Holmes it seemed had fared better. We stood at the end of the bar facing the slaughter-house and he told me that the landlord, one Tom Hedges of Buckinghamshire, had been the tavern keeper for some time. Living with his family, there was nothing they didn't know of the area and, as if to prove it, Richard, the eldest Hedges boy, came over at his father's request. Richard was in his early twenties, with more than a hint of the rural about him both in manner and speech.

"My father says you were askin" questions. Police, is it?"

"Get away with yer." Holmes's accent and speech had changed to that of a South London tough and not for the first time I thought he would make a rare actor.

"My pal and me fancy the livestock business – he likes cattle, but me-self, I likes pigs." I realised that this was one of Holmes's impostures and at once attempted to appear the very model of a cattle fanatic, though I had not the slightest idea of what that might entail.

"Well you've come to the right place, I'll say that, sirs. You could do worse than talk to Mr. Howard. He's a cattle dealer by trade and lodges here." Holmes assumed an attentive air, but waved his stick in the general direction of the slaughter-houses across the road.

"I reckon we might try our luck in the market, have a go like – but we're leery, see? Don't want to be taken for mugs. Is this Mister Howard around?"

"Here he is now, sir" The Hedges boy pointed at a red-faced and burly man who had just arrived at the bar. Thanking the boy with a coin, Holmes tipped his moth-eaten old bowler and winked at me, as if confiding his good fortune with a colleague.

"Half o'best mild please, Cathy."

"Make that a pint, darlin' – and bring it two more for company, will you?" Holmes dropped some pennies down onto the bar and clapped a hand on the cattle trader's shoulder.

"I heard you're the chap to see about cattle and such." Howard's eyebrows went up at this but the arrival of his pint got the better of him.

"Perhaps I am . . . Mister?"

"Wells is the name, John Wells. Me and my partner Bob here – " I raised my cap dutifully. " – we was thinkin' of setting up in business over there (He pointed with his stick again) and young Mister Richard 'ere give us your name – very kindly too, I might add."

"Well, you've really come to the wrong pub, Mister, um, Wells was it?" Holmes nodded good-naturedly as he took a sip of his mild. "Only those slaughter-houses is private, see? You'd need to have your own stock to take there first. They slaughter it for you, like. I'd recommend you saw Abe Rodgett over at The Bull. He works the public side, see?"

This seemed to be an impenetrable barrier to Holmes's enquiry, but he was not to be dissuaded so easily.

"But surely there's some new folks just set up across the way? Why, I heard they were blackamoors workin' there an" all sorts."

A puzzled look came over the man's face at this, but then he looked directly at Holmes, recognition clearly showing on his features.

"Now that's odd, you saying that." The cattle dealer finished his pint and Holmes was quick to catch the eye of the pretty young barmaid, anxious to keep Howard pliant.

"How's that? Odd, you say?"

"Well, odd's the word for it when a gentleman decides he wants his plantation workers to come all this way to learn our ways in slaughterin'. I was saying the same only the other day, to my pal Albie – 'Albie,' says I, 'there's sommat funny here, anyone knows they have cattle in Africa.' Well, I suppose they do. Must have, see?"

It seemed that Pym, with a group of his natives, had descended on the slaughter-house of one J. Poulsett and hired the whole thing as if it were a holiday chalet and not a place of business. Paying the regular slaughtermen off for a week, Pym – for it was certainly he – had taken over the premises for whatever purpose, paying over the odds for a whole week. Thanking Mr. Howard, Holmes tipped his bowler in farewell and hinted he would indeed seek out Abraham Rodgett at the Black Bull, the pub he had mentioned. Outside, however, he made straight for the private slaughter-houses. Discretion forbids me to describe what we saw. Suffice to say, even Holmes seemed moved by the plight of those poor animals. Even at this hour, there were what seemed to be whole herds of horses corralled into the market, and the place had the air of a county fair in places, but a charnel house in others.

We arrived at the slaughter-house of Jack Poulsett at around six p.m. and in darkness to find the place quite deserted. Far from being guarded, there was no sign of any watchman and no lights showed from within. There was a separate entrance to the side where the animals entered and a doorway for the workers, which Holmes deftly unlocked whilst I kept watch. Inside, a tiled corridor led to the killing and cutting rooms, with a small office to the left. This, too was locked and once again Holmes picked the lock. Inside, he lit the oil lamp on the table and began his search.

For myself, I had little to do except listen for any sign of our having been discovered, but perhaps due to Holmes's previous interest in the wastepaper basket at the Pimm Institute, I picked up its equivalent here to find a curious little collection of tiny squares of cardboard at the bottom. These gave the appearance of having been punched out with some uniform object and I remarked upon them to Holmes, who at once abandoned his search in favour of my discovery.

"Cardano! It has to be! Twenty – that figure may prove significant." Leaving me to wonder at this, the detective set about his search anew, going through the drawers of a cabinet file one by one.

The sound of a hammer being pulled back was the first warning we had. Looking to the doorway, I saw a muffled figure holding a large revolver in his hand. My first thought was that it was a watchman, but when he spoke it was with a distinct Continental accent that I could not place.

"You will put your hands up, I think." We did as ordered, Holmes doing so reluctantly.

"You are looking, perhaps, for something?"

Holmes answered instantly. "Yes. A piece of stiff paper or card, the size of a large sheet of paper. The card is perforated in an apparently meaningless fashion." At once I thought of the oddity of the cardboard pieces I had discovered – this must have had some importance after all.

The gunman stayed perfectly still as he considered his reply.

"You shall not find it here, English spy."

"I am English, though not a spy. Your gun affords you no more than mere courtesy in my country – doubtless it is otherwise in Bavaria. I shall continue my search and when I find it, I have no doubt this card will hang you and your paymaster. How is Herr Heinbrunn, by the way?" At the mention of this distinctly Germanic name, the gunman flinched noticeably, but held his pistol steady.

"I will give him your compliments, Herr Holmes, but you will not live to receive a reply." If only I could have reached my revolver without arousing suspicion!

I saw the finger on the trigger tighten and knew I had to act – I was standing directly behind the lamp – I flung my hand out – the lamp shattered on the floor – there was a terrible *bang* – Holmes fell to the floor!

Enraged, I surged forward, desperate to reach this fiend before he could shoot again. A sheet of flame roared up from the shattered lamp, some of the oil from which had spattered the German's trouser leg. Cursing and beating at the flame, he did not see my fist. Though never a boxer, my overhand right had rarely failed me and I had the satisfaction of seeing him crumple back into the hallway. My first thought was for Holmes – my friend lay on his side and I only prayed I had not killed him by my precipitate action. My heart soared though, to find him laughing – the bullet had gone through his hat, missing his head by a fraction of an inch.

"My word, Watson, you nearly parted my hair for good!"

"Holmes! Thank God!"

My joy at my friend's narrow escape turned to passion then as the sounds of the gunman escaping reached our ears. Helping Holmes to his feet, I took out my service revolver, grateful for the heft of the thing in my hands. Resolutely, I charged after the murderous Teuton, determined to bring him to book. Holmes was on my heels as we dashed down the tiled hallway and into the cutting room, the stairs of which afforded us a view of the retreating boche. I took aim but he was too swift for my bullet, which whined off the tiling uselessly. Taking the stairs in a leap, I was hot on his heels when I realised Holmes had paused by one of the long butcher's tables. He was examining some rubber tubing and glassware that he had found, only my shout rousing him from what seemed to me to be his untimely study.

Bursting out into the empty pens behind the slaughter-house, I looked in vain for sign of our quarry, finally spotting him amongst the horses in the corral across the lane. We gave chase, finding ourselves amidst a herd of the beasts, and I had time to wonder if we might have been injudicious in our decision to follow the German agent – for surely he could be nothing but – into that heaving maelstrom of horseflesh and hooves. Twice I found myself jostled by the animals and once a brute of a mare reared at my approach and I should have been trampled beneath its weight had not Holmes restrained me with a timely hand. Suddenly, a volley of shots sounded from ahead and at once the entire herd was surging away from the unexpected noise. Towards *us,* I might add.

To this day I have no idea how I gained the gate, nor what inner strength of force propelled me over, but it is certain that a moment after, several tons of horse crashed against the very gate and splintered it in an instant. I barely made the doubtful sanctuary of a public convenience before being crushed by what had become a surging torrent of stampeding horses. I was afraid for Holmes – had he been trampled? I need not have worried – to my utter astonishment and disbelief I saw him astride a prince of Clydesdales as he vaulted the rail with a jump that would have done Aintree proud, galloping off after his prey like a Hussar at Balaclava. My old wound was, by now, causing me no small discomfiture, so, with a heavy heart and a bitter sense of failure I returned to the slaughter-house to see if anything might be discovered from further examination.

Chapter VII

It was only later, in our rooms at Baker Street, that Holmes told me of his equine adventure. He had, he said, chased down the German to an alleyway, bringing him down with a flying leap from horseback to send the Continental foe sprawling across the flags. As the man was now unconscious, Holmes was able to rifle his pockets to ascertain his identity. His papers gave him as one Carl Heinz Becker of Lindau, a traveller in wines and spirits. Doubtless, Holmes remarked this was likely a fraud designed to draw suspicion away from his real purpose.

"'*À l'œuvre, on connaît l'artisan*', as Fontaine put it." Holmes went to the window to look down on the street as a fresh fall of snow came floating down.

"So he is a spy then?"

Without turning from his vigil, Holmes replied. "Certainly. Wine merchants invariably have about them the tools of the trade: Tasting spoon, lifter – an item resembling a pipette used for sampling – and, of course, corkscrew. Herr Becker was lacking entirely in such *accoutrements*, nor did he have the characteristics of his trade – the man positively reeked of tobacco – any wine taster worth his salt would abstain. Neither were there the slightest trace of stains on his cuff – this man was no dandy, and yet did not use his cuff to dab his lips after sampling? No rural wine merchant this! Indeed, the man was no more a vintner than I a sailor."

"Then what became of him?"

"Lestrade has him now, though I fear not for long. Ah! Talk of the devil! The very man."

It was indeed Lestrade who joined us by the fire. He seemed unusually anxious and refused a brandy as he stood clutching his bowler.

"Well Lestrade, what news?"

"I have the men you asked for, Mr. Holmes, all ready at the Yard. However . . . however, the Director of Criminal Intelligence happened in to the room we were using and – "

"And you have to justify the expense involved?"

"Yes, Mr. Holmes. Quite."

"Then we must make sure," said Holmes, "that we justify every penny."

Going into his room, Holmes returned with a small blackboard, setting it on its easel and flourishing a piece of chalk, rather dramatically in my view. The Faustian extract was reproduced on the board exactly as on the paper. He then produced the paper from the Webb Institute and a piece of perforated card.

"Now, the message. Watson, you found twenty pieces of peculiar cardboard. This brought to mind a rather ingenious cipher devised by the Italian Mathematician Cardano in the sixteenth century. The idea was to write a hidden message within some seemingly trivial piece of text, such as our Goethian Faust here. One then makes a grille from paper and punches a number of holes through it, correspondent with the letters from the secret message. By placing the grille over the innocent text . . . ." Matching action to word, Holmes set the card carefully over the text, and then began furiously circling letters, seemingly at random on the board. Gradually a message appeared, but what Lestrade and I had already seen was this:

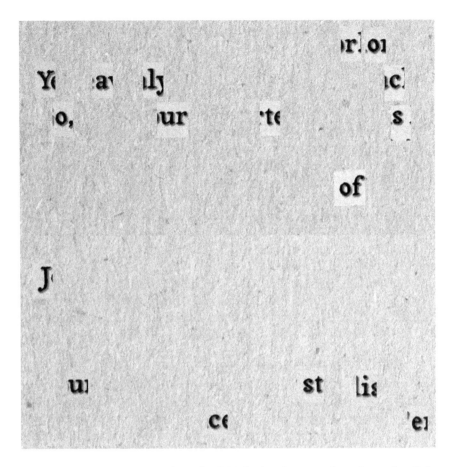

"The Royal Courts of Justice?" I had, of course heard much of the new Courts buildings, which were said to be a wonder of architecture, built to resemble a cathedral.

"The very same."

"But Mister Holmes – what does all this mean?" Lestrade seemed thoroughly at a loss.

Holmes's face was grim and rather pale as he answered the inspector. "It means, my dear Lestrade, that the life of no less a personage than Her Majesty the Queen is imperilled."

The Queen! This was outrageous, beyond contemplation even. "Surely, Holmes, you cannot mean – "

"I do. We must move with caution tonight, gentlemen. I fear a great evil is being wrought at this very moment."

"Then surely we must move to prevent it?"

"All in good time, Watson. If we move rashly, all may be lost. I have made certain arrangements with someone with certain – *connexions* within the Government. We will leave at . . . ." He consulted his watch. "Midnight precisely."

Chapter VIII

It was twenty-five minutes later that we exited the carriage that Lestrade had engaged and found ourselves in a coach-yard to the rear of the vast edifice. Even from this vantage point, the great spire was visible rising into the darkness and, despite myself, a shudder ran through me. Lestrade's men were already there, some in uniform, but others dressed in finery. The smallest must have weighed sixteen stone and many sported cauliflower ears and boxer's noses. Even to my eye, there was no hiding their trade, and Holmes merely rolled his eyes in silent comment.

"Very well. Allow me, Lestrade, to address these men." The inspector seemed doubtful, but acquiesced.

"Gentlemen. My name is Sherlock Holmes. The structure behind you is, as you are no doubt well aware, the new Royal Courts of Justice building, and in a few hours – this very morning, in fact – Her Majesty will be officially opening the new courts. She is to be assassinated as she does so."

At this, a murmur of astonishment went through the ranks, until Lestrade coughed meaningfully and order was restored. Holmes went on. "I must now swear all of you to the most binding oath of secrecy on this matter – and I will then call for volunteers. Inspector, if you please." Holmes held out a hand to summon Lestrade, who produced a piece of paper and cleared his throat before reading from it. The exact details of his speech I cannot reproduce here – suffice to say it was an oath binding the men taking it to their graves.

Thanking Lestrade, my friend continued with his own instruction.

"There is a terrible danger involved, for the assassins are using a particularly murderous weapon, one that can neither be seen nor heard – they are using a malevolent poison of the blood known to science as a 'pathogen'. It causes a disease known and feared throughout central Africa as 'sleeping sickness'. It is invariably fatal and there is no known cure. For this reason, I must ask for volunteers only. There will be, I assure you, no repercussion of any kind on those who are unwilling to take the risk." At this, Lestrade stepped forward and called for volunteers to do the same. To a man, the men all took such a step and it was with evident pride in his men that Lestrade reported that all had done so. Holmes then gave his instructions, outlining a plan to foil the assassins.

I have taken the liberty of quoting from a contemporary account of the events of Monday, the fourth of December, so as to remind readers of the official, public verdict given on that day. Of course, the actual events were never officially chronicled – and with good reason. However, with the passage of time and the recession of the German threat, events have led me to conclude that I may safely reveal what *really* transpired that fateful, far-off day . . . .

It was a grand sight. Every house in the Strand was gaily decorated, and as the Queen and her retinue passed along, the bells of the churches rang merrily, and the crowd of spectators cheered long and lustily. When Her Majesty arrived at the Central Hall, a procession was formed, and first went the builders, Messrs. Edward and Henry Bull, and the architect, Mr. Street. Next came the Attorney General and the Solicitor General, in their best wigs and gowns. Then the Judges, the Lord Chancellor being the hindmost. Next various officials and Mr. Gladstone, and then the Queen, followed by her sons and daughters, the royal attendants bringing up the rear. Her Majesty proceeded to the throne which had been placed on a dais, or raised floor, and, after the key of the building had been presented to her, and then transferred to the keeping of the Lord Chancellor, she read a short address, in which she expressed her trust that the uniting together of the various branches of judicature in this the supreme court would conduce to the more efficient and speedy discharge of justice to her subjects, and that the learning and independence of her judges would prove in the future, as in time past, the chief security of the rights of her crown and the liberties of her people. The Lord Chancellor replied, the Archbishop of York offered up a special prayer, and then Sir William Harcourt, by the Queen's direction, declared the building opened, and the state trumpeters gave a flourish of trumpets to mark the event.

And here is what I recall: Lestrade watched with some bemusement as Holmes detailed men to various posts. Some were to mingle with the throngs of well-wishers and spectacle-gawkers later on, whilst the uniformed constables would, of course, join the ranks serried outside. Each man had a job to do, whether it be to guard a particular passage or exit or, in the case of four particularly hefty constables, protect the Queen's personage from harm. These last were outfitted in the dress of Royal Footmen. Holmes himself had arranged for the two of us to have access to the ceremony from the rather unusual vantage point of the gallery overlooking the hall from the north aspect. The beginnings of the new day began to show through the immensely tall vaulted windows. With a few hours still to the ceremony, we took the opportunity to get what sleep we could in an ante-room, though the plush chairs were hardly suited for beds.

The clock tower at Westminster began chiming the hour for nine and a shout went up below. The last hurried preparations were hastily concluded and various and sundry folk downstairs scurried away, the vast chamber empty for the moment. The last echoes had barely died when a roar went up from the crowd outside. The Yeomen of the Guard hefted their partizans and went to their duties and we were alone for a moment in the great hall. I had the distinct impression of unreality, as if the scene before my eyes was a vast stage of some kind, but then Holmes tapped me on the shoulder.

"It would be better, I think, if we were less conspicuous." Following his example, I shrank back against the stone, making myself as small as possible behind the balustrade.

As described so eloquently above, the procession entered, but was immediately diverted by an apologetic official and, with no small amount of grumbling, the worthies went into a chamber off from the main hall. Next, with a fanfare, Her Majesty was ushered in and was met by a small delegation apparently led by a distinguished, if somewhat corpulent, figure, whose significance was to evade me for some years. This last bowed formally and, after some words, the Queen allowed herself to be shown into a chamber opposite that in which the dignitaries had been led. I began to see that Holmes's plan was being enacted, though I had not the beginnings of any comprehension as to its nature. I was about to remark on this when, tapping my arm, Holmes favoured me with a stern look and a finger to his lips. Indicating I was to follow, he went lightly down the stairs and across to the chamber adjoining that currently occupied by the great and good of the nation.

Holmes tapped softly on the door and after a moment it opened to reveal an odd scene: A short, stocky fellow was being physically restrained by two of Lestrade's rugger players – a *tableau d'incongruité* if there ever was such a thing. Something about the small man seemed oddly familiar, but it was still a shock when Holmes addressed him directly.

"Mr. Pym, I believe – You seem to have lost both weight and age with quite remarkable dispatch. I dare to say that there are ladies who would pay a king's ransom for the secret." I looked closer – it was, indeed Silas Pym!

At that moment, Lestrade entered the room and he seemed uncommonly pleased with himself.

"Ah, Mr. Holmes, I see my men have him. We must hurry, I'm afraid. The Queen will not be kept waiting." Holmes sent an ironic look my way before asking if Pym had been searched. He had not. Holmes's expression assumed an air of urgency.

"Search him from head to toe!" Despite Pym's voluble protests, he could do nothing to retain his modesty as the burly constables ripped at his clothes and searched every item carefully. There was, to my friend's visible dismay, nothing to be found. Somewhat crestfallen, he turned to the inspector.

"It is possible his instructions have been memorised. In such an instance nothing may be done. It is as well," Holmes said to Pym, "that we do not favour the torture method in this country."

Lestrade was anxious now, rubbing his hands nervously. "You have done your best, Mr. Holmes, but I see it has not been enough. We have to let Her Majesty proceed."

"Indeed." Just then, Holmes's keen eye alighted on something and I could see he had noticed a nasty abrasion on the face of one of the constables.

"Constable, if you would, how did you come by that rather unpleasant and so obviously recent wound?"

"Well, sir – it was him there. Hit me, he did, with this." With that, he produced a walking stick from his belt – I saw at once it was Pym's African stick and remarked upon the fact.

Holmes held out his hand and Pym's eyes betrayed him, darting fearfully to the object of the detective's interest.

Inspecting the stick closely, Holmes twisted the monkey's head this way and that, but to no avail. Lestrade's patience was clearly at an end, but then, with a cry of triumph, Holmes pressed both fingers into the eye sockets. With a barely audible click, the stick came away from the head and at once a steel cylinder was visible. From the tube Holmes produced a piece of perforated card which had been tightly rolled to fit. He went to a nearby table, pulling from his pocket the sheet of Faust which he had revealed earlier. Unfurling the card, he laid it over the prose to reveal an entirely different message from the one he had shown us earlier:

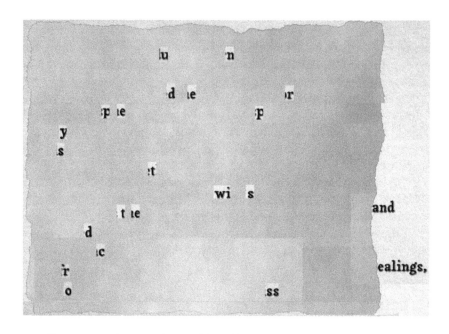

lu   n

                ·d ie   ır

      ;p ie   ·p

  y
  .s

            :t

                    wi   s

        :t ıe   and

    d

      ıc

    ·r   ealings,

    o   .ss

"But Mr. Holmes, what *is* this gibberish?"

"Hardly gibberish, Inspector. Please inform Her Majesty that all will be ready in a very few minutes – but tell the bloated gentleman with her that he owes me a dinner – and not at that atrocious club of his." Without explaining, Holmes rolled up the paper inside the card, handed me Pym's stick, and strode back into the main hall, where I found him vacillating between the lofty stained glass windows above.

"It must be here . . . it must!" Abruptly, he came to a halt below a shield with a yellow bend which featured triple *fleur de lis* flanked by two charger's heads. No sooner had he done this than he was over by the floor and examining minutely a piece of mosaic that resembled the sun's rays, with, at its very centre, a curious design similar to a *fylfot*, or *swastika*, though this was reversed.

I held my breath then as Holmes raised a finger to his lips for silence while waving Lestrade's men over. Reaching into his coat, he drew out his revolver and, with the butt, struck the centre of the mosaic thrice. After a pause, to my surprise the entire panel began to shift, swinging up to reveal the mouth of what seemed to be a tunnel. At once, Holmes took aim and called down.

"Come out at once with your hands above you or I shall be compelled to shoot." In an instant, swarthy figures began to emerge from the chasm and, true to his word, Holmes opened fire.

To my horror, a zombie rose from the ground with a shudder as the bullets went into him, but with inhuman strength and fortitude he grabbed Holmes's leg and attempted to bite into it! Knocking the native away with Pym's stick, I followed this up with a kick to the chest, sending the demented character back into the ranks that were surging up in his stead.

"Lestrade! Watson! We must not let them reach Her Majesty, and do not, for God's sake, let them bite you! They are infected with sleeping sickness!" With that, Holmes had done the unthinkable, diving feet-first into the maelstrom. There was nothing for it but to follow. I found myself in a long, low tunnel lit by oil lamps stretching away into the distance. There must have been thirty of Pym's tribal warriors, all in the fevered grip of the zombie fixation, but there was no time to inspect them. Instead I was thrust into a vicious and desperate hand-to-hand struggle, fighting for my very life against the delirious and ranting natives. I was aware of Lestrade's men behind me and saw one stumble beneath the assault of a cudgel blow from a knobkerry. I wished I had brought my shillelagh, but made do with Pym's stick, which proved its usage as a tribesman reeled from a blow to the face.

We fought then for some minutes, perhaps only few in number, yet they were the longest minutes of my life. I heard a piercing shout as one of the constables was bitten by two of the zombies and drew my revolver, shooting one through the heart. Horrifically, he stood and turned his head slowly to face me, eyes red as burning coals. I levelled my revolver, but, as the man seemed unarmed, I hesitated to shoot again. By some terrible force of will, the man was actually walking towards me. I shrank back against the tunnel wall, but mercifully and he succumbed to the fatality of his wound and fell then, dead. A sudden pain transfixed me and I looked down to find a spear had pierced my side, wielded by one of the spellbound warriors. In agony, I snapped the haft and, with an effort, wrenched the spear-head from my flank, gritting my teeth as the shock began to set in only to see him raising a dagger to strike the fatal blow.

I should have died in that cursed tunnel had not Holmes appeared to shoot the man down. It took all of his remaining cartridges, the zombie finally sinking to the floor after two shots to the skull. Behind Holmes I saw the familiar figure of the witch doctor and shouted a warning, but too late to save Holmes from what came next. The man was wearing his mask, but also he had the claws of a leopard or some such creature affixed to his hands like an evil glove. I saw the blood dripping from the talons – Holmes had been wounded! Despite the shudder of pain that ran through me with every motion, I threw myself forward at the uncanny sorcerer and plunged the head of the spear into his shoulder with the last of my strength.

Shrieking and bellowing with rage, the *juju* doctor spun around and went staggering back down the tunnel, dashing a lantern from its perch as he went. If I thought he was retreating, however, I was sorely mistaken, as he returned from the darkness holding aloft a small decorated skull in one hand and a bottle in the other. This evidently contained some sort of spirit, as he took a swig and spat it at the lamp which lay shattered and burning. In an instant, a wall of fire shot up between us, and I had the distinct image of Holmes wrestling with the frenzied creature, a rictus of a grin upon those savage, primordial features. To see such savagery in a place of justice!

I stumbled forward, keen to help my colleague, but a howl of pain adverted me to the plight of one of the constables, who was being set upon by a zombie, the dull-eyed fiend sinking its teeth into the flesh of his throat with a hollow sound that was neither laugh nor moan. My revolver had been lost in the confusion, but Pym's stick came to good use once more, though it took several blows and I was starting to feel weaker from loss of blood and shock. Holmes was struggling desperately with the witch doctor now and I watched, helpless to prevent the claws raking his back and shoulder. Lestrade then came forth, his face distorted with pain, one arm hanging limp. Another mouthful of spirit renewed the fiery barrier, but without regard to the danger, the inspector raised his good arm and there was a loud report, amplified and distorted by the nature of the passage we were in. The bottle exploded into fragments and with a harrowing scream, the *juju* man was afire, dashing down the tunnel with flame streaming from his body, only to fall some thirty yards distant in a twitching, convulsive heap of thrashing limbs before, mercifully lying still.

I was tending Holmes's wound – a nasty laceration of the shoulder – when a shout went up. Pym had escaped! Brushing my ministrations aside, Holmes dragged himself to his feet and wearily set off after the fleeing villain. I was in no state to continue, so reluctantly accepted the aid of one of Lestrade's men, finally passing out on the way to Barts.

Chapter IX

Dawn broke as dawns must on that long-ago day, and a cold light settled itself on Baker Street. I awoke to find myself confined to bed, and Mrs. Hudson insisting I receive no visitor nor excitement. Despite this, Holmes contrived to find himself in my room on some pretext or other with a bottle of fine Napoleon brandy and, after enquiring as to my health, regaled me with the final chapter of our singular encounter with the *juju* men of Richmond.

I listened in grim fascination at the tale Sherlock Holmes had to tell. Pym – in reality a German agent known as Schumann – had sought no less than the downfall of the British Empire by demonstrating beyond doubt to various factions malcontent with Victoria's sovereignty in Africa and Asia that she was mortal and fallible as are we all. Using his cover as the curator of the Webb Institute, he had devised his dastard scheme when Sir Tristram had fallen prey to sleeping sickness, finally succumbing some days before our involvement. Using the tricks Holmes had already described, Pym, alias Schumann, had convinced a party of native bearers from Sir Tristram's beloved Nkutu tribe that their European friend had been bewitched. Using a cocktail of drugs and some form of hypnosis, it was possible to turn the innocent tribesmen into something akin to the dreaded Zombie of African lore. The *juju* doctor – whom Pym had supposedly found on a trip into the darkest reaches of the East End of London – was no such thing, merely an itinerant dock worker whom Pym plied with money and drink.

Holmes went on then to tell me how Pym had taken infected blood from Sir Tristram to contaminate pigs with the *trypanosoma* parasite, placing some of their blood in the ghastly contraption, knowing I would likely examine it and so discover the presence of the disease. That explained their interest in the slaughter house. The unfortunate bearers were then fed the meat from the pigs to infect them, turning them into lethal carriers of that most frightening of contagion. Set loose, they were to have infected not only Her Majesty the Queen, but many of her ministers and advisers. Pausing in his narrative, Holmes poured for both of us.

Taking my glass, I let the import of Holmes's words sink in before uttering, "The man is a monster!"

"Quite, although it would be proper to say 'was'. I chased him as far as the Thames, but he made the fatal error of assuming the ice was thick enough to convey him across. It was not."

"How, then, were you able to untangle Schumann's cypher?"

"Rudimentary. I used a process of elimination. I knew the plot was timely, perhaps imminent. By carefully perusing the London dailies, I ascertained the events and activities of several prominent people and organisations – the Prime Minister was one, the Home Secretary another. When I saw Her Majesty was due to open the new courts, I simply checked the letters included in the building's full title against the Faustian text and saw it a possibility. From small acorns, as the saying goes . . . ."

Once more I was flabbergasted by Holmes's faculty for reasoning.

"But . . . how could you be sure?"

99

"I wasn't, but the sand was clearly running and the hour was close. I had to take a dreadful chance." There were still points that eluded comprehension, though, such as the business of the tunnel and the second cypher. Matter of fact, Holmes reeled these off in that careless manner that, I knew, concealed his substantial pride in having solved a mystery insoluble to other, lesser minds. By making enquiries, he had ascertained that during construction, the Royal Courts had seen a mason's strike, which led to the employ of German masons. To avoid confrontation with their British counterparts, these Continentals had dug a tunnel leading from New Square, behind the courts. Armed with this knowledge and much encouraged, Holmes began to see how Pym might plan his outrage. When he found the Cardano grille concealed in the agent's stick, he prayed that it would produce an intelligible message and was rewarded with the directions to the tunnel entrance, now covered by marble.

"'*Under Pepys' twisted cross . . . .*'"

"A past Lord Chancellor of some distinction. His coat of arms was, as you saw, above the twisted cross – or should I say *hakenkreuz*?"

I took a healthy sip of my brandy, letting its fire warm my throat. It had been a terrible ordeal, but one which saw the force of Justice triumph beneath a building thrown up to see just such. It had, after all a refreshing inevitability about it.

"So, what of Lestrade's men and the natives?"

"There were five casualties among the former. They are, at this moment in the best of hands at Barts and, it is hoped, may make a good recovery with careful observation. I am told the bites were treated promptly and there is every hope for them. As for Sir Tristam's Nkutu, there are grave fears for their outcome."

My mind was fairly spinning with the whole affair, yet my thirst for knowledge was unabated.

"And what will come of this? It seems the Germans have a lot to answer for."

Holmes assumed a rueful expression. "Pym – Schumann – will be reported as having accidentally drowned. Becker – the other Bavarian we had the doubtful pleasure of encountering at the slaughter house – is under arrest, but I rather think his Embassy will claim him under the international laws concerning diplomatic immunity."

I felt certain Holmes would be fêted for his daring and initiative and voiced this opinion. "The newspapers will have quite a story to relay to the public – I dare say you will be a household name, Holmes."

"Thankfully not. My work requires a certain . . . . *incognito*. Arrangements have been made by an . . . *acquaintance* of mine to keep the whole affair from the press. The German question is on the lips of every diplomat and general alike, and revelation of such a sensational business would inevitably lead to recriminations, perhaps even hostility. And now, my friend, you must rest." We were rudely interrupted by Mrs. Hudson, flying into a spirited Caledonian rage at the sight of the intruder to the sick bay, as it were.

"Indeed he shall, Mister Holmes! The cheek of you! Out! Out this very instant or I shall swing for you!"

It was thus, with a final excitement, that I was able to fall into a blissful sleep in which I dreamed not of ferocious natives, but of Christmases past, sledges and snowmen replacing the terrors that had plagued my waking hours that long ago December.

NOTE

This story is, of course, dramatised. Several events, such as Queen Victoria's opening of the Royal Courts of Justice and the secret tunnel beneath the building are factual, but it should be pointed out that African *trypanosomiasis* was only discovered in humans in the early twentieth century and not identified as the cause of sleeping sickness until then.

The Adventure of the
Headless Lady
by Tracy Revels

"**M**r. Holmes, you must help me! My husband is going to be murdered!"

These frantic words burst from the lips of the striking woman who had appeared at our door early on a summer's morning. She was perhaps thirty years of age, clad in a mauve travelling suit, with a wreath of artfully arranged curls and a fashionable hat. Her fair skin was tinged pink with excitement and distress. She perched on the edge of the sofa like a bird about to take flight, and I sensed that at any moment she might seize our hands and try to drag us from the room, so great was her agitation.

"Mrs. Godwin, most of my clients seek my services after a crime has been committed, not beforehand," Holmes replied. "Do you by any chance know the name of your spouse's intended assassin?"

"Yes, I know her name. I know everything about her. She is shameless, infamous, and deadly."

"Then perhaps you would do better to consult with my friend Inspector Lestrade, or some other worthy representative of the official forces."

The lady shook her head. "They cannot prevent Lady Agatha from killing my husband."

"And why is that?" Holmes asked.

"Because Lady Agatha has been dead for six-hundred years."

The next morning, we were aboard a train, bound for Knights Abbey, where the Godwins resided, he in mortal danger and she in profound terror. The lady had stated her case and departed before luncheon the previous day, and Holmes had spent most of the afternoon in various tasks which – with his usual stubbornness – he had refused to disclose to me. He had not returned to Baker Street until after I retired, and only by merest accident had I heard him up and about long before sunrise. I stumbled down in my robe and slippers to find him brewing coffee with his chemical apparatus.

"I have taxed Mrs. Hudson's patience too many times," he said, "and no matter how princely my payments, she might turn me onto the street if I rang for her at this indecent hour."

"You are going somewhere?" I asked, and felt foolish, for Holmes was clearly dressed in his travelling attire, his long cloak already across his shoulders and his cap resting on his knee.

"To Knights Abbey, where the fiendish spirit of Lady Agatha walks."

"You do not wish me to go with you?"

Something rare and strange passed across my friend's face. I took it as indecision and, perhaps, a hint of guilt.

"In truth, Watson, I had hoped to slip away unnoticed. This case might prove . . . disturbing to you."

"You foresee danger?"

He sipped at his concoction, making a face. I hoped that it wasn't the beaker he'd recently used for testing a new poison. "Of a sort."

"Then say no more. I am coming with you. I am not afraid of ghosts, or spirits, or demons."

"Neither am I. But something more hideous waits at Knights Abbey."

"I will be ready in less than five minutes," I stated. Moments later, as I placed my army revolver in my pocket, I wondered what Holmes could mean by "more hideous". Still, I was resolved that whatever horror awaited, he would not face it alone. He was standing at the door as I slapped my hat to my head.

"You are a good man, Watson, and a far better a friend than I deserve."

That was his final statement of the morning. The moment the train chugged from the station, Holmes slumped in his seat, pulled his cap over his eyes, and dozed. I was far too excited to contemplate returning to the arms of Morpheus. Instead, I slipped into the memories of the previous day, and Mrs. Godwin's strange story.

"I was born and raised in Camford, where my father was an artist. It was at one of his exhibitions that I met my future husband, Albert, and his friend, David Sims. They were both university students at the time. Albert was pursuing a Masters in literature, and David – well, I suppose he was pursuing whatever degree was awarded for rowing and rugby. I do not mean to speak ill of David, but he was as doltish as he was handsome. They both became infatuated with me and courted me in tandem. Albert might not have impressed many girls – he was thin and already going bald, his shoulders slumped from bending over his books – but he was kind, and I knew that if I married him I would be treated like a queen, whereas if I chose David, he would lose interest in me the way a child tires of a toy once its novelty has passed. I feared my decision would cause a rift between the friends, but David seemed to take his rejection in stride and even stood as Albert's supporter at our wedding. Shortly afterward, he left for India.

"Albert and I lived modestly and happily for some five years before – "

Holmes sat up in his chair, holding out his hand. "One moment. You said your father was an artist in Camford. Was your maiden name Avery?"

The lady was clearly startled by this question. She gave my friend a piercing look. "Yes, I was Laura Avery before my marriage."

"Then you are the talent behind *The Nymph's Bowl* and *The Maiden's Abduction,* both in the Pre-Raphaelite school."

Mrs. Godwin blushed. "You are too kind, Mr. Holmes. And I no longer paint, except to give instruction to our young scholars. May I continue?"

"Please."

"It was some five years ago that my husband came into his inheritance – Knights Abbey, a tumbledown manor with a much older, ruined monastery on the grounds. My husband insisted that it was his duty to follow in the family tradition and become the village squire. One of Albert's finest qualities is his sense of obligation, especially to the less fortunate. Thus, he also opened a small charity school in our home, where we board a half-dozen lads whose parents cannot afford to educate them. For some time he was their only schoolmaster, their dear 'Professor'. And then David returned."

The lady began to twist her gloves in her hand. "He came to us without a shilling to his name, so brown and lean and bewhiskered that neither of us recognized him at first. He'd met with ill-fortune, he claimed, though I suspect it was his own idiocy that caused his losses. He was desperate for a position, anything to keep him from begging his bread in London. Albert's heart was soft, and he offered David a place as an assistant schoolmaster, so for the last year David has been living with us at Knights Abbey, though I fear the only thing he properly teaches our boys is how to play games and pull larks.

"David does have a love of history, however, and he soon began digging into the lore of the house and the abbey. One day, he found this paper tucked into an old book. Here, sir – read it!"

I reached into my pocket and pulled out the paper that the lady had given us. It was aged and brittle, torn and stained. Some of the words were illegible, but the gist of the document could, with some consideration, be ascertained.

It was a story from the time of Edward I, the "Hammer of the Scots". Sir Jasper Godwin, a knight and loyal retainer, followed his lord to fight the clans, leaving behind his beautiful young wife, Lady Agatha. The woman wasted no time in cuckolding her husband, luring a dozen different men to her bed to satisfy her wicked desires. Only one, a scholar preparing to take religious vows, resisted her advances. She sent her henchmen to kill him, but somehow he evaded them and made for Scotland, where he told Sir Jasper of his wife's infidelity. Fierce King Edward bid his knight return and deliver justice to the wench, with the scholar at his side to bear witness. When Lady Agatha saw them riding toward the house, she screamed out a curse on the scholar and flung herself from the highest window.

However, she did not die. Her husband rode up to find her broken and moaning on the cobblestones. Without a word, he unsheathed his sword and cut off her head, then rode away, never to be seen again. The scholar, fearful of the woman's curse – for she was rumored to be an enchantress of great power – had her body buried within the abbey, but her head enclosed in an iron box and secreted just beyond the gates, in unhallowed ground. It was said that should the lady's head ever be found, she would rise and take vengeance, manifesting her curse on any man who preferred books to a woman's touch.

Holmes had said little about the paper, other than to dryly pronounce it a "charming" legend. I folded it back and returned it to my pocket, looking through the window, recalling what had followed.

"You may scoff, Mr. Holmes, but it terrified Albert. If he has one fault, it is a somewhat superstitious nature. The boys, of course, were instantly taken with the story, and wanted nothing more than to find the head of Lady Agatha. When they weren't at their studies, they were digging about the old trees like a bunch of little moles. They even destroyed my rose garden, but all David could do was laugh. Then one of them found a picture of Lady Agatha on a wooden panel. The picture must have been tucked away in the abbey vaults for hundreds of years. It was wrapped so tightly that it was well preserved, and David insisted on hanging it in the great hall, where it gazes down upon the boys as they do their work. It is a most disturbing picture. The lady is quite beautiful, but her eyes seem to follow you everywhere you go.

"But now I come to my reason for seeking your aid. Last week, on Saturday, one of the boys dug up an iron box. He brought it to the hall, and I placed it upon a table. Everyone took a seat, anxious to see what might be inside the box. I struggled a bit – It had a hinge, and opened from the side. At last, the heavy panel dropped free and we could see Lady Agatha's head quite clearly.

"Then, Mr. Holmes . . . *she opened her eyes!*"

I had been leaning forward, captivated by Mrs. Godwin's story. My notebook, which I had placed on my knee, dropped to the floor with a thud.

The poor woman nearly flew to the ceiling. Holmes merely raised one eyebrow.

"Did the apparition speak?" Holmes asked.

"No, but the head began to moan, and blood gushed out of its mouth. Everyone screamed, the boys fled in terror. It was horrible, her eyes all wide and red and her teeth gnashing and blood everywhere. Dear Albert fell to the ground, and David ran to him. Somehow I had the presence of mind to slam the box shut. A few of the boys rallied, and together we carried Albert to his room and laid him on his bed. A doctor was called, and afterward he took me aside and told me the worst. My husband, never hearty or strong, now suffers from an aortic aneurism, and any great strain or shock could kill him."

"What of the head?" Holmes asked, a bit brusquely. The lady put her dainty hand to her face.

"While I was with the doctor, the boldest of our boys went up to the box and dared to force it open. He found a head inside . . . but it was a withered, mummy-looking thing, nothing like the vivid lady's face we had all clearly seen."

"I presume, by your earlier statement, that more distressing events have occurred," Holmes said. "That Lady Agatha, now returned from unhallowed ground, is causing mischief?"

"Yes, Mr. Holmes. We have seen her walking."

"Where?"

"On the grounds, every night since Albert fell ill. Sometimes it is at midnight, other times closer to dawn, but we see her in her long gown, carrying her head in her hands. The boys have tried to catch her – and nearly did, one night – but she seemed to shoot up into the trees as they ran toward her. Something fell down from the branches – it was a dress, all covered in blood."

"Did you preserve this article of clothing?"

The lady shook her head. "It frightened the boys so badly they ran away. When they told us of it, in the morning, I went out to search for it, but it had vanished."

Holmes rose, turning his back to his client. "You have, I presume, taken measures to prevent your husband from learning that he is being stalked by a phantom?"

"I have done my best to keep him quiet and confined to his room, but I couldn't stop the boys from talking and Albert from hearing. Two days ago, I sent the children to their homes, telling them they could return when their teacher is well. Already Albert is restless, eager to resume classes. How can I save him? Please, Mr. Holmes, help me!"

Holmes leaned against the mantel, staring down at the empty fireplace. "A priest might be of more assistance in this case. Yet you have come to me instead." He turned, his face sharp and his eyes glittering like steel points. "You have come to me because you know there is no ghost."

"But I have seen her!" Mrs. Godwin cried. "I saw her head come to life. I witnessed her spirit flit about the grounds!"

"Yes, though only after Mr. Sims said an improper thing to you."

Mrs. Godwin gasped and jumped to her feet. She clutched at her throat. "How could you know?" she demanded, her face turning scarlet with embarrassment.

"It is my business to know such things. But tell me – however indelicate – the exact nature of his statement."

The lady resumed her seat. It took her some time to regain her composure, and I wondered if she was about to gather up her skirts and exit our rooms with a slamming of the door. Instead, slowly and nervously, she began to speak.

"It was at Christmas. The house seemed so empty with all the boys gone home for the holiday. We did our best to be merry, just the three of us, but I said how lonesome a home felt at yuletide, without children in it. Albert went to bed soon afterward, while David and I stayed up and sipped sherry by the fire. I was attempting to amuse myself with a book when, suddenly, I felt David's hand on my shoulder, his fingers hot upon my flesh.

"'I could give you children, Laura. Fine sons and lovely daughters. You would not be lonesome again.'

"I pushed him away and raced up the stairs. The next morning, he sought me out in private and fell to his knees. He was in his cups, he said, and would be my slave for life if I would forgive him and say nothing of the incident to Albert. I assured him very coolly that we would never speak of it again, and until this moment I have kept my word. But Mr. Holmes – surely he would not! Albert is his dearest friend – and I have *seen* Lady Agatha!"

"I would like to see her too," Holmes said. "Return home, Mrs. Godwin, and rest assured that I will say nothing of what occurred between you and Mr. Sims. Watch over your husband like a hawk. I will send you notice when I am ready to put your ghost to rest."

The train's whistle sounded, alerting us to our destination. Holmes roused and stretched, then peered through the window as a bucolic village took shape around us.

"I hope Mrs. Godwin received the telegram that I sent last evening."

We disembarked and walked through the station. A deep voice hailed us as we reached the street.

"Mr. Holmes? And Doctor Watson, I presume?" A giant of a man, handsome as Satan with raven black hair and piercing blue eyes, loped up to us. He was dressed in tweeds and heavy boots, radiating the robust life of the countryside. "I'm David Sims. Laura told me you would be here on the earliest train, and I see you've kept your word. A pleasant journey, I hope?"

"An uneventful one," Holmes replied, as I did my best not to wince at the brute strength behind the man's handshake. "Might we trouble you to direct us toward some breakfast before we set out for Knights Abbey?"

The man grinned. "Right this way. Never let it be said that I'm inhospitable!"

There was a bakery nearly, and we settled ourselves on an iron bench outside it. As we devoured some muffins, Sims chattered about the history of the village, how it had seen a half-dozen skirmishes during The Wars of the Roses, and how it lost thirty martyrs to the persecutions of Bloody Mary. He was a font of obscure knowledge, from the number of championships the local rugby club had won to how many horseshoes the blacksmith could make in a day. Holmes was hard pressed to squeeze in a question.

"How is your friend?"

The man suddenly turned serious. "Better, I hope, though it's the devil to get him to rest. He's always been too active for such a frail fellow. I used to tell him that in school – that he'd better sit down and study and leave the sports and the ladies to me. But he's worried about his students. He's afraid if he isn't teaching them every day they'll turn into big dunces." Sims's smile seemed genuine. He began collecting pebbles from the ground, tossing them toward a wall as he spoke. "I've always admired Albert. To tell you the truth, he's more of a man than I will ever be, and look what he's made of himself! A fine home, a beautiful woman to love him, and he's molding young minds. I've never been good for anything but kicking a ball around and flirting with the girls, and you see where it has got me – a life as an underling to a friend whose kindness I don't deserve."

"You are quite the historian," I said, feeling oddly sorry for the man. "You found the story of Lady Agatha."

"Yes, and I've cursed myself for it a thousand times. That damned document," he growled, as I pulled it from my jacket and held it out. "Laura sent me down to bring her a book and there it was, just lying on a table in our little library. It looked old, so of course I was interested. I wish I'd never read it!"

Holmes leaned back, folding his arms. "And the painting? How does it impress you?"

"Why, I don't mind telling you that it gives me the shivers."

"Surely you don't believe in ghosts," Holmes said.

"I thought I didn't, but I've tried chasing this spirit down three times," Sims muttered, "and each time she has given me the slip. She glows like a demon from hell, and she's gone before I can get halfway across the field. If I can't catch her . . . well, I'm at a loss for what to make of the thing." He tossed the last pebble away with a huff. "We'd best start for the house."

"Watson will go with you," Holmes said, much to my surprise. "I would prefer him to consult with the patient first. I have a few inquiries to make in the village – I shall join you in the afternoon."

I was confused by this development, but knew better than to object. I spent the next half-hour in a carriage with Sims, who continued to regale me with a host of facts about Knights Abbey, most of them rather uninteresting. One, however, struck me as significant.

"The property's quite valuable. There's been a rich man from Manchester trying to buy it for some time now. I told Albert, with that much money he could retire and live a gentleman's life in London, and keep Laura in style rather than forcing her to rusticate as a country schoolmistress! But he won't hear to it! The Godwin name means too much."

At last, we arrived and disembarked before a large house with both Tudor and Georgian architecture in its lines. Despite its pedigree, it had clearly seen better days and was now reduced to being sadly shabby, leaving one with the impression that a strong wind could blow the entire edifice down. Lurking behind the building was the roofless abbey, a striking ruin that would make a grand folly in a pretentious garden. Mrs. Godwin met us at the door, alarmed to see that I had come alone. I assured her that Holmes would be along shortly, and she agreed to let me visit her husband.

Mr. Albert Godwin was a pathetic specimen, his yellowed skin pulled taut against his sharp bones. He was bald except for some sprigs of gray hair around his ears, and his hands were twisted with arthritis. Still, he managed a welcoming smile, and his conversation was erudite and witty. There was a gentleness about him that reminded me of stories about medieval saints and holy men.

"I know my time is limited, Doctor," he said, after I had listened to his heart. Not since Jefferson Hope had I heard such a tortured convulsion in a man's chest. "But I would prefer not to be killed by Lady Agatha. Do you know she has cursed all scholars? I worry about Laura, of course. What will she do with this old house, my school, all the debts I've incurred?" He motioned me closer, his voice reduced to a whisper. "I know it was hard for her to go to London alone, but she went at my request. I am not afraid to die, but with so much left undone . . . ."

I insisted that he not strain himself by discussing the matter. Clearly, the man needed rest and a calm mind. At just that moment, Mrs. Godwin tapped on the door and told me that Holmes had arrived. I found him downstairs in the great hall, where a dozen desks were neatly arranged. He was studying the nearly life-sized portrait of Lady Agatha on the wall.

"Her eyes are striking," Holmes said, as I approached. "Walk to one side, Watson. Tell me what they do."

The effect was chilling. "They seem to follow me!"

"Indeed. The lady is always watching." Holmes turned. "Tell me about your patient."

I described his condition. Holmes appeared grave.

"Then we will do well to end this haunting tonight. Could you concoct a mild sedative? Something that will make the gentleman sleep soundly but safely? Excellent. I would like a word with the sufferer before we explore our surroundings."

Holmes promised not to say anything that would upset the invalid. When he came back down, we began touring the extensive grounds of Knights Abbey. Two of the fields near the house had been marked off for rugby and cricket, while others were planted as vegetable and herb gardens. Mrs. Godwin revealed that they employed only a cook, a housekeeper, and a general laborer, as the property was far too expensive to maintain in any grand style.

"Albert would like to do more for the villagers," Mrs. Godwin said, "but I tell him he has done enough by taking in so many of their boys as students! What more could be expected? It costs a small fortune to board the children, but Albert insists."

"She's wasted here, isn't she?" Mr. Sims said, not an hour later, as Mrs. Godwin walked back to the house, leaving us in his charge. "Did you know she was an artist? She gave it up, of course. What good wife wouldn't?" He pointed to a gaping hole beneath a willow tree. "That's where the lad found the box with Lady Agatha's head inside."

"I would like to see the relic," Holmes said.

Sims's face darkened. "You can't. I threw the cursed thing in the fire. I thought burning it would send Lady Agatha back to hell."

Mrs. Godwin served us an early supper, and despite the oddness of the situation, we did our best to be pleasant. Holmes insisted that I regale the pair with tales of his adventures, which Sims especially enjoyed. As the sun set, I accompanied Mrs. Godwin to her husband's room, helping her serve his meal. No couple could have been more devoted or loving.

Careful to be discreet, I took the drug I had mixed and slipped it into Godwin's wine, placing the cup on the nightstand.

"Come dearest, let me help you retire," Mrs. Godwin urged. "You've had quite a day with company in the house."

"And who would have imagined that we would ever entertain the famous detective Sherlock Holmes," her husband chuckled. "And his equally famous friend, Doctor Watson."

I offered a grateful bow and exited their chamber. Just as I reached the bottom of the stairs, I heard a shriek.

"My God! There she is! She's in the hall!"

It was Sims. He was standing in the corridor, jabbing a finger at the massive doorway. Holmes was running to his side, and I hurried to catch up.

"Are you certain?"

"I saw her as clear as I see you! She slipped through there, closed the door behind her! Come on!"

Sims was a man of action. He was to the door and had it thrown open before either of us could move. I heard the rapid patter of Mrs. Godwin's footsteps behind us as we burst into the room.

"There! Look!"

The ghastly apparition swirled around. It was a woman's body, clad in some long, diaphanous dress. Blood stained her shoulders, pooling around the stump of a neck. Her head was cradled between her hands. As we stood, horrified, her eyes popped open and she began to moan, swaying from side to side.

Mrs. Godwin screamed and crumpled to the floor. I pulled my army revolver from my pocket, but just as I leveled it, Holmes smacked it from my hand with a loud shout of "*No!*" Sims broke from our pack, giving chase. The ghostly figure sped away, bolting through an open door at the rear of the hall.

"I could have killed it," I snapped, grabbing my gun from the floor.

"And you would have been a murderer," Holmes said, seizing my elbow before I could kneel to assist the swooning lady.

We flew in Sims's wake, finding ourselves on the grounds between the ruins and the house. There was a terrible cry and then another shrill scream. I froze in my tracks, staring in disbelief.

Two ghostly, headless ladies confronted each other. They were mirror images, each reeling backward, as if astonished to see her twin. For a moment that seemed endless, they simply stared at each other. Sims spun, asking us as to what to do, his face a rubbery mask of confusion.

The second spirit, whose dress glowed with a phosphorescent hue, abruptly let out a most unladylike oath and took to her heels. The phantom from the hall dove forward, tackling her. They wrestled on the ground, kicking up turf and muck before the lady from the hall gained the upper hand and cried out in a triumphant, familiar voice.

"I've got her, Mr. Holmes!"

"Well done, Wiggins! Hold fast!" Holmes moved forward and helped his young assistant retrieve the woman from the ground. I walked closer, shaking my head. Wiggins had been suited up for a supernatural masquerade, his head stuck through an opening in the bosom of the dress, his 'shoulders' supported by wires. Fake arms seemed to hold his head fast to his false body. He grinned at me, then tore off the strange attire and swiped roughly at the heavy makeup on his face.

"I'm no lady!"

"I can see that," I laughed. "Clearly, Holmes, you have competition for the title of master of disguise. But who is this?"

The second woman had ceased struggling and hung limply in my friend's grip. Her strange ensemble had been broken in the fight. Wrapped in an array of rags, wires, and artificial limbs, she resembled a hideous, life-sized puppet.

"I just took a job," she whimpered. "A girl has to eat!"

"She is Miss Anna Martell," Holmes said. "And, until a week ago, she was an assistant to The Great Fedori, one of London's foremost magicians."

Sims snorted like an angry bull. He stared at the woman and at Holmes, his face turning red and the veins in his neck bulging. I feared he would attack both of them, so great was his rage. I tightened my grip upon my revolver.

"Who hired you?" Sims snapped at the woman. "Who employed you to try and terrify the life from Albert?"

Much to my astonishment, a soft voice whispered, "Laura did."

We turned. Behind us stood Mr. Albert Godwin, clad in pajamas and a heavy dressing gown and leaning upon a cane. He shook his head, peering at our strange tableau with watery eyes.

"You were correct, Mr. Holmes. I've suspected it for a long time. Laura no longer loves me – perhaps she never did. She wanted to be free, to sell Knights Abbey and go back to her artist's life. Only she could have created the document and the painting, and hired this actress for the role." He shook his head. "David, I'm sorry I didn't speak out. She was trying to pin the thing on you all along, if anyone should question it. If she'd only been more patient . . . ."

He began to sway on his feet. Sims rushed to his side, and together we escorted Godwin back into the hall, depositing him in a chair.

"Where is she?" Sims snarled. "Damn Laura, where has she gone?"

"It hardly matters," Godwin said.

There was a late train for London and we were aboard it. Miss Martell remained in the custody of the village police, still swearing upon every dead relative she possessed, that she had only been told she was staging a haunting for the amusement of school boys. Wiggins returned with us, proud to have been such an essential element of Holmes's plan. Holmes waited until the youth dozed off before beginning to explain the case to me.

"The fantastic elements of Mrs. Godwin's story seemed all too contrived to implicate Sims. No matter how well preserved, an authentic thirteenth century portrait would not have eyes that, like the Mona Lisa's, seem to follow the viewer around the room – such an effect could only be produced by an artist who understood linear perspective, which was developed during the Renaissance. Did you note how flushed and nervous Mrs. Godwin became when I revealed that I knew of her former career? The document was also clearly a forgery"

"Easy enough," I said, "but what about the animated head in a box?"

Holmes smiled. "That was straight from a magician's repertoire."

"How was it done?"

"A simple enough matter, with some planning. Mrs. Godwin had arranged a special table, with an easily removed panel in its center, in the classroom ahead of time. Beneath it she used mirrors, to give the impression that the space below it was empty. Earlier, she planted the iron box for the boys to find – no doubt that morning she gave one of them the necessary 'clue' that led him to dig it up. Taking charge of the assembly, she made a discreet swap for a special duplicate box, a container which had an opening allowing Miss Martell's head to pass through as she knelt beneath the table, obscured from view. Made up to be hideous with stage blood gushing from her mouth, the spectral accomplice put on quite the show. In the chaos that ensued, Mrs. Godwin rushed forward and closed the box. At this point, Miss Martell placed a grotesque, mummified monkey's head inside to replace her own – this was the artefact that Sims destroyed."

"But how did the assistant get away?"

"A simple enough matter when the entire school was preoccupied with carrying their beloved professor off to his bed."

"Amazing," I said, "how quickly you pinpointed the deception."

"Watson, there was no other possible explanation, as the world is just large enough for the wicked quick, without the added presence of the vengeful dead. I will confess a stroke of good luck in one regard: I went immediately to consult with The Great Fedori about the illusion and learned not only the particulars of the method, but also its most likely performer. Fedori, who has a bit of a fancy for his assistant, was eager to tell me of how she had been lured away from him for some kind of private theatricals in the country."

"But why was the lady unwilling to wait?" I asked. "Her husband is not a healthy man. In another year, she might have been a widow."

"And in another year, there might not have been such a splendid offer for Knights Abbey. I spoke with an agent in the village, pretending to be interested in purchasing the property. He rather indiscreetly told me that I would need to match or exceed the sum offered by Mr. Richard Macintosh."

"The 'Pram Man'?"

Holmes smiled, "Yes, the 'Pram Man' – a captain of industry and inventor of the 'safety perambulator' who currently resides in Manchester. His wealth increases with the regularity of the stork's arrival, but his family roots lie in the gutters of Aberdeen rather than the genteel countryside. He hoped to buy some social status, as well as a quaint old home."

"Sims told me there had been an offer, which Godwin rejected."

"It was that offer which sealed Godwin's fate."

I leaned back in my seat, pondering all that had happened.

"But why did she come to you – wait! She didn't choose to come to you! Mr. Godwin said that he sent her."

Holmes nodded. "Indeed, Watson, he not only sent her, he sent a note directly to me *about* her. It arrived a mere hour before she did. I had just digested its contents when she appeared at our door. He was loathe to accuse his spouse directly. I think he wished to believe in a murderous spirit, but his scholarly mind rebelled against such an irrational explanation for the strange occurrences in his household. It was an intriguing experiment, from my point of view, especially when Mrs. Godwin sprang the traps I placed in her path. There was no indelicate suggestion from Sims, of course, but it was entertaining to watch her craft such an offense on the spot, in response to my bait."

"You could have told me this upon her departure," I said, with perhaps a bit more sharpness than I intended.

"I was in something of a rush to confirm my suspicions about her accomplice, then to make arrangements for Wiggins to play his part. And you are a much more convincing actor when you improvise your lines rather than rehearse them."

The comment rankled. For a long time we sat in silence. Finally, I felt that the one unresolved matter had to be aired.

"Holmes, you implied there was some danger in this case. What did you mean? Was that merely a part of your ploy to use me as a stooge in your little drama?"

There was a small flare of light in the darkness, as Holmes lit his travelling pipe.

"Friend Watson – my words were honest. The danger was to your perception, for I know you hold the fair sex in high regard. You want to think of women as delicate creatures, loving and kind. I did not want to shatter your illusion by presenting to you a sample of the species as cold-blooded as Jezebel or even the mythical 'Lady Agatha.'"

"I would think I had learned that lesson years ago."

"But you are a good man, Watson. One of us must have faith in humanity, even if that faith is occasionally betrayed."

It was a strange, yet sincere compliment. I decided to say no more.

After seeing to the comfort of our patient and assisting Holmes in confining the accomplice, I had joined the search for Mrs. Godwin. There were signs in her room – garments flung about, a broken bag on the floor – that she had departed in some haste. Godwin ordered us not to pursue her, stating that he would leave her punishment to heaven. Miss Martell was soon released, and returned to holding hats, scarves, and rabbits for The Great Fedori.

A year later, we were saddened to learn that Mr. Albert Godwin, the kind and gentle scholar of Knights Abbey, had passed away from natural causes. His wife having abandoned him, he left his estate and the school to Sims, who continues to operate it for the good of poor children and is becoming much beloved as a local historian and captain of the village rugby team.

Not long after Godwin's passing, Holmes halted before the window of an art gallery in London. He drew my attention to a painting displayed behind the glass, a large image in an antique style. It was a medieval scene, of a *la belle dame san merci* plugging a dagger into the heart of a knight whose face bore an unmistakable resemblance to my friend's.

Angelus Domini Nuntiavit
(The Angel of the Lord Declared)
by Kevin Thornton

When I arrived back at 221b Baker Street that Monday after my morning constitutional, Mrs. Hudson warned me that there was a nun with Holmes.

"He asked you to join him. She's only been there a minute or two." I thanked her then proceeded up the stairs.

"Ah, Watson, excellent timing. May I present Sister Fidelma of The Sanctified Order of Mary Magdalene. They have a convent in Whitechapel where they help the poor and destitute."

The lady in question was of middling height and an impossible age to gauge. She had on the simple black habit and white surrounds so common among women of her calling, and the covering of all but her face made her seem timeless. She may have been be a world-weary young nun or a serene senior of the order. She was standing, yet seemed close to collapse. I moved a chair behind her. She almost gave in to the idea, but at the last second she remained upright.

"We help the street whores, Mister Holmes," she said, "the wretched and ignored women that have to sell their bodies to evil men with base carnal needs."

"You are very candid," said Holmes. "There is much to be admired in such directness, but your candour does not help when raising funds for your work. You would do better to see to young orphans rather than old prostitutes. The rich are more munificent to charities that stand them in a glowing light."

"Mister Holmes, I have not come here to be insulted. The work we do is important and valuable, and if you are of the same engrained and inbred attitude of most of the worthies of this city, I shall have to go elsewhere." She looked around for her bag and umbrella, but didn't see them on the stand behind the door. Her exit temporarily stayed, she returned to Holmes as if to give him one more lashing with her tongue.

Holmes was looking at her thoughtfully, waiting.

"Oh," she said. "You have tricked me, Mister Holmes, and rather proved your point. Yes, my temper does get the better of me. I seem to have no patience with the patronising, and most wealthy people seem to be excessively so."

116

"Indeed, you and your convent live close to the breaking point of poverty and are, I fancy, in dire straits."

"How could you possibly know that? It is true, but I did not mention it, nor do I remember us meeting before."

"It is a simple conclusion. I've never seen a rich or finely enrobed nun, but your habit is so threadbare as to be barely held together, indicating that there is not even a spare ha'penny in your budget. I also happened to observe you walk towards our door along Baker Street, and you came from the wrong direction for public transport. The way you walked signalled profound weariness. It would be my estimation that you, still a young lady of a mere twenty-nine summers, set off early from Whitechapel and walked here to save the farthing that the bus would cost. Please, Sister Fidelma, sit down and relax for a moment. Watson, could you trouble Mrs. Hudson for tea, and something to eat?"

"Already here," Mrs. Hudson said cheerfully as she came into the room. "I knew this poor wee waif would need something to bolster her while talking to you two, so I prepared a tray." She laid it on the table and said to Sister Fidelma, "You take your time, my dear. Mister Holmes and Doctor Watson are fine gentlemen who will be able to help you, and when you are done, my nephew and his hackney will be here to take you home."

Sister Fidelma sat down gratefully. "You are too kind, Mrs. Hudson. May God bless you." Then she raised herself slightly in the armchair. "You have proved yourself to be most astute in your observations, but how on earth did you deduce my age – correctly, I might add."

"Sadly that was subterfuge. When you made your appointment to see me, I sent a telegram to a Roman churchperson I know. When I found out your birth name, it was easy to look up the family. Before you became Sister Fidelma, you were known as Therese Greenwood, younger sister and only living relative of Steven Greenwood, the Marquess of Mollington. *Who's Who* lists your brother's date of birth, making him currently forty-four, and notes you are fifteen years his junior."

"It would have been better had you maintained some subterfuge," the nun said, "It would have been more impressive."

"I promise you, Sister Fidelma, that however dismal the truth you seek, I will not conceal it from you."

"Thank you. It is my brother I am worried about. He and I took such varied routes through life. The difference in age meant he was away to University before I had started school, and he then spent some years in the East, where his beliefs and his gods seemed to change with every letter he wrote home. When my parents were lost at sea in 1868, it took two years for him to return to England. I was too young to care for myself, and the estates and banking were all tied up in a trust awaiting his return, so I was placed in the care of the nuns at my school. By the time he returned, my faith had intensified to the point where I knew I had a vocation."

"And your brother?"

"He was a restless soul at first. He has never married, always searching for some obscure truth. However, about a year ago he seemed to have an epiphany and slowly started returning to the church in which we were born and raised. He even mentioned that he wanted to make a donation to our work. He had recently done rather well with some shares and wanted to help my order. I was delighted, of course. I have never asked him before, as he has always seemed reluctant and I have never wanted to put him in a position that would test our familial ties. That he had come to this conclusion by himself was heartening."

"Indeed," said Holmes.

"It has been my custom to see my brother every Monday. He used to come and visit me at the convent, and then we would go for a meal. More typically though, he will send his coachman for me and we will lunch at the manor, the family home." Sister Fidelma smiled. "It was easier that way. Taking me to a restaurant was awkward for him. The Savoy and other such places are uncomfortable with the blatant poverty I display."

Holmes permitted himself a slight smile and a nod.

"Pray continue," he said.

"Then everything changed," said the nun. "A month ago when I was taken to the manor, I was met by a woman at the door, a Miss Yvette LeRoux. She introduced herself as a friend of my brother. At first I was delighted. My brother is shy and introverted, and has never seemed to be one with an interest in women. When he finally came down to join us, he seemed tired and out of sorts."

"'I see you have met my darling Yvette,' he said, but his words did not match his demeanour. 'She calls herself a *therapist*, and among many of her wonderful qualities, she is teaching me how to relax.'

"'Why, that's wonderful,' I replied. 'And how did you meet?'

"'Quite by chance,' interrupted Yvette. 'I was walking past the manor when the heel of my boot broke off. I came to the door seeking help. Your brother let me in, we started talking and I don't think we have stopped since then.'"

Sister Fidelma continued her tale. "To say that I was disconcerted would be an understatement. I asked about her work as a therapist and she was vague to the point of obfuscation. She mentioned Lady Pettibone and Sir Oliver Tuckett, as well as some other names. I cannot recall them, but I do remember at the time how unusual it was that I didn't recognize any of her clients."

"Given your sheltered life," Holmes said, "that is maybe not as surprising as you think."

"Mister Holmes, I lead a cloistered life, not a sheltered one. Of an evening, I find more human misery on the streets of Whitechapel than you are likely to see in a year. I am also the daughter of a Marquess and the sister to one. I grew up in a home where every year I met half the nobility and many of the royals at weekend parties and summer events. Even though I have moved away from that life, it is unlikely that she could list so many ennobled clients, yet I could not recognize a single name."

"My apologies," said Holmes.

"There were a few changes that first Monday she was there, things that at the time I thought insignificant. Added together with what else I have seen, they give me cause for alarm. One of the many reasons I look forward to my weekly visits with my brother is that he puts on a delightful meal. It is the only good meal that I eat all week. Typically there is a roast with all the trimmings, vegetables, some cheeses, and a cake. Steven does very well for himself and we have an understanding that I may take the leftovers back with me so that his largesse may be shared among the other nuns. Imagine my surprise when we were summoned to the dining room, only to find that there was no roast. In its place there were mushrooms from the fields, and roasted nuts. There was a bowl of green leaves that looked as if they had been growing in a ditch, and a puree of something that Miss LeRoux assured me was highly nutritious, and often eaten by the mountain men of far-off Nepal. I don't know how nutritious it all was, but it was definitely tasteless."

"A disappointment indeed," said Holmes.

"Matters seemed to get worse at every subsequent visit," said Sister Fidelma. "By the second week, my brother seemed back to his former health, but it seemed his mentality had lessened. This was a man who scoured the world seeking answers to life's great questions, and he seemed unable to string together two coherent thoughts. Miss LeRoux explained it away by saying that listlessness is one of the initial consequences of learning how to be calm, as all the evil vapours depart the body. When I asked how she hoped to accomplish that, she mentioned a healthy diet, long relaxing walks in the fields foraging for food, and Oriental relaxation techniques."

"On the face of it, all admirable qualities in your brother's fiancée," said Holmes, "for that is what she has become, has she not?"

"Did you read my mind, Mister Holmes? That is exactly what has happened. Last Monday, she informed me that not only had she and my brother become affianced, but also that he was unwell and could not join us for our normal repast. Then she said that Steven had reconsidered his

119

donation to the convent, and would instead be giving his money to a more worldly cause. Ignoring her pleas, I stormed up to my brother's bedchamber. I asked my brother why, after his promises, he was forsaking me. He seemed unable to give me a sensible reply."

"What did he say?"

"That he had seen a guardian angel who had expressly told him *not* to donate to the convent." Sister Fidelma looked as outraged as she could get. Her eyebrows knitted together and her lips pursed. "Imagine that, Mister Holmes. What kind of a heathen angel is that?"

"Setting aside ghostly apparitions, because I am sure there is an explanation for that, did he tell you where he was donating the money?"

"To a charity that Miss LeRoux had found. I asked her what it does, and she told me dismissively that it was a fund to support other charities and that it was a more efficient use of my brother's largesse. She told me it was too complicated for me to understand."

"And that did not sit well with you," I said.

"No, Doctor Watson, it did not. I felt like my whole world had been turned upside down."

"Yes," I said. "Hallucinations can be troublesome."

"Both you and Mister Holmes seem to have dismissed the possibility of my brother actually seeing his angel. I do not. I am sure guardian angels exist, Mister Holmes, at least within the beliefs of my church, and my own faith. My question has more to do with the message of the angel, as well as its fortuitous timing. I suspect my brother is being manipulated, and I suspect that I know by whom, but I don't know how."

"Can you describe Miss LeRoux?" said Holmes.

"She is tall for a woman, nearly six feet with those ridiculous heels that she wears. She has long black hair that she wears straight, parted in the middle, and she has the palest of skin. I would put her in her middle thirties, though my uncharitable thought is she is like mutton dressed as lamb and could very well be some years older than Steven. She is very slender, very sharp. Her face is angular, and she is no advertisement for her food, as she seems unhealthy and wan."

Holmes walked across to the bookshelves and pulled down a vast tome of a scrapbook.

"It is Monday," he said as he began to page through. "Are you not due there for lunch in a couple of hours?"

"I'm not sure. Every week I receive a telegram from Steven confirming that he would be at the manor and that he would send for me. There are times it doesn't happen. Sometimes business takes him away, or he has spent the weekend shooting in Scotland. In those instances, I will still receive a message postponing our little family gathering. This time I have heard nothing. I'm troubled as to what to do next."

"You must go to the manor, and we shall attend with you. Whatever hold she has on him is bewitching enough that he has been transformed from a vibrant intelligent man into a passive sloth." As he said this he paused at a page in his book. "Would you look at this portrait please, Sister Fidelma?"

I went across with her. The picture was on a flyer for one of the more downmarket theatrical establishments and showed a woman as the main attraction of the entertainment. *"She will tease you and please you!"* it said. *"Watch as Madam Mysterio makes you do the things you had always wanted to, but were too afraid to try. Walk a tightrope, juggle, become an acrobat, or a lion-tamer. Madam Mysterio will unleash the powers of your mind and turn you into your most fervent wish or desire!"*

"That's her," said the nun. "My word, that's what's happened to my brother?"

"Well that explains it," I said. "She's a hypnotist."

Holmes shook his head. "As always, Watson, you see only part of the picture. Come – let us away to the manor. Mrs. Hudson's nephew will get a good fee for his cabbing work today."

Unsurprisingly, Holmes was silent as we started the journey. I had learnt it best not to interrupt him in his cogitations. He would reveal all when he wished to – or so I thought. Sister Fidelma had other ideas.

"So is this Madam Mysterio hypnotizing my brother, Mister Holmes, or is he really being guided by his guardian angel?"

Holmes was uncharacteristically gentle. I knew what he thought about the so-called spiritual world, and he would definitely have lumped these heavenly apparitions in with all the other charlatans he had ever exposed.

"We do not have enough facts, Sister, but I think all is not as it seems. There are people who say that hypnotism is a bold new science, that even medical operations can be performed without any anesthetic. A patient merely needs to be put to sleep by a mesmerizing practitioner, and woken up afterwards, free of any pain or trauma. I have my doubts. I believe that a strong-willed man should be able to resist such chicanery."

"And a strong-willed woman," she said.

"Indeed."

"The claims on your theatrical poster seem farfetched," said the nun. "I cannot see how a hypnotist can coerce someone into doing something they had no inkling to do previously – juggling and the like. No one could put me to sleep and turn me into a tightrope walker any more than they could get me to deny my faith in God."

"And there you have the crux of it, Sister Fidelma. Does your brother not seem from your description to be an easily persuaded man, capable of being manipulated?"

"I would say not, Mister Holmes. He has spent his adult years questing for what truths he could find, trying to make sense of the world. I should imagine he has faced many persuasive arguments, each of which he has countered by logic and force of will."

"I suspected as much," said Holmes. "We must wait and see what we will find at the manor, but I am comfortable enough in my theories to be confident that we shall resolve this set of events before the end of the day."

We were quiet for most of the rest of the journey. At one point Holmes started to say something, then thought better of it. He frowned, as if in the midst of a mystery, and then addressed the nun.

"Therese is a French spelling of your name, possibly even Iberian. Do you have relatives from the Continent?"

The nun smiled. "There was much celebrating when I was born. My parents had wanted many children but my mother had six miscarriages between Steven's birth and mine. By the time we arrived at my baptism, which was rushed as I was a frail infant, my father and the parish priest, Father Bonisteel, had spent some significant time wetting the baby's head and could barely stand, let alone write. I was supposed to be named Teresa after the Saint of Avila. Therese was a spelling mistake, so when I professed my vows I started afresh, doing God's work as Sister Fidelma,"

To my astonishment, Holmes slapped his knee in delight. "Well, Watson, what do you make of that? I have sat here pondering Sister Fidelma's unusual christened name, and it is nothing more than a spelling mistake. Let us hope all other questions are as easily sorted today.

The manor house of the Marquess of Mollington was a large and forbidding building done in a mock gothic style. Above the entranceway, four grotesque gargoyles peered down, uninviting and forbidding.

"The second Marquess had four older sisters," said Sister Fidelma, "spinsters all, and miserable souls. Family legend is the gargoyles were modelled after them." She stepped to the door and rang the pull bell energetically, as if summoning her convent urgently to prayer.

Miss LeRoux was dismayed to see us. For a moment she seemed to wish to shut the door. Sister Fidelma, however, marched into the house as if it were her own and sat down on a chair.

"I wish to see my brother," she said.

"Your timing is unfortunate," said Miss LeRoux. "He is resting and lunch is not prepared for today."

"Yet there is a smell of cooking from the kitchen," said Holmes. "Perhaps we might stay for a short while. It is imperative we see the Marquess."

"He has never mentioned you, Mister Holmes, nor you Doctor Watson. I cannot imagine what business you may have with him. Please leave."

"The Marquess's sister is worried about her brother's health and has asked the Good Doctor to attend as a physician. I am here as a consultant. Perhaps I might suggest some form of therapy for him."

"You are not a therapist," said Miss LeRoux. "You are that interfering detective I have heard talk of."

"I am as much a therapist as anyone else in this room, Miss LeRoux – or may I call you Madam Mysterio?"

For a moment I thought I saw doubt in her eyes, but she recovered quickly.

"I am not ashamed of my past, and Steven is aware of my prior life on the stage. He doesn't care."

"Then as soon as Doctor Watson has seen the Marquess, and I have questioned him, we shall leave you to the rest of your life."

The stairway from the foyer upstairs was broad and sweeping. There was a noise from the top and then a man appeared from one of the doors. He was wearing a nightshirt. His hair was longer than fashionable and his beard untrimmed. He was holding his hands out parallel to the ground and for a moment I thought I was having my own apparition of the risen Christ. Then he swayed a little and the nun screamed "*Steven!*"

"Holmes, he must surely fall!" We dashed up the stairs towards him. He nearly did, teetering towards the balustrade, but at the last second he grabbed the top and swung down to his knees on the top step.

"*Angelus Domini nuntiavit Mariae, et concepit de Spiritu Sancto,*" he said, and he looked to the ceiling, smiling beatifically.

"What is he saying?" I said.

"'*The Angel of the Lord declared unto Mary*'," said Sister Fidelma coming up behind us. "'*and she conceived of the Holy Spirit*'. It is a prayer, one of the rote teachings of the church, used to achieve communion with God. What is he looking at?" She shook him by his shoulders. "Steven, what is it?

The Marquess of Mollington pointed up. Though he still smiled like a child in front of a toy store, I noticed dark patches under the eyes. Miss LeRoux's relaxation techniques did not seem efficacious, and whatever was causing this behaviour was not healthy.

"My angel soars and hovers," he cried, raising his hands as if in benediction. "She will guide me along the right path. She is with me now."

Sister Fidelma looked up, as did Holmes and I. There was nothing to see. "Where, Steven?" she said. "Tell me where your angel is! Tell me *who* your angel is!"

The Marquess ducked and then bobbed up again. "She swoops, she soars. Here she comes again. Oh Michael, my Michael!"

"Enough," said Holmes. "Let's get him to bed. It is clear he is delusional."

"You don't believe him?" said Sister Fidelma. "How can you not believe? Look at him! He is enraptured!"

"I believe that *he* believes in what he is seeing. I don't believe it is an angel hidden from us, and neither do you. You are too practical to be taken in by this. If this were indeed a manifestation of a Messenger of God, why does your brother refer to it as *she*, yet call him *Michael*? Why does he get an archangel, and why is it one of the only three-and-a-half angels mentioned in the bible? If this were real, surely the introductions would have been proper, and he would know real things about his angel? This is a charade, and all that is left to do is unmask it."

"You tease me, Mister Holmes, but your logic is correct. My brother is under the influence of someone – or something. This is merely the uncontrolled rant of a man who remembers some small parts of his childhood faith. Has she hypnotized him, Mister Holmes?"

"I believe so, but I believe that she had help."

The Marquess settled into a sleep in his room. Miss LeRoux was waiting downstairs. "You see, he is ill, and I look after him. When he wakes, he will kick you all out, and I shall marry him and be the Marchioness."

"You have hypnotized him," said Holmes, "but you needed help of some sort to lower his defenses. Did you drug him? When I find what you did, I will call the police and you will be arrested."

"You will find nothing," she said. "Go on, search. I dare you. I will delight in throwing you all out of my house and disinheriting *you*!" she said, pointing at the nun. "The Sister-sister who he did not want to disappoint."

"Enough," said Holmes. "I tire of her prattle. Watson, lock her in the library, if you please, so that she cannot disappear."

"Do not touch me!" she screamed and I held back. Sister Fidelma was less restrained. She grabbed Miss LeRoux's arm, twisted it behind her back, and marched her away. I followed, but was unneeded. The nun pushed her through the door where she stumbled into an armchair and sat down rather ungracefully. I locked the door and turned to see Sister Fidelma's shamefaced smile.

"May God forgive me, but I enjoyed that far too much." There must have been a look of surprise on my face. "Do not trouble yourself, Doctor. I have learned to look after myself for my work on the streets. When a drunken pimp comes at me with a broken bottle because I'm trying to persuade one of his coterie to change her ways – well, let's just say there is a time for turning the other cheek and a time to defend God's work most vigorously."

"Most impressive, Madam," I said

When we came back, Holmes was standing in the hall looking around the building. It was a mansion of some twenty rooms or so, and the opulent furniture meant it would not be easy to search.

"What exactly are we looking for?" I said.

"She seemed confident we would find nothing, and as she is a confidence trickster herself, I believe that we need to approach this from a different angle. It is difficult to make someone do something against his nature or wishes, even under hypnotism. She needed to break down his mental barriers before she could start to control him."

"Drugs, then," I said. "I shall check his limbs for needle marks. Maybe she has been dosing him with opium."

'I think not," said Holmes. "I cannot imagine a scenario where she could have come up with a plausible excuse to inject anything into him the first time."

"You're right," said Sister Fidelma. "No matter how smitten he was, he would never let her do that to him. He is scared of needles. Some years ago he broke his leg riding. The doctor wanted to inject a sedative to make repositioning the bone easier. Steven refused, so they anesthetized him the old-fashioned way."

"Rum?" I ventured.

"Whisky."

'Then let us check his liquor cabinet," I said.

"There is no need," said Holmes. "You mentioned earlier about the change in diet at your Monday lunches." He dashed to the kitchen and came out two minutes later carrying a silver serving dish and a triumphant look.

We went into the library.

"I will let you go with a head start before I call the police, if you do one thing for me."

"What are you talking about?" said Miss LeRoux. "It is I who shall call for the police. You have attacked me in my own home and taken over my . . . ." She stopped then, silent as Holmes unveiled the dish.

"It is a simple task," he said. "Eat some of these mushrooms."

"They will make me sick," she said.

"My point exactly," said Holmes. "Now, eat some, or leave this home and never return."

She was gone within the hour.

Based on Holmes's theory, I checked my patient upstairs.

"It is my opinion," I said, coming downstairs, "that all the Marquess needs is time. Time for the toxins to leave his system. Lots of water and bed rest, and you'll see an improvement by tomorrow."

"Will you tell me what happened, please?" said Sister Fidelma. "Why did she poison the mushrooms?"

"She didn't," said Holmes. "The mushrooms *are* the poison. Strictly speaking, they have mind-altering properties. There was an article in *The London Medical and Physical Journal* of 1799 that mentioned a man who picked *psilocybe semilanceata* mushrooms in the park and took them home to his family. The meal caused varied losses of control in his children. In other words, the mushrooms could break past the main barrier hypnotists face, a person's own nature. In the journal article, the family were convinced their youngest child was possessed by the devil as he would not stop laughing for some hours."

"What an evil woman," said Sister Fidelma.

"Quite," said Holmes. "Once your brother had eaten them once, his guard was down and he was easy to hypnotize and manipulate. If you hadn't come to us, I have no doubt that Madam Mysterio would have taken everything your brother owns."

"How can I thank you, Mister Holmes? And you too, Doctor. You have saved my brother, my only family."

"Stay with him," I said. "We shall send a message to your convent."

"Indeed," said Holmes. He opened the door, stepped out then turned suddenly. He was looking up at the vaulted ceiling, and I saw a look of astonishment cross his face. As he stepped back into the hall, there was a tremendous noise outside and one of the gargoyles crashed into the exact spot where he had been standing a second before. Shards from the stonework bounced into the hall, but the mass of the monstrosity, a hundred pounds or more of grotesquerie, lay at the door.

"Holmes," I said, "that would have killed you. What did you see that caused you to step back?"

"I must have had something in my eye," he said. "No matter, there is no harm done."

"It was your guardian angel," said Sister Fidelma. "You looked to the same spot as my brother and you saw your angel. She pulled you back and saved you, didn't she."

"Sister Fidelma, I do not believe in guardian angels." He stepped out of the door past the broken masonry without so much as a by-your-leave, and I followed him to our transport home – but not before Sister Fidelma shouted after him,

"You may not believe in guardian angels, Mister Holmes, but they believe in you!"

I waited until we were on our way. My friend had regained his composure, but this rare opportunity was mine and I would not let it go amiss.

"What if it was your guardian angel, Holmes?"

"My dear Watson, you of all people should know my views on sprites, fairies, and the likes. Angels are the same. I do not believe in their existence. It was, as I said, a fortuitous coincidence."

"Now tell me, Holmes, how that is so?" I said. "I thought you didn't believe in coincidences either."

And for once, Mister Sherlock Holmes had nothing more to say.

The Blue Lady
of Dunraven
by Andrew Bryant

The train rocketed out into daylight. To me, it seemed to rocket, because of the instantaneous transition from the darkness of the Severn Tunnel into the light of day of the Welsh countryside.

"Disconcerting isn't it, Watson."

"Disconcerting?"

"Having just travelled four miles in a tunnel under a river to now find ourselves in another country."

"The transition surprised me."

"It flooded once, the tunnel."

"You did not tell me that before we boarded the train."

"A major emphasis was placed on drainage afterwards."

"I am reassured."

"Do you know what *GWR* stands for?"

"Great Western Railway."

"'*God's Wonderful Railway*'. We just travelled through the future. If a tunnel can be constructed under the Severn Estuary, what else is Man capable of?"

"My experience," I said, "has been that Man is capable of almost anything."

Holmes gave a slight, sideways smile and returned to the present, reading *The Times*.

I looked out the window at the green and mild hills of Monmouthshire. There was little conversation for the remainder of the journey.

We changed trains at Cardiff Station, boarding the Bridgend train for the remaining thirty or so miles of our outing.

Holmes hadn't given me much to go on when this excursion was first proposed.

"Do you believe in ghosts, Watson?" he had asked.

"In the main, no. But I have an open mind and have observed the absolute belief of others in the spiritual world, so perhaps it exists for some, but not for all. Do *you* believe in ghosts?"

"In the main, no. In my experience, thus far, there has always been a rational explanation. Although a mind must always stay open, and be willing to change if the proof exists to make the mind change."

"No Jacob Marley, no bump in the night, no fairies at the bottom of the garden for you?"

"Not without the evidence."

The horse and carriage of the Earl of Dunraven was waiting for us at Bridgend Station. Our luggage was stowed, and we travelled comfortably along the twisting road between low but steep hills occupied only by flocks of foraging sheep.

"It is estimated that there are four sheep to every person in Wales," Holmes said.

"From observation so far I would say it was true."

We passed through the village of St. Bride's Major, a narrow thoroughfare with houses close to the road and farms above on the surrounding slopes. Mid-way through the village was a church with spire on the hill behind a copse, seeming, due to its size, out of place in the small village. A sign at the end of the church lane read "*St. Bridget's.*".

"Why do villages always have such large churches?" I said.

"Because transgressions are so much more difficult to hide amongst a smaller population."

We rounded a curve and started a slight decline, and were soon in sight of the sea – or at least that arm of the sea called the Bristol Channel. Silver-grey and flat calm now, but capable, I knew, of devastating tides and storms when roused.

Holmes pointed to the opposing headland.

"That is Trwyn y Wrach. In English, 'Witches Point'. And that is Dunraven Castle," he said.

Descending into Southerndown Bay, the stone-and-glass mass of the "Castle" stood out on the headland facing us. It was not a true castle, especially not in a land of castles, but more a sprawling manor house with castellations and a small turreted tower. It stood against a background of trees, with its sea-side open to the Channel and to, what I estimated to be, one-hundred-foot high cliffs dropping straight down into the waves.

"This version of the 'Castle' was constructed on the foundations of a twelfth-century lodge, which was in turn built on the ruins of an ancient fort. Some say that King Arthur was born here – the *real* King Arthur, not the one of romantic myth," Holmes said.

"Legend or fact, it is a suitable locale for the birthplace of a King."

"The current Earl's family has lived here for over two-hundred years. Plenty of time for rumour and superstition to run rampant."

"Rumour and superstition?" I asked.

"The Earl explained to me in the letter that requested our presence here: The mystery of the Blue Lady. We are here, Watson, to prove that a mystery is no match for reality."

"While keeping an open mind," I said.

"Of course."

"And just what is the mystery of the Blue Lady?"

Holmes was silent as the carriage moved down between the opposing headlands, onto the flat expanse of the beachhead, and through the gate, opened to us by a coarse gatekeeper who would have been well at home in the writings of the Brontë sisters. We passed the gatekeeper's house and then up again towards the Castle, around the walled garden, and up through the trees to the summit of the headland. The Castle was fronted by a massive conservatory, its panes running with condensation.

The carriage stopped.

"The Blue Lady?" I asked.

"The Earl will explain."

We disembarked and were ushered through the dense, aromatic atmosphere of the conservatory. Small tables and chairs were placed around and under the potted plants and trees. A gardener on a ladder pruned branches from the taller trees up at the glass roof. We were led into the cooler air of the house proper, through the main foyer, and into a sitting room, or parlour, on the sea-side. The room was heavily panelled to mid-ceiling, with portraits of ancestors staring down, almost always disapprovingly it seemed, from above the panelling. The furniture was dark and heavy, befitting a manor and title with an ancient lineage.

Holmes went to the window.

"Clouds are moving in over the Channel. They will bring rain in from the sea," he said.

Already the flat grey of the water was showing scars of silver curls where the surface broke open from the tide and the rising winds.

"You know what they say about our Western coastline, Watson?"

"What do they say?"

"If you do not like the weather, wait one minute."

"Who is 'they'?" I asked.

"'They' – the ubiquitous 'them'."

"I see," I replied, not seeing.

A man came into the room.

"Earl Dunraven," Holmes said.

"Mr. Holmes and Doctor Watson," the Earl replied, shaking our hands.

A young servant girl followed the Earl into the room, carrying a tray with tea and biscuits. She looked a bit of a waif and gave Holmes and me that low-lidded stare of resentment that one sees often from the working classes on the streets of London, but usually not so much out in the country.

130

The Earl was a youngish man, younger than I expected. Titles and their history of privilege seemed to exude age in both their physical and spiritual atmospheres, and it was almost always expected that the holders of the titles and the recipients of the privileges would be as old as their auras and their living quarters. Although youngish, the Earl had a somewhat subdued and haunted air about him.

"We have tea," the Earl said, "but if you wish for something stronger it is available."

"Tea will be fine for us," Holmes said, not consulting me.

The Earl offered us chairs and the servant girl poured the tea. I ate several of the biscuits. "Have the fires started." he said. "The damp is moving in."

"Yes, sir," the girl replied, and left the room.

"How was your journey, gentlemen?"

"Uneventful," I said.

"You travelled through the tunnel?"

"Yes."

"And how was it?"

"Dark," Holmes said.

The polite conversation now over, Holmes leaned forward in his chair intently. "Tell us the stories of both the tragedy and the mystery that brought us here. Starting with the mystery."

The Earl's demeanour became more haunted and withdrawn after Holmes's request. He took on the look of a man completely surrounded by an unwanted, but perhaps deserved, history.

"The Blue Lady?" he began.

"Yes, yes."

"The Blue Lady is the alleged ghost of a woman drowned in a storm one-hundred years ago."

"Drowned under what circumstances?"

The Earl hesitated.

"I know your family's past, as does everyone else round about. Your imminent revelation will be a revelation to no one except Doctor Watson," Holmes said.

"Knowing nothing of the Earl's situation, anything and everything will be a revelation to me," I said.

"The circumstances are this," the Earl said. "My ancestors, having fallen on hard times due to bad investments, turned to the cruel but lucrative trade of wrecking. On the stormiest of nights when every ship in the Channel ploughed headlong in search of safe harbour, my ancestors lit lanterns and paraded across the clifftop. They tied lanterns to sheep's tails,

131

and the running sheep along with the regiment of carried lanterns would deceive a ship's unlucky captain and crew – "

"Luck had nothing to do with it," Holmes interjected.

" – into thinking that our bay was a safe harbour. But the poor souls sailed instead into the rocks and ran aground, breaking up in the waves and spilling their cargo out to be washed ashore where, by right of salvage, my ancestors claimed – "

"Plundered."

" – the contents of the broken ships. They were able to refill the family coffers from the salvaged cargoes."

"And the survivors?" Holmes asked.

"If anyone survived the wreck, they were all killed on the shore by blade or cudgel."

"And the Blue Lady?" I said.

"One ship, thus dashed upon the rocks, disgorged a woman heavy with child. She was found alive on the shore and, due to her condition, brought here to the house. She gave birth to her child, and then succumbed to the injuries sustained in the wreck."

"And the child?" Holmes asked.

"The child was kept and raised in the servant's quarters as one of them."

"And the unfortunate woman, when found on the shore, was wearing a blue dress?"

"Yes, a blue dress with a sachet of dried mimosa flowers and seeds in a pocket."

"The ship that was dashed was inbound from Asia," Holmes stated.

"Possibly."

"Invariably."

"And when did the apparitions begin?" I asked.

"Shortly after her death, according to family legend. And always at night, around about the time that the ship went aground. She is seen as a gliding figure crossing a room in moonlight, or a standing, staring presence waiting at the bed-foot when you awaken in the darkness. But on the anniversary of the shipwreck, she is always seen walking on the clifftop, a lantern swaying in her hand, and crying out the most mournful, baleful sound anyone had ever heard. She is described as crying like a banshee when she paces the cliff. And her presence is always accompanied by the scent of mimosa."

"A banshee would be an appropriate reference," Holmes said, "as you have Irish as well as Welsh in you, do you not?"

"Yes, we do," the Earl replied.

"She was no doubt looking for her forfeited child," I said.

132

"Indeed," said the Earl.

Holmes looked with disdain at both of us.

"And that is the origin of The Blue Lady," the Earl concluded.

"And now, if you would," Holmes said, "your own most recent tragedy, and the reason for our visit."

"Several weeks ago, on the hundredth anniversary of the wreck, my wife, the dearest Countess, saw and heard the ghastly revenant walking and calling out there on the headland."

"Did you see and hear this for yourself?" Holmes asked.

"Not at first. The Countess and I reposed in separate chambers."

"Of course. Go on."

"The Countess allegedly saw the spirit moving along the cliff edge, lantern in hand, wailing out into the darkness."

"Did any of the servants see or hear this spirit?"

"The Countess told them what she had seen. And they saw the Countess running outside, but none of them tried to stop her, and none of them admitted to seeing or hearing the phantom."

"You don't believe them?" I said.

"Servants are not generally renowned for their honesty. Give them half-a-chance, and most are capable of robbing you blind, and then lying about it afterwards."

"Such is the difference between us and them," Holmes intruded.

"The Countess ran outside to follow the shade, and the banshee screamed and bewailed such that I was also awoken and rushed out. But by then the Blue Lady had disappeared, and the Countess . . . I was too late to stop her."

"To stop her?" I said.

"To stop the Countess from going over the cliff," Holmes replied.

"My God," I said, not having been privy, as previously stated, to any of Holmes's prior knowledge of the case.

"It was one-hundred years to the day of the wreck, the day that originally brought the Blue Lady herself into this house," Holmes added.

"Yes", the Earl said. "A remarkable coincidence."

"Coincidence be damned," Holmes spat out.

"A plot?" I said.

"If ever there was one."

"Plot?" The Earl said.

"You requested our presence here to investigate the death of your Countess, so let us begin the investigation. You mentioned in your letter that the Countess was of a spiritual nature, believing in the supernatural, and in an afterlife not so much in Heaven but more here on Earth."

133

"Yes. She believed that some restless spirits, usually determined by their manner or circumstances of death, had been left here to wander among the living, searching endlessly for true rest – true rest for the soul that is."

"The Countess was a devotee of Madame Blavatsky?"

"Yes. The Countess had the Theosophist belief that spirits were the 'shells' of departed souls, and that they could be communicated with under the right circumstances."

"And so, on seeing and hearing the 'ghost' outside, she ran after it to, presumably, make contact with it."

"Presumably. She had been fascinated with the Blue Lady legend since she first heard it."

"And who did she hear it from?"

"The housemaids, I assume. They like to go on about anything and everything frivolous."

"You did not share the Countess' beliefs?"

"Not at all. That is why I wrote to you, Mr. Holmes. The local constabulary dismissed the Countess' death as a fall caused by 'excited delirium' while chasing after an unearthly mirage."

"But you think otherwise?"

"I think that her death had more cause than that. She was a spiritualist, yes, but she did not see things that were not there, and she would not confuse shadows with reality."

"You believe that she actually saw and heard something out there." Holmes pointed towards the cliff.

"Yes, I'm certain of it."

"Our task then, Watson, is to find out just what it was that the Countess saw and heard."

"How will you begin?" the Earl asked.

"To start, Watson and I will spend the night in the Countess' chambers."

The Earl pulled on a satin cord hanging beside the fireplace, and somewhere down in the entrails of the house a bell rang that summoned up one of the poor devils who laboured incessantly to give a good face of civility to an indentured situation – indentured not so much by written contract, but by complete lack of options.

Soon, the same girl who had brought the tea appeared out of nowhere.

Holmes sized her up.

"Our guests will be staying in the Countess' chambers tonight. Ask one of the men to bring up their luggage."

"Yes, sir."

The girl took us to our room.

"Have you ever seen the Blue Lady?" Holmes asked her.

"Many times, sir."

"And heard her?"

"Yes, sir."

"And you believe that she is who they say she is, a remnant of life moaning for her own lost self and for the child she never saw?"

"Yes, sir."

"And why do you believe that"? I said.

"Because everyone knows it's true."

"Thank you."

The girl left the room, closing the door behind her.

"What do you make of her, Watson?"

"Her temperament is not as subservient as her manner."

"Agreed. And she does not believe a word of the physical presence of the departed. It is all ghostly nonsense to her. She is far too practical for it."

"Unlike the unlucky Countess."

"Luck is a word that ought be struck from the English language. Luck is the name applied to the junctions of circumstance, a name applied to the melding of those circumstances into an undeniable reality. There is no such thing as chance involved in the solution of any problem. 'Luck' is the layman's term for the conclusions drawn from a study of the evidence."

"'Luck' takes the guesswork out of logic," I said.

Holmes scowled at the joke. Logic was not a subject for mirth.

"It's more common sense then?" I said.

"Somewhat closer to the truth than 'luck'," he replied.

There were two beds in the room, a grand four-poster, and a smaller day-bed off to one side.

"Choose either bed, Watson. I will be in a chair."

"A chair?"

"I do not plan on sleeping. Tonight will be a night for contemplation and anticipation."

"Contemplation of what?"

"The true nature of our spectral visitor."

"And anticipation of what?"

"A visit from the Blue Lady in the flesh, if she has any."

"I'll take the four-poster," I said.

We dined late with the Earl. The conversation travelled widely but stayed within the boundaries of a particular subject. The metaphysical world.

Holmes raged against spirit boards, even though the Earl was in complete agreement with him throughout. "Collective hysteria" was the explanation for any group of people who had ever seen a ghost. I put forward the notion that certain places with old and tragic histories may hold the essences of past populations and that "collective memory" might be better terminology. Madame Blavatsky's name came up again, more as if she were an enemy of the state rather than the enemy of reason. I suggested that she, being Russian, was actually working for the Emancipation of Labour Group intent on overthrowing governments by spiritual means. Holmes and the Earl were in angry agreement about the validity of Tarot cards. I suggested that we locate the nearest fortune teller to prove or disprove this argument.

Eventually we retired for the night, and I sank into the bed hoping for a night's uninterrupted sleep after the travels of the day.

Holmes sat in the darkened room, in a chair drawn up close to the open window. The rain just beginning to fall.

At some point during a deep and dreamless sleep, I woke to a violent shaking and the excited voice of my roommate.

"Do you hear it, Watson? Do you hear it?"

I *did* hear it. A mournful, sinister moan reaching from alto to soprano, rising to a near scream of grief. It was both a horrible and saddening sound emanating from the soul of the broken-hearted. The sound was a near continuous, unintelligible keening that was carried back to us by the onshore wind.

We both strained at the window and saw through the haze of the rain, moving away from the walled garden, a figure carrying a lantern, the light swinging in the being's grasp. When the lantern swung close to the carrier, a shimmer of blue could be seen in the lamplight.

The figure moved out of sight, beyond the view from our window.

"Come on!" Holmes said.

"Like this?" I said, indicating my nightdress.

"The not-so-dearly departed will be unconcerned with your attire."

Holmes threw open the door and we ran down the hallway in a darkness only just illumined by the generous windows. Down the stairs, and out through the conservatory. The wraith's tune moved away from us, from the house towards the clifftop. We ran around the side of the house to see a lantern moving away rapidly. A faint exotic scent hung briefly in the air before the rain and wind carried it off. Soaked immediately by the downpour, we ran towards the light.

Then the lantern stopped moving.

"We have her!" Holmes shouted back to me.

136

We ran on full tilt until Holmes stopped short of the light and I ran passed him.

"No, Watson!"

As I neared the illumination, the ground under my feet dropped away and I fell sliding on the wet and pitching grass. In that moment I realized that I was at the cliff's edge, but had been unable to differentiate between land and air in the gloom. Below me I heard the sea thundering into the rocks.

I felt two hands grasp my arm and as I lay half-suspended between the clifftop and the drop. I saw the lantern tumble away down the cliff face and into the torrent below. I was dragged back onto the turf and, only then, lying there in my bedraggled state, did I realize how close to death I had been. I was thankful that Holmes was one of those wiry but strong men.

"You saved my life," I said.

"Yes, but since it was also I who roused you out of bed and led you on this chase, it was the least I could do."

"Nonetheless, you saved my life."

"It was nothing."

"It was something to me," I said.

Holmes and I breakfasted early together in the conservatory the following morning, a Sunday, surrounded by humidity and fragrance.

The glum servant girl of the previous day brought us our meals. She would not look us in the eye, and did not speak until spoken to.

"What is your name?" Holmes asked.

"Angharad Morris."

"Would you be so kind as to bring a sprig of mimosa to the table, Miss Morris?"

She hesitated.

"Yes, sir."

She went off into the back of the conservatory, among the tallest trees.

"Why . . . ?" I started.

Holmes held up his hand to stop my question.

Miss Morris returned holding a small pruned branch with several wispy pink flowers attached.

"Thank you," Holmes said.

She walked off without a word.

Holmes crushed one of the flowers in his fingers and inhaled the aroma. I did the same. The smell could be mistaken for a woman's subtle perfume.

"Familiar?" he said.

"The scent from last night's pursuit."

137

"Yes, the Blue Lady and her sachet of mimosa."

"But where did she go? After she abandoned the lantern, where did she go?"

We finished our breakfast, and Miss Morris came back to clear the table.

"Are you to Church this morning?" Holmes asked her.

"Yes, sir."

"Are you in the choir?"

"Yes, sir."

"Did you see or hear anything unusual outside the house last night?"

"No, sir."

"Not a sound or movement?"

"Only the rain, sir. I sleep in the cellar, beside the kitchen."

"Thank you."

The girl left.

"Care to spend the rest of this Sunday morning in church, Watson?"

"It will be an unusual way to spend a Sunday morning," I replied.

"Afterwards we will walk along the cliff," Holmes said, as if the undertaking would be a pleasure for me after last night.

St. Bridget's Church was a twelfth-century Norman structure, the carved tombs of knights and former Earls illuminated in the window-wells under the heavy beamed roof. The minister was raised three steps above the rest of us, and the pews were full. Miss Morris stood with the choir to the side of the minister.

The service was in Welsh, and, although incomprehensible to me in meaning, I was able to gather the intent of the words simply by the tone and inflection of what I can only call the beautiful language. I have heard many tongues spoken, from the Pashto of Afghanistan to the Cockney of London and all places in between, but this lilting ancient sermon transfixed me.

When the sermon was over, the choir began a hymn that covered the vocal range from sublime to reverberating. I looked over at Holmes, who sat motionless, fixated on the choir, drawing in the sound as if it was a religious experience for him. When the hymn was over, he leaned back in the pew, a slight smile on his face.

"What is it?" I asked him.

He did not reply.

We waited a distance from the doors as the parishioners exited and milled about among the old gravestones. Miss Morris separated herself from the others and wandered into the outmost edge of the graveyard. She approached a small, leaning stone, kissed her own hand and placed her

138

hand on the stone. She stood like that for a moment and then walked away down the lane. We waited until she was out of sight and then approached the grave ourselves. The stone was pitted by lichen and exposure, and was unusual in that it did not have a name, or a date of birth engraved on it. This is what was carved into its face: "*Who could understand, In ignorant ease, What we others suffer, As the paths of exile stretch endlessly on.*" And underneath that, a year one-hundred years prior to ours.

We walked out of the churchyard and along the road, turning off at Picot Pool to follow the hedgerows back to the coast and the Castle. We walked past curious sheep and a few cattle, joining up with the mile-long lane that took us to the dovecote and deer grate that marked the rear entrance to the Castle grounds. This lane was the route that laymen and tradesmen were obliged to use.

"Couldn't let the likes of them in through the front gate," Holmes said.

"I believe that we should all be able to enter and exit anywhere and everywhere through the same gate," I said.

"You are in the minority."

We walked down the last of the lane, hearing the sea against the shore before we saw it, and emerged at the beachhead. Then we moved through the gate and up onto the headland where we had our adventure the night before. The headland started to diminish here, sloping down in hollows and ridges towards the beach below. Behind us, a few gardeners worked on the grounds, and some housemaids could be seen moving past the windows of the house in the course of their duties. Holmes went nearer to the cliff edge, while I stayed back.

"Come a little bit closer, Watson."

"Holmes, I . . . ."

"A little closer."

I obliged.

Holmes began to jump up and down on the sod.

"Do you feel that?" he said.

"It feels hollow."

"It is hollow."

"Then is it all that wise to jump up and down on it?"

"The cliffs here are made of layers of limestone with thin sandstone and shale parting layers between. The softer shale and sandstone erodes from between the limestone, and when the stone collapses, part of the cliff face falls into the sea. Just look at the piles of scree down there on the shore."

"I would prefer not to."

"What this means is that the cliff is constantly eroding away from beneath the dense, matted sod that we are standing on. Depending on where you stand, you may be supported just by the sod with nothing solid underneath you. That was how you nearly fell last night. Eventually of course the sod falls as well, and the cliff is in a permanent state of retreat."

I looked down the Channel. A black mass of cloud moved towards us, and beneath that the streaky black and grey scratches of rain. The wind was rising.

"It's going to be a wild night," Holmes said, as we turned back towards the house.

We dined with the Earl.

"My apologies for not breakfasting with you gentlemen. I try not to be an early riser."

"Quite all right. Watson and I went to church and had a pleasant walk back through the fields and lane, and along the cliff top."

The subject of conversation returned again to the contentious world of spiritual and religious belief – or disbelief.

"One can be spiritual without believing in spirits," I said.

"There are different planes of spirituality," the Earl responded. "There is the purely symbolic side as represented by the Christian belief in a resurrection that can never be proven, because you have to die to prove it and are therefore unable to substantiate the claim. Then there is the esoteric side, where a few chosen people – usually self-chosen – can access the spirit world where apparitions walk, incorporeal voices whisper in your ear, and tables levitate."

"It has been my experience, so far," Holmes said, "that the greater the spirituality one has, the greater the chance of being duped. When one *wants* to believe, one *will* believe. The rational mind takes a Cook's Tour of the irrational mind and returns home having had a wonderful time and wanting to live there. But like most holiday destinations, one should never *actually* attempt to live there. It is always disappointing and often disastrous, as was the case with the Countess."

"The servants knew of the Countess' spiritual inclination?" I asked.

"I don't know. What she spoke to them about in private I cannot say."

"It was the servants who told the Countess about the Blue Lady, so one could safely assume that she would have revealed her spirituality to them in turn," I said.

"The servants always know a household," Holmes added, "and everyone in it, better than the masters do. You might be shocked, and perhaps appalled by what your servants know."

"Dear me," said the Earl. "Do you think they tell anyone else?"

"Only their friends, family, and some of the neighbours. It's unlikely that they would tell any others."

"Dear me," the Earl said again.

Holmes had his enjoyment with the Earl, revelling in pointing out the obvious to people who were oblivious to it – especially the gentry, who were oblivious to so very much.

As we dined, the wind rose and banged at the windows while rain pelted the house. A servant fed the fire. After the meal, the Earl's brandy refracted the firelight, an amber iridescence that quivered on everything within its purview. I accepted a brandy, but Holmes refused.

"Wits should never be dulled," he said. "Only enhanced."

"Alcohol can enhance wit," I said.

"Only temporarily. After the initial brilliance has worn off, the drinker invariably becomes a witless wit who unfortunately still thinks that he is witty."

I laughed.

The Earl did not comment on this observation, looking as if he may have recognized something of himself in the remark. Nearly always oblivious of others, the gentry are also generally oblivious of themselves. For instance, mistaking education for intelligence. As an old Army man myself, I had seen many instances where the experienced but lower social class soldier had been forced into a course of action that led to his own death by the blundering orders of an inexperienced, but titled, commanding officer. Experience and common sense meant nothing to those handing out commissions and medals.

As my wandering thoughts came back to the table, Holmes was closing up the conversation for the evening. We bid the Earl goodnight and went upstairs to our room, leaving him a lonely figure at table.

Holmes opened the window, in spite of the weather. "Choose whichever bed you want, Watson. I will be in a chair."

"Again. What about sleep?"

"Sleep is the consequence of an inactive mind."

"Wake me if you need to," I said, settling into the four-poster.

"I am confident that you will be awakened."

True to his word, I was roused by a good shaking sometime in the pitch dark. The rain and wind battered the house, but above those natural sounds I plainly heard the miserable wailing lament of the night before.

"She's at it again," Holmes said, and we ran from the room, along the hallway, down and outside through the conservatory, where the rain was deafening against the glass. Out into the storm we ran, the lantern and its bearer running away from us, the glimmer of blue coming and going as the light pendulumed. We were drenched instantly and buffeted by the tempest sweeping down the Channel into the cliff and across the headland.

"She's going to try it once more!" Holmes shouted back at me.

"Try what?"

"To take us over the edge!"

With the rain and dark and tumult, there was no sense of the cliff. Even looking back at the black hulk of the house, there was no telling the distance from the building to where the cliff fell away before us. All we could do was to follow the jarring lantern and try not to make fatal the near-fatal mistake of the night before.

The lantern stopped, and then tilted on its side.

"Take care, Watson. The trap is laid."

I slowed my run, as did Holmes, when we neared the lantern.

Then, a cry – an exhalation, and a plea.

"For God's sake, help me!"

When nearly on the lantern we both fell to our hands and knees, crawling on the turf, sounding it out for the terminal hollow thud beneath. Reaching the lantern we were both prone, outstretched on the grass, with still no perception of the cliff, only a blurred vision all the same: Air, ground, rain, no differentiation between any. The sound now of the waves below like endless trains roaring towards us.

Looking past the lantern, I saw a small white hand buried into the turf, holding on. Another hand still held the light. There was a wet sheen of hair, and the sense of a body hanging in the air below all.

"For God's sake, help me!" a woman's voice implored.

"As you helped the Countess?" Holmes spat back.

"Repay evil with evil, and let Hell claim you," the woman's bitter reply.

I grasped her hand, but, slick with rain and cold, she did not return the grip. I inched forward trying to hold her wrist.

I felt a hand on my shoulder pulling me back.

"No, Watson! She'll take you with her!"

In spite of my attempts, she slid further and then was gone altogether – a dim shape screaming with the flailing lantern still in her hand, screaming out of sight down into the deafening waves below.

No one had much of an appetite, but we sat at the breakfast table in the conservatory as if prepared to eat. We sipped at coffee instead.

"I had the servant roster checked this morning," the Earl said.

"And?"

"Miss Angharad Morris is indeed missing."

"Her body may be washed up on shore in the next few days, or, due to the ferocity of last night's storm it may be lost forever to the sea. If her body is recovered, you will find the pockets of her blue dress stuffed with mimosa flowers," Holmes said.

"All this time, that girl who had lived her entire life in this house – "

"She had lived *your* life, not *hers*," Holmes interrupted.

" – To think that she would turn on us and bring such tragedy on our household."

"Her view of it, and I dare say the view of many others, is that justice had been served."

"What kind of motive can one have to lure the dearest Countess to her death?"

"The oldest, and in many cultures, the most noble motive of all: Revenge."

"We did nothing to that girl but put a roof over her head and a wage in her pocket."

"Old vengeance cares nothing for modern compensation."

"But why did she do it, Holmes? Why her?" I said.

"I believe that with further investigation the absolute proof of Miss Morris' identity will be revealed with certainty."

"And what is that identity?"

"She was the great-grand-daughter of the Blue Lady."

"How can you know this?" the Earl cried.

"The deduction came in many steps, starting with the fact that all the servants would have known of the Countess' spiritualist notions, making her an easy believer in the Blue Lady legend. You told us yourself that none of the servants had seen or heard anything, which is highly unlikely given the volume of the spirits' wail, Also, none of the servants went outside to help, or to stop, the Countess on the night she chased the phantom. This precluded the culprit being anyone other than an employee of the household. So, without having to look outside, it narrowed the field of suspects considerably.

"Miss Morris was obviously headstrong and not at ease with her social position, but also aware that she had no hope of social advancement and so would remain an employee of this household until she herself was old and infirm. In short, she had no hope for a future other than living out her life as a servant here. Such are the inequities of our society. This would lead naturally to a resentment against the circumstances that forced her to be here, those circumstances being that she was only here because your ancestor killed her ancestor. Of course, all the servants would know the legend, and Miss Morris herself would have been raised on the story, told to her by her own mother and grandmother. A sordid tale that, lodging in the girl's vindictive mind, would fester into a plot of revenge against the masters of her fate.

"I asked her for a sprig of mimosa, and she went straight to the tree, knowing exactly which one it was out of the dozens of species in the conservatory. I suspect that all the generations of mimosa grown here are descended from the seeds found on the Blue Lady's person. This was a minor step, however, as a number of the servants might have been able to identify the flower, but it is the layering on of evidence that leads to the ultimate declaration.

"At some point she would have sewed herself a blue dress, which also alludes to the idea that the other servants were aware of the plot, as such a tailoring would have been impossible to hide in the close quarters down stairs.

"On the one-hundredth anniversary of her ancestors' murder, Miss Morris, lantern in hand, stalked the headland moaning out her grief in order to lure the awestruck Countess out. The Countess followed the lantern into the darkness, fixated on the lantern I'm sure, to where Miss Morris had left it at the very edge of the sod where, with no support beneath it, the weight of the Countess collapsed the overhang and she fell to her death."

"But to where did Miss Morris disappear?" I asked.

"The same place she disappeared to when you and I were fixated on the lantern. The purpose of our cliff walk yesterday was to ascertain the nature of the cliff edge and the terrain adjacent to the Countess' fall. As you saw, the headland starts a decline there with natural hollows and hummocks. While we concentrated on the motionless lantern, Miss Morris was crawling away down the headland at the cliff's edge, invisible to us because of the distraction of the light, the inclement weather, and the darkness of the hour. She would have made her way around through the gardens and back into the cellar to her quarters, the door being unlocked for her by one of her servile accomplices."

"An eye for an eye," the Earl said.

"Biblical justice knows no social boundaries," I added.

"The physical presence of the lantern laid to rest any irrational ideas that the culprit was a 'ghost'. An incorporeal being could only carry the weight of an incorporeal lantern. Since the light had mass, the carrier of it must also have had mass.

"Our visit to church, Watson, was to determine if Miss Morris had the vocal ability to mimic the banshee. As we heard, she had an excellent natural range. An unexpected extra to that visit was the last step in the collection of evidence. Her endearing moment at the gravestone. A gravestone with no name upon it, because no one knew the name. A gravestone with only a seafarer's lament. A gravestone with a death date one-hundred years ago. The confirmation was when she kissed her hand and placed the kiss on the stone. One does not kiss the grave of another without there being a long and affectionate history. I am sure that Miss Morris' mother and grandmother both followed this ritual. This nameless grave could only be that of the Blue Lady. The stone itself likely paid for by the outraged servants of that era, disgusted with the vicious nature of their so-called superiors."

"But why try to kill us?" I asked.

"After the local constables had declared the Countess' demise a death by misadventure, Miss Morris would have believed that she had fulfilled her revengeful destiny, and that there had now truly been an 'eye for an eye'. And then we arrived, looking for some reason other than a ghostly one. She would have known from overhearing our conversations that we did not believe in the supernatural explanation. She donned the blue dress again in order to lead us to our deaths and thereby seal the case forever as a death by haunting. Unfortunately, for her, in the violence of last night's storm she misjudged the cliff's edge, or perhaps there had been a collapse of rock just prior to her luring, a collapse that moved back the true drop. So, by her own misjudgment, she also became a victim of her own plot."

"And well aware of her fate at the end."

"Indeed."

"And the rest of them were in league with her," the Earl said. "I put a roof over their heads. I pay them, and this is how they show their loyalty and respect."

"Loyalty and respect are earned, not bought. Their loyalty is to their own families and to their own histories, not yours."

The Earl sat back in his chair, staring out the window towards where his Countess died, and to where, I believed, he thought that he had been completely and utterly betrayed.

"I'll send the invoice for our services to your solicitor. And, also, a letter to the constabulary giving them the gist of the evidence so their preternatural decision can be reversed."

The Earl did not respond, lost now in his own quite empty world.

Holmes and I went to our room and carried down our own bags. Outside we asked a gardener to summon the carriage for us, which he did begrudgingly. We sat down outside to await it.

"That such a young girl could plot such a murderous course in the name of a one-hundred-year-old misfortune." I mused. "And that she suffered so much in knowing the old history of both her own family and the Earls', even allowing it to lead to her own death. What went through her mind in the time it took to fall from the cliff top to the rocks?"

145

"There is no psychological suffering when the death is your own," Holmes replied. "True suffering only ensues when one must endure the death of another."

NOTES

1 – The Severn Tunnel was opened for passenger trains in 1886.
2 – Dunraven Castle was demolished in 1963.
3 – The Earl of Dunraven title became extinct in 2011.
4 – The Blue Lady is a "real" ghost. (I was born five miles from Dunraven and remember visiting the castle as a child – *Andrew Bryant*)

The Adventure of the
Ghoulish Grenadier
by Josh Anderson and David Friend

"You look tired, Watson," said Holmes across the breakfast table.

"It has been a demanding week," I answered wearily. "I've not been so busy since the scarlet fever outbreak last Christmas."

Holmes puffed on his pipe. "I wish that I were in your position. Things have been wholly uneventful of late."

A month had passed since the case of Lord Timothy Currington and his three secret wives, and with so little to stimulate Holmes's great intellect, I was increasingly concerned that he would take recourse to his seven-percent solution. Indeed, in place of any such incident of import was the trifling matter of Mrs. Hudson's annual holiday to Swanage and the temporary appointment of the pale and portly Mrs. Culpepper. The woman was, in a couple of significant respects, equal to the occasion, but her cooking left much to be desired, and we were much looking forward to the return of our regular landlady.

Holmes took up a knife and jabbed his egg suspiciously. "I would need a hammer to get into this," he muttered.

I was about to reply when Mrs. Culpepper came shuffling in with a tray of tea. "How are your eggs?" she asked Holmes cheerily and placed the steaming cups on the table.

He gave an affected smile. "You have outdone yourself, Mrs. Culpepper."

She beamed proudly. "Then I will fetch the seconds."

My friend's eyes flashed with alarm. "Oh, that won't be necessary. I fear we have worked you too hard."

The lady seemed satisfied with this hasty half-truth and turned to me expectantly. "And yourself, Doctor Watson?" she asked. Her brow darkened with disappointment as she saw how much I had left. "You haven't eaten your black pudding!"

I was not as swift as Holmes. "I . . . seem a little . . . out of sorts this morning." I placed a hand on my stomach. "I must have picked something up from a patient."

"A shame," said our temporary housekeeper and, for a few merry moments, I thought I was finally free. Then she patted my shoulder comfortingly and crooked her head as one would a child. "Such food will do you good, Doctor. I shall bring up some more!"

Before I could stop the woman, she tottered gaily out of the room and I was left with an empty stomach and a plate of pork blood.

Holmes laid down his cutlery with a caustic shake of the head. "I cannot bear it much longer, Watson. It is like spending a weekend with the Spanish Inquisition."

Fortune favoured us, however, and we were saved from any further discomfort by the peal of the bell. A client, it so seemed, had arrived and, after a welcome withdrawal from the breakfast table, he was presently upon us. A handsome gentleman of around five-and-forty years, he wore a royal blue frock coat with a cream waist jacket, and pinstriped trousers. He had black tousled hair mixed with grey, and a silver-handled cane clutched in a gloved hand. He possessed, I thought, the ostentatious appearance of a dandy of the type which was known to frequent the Macaroni Club.

After brief introductions, Holmes seated himself opposite our visitor and surveyed him with a courteous curiosity. "How can we help you?"

The man was purposeful. "My name is Alfred Longhorn. I've heard of your exploits, Mr. Holmes, and believe that only you can help me."

Holmes folded one leg over the other. "Dr. Watson and I will do our best."

The name of our guest, I fancied, was familiar to me. "I've read of you in *The Evening News*. You are a Member of Parliament."

Longhorn nodded. "Yes, for Esher and Walton."

"Previously, however, you were a military man," said Holmes languidly.

Longhorn's broad, pale face creased confoundedly, an expression which was regularly evinced by Holmes's clients. "How can you possibly know that?"

"Oh, he has his ways!" I said with a smile.

"Well, anyone can observe that you have a military bearing about you," Holmes said as though it were obvious. "What is perhaps less apparent is the uneven distribution of weight on your feet as you walk." He pointed to Longhorn's right leg. "You bear most of it there. Hence, it is evident your cane is not merely an accessory, but that it also serves a practical purpose. It cannot have been the result of a sporting accident, since that would only have taken a few months to heal, whereas you have evidently owned that cane for years – the stem is inscribed with the year of its manufacture – and so this, therefore, must be a serious injury." Holmes took a satisfied puff on his pipe and sent wisps of grey smoke swirling across the room.

"Remarkable!" said Longhorn. "Your reputation is not unfounded, Mr. Holmes."

My friend waved the compliment away in a show of false modesty.

"You are correct on all counts," our visitor went on. "I served in the Grenadier Guards in Egypt."

The Grenadiers, I knew, were the most elite type of infantrymen and represented the crème of the British army: They were physically strong, proficient in using rifles, and strategically astute.

"Please tell me the matter which has brought you to our door," said Holmes. "Omit no details in your account."

The man shifted uncomfortably. "A most terrifying thing has happened to me, Mr. Holmes. On Wednesday night at about ten of the hour, I was writing in my study, finishing up a speech I am due to deliver next week. From my window, I saw a figure standing beside the oak tree at the bottom of the garden. It was most peculiar that someone was outside at such a time."

"Trespassers?" I suggested.

"So I assumed. We had gypsies on the estate for some time, and I've only just managed to evict them."

"What did you do when you saw this man?" Holmes asked, and brushed an invisible speck from his lap with the back of his hand.

"Well, I wanted to investigate, so snatched my Webley revolver and headed outside. I must have made a ridiculous sight, hobbling across the lawn in my dressing gown. I reached the tree and felt my slippers squelch into the mud. Looking down, I saw something that made me cold to the bone." He paused uncomfortably. "My brother's coffin had been dug up, and it was standing empty by the open grave!"

Holmes did not even frown. "Your brother is buried on the estate?"

"Yes," said our guest, "and in his soldier's uniform too. We used to climb that tree as children, so I thought it just the place."

"And how did he die?"

Longhorn was suddenly stiff. "Gideon was fighting alongside me in the battle of Tel El Kebir when he was struck in the head with a bullet. I was able to have his body shipped home. I couldn't leave him there."

I nodded knowingly. Having lost close friends and comrades in Afghanistan, I was unfortunately all too familiar with the destructive effects of war.

"So, this man you saw – Was he familiar to you?" Holmes asked.

Our client paused, lifting long fingers to his lips and massaging them absently.

"Take your time, Mr. Longhorn," said Holmes and, tugging on his briar, refilled it with tobacco.

"This is most difficult to say," said Longhorn at last. "You will think me nonsensical."

149

"Not in the least," said Holmes. "I make a point of never having any prejudices, and of following docilely where facts may lead me."

Longhorn took a couple of shallow breaths and a faint, embarrassed smile flit across his features. "The man was my dead brother," he said.

Weighing his words in silence, I rather felt like smiling myself.

Holmes, for his part, was sceptical. "How do you know it was your brother?" he asked calmly. His interest, I could tell, was suitably ensnared, and his piercing eyes never left our guest for a moment.

Longhorn had expected the question and answered it with confidence. "Because Gideon was dressed in the same grenadier uniform that he had worn when he fought in Egypt."

"Is that all?" Holmes pursued. "Never trust to general impressions, Mr. Longhorn, but concentrate yourself upon details."

The man thought deeper. "He was standing completely motionless, with the same brown beard and bearskin hat. And he was holding a rifle by his left side, as though he were standing to attention." Longhorn shifted uneasily in his armchair. "The figure's resemblance to my brother was striking, Mr. Holmes. But, unlike the handsome man I had known in life, the one standing before me was utterly ghoulish. His face was horribly waxen and his body thin and cadaverous, his uniform hanging wearily from him. He looked as though he were wasting away in front of my very eyes. Even more disturbingly, a bloody gunshot wound had been punctured into his temple."

"How curious," Holmes murmured and set down his pipe. "What did you do when you saw this . . . apparition? Did you speak to it?"

Longhorn shook his head. "Before I was able, my legs became heavy and my vision blurred. I seemed to be seeing everything through a thick mist. Next I knew, I was lying on my back on the muddy ground and my wife was there. She helped me back to bed and wired for a doctor. He came the following morning to minister to me." Our client seemed calmer now that he was no longer telling of his night-time adventure. "It was particularly concerning, Mr. Holmes, as I have a history of heart problems. In fact, I very nearly died from it last year. As you can imagine, it has left me with a weak constitution."

Holmes steepled his hands beneath his chin, a pensive expression across his aquiline face. "Did you observe any way in which the figure's appearance was distinct from your brother's?" Holmes asked. "Think carefully, Mr. Longhorn. It is the little things which are infinitely the most important."

But Longhorn failed to remember any such distinguishing features. "He was identical."

My friend's eyes glimmered shrewdly. "Do you suffer from somnambulism, Mr. Longhorn?"

The answer was somewhat curt. "I would have known if I was sleepwalking, Mr. Holmes," said our guest, and his mouth thinned pettishly. "The vision was too vivid, for one thing. I tell you verily that my brother was as real as you or I."

Holmes was unbowed. "Grief can affect the mind in peculiar ways."

"You think I was seeing things?"

"Where there is no imagination, there is no horror," said Holmes. He seemed intent upon pursuing this mode of enquiry. "Did you consume any alcohol on Wednesday night?"

"No," said Longhorn flatly. "It wasn't a result of inebriation, I can assure you. My senses were sound."

Holmes gave an appeasing smile. "I am merely eliminating possibilities. You do, presumably, want me to resolve the matter?"

This seemed to settle our guest. "I would be most indebted, Mr. Holmes."

"Then we must balance probabilities and choose the most likely. It is the scientific use of the imagination." Animated, my friend slapped the arms of his chair and stood up. "I must confess that this has piqued my curiosity, Mr. Longhorn. If you so allow it, Watson and I will visit your home immediately."

Alfred Longhorn accepted this suggestion with grateful relief. "I shall fetch a cab," he said, and left for the street.

"It sounds most interesting," I said to Holmes. "A trip to the countryside and a mysterious phantom."

My friend took his Inverness cape from the coat rack. "And I thought this day would be dull!"

Mrs. Culpepper appeared cheerfully in the doorway and, with a sudden spike of apprehension, I noticed she was carrying a tray of plates. "Now your guest has gone, Mr. Holmes," she said, "I've brought you up some fish stew."

Holmes eyed the bowl uneasily. "I'm afraid we must pass over, Mrs. Culpepper," he said, but softened his words with a smile. "Duty calls!"

Our journey took us over rutted country tracks and rolling hills to the cobbled streets and periwinkle skies of Walton-upon-Thames. It was a welcome change from the cacophony of the capital and its unescapable pea soup fogs, and I spent much time staring out with an appreciative awe. Perhaps it was the beauty of the place and the peace which surrounded it, but I could not countenance such transcendental terrors and felt foolish that we were making it our principal concern. Holmes, however, was

151

working again and I reminded myself that it was cases of this kind which motored his mind and kept him from seeking more damaging distractions.

The manor was an impressive example of neoclassical architecture with its columned portico and bone-white façade. Mrs. Longhorn received us well. She was a tall woman in a white dress and a blue chemisette, with long, auburn hair and an angular face of faint freckles. She escorted us into an expansive main hall where a magnificent chandelier hung from a frescoed ceiling. Sunlight streamed through a bay window at the top of a double staircase and set off the chequered tiles of the marble floor.

"I hope that you can help, Mr. Holmes," she said, leading us through a winding corridor. "My husband has been most anxious and hasn't slept in days. He has enough to deal with as it is. The election, you know. He is determined to be re-elected, though I'm not so sure his health will allow it."

"Perhaps it would be best if he stepped down," I suggested.

Mrs. Longhorn shook her head sadly. "I'm afraid that isn't likely, Doctor. His opponent, Mr. Tobias Quince, would otherwise win and my husband could not allow that."

I had heard of Tobias Quince at my club. By all accounts, he was a man of little personal integrity who would do almost anything to vanquish his rivals.

Alfred Longhorn had gone ahead and was secreted in his study behind an antique desk.

"Thank you, Emilia," he said.

His wife nodded. "I must attend to Iris," she said with some despondence. "The silly girl has lost her purse."

She closed the door and our client waved us into a couple of leather-upholstered chairs.

I couldn't help but notice – aside from a strong stink of whisky – a photograph hanging beside the longcase clock. It featured three soberly-suited gentlemen standing beneath the canopy of a large oak tree: A younger Longhorn, possessing none of the grey hairs which now fashioned his brow, a bearded man of broader chest and fuller frame, and a taller, thinner individual leaning rakishly on a cane.

Holmes had seen it too. "Is this Gideon?" he asked, pointing to the bearded man.

Longhorn seemed surprised. "Yes," he said, giving the picture a melancholic glance. "And that is Francis, my younger brother. He also served as a grenadier in Egypt."

"You didn't mention him," said Holmes disapprovingly.

Our host tilted his head indifferently. "I rarely see him. He was never close to Gideon and me. Francis was a pacifist, you see, and disapproved

152

of our service. Then, when Gideon died, the house held too many memories and he headed to the Congo. Had the deuced notion he could mine for gold. I visited him last Christmas. It was wonderful to see him again after all these years, though it was saddening too."

"What do you mean?" I asked.

Longhorn shook his head lamentably. "Francis had contracted scarlet fever."

"I'm sorry," I said. "I have seen first-hand how terrible such a thing can be." I smiled with what I hoped was reassurance. "It is rarely fatal."

Longhorn looked over to the photograph and his eyes took on a misty glaze. "That was taken just before we went to fight. They were happier, simpler times." He looked away from it with force. "There's no point in dwelling upon the past," he said briskly.

"There is every point, Mr. Longhorn," said Holmes, "for only in the past can the present be explained."

There came a knock at the door and a maid appeared. She was a young, flaxen-haired woman in a grey uniform and carrying a tray of tea.

"Thank you, Iris," Longhorn murmured as she placed it on the desk. "Do you take sugar, Mr. Holmes?"

The maid turned to Holmes with wide, excited eyes. "You've asked *the* Sherlock Holmes to help me find my purse!" she said tremulously to Longhorn. She bowed her head reverentially as though Holmes were royalty itself. "It's an honour."

My friend looked amused and befuddled in equal measure.

"Yes, Iris, run along now," said Longhorn, not unkindly.

The woman walked backwards, her gaze still transfixed on Holmes, and somehow left the room without bumping into the door.

"Iris has a tendency to get the wrong end of the stick," Longhorn explained. He took a sip of the tea and smacked his lips together as though he wasn't sure whether to spit it out again. "I'm afraid making tea isn't a strong suit of hers," he apologised.

"She should meet our temporary housekeeper," I said with a smile, but I caught my friend's expression and quickly returned to more pertinent matters.

Holmes paused in thought. Finally, he said, "Could you show us your brother's grave?"

Longhorn picked up his cane from beside the hearth and led us out through the French window. A sweep of green spread out for a mile, rising precipitously like an ocean wave, before bending low towards a copse. Hedgerows hugged the sides of the garden, a bench had been left in the middle, and a long, tall wall could be seen in the distance. The summer air was thick and scented with honeysuckle, and I was glad that we could spend the day in such spacious surroundings, even though I was not wholly convinced by our client's veracity. I had heard of such visions before, and they were usually caused by a strong but unsettled mind. An alienist, I believed, would be more useful to Alfred Longhorn than a detective. I wondered, however, how long it would be until Holmes came to the same sorry conclusion.

A thin line of soil, graced with marigolds and zinnias, separated the grass from the hedges, and as we strode beside it, I listened to my friend's apparently innocuous questions. He asked about everything from Longhorn's daily routine to his work as a Member of Parliament to how he had his dinner prepared. Even the topic of marriage was not prohibited and Holmes soon learned the year of the couple's wedding and whether they shared the same social circle. It was my friend's belief that he must know everything if he was to discover the very something which would reveal the truth.

Longhorn pointed to a knobby oak tree. "That's where I saw him." He said it mildly, without a trace of embarrassment.

I followed his finger, almost expecting to see the ghost of which he spoke, with the withered face and deathly wound. Instead, near the muddy patch surrounding the open grave and the plain empty coffin abandoned beside it, I noticed another man entirely, round and ruddy, crouched on all fours beside a nearby rhododendron bush and arranging rocks into a pattern on the grass.

"Who is that?" I enquired.

"Oh, it's Mr. Eldritch," said Longhorn.

I could feel Holmes bristle beside me.

We had already experienced the displeasure of working alongside Bernard Eldritch, a detective of dubious distinction who was obsessed with psychical phenomena, during a case in which a medium had been murdered during a séance. Eldritch had believed the culprit was a vengeful spirit, but Holmes proved otherwise. As detectives, the pair were the very antithesis of one another. Holmes, of course, took a rational, empirical approach to problems, while Eldritch consistently believed the causes to be supernatural.

"Let me introduce you," Longhorn said hospitably.

"There is no need," Holmes cut in. "We are already acquainted."

Our host was pleased to hear this. "In which case, you should get along just fine."

Eldritch must have heard us, for he shuffled to his feet and brushed dirt hastily from his shabby black suit. His sallow complexion and prematurely grey hair made it look as though it had been he, and not Gideon Longhorn, who had awoken from death.

154

Holmes and Eldritch appraised each other coolly.

"Has Gideon made another appearance yet?" Longhorn said to the large man. He could have been asking about the weather.

Eldritch fiddled with a medallion hanging glitteringly from his thick trunk of a neck. "No, I am afraid not. But I hope to call upon his spirit by using this." He pointed a chubby finger at the rocks underfoot. They were arranged into the same shape as the medallion.

"What is it?" I asked.

"It is known as a *pentacle*," he explained with all the pomposity of a preening poet. "It has been used for centuries to summon entities from the spirit world into our own. Unfortunately, when we open such a channel, evil spirits may also travel through. By standing inside the pentacle, however, I shall be protected."

Holmes was typically dismissive. "I find it hard to believe that a few rocks can possess such mystical properties."

"Then you must open your mind," said the other man, and I looked at his rival with amused anticipation.

Holmes's face split into a thin, mocking smile. "Mr. Eldritch, I deal in facts, logic, and reasoning. I believe in what the eyes can see and what the mind can comprehend."

Bernard Eldritch did not seem surprised by this cynicism. Indeed, it was as though he had been asked his favourite question of all. "There are mysteries which transcend the limits of human understanding. Perhaps even *yours*, Mr. Holmes."

My friend, however, was undeterred. "If there are, I have yet to discover them."

"Then how do you explain what happened to Mr. Gideon Longhorn?"

This was something I also wanted to know and turned to Holmes expectantly.

"I admit that I cannot explain it at the moment," he allowed, "but only because I have insufficient data, not because it can be attributed to anything otherworldly. You, Mr. Eldritch, prefer to fill any gap in your knowledge with the fantastic, while I favour only the credible and corporeal."

"After all," I put in, for I was feeling just as sceptical, "it is a capital mistake to theorize in advance of the facts. Insensibly, one begins – "

"Ah!" interrupted Eldritch and I looked at him sourly for doing so. He gestured a thick hand towards the ground. "Notice that? Just this moment. There is a perceptibly strong spiritual energy in this spot." He was bobbing his head excitedly. "I have a feeling in my stomach."

"Perhaps you are suffering from a digestive ailment," Holmes said wryly.

The other man was not amused. The otherworldly energy of which he spoke, however, seemed to have dissipated and he became calm again. "If you so wish it, Mr. Holmes, we could have a wager," he offered. "The man who cannot solve the case by the end of the day must leave the premises at once."

I did not expect Holmes to agree to this preposterous gambit – he generally found such things undignified – and yet I was surprised to see how earnestly he accepted. Now with even more incentive to solve the matter, Holmes moved away from the supposedly second-sighted sleuth and towards Gideon Longhorn's empty grave. Focused again, he hunkered upon his haunches to inspect the mud and the displaced soil lying on the edge of the hole.

"Unfortunately," he reported, standing upright, "the rain from yesterday must have washed any footmarks from here. That leaves us, I am afraid, with precious little evidence."

It was, admittedly, not the most auspicious of starts.

Eldritch flashed a self-satisfied smirk. "The dead do not leave footprints, Mr. Holmes," he said and, chuckling wryly, wobbled off to speak to the gardener.

"At the very least," I remarked to Holmes, "he's right about one thing."

After thoroughly exploring the area around the grave, and looking at the coffin as well, seemingly without making any useful discoveries, Holmes elected to explore the estate without the guidance of our host and I followed him eagerly around its edges for the next few hours. He was keen to discover any means of entry – perhaps a piece of climbing rope left dangling next to a fence or a conveniently positioned tree – so we made our way to the wall circumvallating the grounds and inspected it solemnly. His eyes were unblinkingly attentive and he paused every so often to check the brickwork before darting off again with renewed and irrepressible energy. I followed on his heels, trying my best to keep up with his loping strides, but it was like hurrying after a bloodhound.

Holmes came to an abrupt halt and lifted a finger towards a birch tree. "This has a branch which overhangs the wall. It is a perfect way by which someone could have vaulted over. See if you can climb it, Watson."

I looked at my friend with unalloyed alarm. "You want me to . . . *climb*. . . ?" I asked, in the weak hope that I had been mistaken.

"Of course, Watson," he said casually. "It should not be too difficult for a man of your physical type."

"But – "

"Come now, Watson," he interrupted. "It's simplicity itself."

I lifted a weary head and wished that I was again sampling Mrs. Culpepper's unprepossessing black pudding. I knew from considerable experience, however, that any argument with Holmes would be foolishly futile.

Climbing the tree was even harder than I had anticipated. Its trunk had few cracks or crevices into which I could leverage my foot, and I almost lost my balance several times as I heaved myself up. Had I fallen, I most certainly would have broken several bones. After a while, despite my best efforts, I had only managed to make it halfway to the top. I could only concede defeat and clambered clumsily back down. It was a relief to have my feet planted securely on *terra firma* once again.

"You made it look effortless," Holmes said with a patronising pat on the back. "Your army days haven't gone to waste."

I was gasping for air and my arms were smarting. "I didn't even make it to the top."

"Nonetheless, you demonstrated that no man could surely have scaled such a tree. The culprit – and, despite what our friend Mr. Eldritch says, there must have been one – did not come from outside the grounds. We must then, Watson, look inwards for an explanation."

Returning to the lawn, we found Alfred Longhorn and his wife sitting on a bench and surveying their surroundings with uncomfortable apprehension. His head was leant against her chest and she was whispering something reassuringly to him. It felt awkward to witness so intimate a scene and I wondered whether we should leave the couple to their ruminations. Holmes, on the other hand, was sprite and unconcerned and sauntered easily towards them. Mrs. Longhorn noticed us and, rising from her seat, bowed her head politely and walked away.

"Emilia has been wonderful these past few days," he said. "She has tolerated my moods with the utmost patience. I've been rather short-tempered of late, you see." He sighed. "I just wish that I could tell her the truth. If anyone deserves to know, it's her."

Holmes regarded him with a penetrating gaze. "The truth?"

Something about our client had changed. He chewed his lip distractedly. "Speaking to my wife just then, I realised I wanted to be free again."

"Free?" I said with some surprise. "You mean you intend to divorce her?"

Longhorn winced at the thought. "No, of course, not. I mean to say, I don't want to live as I have. In fear. With guilt." He leant forward conspiratorially, though there was no one to hear him as the lawn was too wide, and set his elbows on his knees. "I've never told this to anyone

157

before, Mr. Holmes, but I think it could be crucial to your investigation. I have lied, and I hope you will not think less of me because of it."

Holmes seated himself beside our client and looked at him with eager expectation. "Rest assured, you will not be judged by us."

There was a terrible look in Longhorn's eyes. "Even now, the memory is uncomfortably vivid," he said. "I was in camp – Gideon and I were stationed at Kassassin at the time – when something woke me in the middle of the night. A sound seemed to be coming from outside my tent. I thought, of course, that someone was lurking there. At the time of which I speak, the region was rife with bandits and a few weeks earlier we had been raided, so naturally I assumed they had appeared again. I grabbed my rifle and headed out of the tent. There was a particularly bad sandstorm blowing through the desert that night which made it impossible to see much further than ten feet in front of me. I somehow spotted a figure prowling next to our tent. He had his back to me and I could not see his face.

"After all that had happened, our Lieutenant General had given us strict orders to shoot any intruders on sight. Not wishing to disobey him – he was a formidable man and had dismissed many for insubordination – I snuck up behind the figure. War makes a killer of even the most peaceable man, Mr. Holmes, and it was with a chilled indifference that I squeezed the trigger. The bullet hit him in the forehead and he sunk insensibly to the ground. When I rolled the body over to check for death, I discovered that I had made the most unforgivable mistake." Longhorn took a breath, as though summoning some inner strength. "It was Gideon," he said shortly, and shook his head with rue anew. "I had killed my own brother."

With that, he leant back on the bench and a thin breeze blew away his words. It was unconscionable, but I knew it to be true. Such misfortune in the military was not as rare as it should have been. It seemed almost impossible, however, as we sat in the calm of the garden, with only the starlings breaking the silence. My own thoughts on war, and whatever else I had done abroad, swung somewhere between grief and gratitude, but I always tried to focus on the friends that I had saved. For Longhorn, cruelly, it was the very opposite, and he was forced to dwell forever on the one life he had so inadvertently lost.

Holmes, unaccountably, remained impassive. "What happened next?" he asked.

Longhorn seemed to have forgotten we were even there and stirred with surprise. "The gunshot had disturbed some of the men from their sleep and they emerged from their tents with rifles."

"And what did you tell them of your brother's body?" Holmes asked.

"I panicked," admitted Longhorn truthfully. "It could have meant court martial, after all. Now, of course, I consider it to be a worthy fate and one I wish had been brought upon me. At the time, however, I simply lied. I said that Gideon had been shot down by a bandit who had since absconded."

Holmes looked perplexed. "Why would your brother be wandering around the camp at night?"

"Well, you see, Gideon was quite nocturnal and would go wandering. He said he liked the air. It was certainly more tolerable than in daytime."

"It's not, then, out of character to find his ghost about at night?" I said, in the full knowledge that such a question was ridiculous.

"Precisely," he said. "He's punishing me, I know, for what I did to him."

Holmes had heard similar proclamations from previous clients and treated this one with the same weary patience. "I believe we should eliminate the natural causes before we lead ourselves to a supernatural explanation, Mr. Longhorn."

It seemed our host had talked himself into believing the fantastic, and the hope which had caused him to hire Holmes in the first place was fast receding. "If I didn't perceive the ghost of my brother, Mr. Holmes, then what was it?"

"Someone," my friend assured him, "who knows of your secret."

This, however, only made Longhorn even more unsettled. "But I have told no one until now! Why would I? It would destroy my career. Who would vote for such a murderer?" A hollow laugh of hysteria escaped him. "And I mustn't tell Emilia. She would never forgive me. Indeed, I cannot even forgive myself!"

"You cannot know with certainty just how she shall react," Holmes pointed out. "You may be troubling yourself unduly. Any truth, in my experience, is better than indefinite doubt."

He clapped a consoling hand on the man's back and I knew he would offer no further counsel. Instead, he stood up with energetic purpose and cast a glance around. "Where does the gardener keep his tools, Mr. Longhorn?"

I could not see the logic in such a question and neither did our host. "Why do you ask?"

"Because," said Holmes briskly, "whoever dug up your brother's grave made a tidy job of it."

Longhorn led us onto the other side of a copse where a little ramshackle hut was positioned discreetly away from the house. The gardener was bent over some begonias, his flat cap shielding his eyes from the searing afternoon sun. Holmes yanked down on the handle but the door would not open.

"Oi! You can't go in there," said the gardener, and shook his head so thoroughly that his chevron moustache could have fallen off. "That's private!"

Longhorn stepped out from behind me and raised a placating hand. "It's all right. I'm here too." He looked at us apologetically. "I don't think he's been here very long. My butler recruits such people."

Holmes interrupted, surprising me when he seemed to lose interest in the shed. "It's locked," he explained. He leaned forward to look at the door with concentration, as though his very gaze could prise it ajar. "We must look elsewhere. Perhaps the staff can tell us more. Shall we return to the house?"

We did so and, with Longhorn's permission, we took ourselves into the narrow, labyrinthine corridors that lay below the manor.

"Should we not focus upon Gideon's accidental death?" I asked, once more having to keep pace with my friend's vigorous strides.

Holmes, however, seemed to have taken Longhorn's story at face value. "Crime is common," he said. "Logic is rare. Therefore, it is upon the logic rather than upon the crime that we should dwell."

His interest in the matter of Gideon Longhorn's ghost did not surprise me. Holmes had often been drawn to the *outré* and original, from the case of Victor Furnival and how he died of fright to the comical code of the fifteen stick figures, and it was this same peculiarity which had entranced me too. I was grateful, therefore, that we would not be treading through the arid sands of Egypt, but could stay in the Surrey green and investigate an incident which seemed to defy even the most logical of natural laws.

There were, however, a number of obstinate obstacles in our path and one of these was the chattering chambermaid who believed we were there on her account.

"Have you found my purse yet?" she asked Holmes as she passed through a corridor.

"Not yet," he said politely and carried on into the servants' hall.

Sitting at a long table, enjoying their lunch, were the butler, cook, a couple of footmen, and three scullery maids. The butler, old and stout with iron-grey hair, stood up respectfully and bowed a head to Holmes.

"My name is Henderson, sir. How may we help you?"

"We are here to assist Mr. Longhorn in a personal matter," said Holmes. He glanced down at their servants' plates and his eyes gleamed gluttonously. "Would it be inconvenient if Dr. Watson and I dined with you all?"

The butler took a moment to react. "Not at all," he said, and nodded to the cook.

Having spent the last several days subjected to Mrs. Culpepper's fish stew, Holmes and I couldn't help but smile at the sight of beef casserole.

Afterwards, my friend was focused again and began asking the staff for their opinions of Mr. Longhorn.

"He's a wonderful man," said the cook, a corpulent woman of middle years with grey hair in a bun. "He treats us like his own family, he does."

Everyone nodded in earnest accord.

"I've been here since the Longhorn brothers were children and Mr. Silas was still alive," said Henderson reminiscently. "It was a terrible shock to lose one of them."

I could see that one of the scullery maids wanted to say something and gestured for her to do so. She was a slight, diffident girl who spoke in a low voice and never looked up. "These past few days, Mr. Longhorn hasn't been himself. He's been acting all nervous."

"I see," said Holmes, as though she had said something of considerable import. He knew to behave appreciatively of any information on offer as it invariably precipitated even more. "Aside from Mr. Longhorn's anxious behaviour, has anyone noticed anything out of the ordinary of late?"

They all shook their heads.

Holmes tried a different tack. "Your master believes he has seen a ghost in the garden."

He said this simply, as though he were speaking of nothing but a bullfinch.

I had expected this to be news to the staff, but none of them seemed surprised. I wondered how well they knew Longhorn and whether such stories were considered to be consistent with his character.

"The incident of which we speak apparently occurred on Wednesday last," said Holmes. "If I may be impolitic to ask, where were all of you?"

"I was mopping these floors," said the scullery maid.

"I was cooking supper," said the cook.

Henderson confirmed this. "We were all in sight of each other."

Holmes rose from his seat. "Thank you for your time – and for the delicious food," he added, smiling generously at the cook.

"A popular man," I remarked to Holmes as we left the servant's hall.

"So it would seem, Watson. So it would seem."

I was beginning to feel increasingly disillusioned with our lack of progress and the paucity of physical evidence. We had seemingly discovered very little during the course of our investigation thus far: No footprints were found beside Gideon Longhorn's grave. It looked unlikely

161

that anyone had trespassed upon the estate. And the domestic staff couldn't seem to tell us much beyond the fact that their master had been acting nervously and consuming copious amounts of alcohol in the last couple of days.

I wondered, in fact, whether Holmes, despite his unparalleled powers of deduction, could indeed unravel the mystery by the end of the day. It would be difficult to concede any ground to Eldritch, but what if the strange little man was actually correct? Could Gideon Longhorn have really climbed out of his own grave? As each rational explanation was dutifully dismissed, such supernatural solutions seemed distressingly probable. Holmes, it behoves me to mention, was often uncommunicative during cases, and I usually found such reticence to be singularly irritating. I would have been delighted, therefore, to discover that he was withholding something significant from me again. However, as the afternoon sun became weak and watery and wilted behind the brow of the hill, I felt all hope fade with it.

Night soon shrouded the estate in darkness and all was quiet. In the study, Alfred Longhorn was seated again behind his desk, one hand curled around a glass of whisky while the bottle itself was gripped in the other. Holmes and I entered demurely to find Bernard Eldritch standing beside the longcase clock.

"Have you managed to shed any light on the matter, gentlemen?" asked our host.

"We have discovered some curious particulars," Holmes allowed.

I was surprised. To my mind, we had learned nothing substantial during the entire afternoon.

Eldritch lifted his chin smugly. "You can deny it all you wish, Mr. Holmes, but we are dealing with the supernatural. Eventually, you will come to your senses, I am sure."

Holmes was unruffled. "Mr. Eldritch, time has not yet been called. It is only eleven of the clock, and not yet the end of the day. Our wager still stands."

"Well, you haven't long," he said complacently and thumbed the clock in warning.

"I am perfectly capable of telling the time," said Holmes.

"Glad to hear it," was the other detective's injudicious rejoinder.

I was about to answer myself, and remind the man just how many apparent imponderables my friend had managed to solve, when I noticed something stir just out of the French windows. I must have uttered an incredulous cry, as the other three turned their heads in alarm. I drifted forwards for a closer inspection and felt a chill ripple across my back. By the thin sliver of moonlight, I could discern the shape of a figure standing across the lawn beside the oak tree where the grave of Gideon Longhorn was known to lie.

Our client was also gawking across the garden and had similarly made the association. His glass dropped onto the carpet with a dull thud and he tugged open the drawer of his desk. I was not surprised, but rather comforted, at the sight of his Webley revolver. He drew it level and strode to the window with an unaccustomed confidence. Perhaps it was our presence, or maybe he was feeling defiant, but Alfred Longhorn seemed braver now than at any point during our brief acquaintanceship. I could certainly perceive the steely calm of a soldier as he threw the windows wide and challenged the darkness.

"It's there," he murmured grimly and moved onto the grass.

Holmes didn't seem to notice anything amiss and watched the man with only a mild interest. He seemed, in fact, so sure that there was nothing remotely preternatural taking place that he was almost detached from the proceedings. I, on the other hand, was not so stoic and stood a few steps back from Longhorn as he moved implacably off the lawn and closer to whatever apparition had somehow appeared.

And that was when I saw it myself.

The branches of the tree hung low as though protecting the figure from the heavens above. The grave was open still and standing resolutely beside it was the ghost of Gideon Longhorn. He was holding his rifle erect, his uniform resplendent, just as Alfred had described him, with a bearskin hat pulled low across his brow. Jagged shadows cut across a broad, brown face and he seemed to be staring in unspeakable fury. His lips were pinched tight as though they might split apart and scream of all that Hell had handed him.

Even Eldritch was watching with his jaw hung loose. "What are your eyes telling you now, Mr. Holmes?" he asked in an excited whisper.

Longhorn drifted cautiously towards the spectre and trained his Webley upon it with a trembling hand. "What do you want from me?"

The ghost did not utter a reply and instead glared back at him impassively.

"Have you not tortured me enough?" Longhorn cried.

Eldritch spoke up with an unexpected authority. "You may as well throw your revolver away, Mr. Longhorn," he said. "Spirits cannot be wounded by bullets."

The ghost marched forward slowly, bearing down upon Longhorn, causing him to scuttle backwards. His finger curled instinctively around the trigger of his revolver. "Get back! I am warning you!" he shouted, trying to disguise the quiver in his voice.

"I would not advise that, Mr. Longhorn – " said Holmes.

A deafening crack echoed through the trees. The shot seemed to have no effect on the ghost, however, as it continued its imperturbable advance.

"This has gone on long enough," said Holmes sternly, and stepped in front of the ghost. "Stop this now!"

I watched with a cold shock as he tugged off the figure's beard and bearskin hat.

Despite the low light of the moon, I immediately recognised him from the photograph on Longhorn's wall. It was the face of the other brother, Francis Longhorn.

Back in the study, our client swigged a glass of whisky in an effort to calm his nerves. Francis was sitting shamelessly opposite. The resemblance to his brother could be seen in the black, rumpled hair, the broadness of his face, and the earnest way in which he slid his fingers across his mouth. I had locked the French windows and was standing with my back to the door in case he tried to affect a hasty escape. After all, it was not as though he could really walk through walls. Holmes, meanwhile, was stood silently in the corner and allowing himself to be forgotten. It wouldn't have made much difference, however, if either of us had spoken. Alfred, certainly, was uninterested in addressing anyone but his brother, and did so with a mixture of anger and bitter incredulity. Francis remained silent and so it appeared, even now, as though his brother was the only one who could see him.

Eldritch was standing, once more, beside the longcase clock and somehow found a moment which was not filled with Alfred's virulent reproaches. "I was mistaken, Mr. Holmes," he allowed, and even the brothers turned to him curiously. He fished a fat hand into his pocket, produced a few coins and slapped them down onto the desk. He was, it seemed, dignified in defeat. "However," he went on, spoiling himself somewhat, "this case may have had a rational explanation, but that doesn't mean that they all do."

Holmes stepped forward and, for a moment, I expected him to issue a cool and callous retort. Instead, to my surprise, he seemed to suppress his more abrasive tendencies, and looked upon the rotund detective with something like respect. "Indeed, that is so," he said at last.

I stared at Holmes in surprise and it took me a few befuddled moments to realise that he was actually being diplomatic. This, I concluded, was just as rare as any redoubtable ghost.

Bernard Eldritch seemed similarly stricken. "Er, yes, well, maybe, perhaps," he said, suddenly without the strength of his convictions. "But who really knows, eh?"

He gave a subdued nod to our host and shuffled shabbily out.

Longhorn took another gulp of whisky and looked at his brother again. His outrage had subsided somewhat and he was ready to speak some sense. "What is the meaning of this cruel trick? Can you tell me that?"

Francis remained impassive. "I couldn't let you forget what you'd done," he replied. "I wanted you to suffer as I have."

Our client leant forward and drummed a finger against the desk. "I've had to live with Gideon's death on my conscience for five years – every day of which I thought of him."

His brother blew out a bitter laugh. "You deserved it all the same."

"You knew I suffered from a bad heart. You could have killed me!"

There was something I didn't understand and I lifted a hand to stop Alfred from fulminating further. "Where did you put Gideon's body?" I asked his brother.

Francis, his arms hanging exhaustively off the chair, could barely summon the strength to reply. "After I dug him up, I made another grave in the woods. It was respectfully done, and all the better without Alfred there."

There was, I concluded, far more dividing them than a desk.

I did not bother to point out, however, that disturbing a grave was a criminal offense. "But how did you know the secret of Gideon's death?" I asked instead. "Mr. Longhorn never spoke of it to anyone."

Francis's mouth curved grimly but, even so, it was the very opposite of a smile. "Oh, but he did. He just cannot remember doing so. Last Christmas, Alfred, during your visit, you became drunk and confessed everything to me."

Alfred Longhorn stared blankly at his brother, and in that moment he seemed to recall, dimly, a night of sinful secrets and god-fearing guilt.

"It's getting late, Mr. Longhorn," Holmes said eventually. "Watson and I must return to London."

I was not sure it was right to leave the brothers together, but Alfred seemed soothed by his words and finally pushed the whisky away. "I apologise for dragging you into my domestic affairs, gentlemen." He stood up and gripped Holmes's hand. His eyes were bloodshot, his brow creased wearily, but his fear had gone and I knew the anger would too. Holmes, I felt, had afforded him absolution. My friend may not have believed in such spiritual matters, but he often delivered his own kind of peace.

"You look tired, Watson," said Holmes across the breakfast table.

"It was all that talk of ghosts and grave-robbery," I complained. "It was playing on my mind until morning."

I folded up *The Illustrated News* and tossed it aside. Nothing within its page could quite match the events of the day before.

"Do you think Alfred Longhorn will confess to the police? He did, after all, kill somebody."

Holmes lifted his head and considered it. "He will do the right thing, I'm sure."

I took a sip of tea. "How, then, Holmes, did you know it was Francis?"

It was a matter which had been bothered me since we had left the manor. The removal of Gideon Longhorn's body had led my friend to discuss the Burke and Hare murders, always a favourite topic of his, and he had spoken of nothing else throughout our journey home. Now, however, he returned to the case which had so confounded us.

"My suspicions were first aroused by the photograph on Mr. Longhorn's wall. I observed how his brother, Francis, was holding a cane in his left hand. A right-handed person would not do such a thing. The supposed ghost was also left-handed: He was carrying the rifle in that hand when we confronted him last night."

I was sceptical. "A lot of people are left-handed," I pointed out.

"It is not as common as you think, Watson. But yes, I grant you that I could not predicate my hypothesis solely on such evidence. That would do no good at all." He let out a plume of purple smoke.

"Tell me, how did Francis get into the estate? We proved it was unlikely anyone from outside could have gained entry."

"We did, yes, due to our little experiment. It follows, then, that Francis had been inside the estate all along."

"How then did he go unnoticed by his brother? Mr. Longhorn would surely have become aware of his presence." I paused. "Unless," I suggested, "he was in disguise."

"You have turned over an ace, Watson," he said. "He was the gardener." Holmes sucked on his pipe again. "When we saw him in his flower patch, I observed red rashes on his lower forearm."

"I did not see them."

"Because you were seeing and not observing, Watson. Is that not so? When he was pulling on the roots, his sleeve rode up his forearm and exposed the skin. And what do such rashes indicate?"

"Scarlet Fever!" I said at once. "Its symptoms are a sore throat, swollen glands, and red, bumpy rashes on the skin."

"And Longhorn, you will recall, had told us how Francis had contracted it a few months ago."

"Yes, I remember there was an outbreak here too."

"It was those characteristic rashes which I observed on the ghost's wrists and lower forearm. Not only that, but like Francis and the ghost, the gardener was left-handed. He was planting rhododendrons using that hand, while the mound of mud which he had dug up from Gideon Longhorn's grave was lying on the right-hand side of the hole."

"Because," I finished, "a left-handed person would naturally shovel it to that way!"

"Quite so. Now, the chances of someone being left-handed are slim. But the likelihood of them being both left-handed *and* suffering from scarlet fever are slimmer still. It is all a matter of probability, Watson. Francis Longhorn, we know, fulfilled both these criteria, as did the gardener. Therefore, they had to be the same person."

I still found it all slightly implausible. "But surely Mr. Longhorn would have recognised the gardener as his own brother."

"He told us he did not employ his own staff, remember – that was done by his butler, Henderson – so they would seldom come into contact with one another. Besides which, Francis wore a flat cap and a false moustache. When I recognized the disguise, I didn't press to enter the shed."

"And Alfred Longhorn's bullets didn't injure him at the grave – "

" – because he'd gained access to the house and substituted blanks. He knew that he was safe – and his seeming imperviousness to gunfire would only emphasize that he was a ghost, and heap further fear and punishment upon his brother."

"But how did he gain possession of the grenadier uniform?"

"From his brother's body. Francis kept it well-hidden in the shed, which was why he didn't want to allow us to access it. He weighed slightly less than Gideon, so it made him look properly withered and, as it happens, more like a corpse."

"And what of the ghost's face?" I said, unnerved at the recollection. "It was ghoulish!"

"Well, Watson, although we have never looked into a lady's purse, we can imagine the miscellany it may contain."

"A hand mirror?" I suggested. "Rouge, face powder . . . ." I smiled with sudden realisation. "The chambermaid's purse! You think Francis stole it?"

"Doubtless. He used the powder to produce a ghostly effect and had liberally applied rouge or lipstick to his temple to create the impression of a bloodied bullet wound."

"But why would Francis disguise himself as the gardener when he could just as easily have accessed the manor by visiting his brother?"

167

Holmes put down his pipe. "Because if Mr. Longhorn had met him again, he may have remembered his confession, and would therefore know immediately that his brother was behind the hoax. As the gardener, Francis was completely incognito. No one knew he was there."

"Marvellous, Holmes!" I said. "It is just a shame that we couldn't find the chambermaid's purse. She would have been most pleased."

"On the contrary, Francis had kept that in the shed too. I got it back to her before we left."

Although I had been privileged enough to witness my friend's prodigious powers of perspicacity countless times throughout the years, they still never ceased to impress me. I leant back reflectively in my chair and, with another case closed, began searching through the morning's correspondences.

"There's been a wire from Mrs. Hudson," I said, and winced. "Her sister is ill, so she won't be back for another few days."

Holmes's face folded into a frown. "A few days?" he said with something approaching anguish.

At that moment, footsteps alighted the stairs, and I hung my head in disappointment. Even in battle, I had not been so brave.

Mrs. Culpepper bustled through the door with a tray of breakfast plates and regarded my friend concernedly. "Are you all right, Mr. Holmes?" she asked. "Anyone would think that you had seen a ghost!"

The Curse of Barcombe Keep
by Brenda Seabrooke

The day was braw for late September and I was glad after luncheon to sit in front of the crackling fire with a journal while Holmes did the same. The afternoon stretched comfortably before us, but it was not to be. At the knock on the door, I glanced up at Holmes, but his attention was on the paper before him. Footsteps on the stairs held no interest for him.

I buttoned my coat and stood as a lady swathed in a black cape entered. Holmes stood then as well, though he didn't button his coat in time.

"Lady Northington," Mrs. Hudson announced while taking her cape, revealing a black silk dress trimmed in delicate braid. She wore a fashionable hat which meant that her mourning was recent. I was glad to see, though it had feathers, an entire bird was not perched on the crown. She was of medium height with smooth brown hair drawn back on the nape of her neck.

"My condolences for your bereavement, your Ladyship," Holmes said as he ushered her to a chair.

She inclined her head and removed her gloves. She wore a wedding ring of plain gold and no other jewelry.

"I trust your loss was not your husband," Holmes said.

"No, it was not." Her voice was pleasant. She glanced at me.

"I am glad to hear it. Forgive me, your Ladyship. This is my colleague, Dr. Watson."

I bowed and she nodded. We sat and she touched her ring, looking at us but saying nothing. Her eyes were brown and sorrowful.

"You are afraid for someone," Holmes said. "Your husband, perhaps?"

"How – how did you know?"

"You wear your sorrow like your mourning. If it were your child, with that much worry, you wouldn't have left it to come here."

"That is true." She paused and seemed to be considering her words carefully. "My husband never had a thought of inheriting the title or the manor house. We had a comfortable living in Devon. His cousin, Roderick, was always the heir, but even he did not expect to inherit so soon. Their uncle was in perfect health until he fell down the stairs last April. He had no children. His wife had died the year before. Poor

169

Roderick didn't last but a few months before he, too, fell down the selfsame stairway three weeks ago, and my husband inherited."

"These deaths were investigated?" I asked.

"Yes. They were both ruled accidents."

"And this cousin was also in perfect health?" I asked.

"He was. His death was totally unexpected. After the affairs were settled, we moved into the manor house with my husband's youngest brother, Gerald, and his wife, Helene."

"Youngest brother?" I asked. "There is a middle brother then? Where is he?"

"Frederick was with his regiment out in Burma – last we heard from him." She paused.

"What brings you here today?" Holmes asked after a minute had passed.

"I had an appointment in London and thought to ask you – to consult you."

"There have been no more mishaps?" I asked when Holmes didn't.

"Well, perhaps. My husband tripped on the stairs Sunday night, but was able to catch himself."

Holmes steepled his fingers. "I see. In six months those stairs have been the scene of three accidents, two of which were fatal. You have some concerns that they may not have been accidents."

Lady Northington pressed her lips together and her eyes welled with tears. Before I could provide a clean handkerchief, she removed a black one edged with black lace from her jet-beaded purse and dabbed at her eyes. We waited for her to regain her composure.

"Do you know what to do about . . . well . . . *curses*, Mr. Holmes?"

He managed not to shout with laughter. "No, I do not. I think you need the clergy for that."

She turned pale. I thought for a moment she might faint, but she rallied. "The house is cursed."

"Indeed." Holmes nodded.

Lady Northington thought he was sympathetic. "Yes. During Cromwell's time, a Roundhead was caught looting the house. He was hanged on the spot by the Cavaliers, but not before he cursed the house and all the lords of the manor. When King Charles regained his throne, the fifth Lord Northington, upon his return to the house, fell down the stairway and died.

"From 1660 until now, no one has fallen down the stairway or died in a peculiar accident?" I thought that was a long time without mishap with an active curse in place.

170

"Since the fifth Lord's death, each new lord had the house blessed on his ascension to the title. My husband's uncle did not believe in curses and refused the blessing. Cousin Roderick was the same. Last Saturday, my husband had a – a curse remover come and chant prayers on each step of the stairs."

"And the next night your husband had his accident. You are concerned, but not afraid for him to be left there today. Why, I wonder, is that?"

"Your husband was injured and is staying in bed," I deduced.

"Excellent, Watson. Otherwise, her Ladyship wouldn't have left her husband's side. Is that not the case?"

Lady Northington stared at the two of us. "You seem to know everything already."

"It is our business to read the signs. I am a consulting detective, and my colleague is a doctor."

"It is true that my husband's ankle was twisted. He will not be taking the stairs for at least a week, according to Dr. Oliver."

Holmes nodded. "It seems the removal of the curse did not entirely work."

"Yes, that is undoubtedly true. With my husband safe, I took the liberty of coming here. I have read of your cases."

"Quite right."

Lady Northington leaned slightly forward in her chair. "You'll help us end this accursed curse?"

"Indeed I will."

She looked inordinately relieved. I didn't know how Holmes would do it, but clearly he was ready for the challenge.

"Take some notes please, Watson."

I reached for my notebook, always at hand, and the pencil tucked into it. Holmes wanted to know where everyone was at the time of the three falls.

"My husband and I were in Devon for the first two deaths. We went to Gloucestershire for both funerals, but after the first one returned home. After the second, we remained there."

Holmes ascertained the whereabouts of the rest of the family at the time of the deaths in April and a few weeks earlier. The middle brother, Frederick, was in Burma with the Army. Gerald, the youngest brother, was in London staying with his wife's relatives. I wrote down their address.

"Excellent," Holmes said. "I have some business here this afternoon, but we shall be on the train to Gloucestershire as soon as possible. Lady Northington, I must ask that, after your return, you stay in the room with your husband. Do not go down to dinner, or leave his side for any other reason."

She was puzzled but agreed.

"I trust the stairs are not in use for the present?" I said

"No, everyone is using the servants' stairs."

"Please give Watson any relevant details. I must excuse myself."

I continued eliciting the whereabouts of the servants in the household, and then saw the lady downstairs.

Mrs. Hudson bustled into the hall with a packet for the lady's return to Gloucestershire. "Ginger biscuits," she said. "These will help with your journey."

"How thoughtful!"

"It was at Mr. Holmes's behest."

That was odd. Holmes was unfailingly polite to women, but I hadn't known of him to be so concerned with their appetites outside of his presence. I saw the lady to her waiting cab and returned to find Holmes writing out telegrams.

"She seemed much relieved that you're on the case, but why did you tell her to remain with her husband? Do you think she can protect him from a ghost or a curse? Wouldn't a footman be a better choice?"

"Come now, Watson. Do you expect the Roundhead to appear and grapple with a footman?"

"No, certainly not. I don't believe in ghosts or curses."

"Perhaps this case will make a believer out of you," he said without looking up.

I waited for him to continue, but he did not. I went to my room and packed a bag, adding my Webley just in case.

Holmes was in and out of the sitting room and his bed chamber as he waited for answers to several of his telegrams, but before all of them had returned, he sent one more as we left for King's Cross.

We had the compartment to ourselves after the first stop, and I sought to question him. "Really, how do you expect to foil a two-hundred-year-old curse?"

"It will be revealed in good time."

I suspected he hadn't a clue, hence the plethora of telegrams searching for information about the family and the manor. "You don't even believe in curses either."

"Of course I do. Anyone can lay a curse on anyone." He took out one of the telegrams delivered to our rooms before we departed and read. "'*A curse shall befall each Lord of Barcombe Keep. Let them fall as I fall.*' Uttered by Willy Beedles just before he was hanged in the stairwell."

I gaped at him, amazed at the information that he could obtain. I would have laid a bet that he did not believe in curses any more than he believed in ghosts or banshees or magic lamps. "You cannot possibly give this any credence."

He raised his eyebrows. "Why would I not? It has been well-documented by a number of sources."

"You are the most rational being I have ever met. Curses are not rational – especially curses uttered by a Roundhead over two-hundred years ago."

"We shall see, Watson, we shall see. Tell me, did you notice anything about Lady Northington?"

"Beyond the fact she's an attractive, intelligent, well-spoken lady in double mourning? No. Surely you don't suspect her of an attempt to get rid of her husband." I was attempting levity. I didn't like Holmes going in that direction. Suspicion of the wife was in my experience the wrong spouse.

"My dear Watson. Such a thought never entered my mind. If that were the case, she wouldn't have consulted me, but carried out her schemes and hoped the constabulary didn't winkle it out. No, her concern was genuine."

"I'm glad to hear it."

"This case is complicated at the moment, but I suspect it will prove to be something simple in the end. Now I suggest we get some sleep. We are staying at Barcombe Keep, and may not get much there."

He closed his eyes and was instantly asleep. I followed soon after. We awoke as the train approached the village of Barcombe.

"Interesting name, "Holmes remarked. "My research revealed that *Bar* comes from *bere*, meaning *wood*, and *combe* from the Welsh *cym* meaning *valley*. The Keep dates back to about the twelfth century, but was hit with bombards during The War of the Roses. It remains a ruin. The present house dates from 1490 and has gone through several renovations. The latest was a half-hearted Palladian make-over of some of the inside – notably the entrance. I think money became a problem and the work was abandoned."

The train halted at the station and he went inside, I assumed, to pick up a reply to one of his telegrams from the station master while I found the carriage from The Keep.

Holmes smiled with satisfaction as we climbed into the coach.

"Did you get the reply you expected?" I asked when he didn't enlighten me.

"Oh yes. This carriage is the height of comfort."

"Not a height we usually reach." We hired our vehicles from whatever was available, often a dog cart, unless the client offered

173

transportation. I sank into the soft, cushioned comfort and remembered his errand. "What did the telegram say?"

"About what I expected, but we must not theorize ahead of the facts."

"Really, Holmes, I should have the same information you have in order to solve the curse of Barcombe Keep."

"We need to keep an open mind. With this information, I fear that you would veer toward a solution. Indeed, your mind might be forced to that conclusion."

I was irritated with him. "And yours is not?"

He snorted but did not deign to reply. I was not the one believing in curses. We fell into an uncomfortable silence.

The night was dark and the hour was late when we reached the door of Barcombe Keep, a hulking stone-and-plaster house. Except for the entrance, it appeared to be primarily half-timbered Tudor trim and mullioned windows. I expected to see arrow slits but later, in the morning light, some windows proved to be wide with views of the lake and wood, thanks to the partial Palladianizing.

The heavy door swung open to a large room with paneling painted in grand scenes from mythology divided by marble pilasters. The butler, Jayson, saw to our cases and coats.

Holmes asked him if he was on duty when the three falls occurred. "Yes, sir. It was my misfortune to find them."

"All three of them?" I asked.

"All of them. I won't be forgetting for a long time."

He showed us where all had been found on the marble floor. "All but the present Lord Northington. He managed to catch the banister rungs and stop himself about halfway, giving his ankle a nasty wrench."

"Did you see anything that might have caused these falls?"

"It was dark. The small lamp by the door were the only light. His Lordship gave orders after his fall to keep the room lighted at night."

I noted several small lampstands that had been placed about the room to cast their light upward, but the great chandelier had not been lit.

"Everyone in the household is using the servants' stairway for now, until this curse is lifted." He gave Holmes a meaningful look. I hoped that no one expected Holmes to do *that* job. No matter what Holmes said about believing in curses, I was sure he was here to solve what may have been two murders and an attempted murder.

After being told that we would see Lord and Lady Northington in the morning, we were shown to our rooms by the housekeeper, Mrs. Boone, who was nervous when Holmes insisted on using the deadly stairs. He went ahead and the maid and footman with our bags had to follow. I was behind him. We held onto the smooth banister and took each step carefully up the curving stairs. I don't know what Holmes expected. A banshee to rush screaming at us? The ghost of the hanged Roundhead to push us backwards.

As I rounded the curve I saw the maid, clearly terrified, turning her head from one side of the stairs to the other and the nervous footman looking behind him on every tread?

"The curse appears to be specific to the Northingtons," Holmes said over his shoulder. "You have nothing to worry about."

That did nothing to alleviate their fears. The maid gasped as the footman gulped.

We reached the upstairs hall without mishap and were shown to our suite, where a welcome light repast awaited us on trays in a sitting area between rooms.

It was now ten o'clock. I anticipated an early turn-in, but it was not to be. Holmes ate half of his meal and then chided me to finish up.

"Surely you don't expect anything to happen on our arrival."

"Indeed, I expect just that. The entities responsible for the accidents will not expect us to be ready for an incident."

I hastily swallowed the last of my tea. "Nothing's happened so far." I gave Holmes a look and removed my coat preparatory to getting more comfortable when we heard a scream. Holmes grabbed a lamp as we rushed into the dark hall. I raced after him, expecting to see a twisted figure lying at the bottom of the stairs.

Instead, we confronted a woman, her face contorted as she stared at a figure slowly turning at the end of a rope hanging above the stairwell from an upper bannister.

As her cry soared over the scene, I took her by the shoulders. Her hands grasped my shirt. I should have grabbed my coat before leaving our rooms, but this was an emergency. Propriety was of little import in the face of terror. "It's all right now. You're safe."

My words failed to comfort her. A fresh scream burst forth. She seemed not to see me.

"Madame, I am a doctor. Please pull yourself together."

"Is it my husband?" she rasped out, her throat no doubt hoarse from the effort.

"Decidedly not." Holmes had put down the lamp. He had found a cane somewhere and used it to attempt to hook the figure's feet.

"Then who?" the woman cried out.

"No one living," Holmes said.

The woman slid down in a faint. I caught her before she hit the floor.

"See to her, Watson. She will be Helene, Brother Gerald's wife. I have work to do."

"But who is the hanged man?"

"No one."

Doors opened along the hall as the Northingtons straggled out in dressing gowns and the servants rushed down the back stairs.

Jayson and Mrs. Boone, the housekeeper, were in dressing gowns as well, but their hair was not rumpled like the maids and footmen.

Only Lord Northington was absent because of his injury.

Mrs. Boone ushered everyone into a nearby empty bedroom while I carried the fainting woman to a sofa along one wall of the hallway. A maid brought tincture of lavender. Several sniffs of it brought her around.

"Keep her warm," I told the maid.

I made my way into Lord Northington's room, where I introduced myself. He seemed like a likeable fellow, quite irritated with being forced to recover in bed. His wife explained the event to her husband while I ascertained that his Lordship was unhurt, in case he was supposed to be the intended victim while everyone else was lured out to the hall. It would not be the first time that we had encountered such a ruse, but he was as well as could be expected following his recent accident. I returned to the scene on the stairs.

Holmes and Jayson directed two footmen, one with a knife to cut the rope, and the other below to catch the figure hanging from it.

The footman sliced the rope and the body fell on the footman. He yelped and disentangled himself from it.

I descended the stairs to study the victim.

The footman laid the body on the floor and stepped back, ready to be of service but staying as far away as he could go while still remaining in the hall. "He's . . . he's – " babbled the young man.

"A man," I said. "Why are people afraid of dead bodies? They are the safest beings on the planet. They can no longer hurt anyone.

I reached to turn him over. The body was surprisingly light as it rotated, and I recoiled at the dreadful rictus facing us. I'd seen the horrors of war, but never anything this grotesque.

"I told you, Watson, it is no one. It is a guy – just clothes stuffed with what looks like old sheets."

"Beg pardon, sir," the younger footman said. "Them looks like the gardener's clothes,"

"Indeed." The face was limned with charcoal. Its mouth was drawn back to show huge teeth. The eyes bulged, the nostrils flared. It was hideously ugly.

"Show this linen stuffing to the maids and see if they have any knowledge of it." Holmes unbuttoned the coat and trousers to reveal the bunched-up sheeting. Jayson took it from him. I noticed that he was wearing gloves.

We went into the Northingtons' room to check on their condition. Holmes introduced himself and, finding that all was well, we returned to own suite..

"What are you thinking?" I asked.

"I'm thinking this is a complicated case that will be revealed as simple."

"You said that before. Do you still believe in the curse?"

"Of course. Look to your shirt, Watson." He went into his room.

What did he mean by that? I had removed my coat earlier, but when the screams began had not stopped to don my dressing gown. I looked at myself in the mirror and discovered smudges on the white cloth. I concluded that they must have got there when I examined the guy.

I retired then, but sleep did not come soon. I was baffled by Holmes's continued insistence in his belief in curses.

Morning brought knowledge that the sheets were from the mending room. I joined Holmes as he questioned the staff. The rope was from the barn, and could have been picked up by anyone at any time. The knot was common and revealed nothing. The rough clothes, including the worn boots, were from the gardener. At his cottage, the man's wife, a plump woman with serious grey eyes, said that she hadn't noticed any missing garments but they might have been taken at any time from the clothesline behind the cottage. The boots were kept in an outside box.

"I telt 'im dinna be traipsing yer mucket boots on me clean flaer," she explained. "Leave yer clarty boots outside, I likes ma flaers ta be clean."

"Quite right," I said. "Cleanliness is important."

She looked at me for a second. "If you sayin, sir."

I had no answer for her, and we took ourselves back to the house after a walk around the gardens and a smoke.

Later in the morning, Holmes talked to the members of the family. Helene was the thin blond with an aristocratic nose and blue eyes who had found the guy. When she smiled, which was rare on this grey day, winsome dimples flashed in her cheeks.

"I left my room last night to see how my sister-in-law was feeling after her journey to London. I have ze premonition something was to happen. I worried and wanted to see if she needed anything for the night. I didn't want her to venture onto ze stairs."

She spoke with a faint trace of a French accent. I had a feeling she clung to it because it set her apart from the English.

"A bit of French snobbery, eh, Watson?" Holmes said later.

"Possibly. I have noticed this affectation before."

"Last night," Holmes said, "Brother Gerald had already retired to their rooms at the far side of the house. When he responded to the screams of his wife, he wore a dressing gown over his night clothes. In all the household, only Helene was still in her mourning dress. Do you not find that strange, Watson?"

"Not if she were going to check on her sister-in-law. It makes perfect sense to me. She felt something was about to happen. She remained dressed in case she needed something from another part of the house."

"Why did she have this premonition, do you think?"

"People have them. My great-aunt always knew when a family member had died."

Holmes steepled his fingers, an indication that he was thinking. "Yes. Premonitions sometimes can be convenient."

We spoke to the staff. Everyone, including the butler, was convinced that the curse was still in effect. The curse remover had only thwarted it briefly, and they were certain it would strike again any time now.

"Could be wunna us," a kitchen maid called Daisy said, her eyes wide with excitement and fear as she plucked at her apron.

The servants didn't feel themselves exempt from the curse. "Stands to reason donnit?" said the footman. "The guy was a warning to us," he explained. "He were dressed like us and stuffed with sheets ironed in the laundry. Clear as a picture."

We retired to the library to speak to remaining family members.

Gerald, the younger brother, came in from riding, explaining that nothing could keep him off his horse except foul weather. He was smaller and less well-formed than his Lordship. "That confounded curse!" He slapped his leg with the riding crop. "All those centuries without mishap and suddenly my uncle's lack of belief in it caused it to attack. And my cousin's as well. Like they were daring it."

"It couldn't have been someone with a grudge against the family?" I asked to steer him in a different direction.

He brushed off the suggestion. "I know of no one. My uncle was a kind man, well-liked in the valley. The only hate ever evidenced toward the family was from the Roundhead who cursed us."

"That was over two centuries ago."

He bowed his head in acceptance. "A curse is a curse."

"What do you make of him?" Holmes asked me when we were alone.

"He, like everyone else here, believes in that curse."

"Yes. Very much so."

"I don't know why you are so enthralled by it. We know very well a curse didn't cause those falls. And it didn't cause that guy to hang from the stairwell."

"How do you know that, Watson?"

"Because that was real rope, real clothes belonging to the gardener, sheets from the sewing room, and a face drawn on by a human using charcoal. Those are facts, not superstition."

"You are correct. They are tangible facts."

"I'm glad you agree with me."

"But who is to say that a curse didn't *cause* it to happen?"

"Really, Holmes. You are not treating this case seriously."

"Am I not?"

We fell silent, until Lady Northington came to the library, questioning whether she should arrange for an exorcism.

"I am neither clergy nor an exorcist, my Lady."

"It would make the servants feel more comfortable," she said.

"And then if something else happens, they will feel more afraid, as if there is nothing to be done. I think you don't want that to happen."

"I do not. I see what you mean. The curse remover didn't work. Since none of the family were on the stairs, the servants now think the curser caused the guy to happen."

"Do you believe this, your Ladyship?"

She bowed her head. "I don't know what to believe."

"Stay in your room and avoid the stairway," Holmes said. "The curse seems only able to operate there."

After she left, I chided him. "Surely you know you are dealing with murder here."

"A curse is a curse, Watson, as Gerald said."

By noon a drizzling rain darkened the day. Holmes and I dined in our sitting room. This might have been construed as rude, but Holmes had told everyone to keep to their rooms. The family avoided all stairs while the servants scurried around in pairs using only the back stairs, and as little as possible.

Holmes and I ate silently, listening to the patter of rain until he folded his serviette and slid it into the silver ring engraved with the Northington coat of arms. I had just done the same when a knock sounded at the door.

"Enter," Holmes said.

Lady Northington rushed into the room, her face pink with the exertion. "Oh, Mr. Holmes, I've solved the case. Jenny, my maid, just told me that the gardener's wife was a Beedles before she married."

"Calm yourself, your Ladyship," I said.

179

"Jenny is mistaken," Holmes said. "Her maiden name was not Beedles, *but Peebles*. She is from Scotland, as is her husband."

"All the best gardeners are," I said. "Even in this foul weather, I can tell the work of a master gardener." I was loath to put blame on the man. "It would hardly be a trick of the gardener to make a guy out of his own clothing and boots."

"I guess not. I will have to stop Jenny before she tells the others."

"She was quick to blame Peebles," Holmes remarked when she had returned to her rooms.

I laughed. "She would be hard put to find a better gardener. My guess is that she is clutching at straws. Peebles and Beedles may sound similar to one not accustomed to a Scot accent."

"Yes, she no doubt is. She's desperate to get this business cleared up as I am before there is another death."

While I didn't see that he was doing anything useful, I knew from past experience not to push. Much of his method was related to fierce thinking and smoking his pipe. I hadn't seen him with the latter. Maybe this case was more than could be measured in pipes.

That afternoon, we were in for a surprise when the middle brother, Frederick, unexpectedly returned from Burma. He sent for us as soon as he learned of the events of the weekend, and last night's occurrence on the stairs. Holmes and I hastened to the library where he awaited us.

He was about thirty, as erect a young man as one would expect from an army officer. He was casually dressed in trousers and soft coat. He stood against the fireplace, one arm leaning on the mantel. Like his brothers, he had dark hair and eyes.

"So you are Sherlock Holmes. I have heard of you. Word gets around. Even in Burma."

"This is my colleague, Dr. John Watson, late of the Berkshires.

Northington inclined his head. "Nasty business, Maiwand."

I returned his nod. "It was that."

"You didn't just arrive from overseas," said Holmes. "My information is that you arrived back from Burma several weeks ago – just before your cousin's death, as a matter of fact. Why the delay in visiting your family?"

"There is a certain young lady I desired to see. And then I spent a bit of time in Aldershot."

Holmes nodded as if he had known all of it previously.

When we were alone, he admitted he had already confirmed the whereabouts of the middle brother from the one of the telegrams that he received at the station upon our arrival. "He was as he said, visiting a lady and after that in Aldershot. The army keeps up with its officers on leave."

"This, then was the information that you withheld from me so that I wouldn't be predisposed to suspect him. He could have been responsible for the murder in a few weeks ago, as well as last night's folderol."

"He could have been, but he wasn't. And I would hardly call what happened last night 'folderol'. More like a desperate play to provoke a reaction. In any case, I believe that I now have all the information necessary. We must now seek confirmation. Now let us have a nap so as to be ready to end this curse."

"And solve the murders," I added.

"Those, too."

As the afternoon waned, the rain hardened to flinty chips that fell with a staccato rhythm. After a light repast, we settled down in front of the fire in our sitting room. I dozed and I assumed that Holmes did as well, though every time I jerked awake he was staring into the flames. At about half-past-nine, he arose.

"It is time."

"Time for what? For the curse to strike again?"

"Yes, I think exactly that. Come, we must conceal ourselves. And bring your Webley."

He strode to the door and opened it silently. I pocketed my revolver.

In the darkened hall, Holmes insisted we wrap ourselves in a pair of dark traveling rugs that we'd brought to our rooms earlier that afternoon, in order to blend into the shadows. The lamp in the hall had burned out, and none of the servants seemed to have wanted to attend to it at this hour. I made myself small behind a chair with a view of the stairs. Holmes concealed himself in the shadow of a large chest from a previous century.

Outside, the storm worsened, striking with howling wind, thunder, rain, and flashing lightning. If there was a curse, this would be the time that it would appear. The noise would cover the sound of any movement. The darkness would cloak nefarious activity.

At half-past-ten, the storm settled down somewhat but every now and then it renewed its frenzy. It was a night to be tucked into a warm bed, not lurking in a lord's hallway. The floor was hard. Our positions were cramped. A clock somewhere in the vast reaches of the house chimed eleven times.

Sometime before midnight, a dark hooded shape entered the hall where Holmes and I waited. I couldn't tell if it were man, woman, or wraith as it glided down several steps and bent to some task. I couldn't see what the task was but it did the same on the left and right side of the step.

The shape straightened and continued down the stairs and out of our sight.

A door opened and closed somewhere among the multitude of bedrooms in the ancient house and a tall erect figure strode down the hall in the direction of the stairs. It was, I ascertained from his movements, Frederick.

As the figure neared us, Holmes rose from his concealment and put his hand on its arm.

Frederick, trained in eastern warfare where a breath could mean your last one, didn't make a sound. Holmes whispered something in his ear and Frederick nodded.

He started down the stairs, and had only taken a few steps before he tripped, letting out a yell as he fell to the floor below and lay unmoving. As I started to go to Frederick, Holmes directed my attention to a small dark figure ascending the stairs. We backed into a shadow. The figure stepped around Frederick's body and bent to one side and then the other at the fifth stair from the top.

"Your Webley!" Holmes whispered. .

I pulled it from my pocket. "Halt or I'll shoot!" I cried. My voice sounded loud in a sudden lull in the storm.

At the same time Frederick rose from the stair where he had been lying. The figure before me uttered a moan as Frederick grasped its arm.

"Do not attempt to faint again, Madame," Holmes said.

Behind me, he lit a lantern and set it on the chest. Frederick flicked the hood off the figure and I found myself staring down at Helene. In her hands she held a gossamer strip of fabric which had been tied to the banisters on each side of the stair.

"Helene!" Frederick said in horror at what his sister-in-law had tried to do to him, along with the realization of what she must have done to his uncle and cousin, and to have attempted on his brother.

Her name was echoed by her husband, Gerald, when the rest of the household, hearing Frederick's cry, came on the run, including Lord Northington, walking with the assistance of his wife and the aid of a cane.

"Why did you do it, Helene?" Lady Northington said.

"I should be the countess!" she hissed at her sister-in-law.

"We were fond of you," replied our client, aghast. "You killed two members of our family. You tried to kill my husband, and tonight his brother."

"You do not know what it's like to be a poor relation! To have no home!"

"You had a home here," Lord Northington said, looking lordly in his burgundy dressing gown with the crest on the pocket as he leaned on his cane.

"It is *your* home!" She spat the words at him. "I wanted my own!"

"No," Holmes said, "You wanted his Lordship's home, and you didn't care how many you killed to get it."

Lord Northington looked at his younger brother, Gerald. "Were you part of her schemes?"

Gerald shook his head, looking dazed and shocked. He denied knowing anything about his wife's activities, even as the rest of the servants crowded into the hall from above stairs.

"I have found no evidence to implicate him," said Holmes. "His wife procured the clothing and made the hanged guy. Mrs. Peebles told me she often came by with suggestions for the garden as if she were the lady of the manor. She would have known that the gardener's boots were never allowed in the house, and when the washing was hung on the line behind the cottage. She could have procured sheets during a nighttime ramble. It was simple to tie the cloth across the stairs and send notes to her victims, then retrieve and destroy them while the household was in disarray. Did you not get one asking you to meet your brother in the library?" Holmes asked Frederick

"I did. I thought it odd under the circumstances, but thought maybe he wanted to speak to me in confidence away from others."

Holmes nodded. "Exactly what she wanted you to think. The library was chosen because it's near the accursed stairway. You wouldn't have used the servants' stairs."

"It might have worked if Holmes hadn't been on the premises with his finger on the pulse of the household," I said.

Frederick almost shivered, but managed to keep himself under control.

"I don't know if you were involved in these murders or not," his Lordship told Gerald, "but I don't want you at Barcombe Keep. You must leave on the morrow. Keep your wife locked in her bedchamber tonight. I'll send for the police then."

"I shall sleep in my dressing room. I swear I did not know what she was doing," Gerald said. "I thought she was visiting friends in April and earlier this month."

"She was impersonating a maid and committing murder," Holmes said, "but it is possible that you didn't know. Not every spouse realizes that he or she is living with a cold killer."

Gerald took his wife's arm in a firm grasp and led her away.

Jayson sent the servants back to their rooms. They were puzzled and confused. "Do that mean there ain't no curse?" one of the footman asked.

"It does indeed," the butler assured him.

His Lordship thanked Holmes and me. Holmes inclined his head. "Just to be safe, keep your doors locked tonight."

"How did you know it was Helene," I asked him when we were alone.

"Your shirt told me."

"My shirt? How is that possible?"

"When we found her, after she had screamed at supposedly discovering the guy, she grasped your white shirt. Remember that I told you it was dirty? She'd had no time to clean the charcoal from her hands from constructing and hanging the guy. When you rushed to her aid, your shirt was clean – I had just seen it. She had the misfortune of encountering a gentleman *sans* coat coming to her rescue. The marks wouldn't have been noticeable on the dark fabric of a coat, or even a dressing gown."

No doubt everyone slept better knowing the curse was a lady – all but that particular lady. By morning the storm had ended, leaving a drenched valley with many downed tree limbs. After a subdued breakfast, we heard a cry outside.

"Your Lordship! Come quickly!"

It was the gardener. The members of the family and the household poured out of Barcombe Keep. A groom brought a trap for Lord and Lady Northington. The rest of us trailed it down the long drive where some of the groundskeepers were gathered around a soaked bundle of clothing.

I stepped forward and examined the clothing that contained the remains of Helene, felled by a huge limb from a giant oak.

Holmes examined the surrounding ground, but the rain had washed away any footprints or other clues. Only the groundskeeper's footprints were visible walking toward the body and then away.

The coroner was called, but Holmes and I left before he arrived, after a word with his Lordship.

"I shall tell the coroner my sister-in-law went for a walk early this morning and a limb must have fallen as she passed under it. She was in the habit of walking early."

"That part is true," Holmes said, "though I suspect she left on her walk soon after we retired last night."

"It was a most unfortunate accident," his Lordship said. "You understand?"

"Indeed," I said. The three of us looked at each other but did not voice our thoughts.

"Perhaps a remittance is in order for your younger brother. I hear Australia is lovely this time of year," Holmes said.

"I shall see to it – a change of hemispheres as a balm to the bereaved."

I wasn't sorry to leave the formerly accursed Barcombe Keep behind us. We boarded the train for London and settled ourselves. As we pulled away from the station, I opened a journal that I had brought for the return journey.

"It was just as I told you," Holmes remarked.

"And that was?"

"A complicated case that proved to be simple."

I looked up. "How can complicated be simple?"

"It was a complicated case involving the use of an old legend to cover a series of murders. But it was a simple case of murderous greed by a small woman who might never have been suspected if only she had waited to commit the next murders. Frederick's return stirred her to act precipitately, and she decided to try and kill him last night as well, before he could return to Burma. Otherwise, she would have targeted Lady Northington next. Then she would have made arrangements so that the Lordship's mourning would apparently lead to his suicide caused by grief. Frederick would have been dealt with sometime after that, leaving her husband, Gerald, as the eventual possessor of the estate."

"I say, Holmes, you sound like a murderer."

"Not I, Watson, but I have to think the way they do to catch them. I must say, Helene is one of the more cold-blooded woman that I've encountered."

He gazed out the window at the sodden landscape as we passed by.

I remembered the small figure of the murderess. So innocent-looking with those yellow curls, those dimples, those clear blue eyes.

One more aspect of the case needed clearing up.

"Tell me – is there any time that you've ever believed in a curse?"

"Indeed, I have."

I was skeptical. He had to be pulling my leg, but there was no hint of humor in his austere face and penetrating eyes. "How is that possible, when we've just seen that the curse was engineered by that murderess?"

"I believe that curses can be laid, so that the effects ripple through the real actions of men and women. I don't believe that something supernatural causes things to happen, but sometimes, if the cursed is a believer, it can seem as if the curse is real. Amongst primitive peoples, a curse is often a death sentence simply because the victim believes it to be so."

"Most of the inhabitants at Barcombe Keep believed in it."

"They did, but the curse was only directed at the Northington family, so that the others, such as the staff, were safe from its clutches."

"You knew all along the human factor was at work."

"Of course. But if the subjects believe in the curse, it can be as deadly as a poison dart. In this case, the dart was a bit of gossamer stretched across the stairs."

185

"What about the guy? Why something that was so obviously constructed by a human hand?"

"Yes, that was a mistake, but I think that Helene did it to show the curse was still in effect following the curse remover's visit and his Lordship's escape. It served its purpose. The servants now had something tangible to frighten them, and the family was shaken as well."

"Why would she do it? Surely it was impossible to think that she could get away with it."

"She stated her reason: She wanted to be the countess. She had three more to kill before she could reach her goal, and then her husband would become the Lord of the Manor."

"Three? Lord Northington and Frederick. Who was the third?"

"Lady Northington."

"Why? She cannot inherit the title."

"No, but the child she is expecting would, if it's a boy."

I stared at him. "How do you know that?"

"Simple deduction, my dear Watson." He crossed his arms and smiled at me.

"What kind of doctor am I? I didn't even suspect."

"Come, come. You didn't miss anything. I spoke to her cabby while you took notes upstairs in Baker Street and, for a hot cuppa and one of Mrs. Hudson's excellent scones, he told me the traffic that morning in Harley Street was thick as thieves. Her Ladyship had obviously been to a consultation."

"And that's why you asked Mrs. Hudson for ginger biscuits. Ginger would be a restorative."

We were quiet contemplating the events of the last two days.

"Do you think Gerald was involved in the scheme?" I ventured.

"It is a possibility that the other Northingtons must always consider. I think they believe that he killed Helene. I saw bruises on her throat, but with that great limb and its branches, proof would be impossible either way. The family will certainly be safer with him in the Antipodes."

"There's plenty of scope for criminal activity down there," I said.

"The family will bury her at The Keep and hope she and Gerald will be forgotten."

No doubt she has been forgotten by all but a few who tell chilling stories in the night. And by me, recounting the story these many years later. I remember most vividly my shock at the thought that Sherlock Holmes believed in supernatural curses. I was relieved to learn his cool rational intellect was still extant.

The Affair of the Regressive Man
by David Marcum

Part I: A Short Series of Deaths
Rooted in the Past

Sherlock Holmes's investigations were never as limited in real life as those presented in my published versions, wherein the beginning and middle lead to a resolved ending. Instead, we would occasionally hear more of former clients, sometimes arriving on our doorstep with a new problem, or presenting some aspect of continuation to their original investigation.

The matter which I will now recount seemed to be routine when it occurred – if a matter of murders can ever be called that. And yet, there was a loose end that led to a most unusual epilogue, and possibly the strangest story that was ever narrated to us in our Baker Street rooms. It resulted in our remaining awareness of this case even to the present, and while I consider it to be the merest moonshine, I would be remiss if I didn't make some record of it, although it will rest in my dispatch box like so many others, as one of those for which the world is not yet prepared.

The audience laughed, as did I, at the antics of the commanding figure upon the stage. The play was clearly a success, with the promise of a long run, and I was glad that we'd received tickets – however mysteriously that they had been sent to us. Once again the audience reacted with great amusement as the lead actor, in his role as Petruchio, twisted the ears of Grumio, his manservant. Clearly this interpretation of *The Taming of the Shrew* was intended to emphasize physical humor in addition to the clever plot.

As the business continued on stage, to the immense pleasure of those around me, I glanced toward my left to see that my friend, Sherlock Holmes, was not sharing the same sentiment as those surrounding him. I wondered if he, with his great knowledge and experience with the works of The Bard, had some objection to the presentation, or if he was still vexed by the manner in which we found ourselves at the Lyceum that night.

That afternoon we'd received a sealed envelope, delivered by a messenger that we knew slightly from a previous matter. It simply had our names written on the front, with no other information provided, and contained two tickets to that evening's performance. It was quite puzzling, I knew, but I felt fortunate, as this was the most popular event in town at present. While I understood that it was possible that we were being lured to the theatre for some sinister purpose, I also felt that we had simply been gifted with the tickets by a former grateful client who wished to remain anonymous.

Holmes had been intrigued as well, and any suspicion that there might be an ulterior motive was simply one more reason for him to elect to attend. And yet, now that we were here and the play had begun, I saw that he wasn't going to allow himself to simply enjoy the performance. Rather, he was even more alert and watchful than usual.

That evening, as we were conveyed by hansom from our Baker Street rooms to the theatre in Wellington Street, his lips had been pursed, and I had initially taken it for simply a peevish mood. "They are billing this as the three-hundredth anniversary of the play," he'd said, in a rather irritated tone, "but there is no evidence that it was actually written as early as 1888. It's much more likely to have been initially performed in the early 1590's."

"Leave it to Irving to discover an unusual aspect that will sell tickets," I said, rather feebly, not knowing how else to respond. "There's talk of him receiving a knighthood, you know." When this elicited no response, I tried a different tack. "The reviews have been tremendous. This actor playing Petruchio – Myrddin, I think is his name. Sounds Welsh. – has seemingly appeared out of nowhere, and they say that he *becomes* the part – an amazing skill for one so young. And Jenny Sheridan, who plays Katherina, brings an amazing reputation with her back to England from all those years spent in America." I faded away for good, as I saw that Holmes wasn't listening.

Now, as I considered this, I wondered if I had let myself sink into the performance just a bit too easily. Perhaps, like Holmes, I should watch and enjoy, but observe a bit as well.

On stage, there was a long bit of dialogue between Hortensio, Grumio, and Gremio, while Petruchio stood a step or two away. I noticed that his attention seemed to be elsewhere, as if he were listening to another conversation instead of the one directly before him, which should be claiming his full attention. I found it rather distracting, and wondered if this was a choice that he had made as a performer. If so, I decided that it was a poor one from an actor who had been so fulsomely praised by the critics.

Just in that short time my mind had wandered, I had lost the rhythm of the actors' quickly paced lines, and leaned forward a bit, listening more intently, trying to find my way back. Grumio was saying, "O this learning, what a thing it is!" when I heard a woman scream.

188

We all heard it, as a matter of fact. It was muffled but shrill, and came from somewhere backstage. It was unmistakable, and the actor speaking seemed to physically stumble for a second as his voice lowered and then paused. Then he tried to resume his lines, but stopped again after only a few words. A couple of people in the audience twittered nervously from different parts of the house, for the scream had been so unexpected, and so very real. I knew that nothing like this was written into the play, but many productions chose to add unusual aspects to make their version different. Perhaps the Shrew was meant to be heard screaming off-stage. But no – this was clearly unplanned, as the actors suddenly lost character and appeared to be nonplussed.

I looked from right to left, noting the confusion on a number of faces in the audience. Holmes was sitting forward on his seat, as was I, his expression like that of a hound about to be released for the hunt.

The curtains at the right side of the stage billowed and moved, in that curious way that they do when someone behind them is trying to find his or her way onto the stage and cannot locate the correct space. Then a middle-aged woman – decidedly in modern dress and not representing sixteenth-century Verona – stepped out and peered toward the audience, her eyes nearly squint shut. "A doctor," she said, her voice low and hopeless. "Is there a doctor?"

At that point, Petruchio – or rather, the actor playing him – took a step forward and seemed to look directly toward me. "Dr. Watson," he called in a commanding voice, to my great surprise. And then, "Mr. Holmes. You are both needed. Please come backstage."

Without a second thought, Holmes was on his feet. Since he would have to pass by me to reach the aisle, I stood as well, although my thoughts were still vainly trying to catch up with the events that were unfolding. Together, he and I approached the stage and, finding the entryway to the right, went up the short set of steps and into that mysterious and decidedly unromantic area that is the backstage of a theatre.

After the brightly lit stage, supposedly representing a sunny plaza in Verona, the darkness behind it required a moment of adjustment. I had been backstage before at many theatres over the years, sometimes as part of Holmes's investigations, and other times on my own business, so I wasn't surprised, either by the shabby spaces filled with props, the hanging flats and myriad ropes running up into the darkness, or the smell of slightly unwashed bodies and makeup suddenly clustered around us, mixing with the general odor of the building – a cellar-like smell, augmented with the scents of canvas, paint, and freshly cut wood.

We were caught up short by the crowd of people, and as my eyes adjusted, I could see that they were various cast and crew members who had apparently been standing in the wings, watching the performance. To my left the bright lights of the stage were visible, with the four actors and the woman standing there, peering in our direction. Even as I looked that way, I saw the great curtain beginning to swing shut, cutting off the audience's view. Turning back toward the dark recesses of the theatre, I was aware that the mutterings of the seated crowd became more muted when the curtain closed.

A tall man stepped forward and the crowd of actors and stage hands parted around him. Gesturing us forward, he said, "I'm Grimley, the stage manager. Are you the police?"

Holmes shook his head. "I am Sherlock Holmes, and this is my associate, Dr. Watson. We were called forward from the stage by one of the actors – "

"I've heard of you," the man interrupted. He was tall and thin, with thick wild eyebrows combed upwards across his forehead. He was blessed or cursed with unusually broad and prominent cheekbones. He had an excessive amount of Macassar oil on his head, laying his hair straight back and giving him a rather Mephistopheleseian appearance. "This way."

Holmes glanced at me with a curiously amused expression. I knew what he was thinking – how quickly life could turn.

We were led deeper into the building, to the row of dressing rooms. One with a star affixed crookedly on the door had a large stagehand standing in front. Grimley waved him aside and threw open the door.

From the wafting smell of perfume that rolled our way, it was easy to determine that this was a woman's room. That was confirmed by the view through the door of various gowns and related accoutrements and appurtenances tossed about – on the backs of chairs, on stands, and on the floor. However, all of this was of no significance when compared to the body of the woman slumped in a chair before a dressing table.

After knowing Sherlock Holmes for so many years, and having been involved in the examination of so many scenes of violence – both in association with my friend's investigations, as well as sometimes doing occasional work for Scotland Yard as a part-time police surgeon – I was well aware of the importance of causing no disturbance to any of the evidence. And yet, my oath as a physician required that I step forward to ascertain whether any signs of life could be coaxed from the poor woman's body. I stepped carefully into the room, aware that my movements could obliterate some fingerprint or speck of ash that might provide Holmes with the solution to the mystery. But I had no choice.

I leaned over the woman, but it was immediately clear that she was beyond my aid. There was no pulse and the pupils of her open eyes were fixed and dilated with that flat sheen on their surface that only manifests itself for the dead. Her skin was cool, and clearly the scarf knotted around her neck was so tight that the end had come quickly.

She had been beautiful once, but the bloom, as they say, was rather off the rose. Up close, it was easy to see that Jenny Sheridan – and it was certainly her, the famous actress who had traveled from England to America as a girl, finding fame and fortune, only to now return in triumph to the long-abandoned land of her birth before encountering a violent death – had known that her beauty was fading. Her hair was just a little too black, and her make-up – even for the stage – was a trace too thick.

I moved back with a shake of my head, and Holmes carefully shifted forward. He seemed to waste very little time on the corpse, other than to look closely at her face, hands, and clothing. He did examine the knotted handkerchief at her throat, and made a soft exclamation at something he discovered in her tightly curled right hand. Then he turned his attention to the floors and strewn items around her.

I don't know how much time passed, but surely not a great deal. It seemed almost immediate that there was a rustle of shifting bodies outside the dressing room, and then the door was filled with our old friend, Inspector Bradstreet. It was no surprise to see him, as he was normally located just a few blocks north at the Bow Street Police Station.

Holmes straightened at that moment, a look of disgust on his face. "Bah! Too many people in and out, all of them but the killer having legitimate business, most likely. There's no easy way to determine who the murderer might have been." He glanced toward the newcomer. "Good to see you again, Inspector. I thought that you'd have been around to Baker Street by now regarding that Haverley business."

"Planned to at the first of the week, Mr. Holmes."

"Let me save you a trip. Confront the groom about the house in Cavenagh Street – specifically the mews. Don't act as if you don't know – let him believe that you already have the whole story."

Bradstreet nodded. "That makes sense. I know just how to handle it." He stepped forward. "What's this, then? Is that Jenny Sheridan? I was here for a performance not a week ago."

"It is indeed. She's returned from America to meet a bad end." He looked toward the door. "Do you have any help?"

"I do," nodded Bradstreet. "Knowing that it's a theatre job, I brought a full passel of constables, and Inspector Jones is on hand as well. He's with the audience, making a list of names and finding out what they saw or heard, and if anything was strange on that side of the footlights."

"An excellent task for him," smiled Holmes.

At that time, March 1888, it was still several months before I would formally meet Inspector Athelney Jones, so Bradstreet's grin at Holmes's comment held no significance for me.

Bradstreet nodded. "What do we know?" he asked.

"Not much. During the early part of the performance, there was a scream. Then a woman came on stage and asked for a doctor. Watson and I were summoned – by name – by the leading actor. We hadn't been here long when you arrived."

Bradstreet took a moment to examine the body before turning back our way. "I suppose we should question the primaries – although at this point we won't learn a lot, I fear."

Holmes nodded and walked to the door. He opened it, calling, "Mr. Grimley? Come in here."

The stage manager appeared, entered, and shut the door behind him as directed. In the brighter light of the room, he seemed less intimidating and more nervous than in the mysterious shadows behind the stage.

Holmes introduced him to the inspector and then said, "Who discovered the body?"

"Her dresser, Mrs. Wick," was the reply. There was a nervous tremor in his voice. "Jenny – that is, Miss Sheridan . . . ." His eyes cut toward the dead woman – for the first time since he'd entered, I noted. He swallowed noticeably and said "Miss Sheridan was due for her first scene soon."

Holmes frowned. "To your knowledge, did anyone have a reason to kill her?"

"None at all. She's been a delight since her arrival." His words were belied by his tone, which implied that she had been anything but pleasant.

Bradstreet caught it as well. "No need to refrain from speaking ill of the dead," he said. "What did you really think?"

Grimley blew out a breath and seemed to collapse a bit. "She was every bit the shrew that she portrayed on stage. Demanding. Critical. Impatient. Arrogant. Hateful to the others. I regretted that she was chosen for the part, but my advice was ignored."

"You are allowed a vote on such matters, then?" asked Holmes. "Very democratic of Mr. Irving." He looked around. "Where is he, by the way? And his business manager, Mr. Stoker?"

"I am not allowed a vote," said Grimley with a frown, "and they are both out of town. Neither likes to be away, and never at the same time, but they are meeting with a new playwright in York who refuses to travel." He lowered his voice. "I'll never hear the end of this."

It seemed that Bradstreet might have had a few more questions, but Holmes interrupted. "That will be all for now, Mr. Grimley," he said. "If you'll send in Mrs. Wicks."

"Certainly," said the tall man, giving a second and final glance to the dead woman. Then, without further comment, he stepped outside.

"You have an idea, Mr. Holmes?" asked the inspector.

"Nothing definite," he replied. "The room is a mess, but I believe that the dresser, Mrs. Wick, will confirm that to be the normal state of affairs. There is nothing that can be determined from footprints on the floor – too many people have been in and out of here, as would be expected in a leading lady's dressing room."

"No footprints left by Persian slippers of two different sizes this time, eh?" grinned the policeman.

"Sadly, no," replied Holmes with a smile. "Sometimes we aren't that lucky. There is something to be determined however, from the scarf that is tied around her throat, and more importantly, from what she has curled in her left hand."

I hadn't noticed anything there, but reminded myself that I had been more interested in seeking any remaining signs of life. Bradstreet stepped forward and leaned down, reaching to uncurl her fingers. Clutched there was bright golden button.

Bradstreet lifted it to the light, turning it this way and that before handing it to me. It was oversized, constructed from some sort of gilded metal, and looked rather cheap. The stylized figure of a Paladin was stamped into it. I returned it to Bradstreet, and he tucked it into his waistcoat pocket.

Holmes spoke. "The button is from a costume. More about that in a bit. The handkerchief is tied in a common knot, pulled tight while she struggled, and then knotted after when she was still. There is something additionally sinister about the emotion that would cause someone to tie off the scarf when the deed was done, rather than simply carry it away. Please take note of the color."

While Bradstreet and I did so – seeing a dull and vaguely familiar plum hue – there was a knock, and then a constable opened the door to allow a small woman to pass him. She was the same who had fumbled so when trying to get through the stage curtain to announce that a doctor was needed. From my seat in the audience, she'd seemed shaken and distraught, but now she was quite composed, her mouth fixed in a tight scowl that ran along deeply grooved lines, surely set in place by that expression over many unhappy years.

"Mrs. Wick," said Holmes, stepping forward, using a sympathetic tone. "We're so sorry for the loss." When necessary, he could be the most polite of men, especially to women. It often worked to calm them, or gain their confidence – but this one was having none of it.

193

"It means nothing to me," she snapped. "I knew when I met her that she'd come to a bad end. Never satisfied with anything. Always complaining. Always trying to set one person against another, just to keep something stirred up."

I was torn between surprise at her speaking of the dead in such candid terms, especially in the very presence of the recently deceased, and a bit of admiration that she was apparently completely willing to express her mind.

Her accent was of a decided Liverpudlian cast, and I asked, "You are obviously British. Did you know Miss Sheridan previously in America?"

Mrs. Wick shook her head. "Not at all. I was hired two weeks ago, when she arrived here and began rehearsals. Her American dresser had refused to come with her – no surprise, I'm sure."

"Having known her for a fortnight," Holmes interjected, "you seem to have formed a strong opinion."

"Indeed I have. She wasn't ever happy unless there was some kind of trouble going on. Insulting the costumes. Complaining about the food. Turning the men against one another."

"Really," said Holmes with a conspiratorial smile. "How so?"

That seemed to be the key to unlocking her confidences. "She flirted with all of them – from Grimley to Myrddin, to Mr. Irving himself. Of course *he* had no part of it, being smart enough to see through her type, and she realized that she was wasting her time. But she seemed to enjoy teasing Mr. Grimley, who was very interested in her, with all the time she spent with young Mr. Myrddin – and her more than twice his age!"

"And how did Misters Grimley and Myrddin take that?"

"Grimley was angry at first," she replied. "I often saw him watching the two of them from darkness as they would leave together. But about a week ago, she threw over Myrddin and began dropping crumbs to Grimley again. He's followed her like a dog since then – but oh he hated her for it!"

"And what did Mr. Myrddin do when he was supplanted?"

Mrs. Wick looked confused, and Holmes amended his question. "When he was replaced by Mr. Grimley?"

"Truthfully, he didn't seem to care one way or the other – which bothered *her* more than she wanted to let on." And she nodded toward the body.

"Do you have any idea who could have done this?" asked Bradstreet, cutting to the bottom line, like the steadfast policeman he was.

"Not at all," the woman snapped, her willingness to gossip slamming shut.

"You were the one who found her?"

194

"I was. It was time to make sure she was ready for her first entrance."

"You screamed," stated Holmes.

"I did." She said it rather defiantly, as if admitting a weakness. "It's not what one expects to find, is it?"

"Why didn't you find someone backstage to ask for help?" I asked. "Why come out front onto the stage?"

She seemed a bit puzzled. Then, "I knew this lot. There's no one back here who could help. I thought that she might still be alive."

Bradstreet then asked, "Did you see anyone else nearby when you went into her dressing room? Or right after you came out?"

She shook her head. "They were all crowded up front, watching the stage. There's a lot of funny business worked into the part where Petruchio first arrives, and they all like to stand there and watch it. And I suppose a lot of the girls want a look at Corvidien – he takes off his shirt then, you see."

I raised an eyebrow. Clearly the modern interpretation of Shakespeare was different than it used to be.

"Did you see any strangers backstage?"

"Not a one."

At the mention of strangers, Holmes interrupted. "The man at the stage door would know if anyone was here that didn't belong. What is his name?"

"Amos," she said. And then, "He's a drunk. He can't tell you anything."

Holmes nodded toward the door. "Thank you, Mrs. Wick. Would you please have the constable summon Amos?"

She nodded and then took a single step toward the dead woman. She stood for ten or fifteen seconds, just looking, before making an impatient noise like one hears from the lips of a cab horse forced to stand too long in one place. She opened the door and stepped outside.

"Could she have done it?" I asked when the door shut. "She had a reason to be in and out of the dressing room. After the murder, she could have screamed to divert attention, knowing that someone could walk in at any second."

Holmes shook his head. "I doubt it. She's too small to have held the scarf tight enough to kill. If there had been a wound on the head, perhaps, to knock the victim unconscious first, I might have entertained the notion, but as it is . . . ."

"Do you have any ideas yet, Mr. Holmes?" interrupted the inspector.

Holmes shook his head. "These are early days, Bradstreet. But I suspect that before it's over, we'll need to know more about Miss Sheridan."

195

The door opened to reveal Grimley once again, now leading in a shabby old man in worn but clean clothes. He looked as if he would have been tall sometime in his past, but he was now bent and downtrodden. There was a distinct smell of alcohol about him. His hair was shaggy, and he kept his gaze toward the floor as the stage manager stopped him before us.

"This is Amos Lee," he said. "He sits at the stage door." He glanced at the man beside him with distaste. "Mr. Stoker hired him. I thought that I should come along – in case I can help answer any of your questions."

I was uncertain as to why, until the old man lifted his head, revealing a tracheostomy centered at his throat where his Adam's Apple would have been. I had seen a few such patients in my career, left with an opening to breathe when their larynxes had been removed due to various types of cancer. I was surprised that Amos left his uncovered, as most patients chose to mask the open hole to their trachea with a small cloth affixed to their collar.

I glanced to one side, where Holmes looked upon the man's neck with scientific interest, while Bradstreet tried not to look at all.

"Amos, is it?" asked Holmes. The man nodded. "How long have you worked here?"

He held up two fingers, and Grimley translated. "Two months." He sniffed. "He is apparently some sort of veteran with a background in the theatre, and he had a letter of reference for Mr. Stoker. I don't know what it said."

"Very good," replied Holmes. "Did you have any dealings with Miss Sheridan?"

The old man shook his head vigorously. I realized that he'd never once looked toward the body.

"And did you see any strangers backstage tonight?"

Again he shook his head, but not with such intensity.

"If I may," interrupted Grimley. "Amos sits by the back door, but his duties are minimal." He gave a look of frank disgust toward the man beside him. "He . . . falls asleep, you see, and is sometimes derelict in carrying out his responsibilities. Mr. Stoker has been informed about this – " Again he turned toward Amos, to see if his words were having any effect. " – but so far to no avail. Therefore, I've taken to keeping the stage door keys with me, and locking the door during the performances. We've had a problem backstage with petty thefts, you understand, and I don't trust that Amos is the man to make secure the premises."

"You lock the door?" asked Bradstreet, turning his head. "Isn't that a bit dangerous in case there's a fire?"

I knew what he was thinking. He had been with us at the tragic burning of Exeter's Theatre Royal the year before, when scenery, ignited by a gas burner, led to the death of nearly two-hundred people. Holmes, Bradstreet, and I had been there on other business when the fire broke out, and it was only chance that had placed us near the scene. Without Holmes's extreme bravery, leading the panicked people in the theatre to safety through the smoky darkness, and Bradstreet's great strength in prying open the stage door from the outside, the death toll could have been much higher. The true story, involving the facts that Holmes uncovered afterwards, may never be known, but their actions there that night should be.

"Sir," replied Grimley, affronted at Bradstreet's reaction. "We don't discuss that word here. It's bad luck. And in any case, if such a thing *were* to happen, then I would simply make my way to the stage door and unlock it. And that," he added, "will continue to be the procedure until we have a more responsible doorman."

Throughout this castigation, Amos simply stared at the floor without comment. Holmes had been looking at him, certainly cataloging countless details, but I saw nothing more than a broken old man.

"Amos," said Holmes. The old fellow looked up at the sharp tone. "You've let this man speak about you and for you. Do you have any knowledge of the lady's murder?"

Amos did a curious thing. He seemed to be swallowing, his throat working and his mouth open. I had seen this before from others who'd had the same surgery. By literally swallowing air, these people were able to *belch* words. Bradstreet's eyes widened when Amos rattled an emphatic and frog-like, "No!"

With nothing further to apparently be said, Holmes nodded and waved a hand toward the door. Grimley led the old man out.

Bradstreet shook his head. "What to do, gentlemen? There must be hundreds of people out there – "

"Oh, many more than that," interrupted Holmes.

Bradstreet rolled his eyes. "One way or the other, it's too many. Jones may spot something, but we'll likely have to question each and every one, and still we might not turn over the right leaf."

"But lest you forget, Bradstreet," said Holmes with a smile, "we have yet to meet one of the primary players in our little drama – the owner of the button and the handkerchief."

The inspector smiled grimly and said, "Let's do that, then." Holmes stepped to the door, opened it, and said something quietly. In a moment, a constable appeared in the door, ushering in the leading actor, Myrddin. The officer then backed out and pulled the door shut.

197

He was even taller and more broad than he'd appeared on stage. He was quite handsome, and had a most commanding presence for one so young. He was in his mid-twenties, although his eyes seemed older, as if he had seen much that had given him some sort of additional wisdom. Unlike Grimley, who had only looked twice with discomfort toward the dead woman, Myrddin stared frankly at the corpse with no signs of squeamishness. Rather, his expression seemed markedly sad.

However, in spite of the young man's confidence, what was noticeable to both Bradstreet and myself was the fact that his costume contained several pieces that perfectly matched the coloring of the murderous scarf, and missing from his waistcoat was a golden button, seemingly identical to the one found in the dead woman's grasp, if the others were any indication.

The actor looked toward the woman and then back to the three of us, facing him. He shook his head. "A terrible loss," he murmured, his voice deep and rumbling. Like many who have trained for the theatre, he projected clearly even when speaking in soft tones. His voice filled the room in a way that somehow seemed somehow disrespectful.

"We understand," said Holmes, "that you've had a somewhat special relationship with the woman since she arrived here."

Myrddin shook his head. "Nothing so special," he said. "In the theatre, people are simply ships that pass. From what I understand, she has most recently been associated with Mr. Grimley. Perhaps you might turn your attention that way."

"We shall," said Bradstreet, clearly disliking the man. "These is simply a preliminary to the larger investigation." He took a step closer. "Myrddin. That's unusual. What's your first name?"

The man smiled. "I have no other name. No need, really. I find that 'Myrddin' suffices for the present – and isn't living in the moment the secret of life?"

"I'm always looking backwards," said Bradstreet with a small laugh.

"What a coincidence," said the actor. "So am I."

Bradstreet frowned. "I'm certain that somewhere, your real name is recorded – likely along the lines of Ernie Smith, or something similar. Can't blame you for taking a stage name – but you *will* tell us the truth."

He reached toward his waistcoat pocket, and then paused, his fingers resting there. "Where did you lose your button?"

Myrddin didn't bother to look down. "I don't know. I realized that it was missing before the performance – too late to have it repaired. I'd hoped that it would add to the notion that Petruchio is a traveler arriving weary in a new town." He glanced toward the dead woman. "If you ask,

198

there must be a reason. I take it that it was found here? On the floor, perhaps?"

"In her hand," said the inspector, pulling it finally from his pocket. "I believe that it is a match for the others that you're wearing – as is the scarf that killed her, which is clearly another piece of your costume."

Myrddin nodded. "I saw that." He smiled. "It looks bad for me, doesn't it? But I know that it all turns out all right in the end."

His indifferent attitude surprised me, and it irritated Bradstreet. I glanced toward Holmes, who was oddly silent, watching the actor carefully.

"Your accent intrigues me," he said. "I hear traces of London, but there are parts I cannot place."

"I am originally from London. I have traveled a great deal."

"Indeed. And I see that you write a great deal?"

Myrddin smiled again. "You observed this, perhaps, from the rubbing on my cuff?"

"Not at all," replied Holmes. "You are in a costume – nothing could be determined from that. Rather, you have ink stains on your fingers – some quite old, and a lot of them."

The man didn't bother to look at his hand. "So that's it. I thought that you'd made a rather clever deduction."

"And you are a writer?" Holmes asked. "Fiction perhaps? Or plays of your own?"

"Something like that."

"Do you have anything to add," interrupted Bradstreet impatiently, replacing in his pocket the button that he'd twirling in his fingers throughout, "about the murder?"

Myrddin shook his head. "I did not kill this woman." He turned toward my friend. "Mr. Holmes, I assure you that I did not. Please use your powers to clear me."

"Can you then provide any other information that will assist us?" asked Holmes.

"I cannot, other than my belief that this was due to something in Miss Sheridan's past – most likely connected to America."

"And why you think that?" asked Bradstreet.

"It simply seems likely. She has spent her whole adult life there, and she was only here for a few weeks."

That seemed to be enough for Bradstreet. Calling the constable, he had Myrddin taken into custody pending further investigation. When they had gone, he turned to us in a strangely explanatory manner. "I have to hold him," he said. "The button and the scarf. Possibly he's been framed, but that type – those actors – might flee at the drop of a hat."

"Oh, no doubt," said Holmes in a way that indicated he didn't actually agree. "In the meantime, you can continue organizing your data here, while Watson and I pursue a few other paths of interest."

Clearly Bradstreet wanted to ask further questions, but Holmes was obviously and suddenly finished with whatever he hoped to accomplish at the theatre, and ready to move on to something else.

Taking a last look at the dead woman slumped in her chair, and wishing Bradstreet a good evening, I followed Holmes outside. In the hansom back to Baker Street, he made no comments, and after our arrival, he set about sending a number of telegrams before sinking into his chair by the fire, smoking and staring into the distance. I murmured good night and went up to my room.

I had no rest that night, having trouble falling asleep, and then dreaming not of the dead woman, but rather the strange and compelling presence of the actor, Myrddin. As I slept, my mind seemed to see what I had missed while awake – he had an odd manner when questioned, as if he knew much more than he had told. I wondered if his arrest would serve to make him reveal his whole story.

It was very early – a subsequent verification of my clock showed that it wasn't quite six – when I was shaken awake by Holmes. "Hurry, Watson. Bradstreet has sent a cab. There has been another murder."

I knew better than to ask, and sooner than I would have liked, we were rattling back to the Lyceum. Holmes informed me that the cleaning women, who arrive at the theatre quite early indeed, had found a body lying in the center of the stage – Mrs. Wicks, the dresser of the dead actress. Her throat had been cut.

"And," said Holmes, "Bradstreet hinted at a further complication – something that he didn't share in his wire."

The cab pulled up in Exeter Street, at the stage door. A constable met us and then left us to find our own way to the stage. Bradstreet, as well as several other members of the force, were standing around a small body piteously highlighted by the stage lights.

She was staring straight up, with a terrible surprised expression on her face. Except for one great splash across her thin chest, there was surprisingly little blood.

Holmes looked back and forth, an expression of irritation on his face. "There were no footprints, Mr. Holmes," explained Bradstreet without preamble. "At least nothing of note. She was just lying here when the cleaning women turned on the lights. They all clustered around her, as did the passing bobby they called inside."

I could see that Holmes wanted to disagree, believing – and almost certainly correctly – that he would have been able to see some clue. "If you don't mind," he said, and then he proceeded to prowl around, sometimes upright and sometimes on his hands and knees, in ever-widening circles around the corpse. Finally he stood and rejoined us, commenting, "You indicated that there was something unusual."

Bradstreet put a hand in his pocket and withdrew a metallic object that shone in the high lights. "This was wedged in her mouth."

He handed it to Holmes, who looked at it front and back before passing it my way. It was a coin, rather sizeable and solid. Quite worn and faded, much of the imagery was rubbed away over the passing years. On the front was a woman facing to the left, her hair pushed back by a band stating "*Liberty*". The back, much more worn than the front, had the remnants of something at the top that was just readable as ". . . *States of America*", above a shield surrounded by an olive branch and a stalk of grain. The shield contained seven stars at the top, and seven vertical stripes at the boom. Something like a bee-hive capped the shield, while along the bottom were the words "*Twenty Dol.*"

"States. Dollar," I said. "An American has done this thing."

Holmes smiled and shook his head. "In a way. In spite of the initial similarities, this is *not* a United States coin. Rather, it's a twenty-dollar gold piece from the Confederate States of America – the word '*Confederate*' being what's worn away at the top there. The seven stars and the seven stripes represent the seven traitorous states that seceded from the Union 1861. Apparently they were unoriginal enough to come up with coinage that was too different from that of the true United States to the north."

He took back the coin and handed it to Bradstreet, saying, "Of more interest is that it was found in her mouth."

The policeman nodded. "She was trying to blackmail someone."

"The killer," I agreed. This was not the first time that we had encountered a coin left in a victim's mouth.

"I regret this," said Holmes. "I had received several wires very early this morning from America, but chose to wait until daybreak to act. Possibly this could have been prevented."

"I doubt it," said Bradstreet. "She probably didn't wait long at all before approaching the murderer. Clearly she knew more than she told us."

"At least," I said, "this clears Myrddin. He is in jail." I glanced at Bradstreet. "He is, isn't he?"

"Yes," agreed Bradstreet. "In the cells just up the street." He looked at Holmes. "You say that you can put an end to this?"

"I can. Let us proceed to Seven Dials, where all will be revealed."

Bradstreet had a constable go down to the Strand to procure a growler. Then we set off, up Bow Street and then along Long Acre to Mercer Street. There was no activity that early until we passed the brewery, where the workers were beginning to arrive for the day, and deliveries were already going out. The air changed as we crossed Seven Dials – a literal smell of decay and corruption that held even as we continued into nearby Lumber Court. Stopping before a shabby old building, half-collapsed upon itself, I felt a hundred angry eyes upon us from the surrounding dark and broken windows, and was glad that I had brought my service revolver, and also for the presence of the constable who had traveled with us.

As we stepped down, a wiry boy of ten or twelve approached. It was young Edwin Hopper, one of Holmes's more bold Irregulars – a lad who wouldn't have been fearful of spending the night in such a neighborhood. "'E's still here," was his announcement, while cocking a thumb toward the structure behind him. Without further comment, he melted into the shadows, and Holmes led us inside the filthy building, advising us to climb carefully and stealthily to the third floor.

What followed was accomplished without drama. Bradstreet easily forced the indicated door to find Amos Lee, the keeper of the stage door, asleep on a filthy pallet on the floor. He blinked in confusion, and then reached under his stained pillow, pulling out a straight razor while simultaneously struggling to his feet. Holmes brushed past Bradstreet and kicked with his foot, sending the weapon flying to the far side of the room. The constable then took charge of the man and led him outside. "He's stronger under these old loose clothes than he looks," he grunted.

A search of the room revealed a number of interesting items, including various clippings and theatre programs relating to Jenny Sheridan going back twenty years or more, to when she was a rising star on the American stage. On top was the news story that had appeared in the London newspapers when her triumphant return was announced.

"But why would he have had such an interest in her?" asked Bradstreet as we carefully made our way down the quivering staircase.

"Because he was her husband," replied Holmes.

We were outside before he could elaborate, and only after we were at the Bow Street Police Station did he explain.

"I agreed with Mr. Myrddin that this crime had its roots in the victim's American past," explained Holmes. "Last night I sent messages to several men that I trust in the United States, with instructions to quickly obtain a broad biography of Miss Sheridan. While you slept, Watson, I kept vigil as their various responses trickled in, and subsequent replies were made. A picture was quickly painted of her life – from when she had arrived in the United States as a young lady not long after their Civil War, and through her rise in the American theatrical world. One thing that was mentioned was that she'd been married to another actor – a reprobate Southerner named Calvin Tyrell, considerably older than she. Their relationship would burn hot and cold from year to year, but she never seemed to shake him. Then, his fondness for drink, as well as a terrible throat cancer, seemed to be the necessary wedge to separate them – at her insistence. She made it clear that she would not be playing the part of the doting wife to nurse him back to health.

"The husband was known to have survived his illness, but he apparently vanished from the scene. However, my interest in him did not diminish, as I was aware that he might have been involved in this current matter.

"When we spoke to Amos Lee, I could see that his worn clothing was clearly American in cut and design, although it had certainly seen better days. Here then was an American, although I couldn't confirm it by hearing him speak. I had believed that the roots of the crime lay in the actress's American past. After receiving more specific information regarding Jenny Sheridan's former husband, I realized that his illness matched that of Amos Lee's affliction. Fortunately, I had set some of my Irregulars in place to follow various principals when they departed the theatre last night, so I knew where to place my hand upon him.

"Sadly for Mrs. Wicks, it didn't occur to me that the interior of the theatre needed to be watched as well. If she never left, she couldn't be followed. She must have seen Amos Lee, as Calvin Tyrell calls himself now, commit the murder – or at least she knew that he was in the vicinity when it occurred. Possibly she had seen or heard something that revealed his past connection to Jenny Sheridan. Later, after she discovered the body, she likely believed that she could make something from the situation, and informed Tyrell of what she had seen or knew. Late last night, they met in the theatre – she thinking to be paid for her silence, and he intending to eliminate her threat. Theatrically, he left the coin – a souvenir of his days in the Confederate Army – in her mouth signifying that she was a blackmailer. Then he departed, where he was followed by young Edwin Hopper, who had sent word where the man lived.

"When I saw the coin found in Mrs. Wick's mouth, I knew that this southern American, Calvin Tyrell, living as Amos Lee, had killed to protect his secret. It was really quite simple, but finding the solution wouldn't have been possible without making use of modern communications."

"Not quite so simple as that," rumbled Bradstreet. "Noticing the American clothing, for instance . . . ."

Later, through much tedious questioning as Amos Lee – Calvin Tyrell – attempted to communicate, Holmes's conclusions were verified. He was Jenny Sheridan's former husband. Knowing that she was coming to England, he'd arranged to travel there first, bringing with him a letter of reference in order to obtain employment at the Lyceum through the business manager, Bram Stoker. Then, his appearance much changed from when he'd known her, he'd settled in to wait for his chance to plead his case.

However, when he'd finally revealed himself, she'd treated him with great disgust. This he might have been able to take, as it was nothing new, but she began to fraternize with both Grimley and Myrddin, with the seeming intention of throwing it in her former husband's face. He'd confronted her several times, but she'd only laughed – clearly, in spite of their years apart, there was still some connection between them wherein she gained some twisted joy from getting a reaction out of the old actor. He realized that no one knew their connection, and he resolved to kill her – and to frame Myrddin in the process.

It was a simple matter to slip in during the performance, when everyone was gathered at the front to watch Petruchio. Jenny Sheridan never suspected his intent until the scarf stolen from Myrddin's dressing room was pulled tight around her throat. Then Calvin Tyrell knotted the cloth and slipped the unusual button, obtained in the same way, into her hand. He stepped out, unaware that he'd been seen by Mrs. Wicks. Soon after, he heard her scream – the body had been discovered. He waited around the theatre the rest of the night, as was his duty, and he was most surprised when Mrs. Wicks – who normally would have left much earlier – found him and said that she knew what he'd done. She demanded payment for her silence and he led her to the stage – the curtain was pulled, and it was as private as anywhere – and before she had a chance to elaborate, he killed her, placing the coin in her mouth – the only coin that he had with him at the moment, and one with great sentimental attachment, but a necessity, he indicated, when taking care of a blackmailer. "It was . . . a matter , , , of honor," he croaked.

He said that last statement in his curious and unusual way of speaking – a labored and painful thing to watch. After we had finished interviewing him, the entire distasteful situation became rather too much, and Holmes and I excused ourselves, wishing Bradstreet a good day and then returning to Baker Street.

Part II – The Past is Relative

The case had ended and the guilty man was discovered. And yet, I have debated whether to include what occurred next. Nothing is added in terms of the investigation by what I am about to relate – there was no additional killer, or fact whatsoever that added anything to what we already knew. But I would feel the matter incomplete if I didn't record the singularly unique narrative that was subsequently shared with us by one of the participants in the seamy Lyceum murders. The reader may, after reading the rest of this account, simply choose to disregard this addendum and instead accept only the first part as the whole and complete narrative, dispensing with this segment as pure speculative fiction, grafted onto my notes by some well-meaning but misguided and supernaturally obsessed literary agent. But to be complete, the entire tale must be told.

The following morning, Sunday, I awoke to find that the spring rains had set in. My bedroom window, which normally provided a rather bleak but unobstructed view of the buildings to the rear of our house and of the small yard where our lone plane tree eked out some sort of existence, was instead replaced by a constantly varying pattern of runnels of water, thrown there by the unceasing squalls. Occasionally the window would rattle under a fresh assault of wind, to be immediately followed by spattering of drops that sounded as if someone had tossed a handful of shot against the glass.

I dressed warmly, thankful that there were no plans afoot for me to leave the comfort of my fireside chair. Picking up the Clark Russell novel from my bed-stand where I had lain it the night before, I made my way down to the sitting room.

After a satisfying breakfast, I steered my way for my chair, as according to plan, carrying the book, a handful of newspapers, and a refilled coffee cup. Settling in, I had just unfolded *The Times* when the doorbell downstairs rang.

Holmes, who had yet to make an appearance, briskly opened his bedroom door. I saw that he was fully dressed. As he purposefully stepped to the door at the landing, he said, "I have invited a visitor." Then he was descending the stairs, while I refolded my newspaper and set it aside with a sigh, vowing that my planned day would not be altered.

In moments he had returned, and with him was Myrddin, whom I had first seen little more than thirty-six hours earlier, when he made his initial entrance as Petruchio. Since then he'd been through a harrowing experience, spending a night in the Bow Street cells suspected of murder, but now he seemed little affected. Smiling and shaking my hand as I rose to greet him, he gratefully accepted our offer of coffee and seated himself where directed in the basket chair before the fire. Then, while the storm raged outside, one of the strangest conversations that I was ever to witness in those Baker Street rooms began.

"Thank you, Mr. Holmes," said our visitor. "And you too, Doctor. I've been admirers of you both for so long – since I was a boy. I'm simply thrilled to be able to make your acquaintance now, even under such terrible circumstances." He lowered his head. "I knew that you would clear me of the charge."

I muttered something about being glad that it had worked out, and then Myrddin looked toward Holmes, who was silent for a moment as he fussed around, getting his pipe satisfactorily lit. After taking a long draw, he pulled it from his mouth and, using the stem as a pointer, directed it toward our guest. "It was you that sent us the tickets."

Myrddin raised his eyebrows, with surprise and seeming delight. "You knew? May I ask how?"

Holmes frowned. "I was inclined to credit you with the act immediately after the murder was announced, when you turned toward the audience and requested our assistance. I didn't mention it Friday night, as the inspector was already suspicious, and this was our business. It was possible, of course, that you had simply seen and recognized us from the corner of your eye while on stage – particularly as you had a bit of time while the other actors conversed without any lines required from Petruchio. I was an actor once myself, for a time, and I know that casting covert glances toward the audience is unavoidable, even if not good form. Still, someone had sent us anonymous tickets, and why not you? If you already knew that we were there due to your efforts, then asking for our assistance when Mrs. Wick screamed was no great trick. I confirmed with the ticket office that you had requested those particular tickets for complimentary use, although you chose not to have the theatre deliver them, or for them to be held at the box office until the performance. The question is, *why* did you want us there, before the murder diverted our attention?"

Myrddin continued to smile, but it had become faintly brittle, as if he were thinking furiously while continuing to present an easy-going front. Finally the silence became awkward, but both Holmes and I knew the value of such as that – often someone would nervously try to fill it, revealing more than they meant to. It was a useful tool.

"I invited you both," Myrddin finally said, his voice now lower, and rather strained, "because I already knew that I would need you to clear me of the murder."

Holmes's eyes narrowed, and I asked, "You *knew*? That you would be charged with murder before there *was* a murder? You knew that there *would* be a murder?"

He nodded.

"Then for God's sake, man," I cried, "if you knew, why didn't you do something to prevent it? Had you already seen some indication that Miss Sheridan was in danger? Some implied violence? Some overheard conversation?"

"No, Doctor. Nothing like that." He took a deep breath. "I didn't really know any details of the crime until I read in this morning's newspaper that you had both unmasked the killer on Saturday – yesterday."

"Did the police not explain what happened when they released you yesterday morning?" I asked.

He smiled. "I won't know for sure what they tell me until yesterday."

For a moment I thought that I had misunderstood, but his statement was clear enough. "Yesterday? You won't know . . . until *yesterday*?"

"That's right," said Myrddin. "Saturday is your *yesterday*, Doctor Watson. For me, it's my *tomorrow*."

Holmes looked intrigued, as if a chemical experiment that had been performed a thousand – nay, a million – times, had been repeated yet again, this time producing a much different and unexpected result. I was becoming irate, attempting to understand the actor's riddle.

"What are you trying to tell us, Mr. Myrddin?" asked Holmes.

Myrddin drained his coffee cup and set it aside. Then he pushed back into the basket chair, carefully placed his hands on the arms, and looked from one to the other of us.

"I live with a secret, gentlemen. A vast and complex and dangerous secret. I sometimes share it with others. I have decided to share it with the two of you. I . . . You see . . . ." He licked his lips, and then retreated. "I sometimes tell this to people – those that I have learned that I can trust. Those that I know will help me in the future – *their* future. My past, you understand." He looked at Holmes, and then me. "Ah, I can see that you don't. Not yet. You have helped me already, Mr. Holmes – in addition to clearing of Jenny Sheridan's murder . . . yesterday. That is, you *will* help – over twenty-five years from now." He suddenly appeared nervous, the first time I'd seen such a reaction for the normally steady young man. "It's very confusing."

"Go on," said Holmes, watching him closely.

"It's . . . it's difficult to explain. And difficult for others to comprehend," he said. "One would think that by I'd know by now how to relate the strange circumstances of my existence – "

"And those would be . . . ?" Holmes pressed once again, a touch impatient.

Myrddin nodded and cleared his throat. "Yes. Right. The fact is, gentlemen, that I knew there would be a murder before it occurred, Mr. Holmes, and that I knew you would clear me."

"You *knew*," I asked, still trying to grasp the implications of his outrageous story. "*Past tense*? You say that as if . . . ." I leaned back, fascinated to see such a sincere but mad conceit up close from someone who had initially appeared so sane. "You . . . you believe that you can see into the future? That you can predict events before they occur?

"Not exactly *before* they happen, Doctor," said the young man. "Instead, I prepare myself for what has already happened. *Your past* is *my future*. For I am living my life backwards through time."

Needless to say, a silence fell across the room. Myrddin's gaze pivoted from one of us to the other and back again. I settled back with a frank snort of disbelief while staring with fascination at the sincerity of the man's expression when making such an outrageous statement.. Meanwhile, Holmes looked at him as if he were facing a predatory animal that might make an unexpected move. Finally he spoke.

"You say that you have shared this before with others. Perhaps if you begin at the beginning, your . . . *interesting* experiences will make more sense to us."

Myrddin nodded, and seemed to relax a bit. "I don't expect you to believe me. There's no reason that you should. But I'll tell you anyway, because . . . because I know that you and I will meet again. We *have* met again, Mr. Holmes, from my perspective, although you don't know it yet – it hasn't happened to you, and won't for years to come – and you will remember me then.

"Today is Sunday. Yesterday – Saturday, *your* yesterday, and *my* tomorrow – you won't yet know this story that I'm about to tell you yet, because you're moving *forward* in time, and on Saturday, this conversation will still be in your future. But after I tell you today, from this day forward, you *will* remember it as you go into the future, and recalling me from today, and this conversation now, will be of benefit when we meet again, and when I need your help in your future – which is my past."

I closed my eyes, trying to order my thoughts. Myrddin saw my confusion.

"Imagine, Doctor," he said, looking at me, but speaking to both of us, "that time is like a series of fence posts, one after another, stretching from far to the left, out of sight – that's the past – and just as far to the right. That's the future. Time, as you and almost everyone else knows it, walks along those fence posts, steadily from left to right, one after another, moving from the past into the future, minute after minute, day after day, year after year. Each post represents a minute, or a year, or a century, or however you want to view it. But nearly everyone inexorably follows that path from left to right."

"This is a given of the universe," said Holmes. "It is entropic. Time flows forward. Order declines into disorder. As time progresses, entropy controls. It increases – that is Newton's Second Law. Levels of high energy decrease and dissipate – that is the essence of the Third. What is uphill works its way down, slowly or quickly. Mountains are worn down and out into the sea – not the other way. Stars burn and send their energy into the cosmos until they are extinguished. The process doesn't work in reverse. Wood doesn't *un*-burn. An egg dropped on the floor does not suddenly rise back to the countertop and reassemble itself.

"And yet," Holmes continued, with a gleam of interest, "*you* assert that you are walking in the opposite direction along the fence, contrary to the unwinding of the entire universe. A most original conceit."

Myrddin nodded. "I do so assert it. I am *doing* it. It has been my whole life. How old do you think that I am?"

I felt that I could answer this with confidence. "No older than twenty-five."

"I am fifty-three years old," said the actor. "I was born in 1941, here in London. For the first couple of years of my life, I believe that I grew as any child would, both physically and mentally. When I was two, there was an . . . an *incident*, here in London, and my parents were killed."

"When you were two," interrupted Holmes. "So by your statements, you would assert that you were two years old in 1939 – two years *before you were born in 1941?*"

"That's correct," Myrddin agreed.

"Fascinating," muttered Holmes. He leaned back, thinking furiously. I didn't know if the idea itself was of such interest, or if – like me – he was intrigued at the elaborate beliefs of the man and the calmness that was exhibited by someone so clearly mad.

"How can you be fifty-three?" I asked, a tone of skepticism creeping into my voice that I tried unsuccessfully to hide. "You are clearly in the midst of your third decade – no more."

"I know that I am fifty-three, Doctor, in the same way that you know your age. You count the years that have passed from the date of your birth. I was born in 1941, and – living backwards – have passed through fifty-three cycles of the earth around the sun to reach this date, here in March 1888, when we are all now together in this room, having intersected in this place and time to carry on this conversation."

I waved my hand, a feeble gesture as if warding away an insect, not knowing what argument to make. He continued. "I know that I don't look my age. It's a curiosity of my condition. I seem to have reached a certain point and stopped aging altogether – or at least the process has been so significantly slowed that I can't tell the difference. I suspect that – barring an accident or illness – I'll continue living into the past for quite a long time before I eventually become an old man." He looked around. "Might I have something a little stronger than coffee?" he asked. "I have a great deal to carefully explain."

I arose and offered brandy or whisky, and he chose the latter. I poured one for myself, despite the early hours. Holmes declined.

Back in my seat, I took a sip, as did Myrddin. Then he began share his curious story in greater depth.

"As I said, I was born in 1941, the only child to my parents. I know very little about them. They were from somewhere north – if not actually in Scotland, then very close. As I said, there was an – *incident* – in 1939, when I was two years old, resulting in their deaths. More than that you don't need to know. I was placed with a friend of my mother's – a morose woman who felt it was her duty to raise me. It turned out that I was supposed to go with her when my parents died – they *knew* it was going to happen.

"This woman – we'll call her Margaret – was curiously reticent when relating facts about my past – thus my ignorance about my parents. If your parents had died in such a way, and you knew nothing of them, you could do research on the incident that killed them, and then back-track to find out their identities and their origins. I didn't have that luxury. When I was old enough to understand my backwards journey through time, I had no way to do any such research. By then I was living in the early 1930's, and then after that the late 1920's, and the incident would not occur for years. How could I search the newspapers for facts about their deaths when it hadn't happened yet?

"Margaret didn't send me to school, but rather taught me at home – and surprisingly well. I learned mathematics, and literature, and a number of other subjects, some rather advanced. Philosophy, for instance, and religion. The more complex sciences weren't ignored either – physics and chemistry. But *history* – that was the most important subject of all for someone like me, as I walked backwards into it.

"For several years, that was my only existence – Margaret and me and our little cottage. We lived far from any town or village, and I saw no one else. Early on, with memories of my own parents so hazy, I'd thought of this woman as my mother, but she was quick to point out that she was not. Of course, by then the nature of my curious existence had been revealed to me, and I found that Margaret was making the same backwards journey. My parents had been the same – that was how they knew when they would die – and that there was no avoiding it. It was set history, you see, and they expected it – and believed that they couldn't change it.

"There are others like us who swim upstream through time – the ones who don't go mad because of it and end their lives early before they really even begin – and we are known to one another. Some of us, anyway. There are probably more who never reveal this gift – or curse. We generally try to keep our existence a secret, even from each other, because there are some among us who never stop trying to profit from this unusual ability, and they are jealous and fearful of the rest of us who might do the same.

"I have no idea how old Margaret was – whether she was like me and had aged very slowly, or if she was progressing at a normal rate. She looked to be about seventy when I was ten or twelve, which would place her date of birth around the year 2000, I suppose. But if she was aging very slowly, she could have been born much further in the future – perhaps hundreds of years from now. She died of a sudden illness when I was ten years old, without telling me much that I still needed to know.

"But before she passed, she taught me a great deal about how we moved through time, and how to comprehend the seeming paradox of it, and tricks to survive it. She showed me how I could leave hints for myself from within the present, buried in the past like guideposts as I moved in that direction. Margaret explained how to devise a code that only I could understand. When she was certain that I understood it completely and would never forget it, being able to read it as easily as you do the English alphabet, I learned that I could leave messages for myself – in hidden diaries where I know to look, written by myself in the past to be discovered in the present, or as coded lines in the *Personals* column of a newspaper.

"I also found that I could think of some date in *my* future – *your* past – and in that way send myself a message of sorts. For example, say that in 1920, after having done research as to what present banks were around in 1900, I could *think* of that bank and a certain date in that year with great intensity, until it was unforgettable to me. Meanwhile, time flowed, and I would keep reminding myself of it, year after year. 1920, 1919, 1918, and so on. When I reached 1900, twenty years older and two decades into the past from when I made that initial memory, and having remembered that date and bank specifically for so long, I could go there and obtain a safety deposit box, placing vast amounts information in it about what had occurred over the last twenty years – extensive diaries and notes of things that I would need to know about my own life. Meanwhile, back in 1920, in the present where I was still twenty years younger and had just spent so much effort to think of that date and place, I could then go to the bank, access the safety deposit box (which would have been maintained for all of those twenty years) and open it to find the information that my older self had placed there in 1900, sharing what is going to happen to me over the next two decades between 1900 and 1920 – people that I needed to remember, jobs that I would hold, and so on. I knew that it *would* work because it *did* work!

"In the meantime, having been able to read the history books and old newspapers along the way, I would know the greater world events as I went into them. That was where my trained memory was so useful. Obviously once I had seen today's newspaper and moved a day into the past, I could not go back and recheck it to confirm some fact, as you would in that pile of papers over there. The newspaper I had just seen was now lost in tomorrow and doesn't exist yet, and I was going the other way. Therefore, I practiced recalling all that I could. As I learned to remember more and more, and as I absorbed history from the books and newspapers, and from actually *seeing* it occur, I began to understand the patterns, and how it all flows and weaves together."

I cleared my throat. "How does this work? How does one move back into the past? How can you go through this day now, in the right order from morning to night so that we can sit here and converse with you in the same direction, and yet wake up yesterday?"

Holmes nodded. "Good, Watson!" he murmured.

"That's an excellent question, Doctor, and it's hard to explain," Myrddin replied. "I believe that it has something to do with the earth rotating on its axis, and portions of it passing through darkness and facing away from the sun – or so it seems. I do live each day forward, from morning to night as you both do, but something about passing through night moves me one day into the past. It's not a sudden snap from today to yesterday. Rather, as each new day begins, reality seems to coalesce and I realize from various clues – calendars and newspapers and seasons moving in reverse – that it's yesterday now instead of today."

He paused to take a sip of whisky, and I couldn't help remarking, "Good Lord, man! With such a . . . a gift, you could make a fortune. You could rule the world!"

He smiled. "One would think so, Doctor," he said. "But it isn't that easy. To become rich, I would need to do certain things today – place an investment, for instance – and reap the benefits tomorrow, and so on into the future. Instead, whatever I do today is lost to me as I go in the opposite direction. I've tried what you suggest – sending a memory message to myself in the past to place an investment that I can reap now. When the investment matures, I may have something extra today, but then I'll be one more day into the past, where the investment is diminishing, and I'm moving away from the direction where it grows. I can leave notes for myself telling me where to go when I wake up yesterday – something like '*You are still working at the Capitol and Counties Bank on Wednesday, March 9th*' – so that, on Thursday, March 10th, I'll know where to go, instead of awakening yesterday to find my immediate future a mystery.

"Since I'm *not* rich now, apparently I've yet to send a successful memory message to myself about some wise investment. My past self does hide some money in the past in my safety deposit boxes, or my other hidey-holes, that I can access now – a gift from my past self to my present self, in the same way that you set aside money for the future. But I'm careful not to take too much, as spending a lot today will leave less for the version of me who might need it tomorrow – *my yesterday*."

I groaned, barely able to follow this convoluted explanation. I glanced at Holmes, who appeared to be fascinated. "Thanks heavens," he murmured, "that Professor Moriarty doesn't know about this," he said, adding to the amazement that I was already feeling from our client's story. "He would find a way to turn it to his advantage."

"Or with such a thing to ponder," I added, "he might have never felt the need to turn to evil at all."

Holmes realized that his pipe had gone out and he set it aside. "You've explained how knowledge of the past – your *future* – is of no use toward your own acquisition of wealth, but what you do know of what's to come – and that's if I tolerantly accepted the authenticity of your tale! – would surely be of use to the British Government, which is always involved in preparing Britain for upcoming future conflicts, which some of us are certain cannot be avoided. If you truly had information about the next forty or fifty years, it would be your duty to share it."

Myrddin shook his head. "That isn't a good idea. Suppose I were to tell someone within the government of an important battle ten years from now – and that is purely hypothetical. At first it's simply on the edge of his awareness, something vague, like a birthday months from now that he needs to recall in order to buy a gift. But as it gets closer, he begins to see how the events of history are unfolding, leading inevitably to that moment in time. He begins focus on it, however little at first, and his own interest begins to emphasize and even accelerate events, making it not only certain, but possibly worse than it would have been otherwise – because of my initial influence.

"His own interest in that event begins to have more and more of an unintended effect on *other* events. He convinces other men in positions of power to prepare as the battle approaches, before they should even know about it, and to direct resources in that direction which might have gone another way – possibly from somewhere that can't afford to lose those resources. This information might give that man a reputation for wisdom or prescience that he might not otherwise deserve, causing people to grant him more relevance and influence than he's supposed to have. Perhaps along the way, some new weapon is developed to end the battle more decisively – something that might not have appeared quite so soon if this man had never known so early about what to expect. The new weapon could itself nudge history in yet another wrong direction.

"And as I travel *away* from that future – my *past* – in ignorance, might it not change behind me, reweaving in a different way from how I remember it because of what I revealed?"

"But," I interrupted, caught up in his idea, "how do you know that your revelation of the foreknowledge of the battle, given to England in order that we might prepare, isn't the way that history and time are *supposed* to unfold? Perhaps it is part of the overall plan that you were able to intercede on our behalf and tell us what you know."

He shook his head. "Margaret was adamant in teaching me just how much or how little that I could attempt to nudge history. She always believed that time is like a river in a deep channel – no matter what temporary diversions impede the true flow, it will always correct itself – sometimes violently. What has happened *has* happened. But I'm more fearful. I think that it *could* be changed, and what I had observed as I passed backward through the future might have come undone and reknit itself into something else. Perhaps something that I've already done – some inadvertent and seemingly small action – has already changed what happens, and since I'm going the other way, I'll never know.

"It's one thing to for the older version of me, somewhere in the past, to write a coded message back to myself, left in a safe deposit box or other hiding place, about something that has already happened to *me* so that I can be prepared – about what to expect concerning an ongoing task at whatever job I'm walking into, or that I should learn Petruchio's lines because I'm going to be in a play at the Lyceum, and on what date I'll attend the audition and be hired. But pulling at larger threads in Time's Tapestry either fails, or might be a very bad idea. Possibly time might correct itself in ways that we cannot imagine." He took a final sip of whisky and set the empty glass down beside him. "No," he said. "I don't think that I'll be offering any advice about your future."

"'*Your* future'," I noticed sarcastically. "Is it so different than your own?"

"It is, Doctor. My future lies the other way. 1887, and then 1886, and so on."

"Can you foretell just how far you will be going?" Holmes asked. "Have you tried to determine just how far you exist into the past? A mention of yourself in the historical record, for instance?" I tried to see any emotion in the question – belief or skepticism, or anything in between – but there was nothing. "Have you foreseen the records of your own death, as you said was the case for your parents?"

"I have not. Every one of my attempts to 'remember' something, and send a message to myself farther and farther into the past, has been successful, no matter how far I push. I've left messages as far back as I can at businesses that were in existence in the deep past – a few banks and financial institutions, for instance – but I must wait to explore further. In the meantime, I've left myself increasingly comprehensive notes about yesterday, and the days past that. I know where I will be in a few weeks, before I obtain the job at the Lyceum, and what name I'll call myself. And beyond that, and beyond and beyond, versions of myself have left very detailed records of what I'm to do. The information continues to grow, and the tiniest of details are being painted in. My path is set. As I progress into the past, I'll keep leaving more detailed messages, filling in the blanks – I know this because I receive so much information now, so I must be taking a great deal of time to send it to myself, and I must be very good at it. And if I have questions, I simply think of a date in the future and remember it when I get there, and then I find out the answer, write it down, and leave it for me to come across here in the present.

"Acting is just one thing I will try. I know that I will become a doctor, and an engineer. And in spite of what I said about sharing information now about the future that lays behind me, I begin to see that I may be the one who *causes* history to happen along the path that it's already occurred. I've already seen some signs that I've done so."

"Indeed? In what way."

"Perhaps you've heard of the Confederate battle plans found by the Union forces, wrapped around three cigars, before the Battle of Antietam in 1862?"

I had. Holmes had not.

"Finding the plans allowed the Union to decisively defeat the Confederate forces at that battle. Would it surprise you to learn that I have been told in a message from a future version of myself (in the past) that I will be the one responsible for wrapping those cigars with the plans and getting them to the Union Army's attention?"

"So, along those lines – assuming any of this to be true," said Holmes, "you've already been trying this on a more limited scale, by sending a message to the version of yourself last Friday, to make sure we attended the theatre by arranging for our tickets."

Myrddin smiled. "That's right. It occurred to me to 'remember' it last Friday.

215

I tipped up the last of my own whisky. "Outrageous," I muttered.

Holmes, meanwhile, simply smiled tolerantly. "Have a care, Mr. Myrddin – or is that your true name?"

"True enough for now." He smiled.

"Your interest in affecting history," continued Holmes, his tone darkening, "sounds suspiciously arrogant. Power corrupts. And if you wish to enlist my aid for whatever it is that will assist you years from now, you're not leaving me with a very favorable impression today."

The smile seemed to wash from our visitor's face, as if realizing for the first time that his actions as described – or as he believed them to have occurred, at any rate – were bordering on something more malicious – or omnipotent – than the simple study of history while passing through it. He sat quietly for several minutes, and then nodded thoughtfully.

"You are right, of course. And you *will* give me more good advice when we meet again – in Chicago, in 1915. You will be surprised to see me again – but you will know me. Please recall this conversation, so that I can confirm to you then that I listened."

I was still trying to comprehend this story, and wondering if Myrddin were a danger to himself or others, and whether I should seek a constable in order to have him committed. He looked at me knowingly. "I am not insane, Doctor, I assure you. I am simply living something beyond your comprehension – until now. After this, you will know something about the way the world works that is hidden from most men. I don't understand it either, but I assure you that it's true."

"You say that others with this condition sometimes go mad," I said. "How do you know that you aren't already?"

He smiled. "I was fortunate to receive a good understanding and a solid grounding. And my quest for knowledge as I move back through time only expands my comprehension of the overall *patterns* of time."

"Surely knowing everything that will happen must become vastly boring. What will you do as you go back to keep things fresh, where there are no surprises?" I asked, curious to see how elaborate a structure he had constructed to support this madness.

"I have a theory," he said. "So many legends from the past – from all cultures around the world – hold a common belief in some sort of magic. And peeling away the froth on top reveals a great similarity in the stories, no matter what part of the world they originate. I believe that in the past, magic – *true magic* – existed, and that the farther one goes into the past, the more there was. Perhaps it was a substance of limited quantity, and in 1888 is has been nearly depleted, and any that remains will vanish entirely in the near future. But I'm going the *other* way, upstream *toward* the source – should it actually exist." He stood. "Knowing that it might be there and with the benefit of 'hindsight' and research along the way, I hope to find it, and learn it, and understand it – *and maybe master it!*"

He fell silent. What he had to tell us was finished. Holmes and I stood then too. "I only know some of what happens on Friday night – the theatre and the murder – from the little that I've read in today's newspapers and my notes to myself from yesterday when I was released. For you it's already a memory. For me it has yet to happen – the murder is two days in my future. I wish you both well – until we meet again last Friday, and also when you and I will continue this conversation in 1915, Mr. Holmes."

With that, Myrddin – or whomever he truly was – bowed and shook our hands, and walked out. We made no effort to follow, and in a moment we heard the street door close.

Holmes looked at me with a quizzical smile. I knew that he was asking what I thought.

"Utter rot," I said. "The man is insane."

"More likely an author," countered Holmes. "You'll recall that I did note the excessive ink on his fingers. He would have had us decide that it comes from constantly writing notes and diaries to himself and hiding them in safety deposit boxes for discovery yesterday and yesterday – or from his perspective, tomorrow and tomorrow. In fact, he's no doubt concocting this and other fantastic tales in the hopes of some sort of literary success."

"It will never happen," I said. "His premise is too confusing."

"Amen to that, Brother Watson," replied Holmes, and we both laughed.

I settled back in to my chair, turning my attention to the newspapers. And yet, my thoughts continued to return to Myrddin's amazing tale, and I found myself pondering various versions of him at different places along the fence posts of time, leaving hidden messages to be found decades later, or making memories for himself to be recalled when he was much older – in the past – requiring a certain action to be carried out. I tried to picture myself on such a fence, various versions of me in the past, present, and future, communicating with each other. At times I could almost understand – a version of me the week before had bought cigars and left them on the mantel so that I might find and enjoy them today – a thoughtful little gift from my past self to the present version. If such a person as Myrddin could travel backwards through time, mightn't he, and others like him, develop, by sheer necessity, just such a complex system as he'd described?

Throughout the day, I would glance at Holmes, ostensibly working at his chemical bench, but instead he was motionless, lost in thought. I knew without asking that he was pondering the same questions as I.

217

We never spoke of the matter again, but it still occasionally haunts my thoughts. And every once in a while, when I see Holmes studying the personal columns as he so often does, I wonder if he's trying to spot a coded message placed by the version of Myrddin on that particular day to be found days or years from now when a younger version of himself searches through an old newspaper in order to gain valuable information along life's journey.

But of course Holmes isn't looking for anything like that. To do so would be to acknowledge some sort of validity to Myrddin's ridiculous tale, and neither Holmes nor I are that foolish.

The Adventure of the Giant's Wife

by I.A. Watson

"All this landscape were becos' of a marital dispute," the dour guide who led Holmes and I up the steep slope beside Carr Beck informed us. Mr. Slaithwaite had evidently taken Londoners on walking tours up to Burley Moor before. "At least that's what t' legends say."

The slushy remnants of a fading late winter made the ground treacherous. I was glad of my walking cane. The sharp wind off the peaks above us made me gladder of my Burberry.

"Burley Moor, y'see, and Ilkley Moor up there, are both rightly part o' Rombald's Moor," the local went on. "And Rombald, well, 'e were a giant, back in t' olden days 'afore t' Romans ivver come."

I glanced to see how Holmes was taking the impromptu history lesson. His attention seemed transfixed on the local landscape, the wild ridges and sudden valleys of the Yorkshire hills.

"Well Rombald, 'e were a fierce old monster that fritted [1] everybody. When 'is temper flared there were storms. 'E tossed around lightning and 'ole mountains. So they reckon, in the stories. But . . . 'e 'ad a *wife*."

Holmes paused momentarily to examine an ancient waystone, half-lost in a clump of vervain. Under frost and green mould the rock had prehistoric cup and ring carvings. There are more than four-hundred such stones scattered about the area, and many more lost over the years. [2]

"Supposedly, this Rombald's missus weren't the sort t' put up wi' much. And one day, these two get into such a fight over 'is burned dinner that she starts tossing 'uge rocks at 'im. Old Rombald, 'e legs it off t' try and get away from 'er. And 'is wife, she runs after 'im, chucking 'ills at 'im." Slaithwaite gestured round the cold misty incline. "And this is what they left, 'im crashing through and splitting mountains into valleys, 'er lobbing giant boulders after 'im. We're heading to t' Great Skirtful of Rocks, what fell out of 'er pinny [3] as she chased 'er man. Over yon's the Little Skirtful of Rocks, and below us the Skirtful Spring. Up there over that ridge is't famous Cow and Calf Rocks, what Rombald broke as 'e scrambled away. There were a Bull Rock an' all until eighty year or so back, that got quarried away to build Ilkley. But point is, according to t' owd wives tales, all of this were caused by a 'do-mestic incident', as they calls it." Slaithwaite breathed before his punchline. "And *that's* why tha' don't go peeving a Yorkshire lass."

"We're not hunting Burley's first giant," Holmes acknowledged. It was the first indication that he had been listening to the fellow at all.

Slaithwaite became suddenly shy. "Well," he responded, a little abashed by my companion's sudden attention, "it's only a bit un a story, like."

"But we *are* here seeking giants," Holmes reminded us. "And one of them a murderer."

It was true. In Holmes's Inverness coat pocket was the letter that had brought us to this wild Yorkshire landscape chasing an unconventional killer:

Stephill Farm,
Burley Woodhead,
West Riding, Yorkshire.

Mr. Sherlock Holmes
221b Baker Street
London

10th April, 1888

> *Dear Mr. Holmes,*
>
> *Knowing your acuity and memory from long back, I have no doubt that you will remember me, Samuel Rudd, who worked in your father's service as stable boy at his estate in Mycroft [4] up to his passing. Since then I have received a groom's position at Stephill Farm stables near Burley-in-Wharfdale and have worked there these dozen years.*
>
> *I hope you will pardon my letter, in which I am forwarding details of a troubling and unpleasant series of events that have recently disturbed our quiet little farm, concerning the death of its owner, Mr. Lister.*
>
> *The former proprietor of Stephill, Mr. Giles Packworth, died in the summer of 1887. He had no remaining close relatives, his son having been lost in the Indian Hill Wars, so the estate was sold – farm, stables, and pastures – to Mr. Hogarth Lister of York. Mr. Lister had made his money in coal but now wished to retire and breed horses.*
>
> *Mr. Lister took up residence in September of last year, and there was, if I may be so bold as to admit it, some tension between the town staff that came to Burley Woodhead with*

Mr. Lister and the people who had been in service at Stephill during Mr. Packworth's time. Indeed, Mr. Lister dismissed some of the older staff for getting into disputes with the newer folks. Not wishing to speak ill of the dead, but Mr. Lister was not an easy master.

Mr. Lister was not popular with the local folk. An antiquarian, he organised a dig into one of the old barrows up on the ridge, looking for burial treasures, despite the protests of the people of Burley Woodhead. Indeed he had the right, having permission from the landowner Mrs. Duexbury, but it was a controversial thing and led to bad feeling in the neighbourhood and a distance with some of the gentry.

This excavation took place in early March, as soon as the frosts first passed and before the late frosts we have now, when the ground could be cut. A wedge was sliced from the tump and some old metal bits and shards of broken pot were discovered, but no treasure trove. For several nights afterwards the horses were disturbed, and since then the main house was awoken by loud thumps as of someone rattling the shutters and tossing stones onto the roof.

Mr. Lister was angered by what he spoke of as "ignorant country tricks by feeble-minded yokels". One of the young grooms was blamed and dismissed without references, but the noises went on. There was a small fire in the hay-barn but it was discovered and doused before it could spread. A few things in the big house were tampered with, moved, or disappeared, including a clock that had belonged to Mr. Lister's late mother. Mr. Lister complained to the bobby from Burley-in-Wharfdale, and was angry when nothing was done. Some of the more superstitious of the staff, including Mrs. Ophelia, our housekeeper, were convinced that the house was haunted and Mr. Lister cursed because he had opened and disturbed the tumulus.

Mr. Lister was a man of fixed habits. He rose early and walked his dog, leaving the stables at six sharp and returning for his breakfast at seven. He was fit for his age, which was around sixty, and in apparent good health. On Monday, 2nd April, he left as usual on his constitutional but returned early, hastily, and as pale and scared as I have even seen a man. I was walking one of our broody mares in the long pasture when he hastened down the hill.

I asked him what was wrong, worried for his heart. He replied that he had seen ghosts, giant ghosts, and that one of them had killed the other.

Now, there are stories about Ilkley and Rombald's Moor (which Stephill Farm edges onto) and of sightings of such spectres. Children here dare each other to go up onto the tops at dawn and look for the phantom. I tried to reassure Mr. Lister that he had not seen aught that many others hadn't perceived over many years, but he was curt with me and threatened me with dismissal. These ghosts, he insisted, were unlike any other, and he was certain that they had acted out murder. He had seen one, a woman, creep upon the other, a man, unawares, and strike him down with a blow from behind. The attacker had then fallen upon the downed spectre and had hit him repeatedly upon the head, perhaps with a rock.

Mr. Lister was convinced that he had seen some apparition, and that it was some portent of doom.

He spoke no more of it after that morning, and for eight days he did not take his morning walk. Yesterday, the day after Easter, he vanished before breakfast without word. When he was missed, Mr. Slaithwaite our Head Groom organised a search. I was amongst those who took the steep track past the lower tarn towards the barrow and stone ring up there.

It was the dog's barking that led us to the place where Mr. Lister had fallen. He was dead. He had tumbled down a steep slope and might have hit his head going down. That was the policemen's conclusion at first, but the police doctor has since said that the cause of death was several blows to the skull, which would be hard to take on a fall of no more than twenty feet.

Some of the local lads blame the curse and the "moors knockers", and I admit to a bit of a tingle of fear myself when I remembered Mr. Lister's fright of the week before, and that he might have somehow seen a phantom prediction of his own passing. In the village they are saying that it was a punishment on him for disturbing the tumulus.

When I was questioned by the inspector of police who came out from Ilkley, I mentioned that I had been in service to your family and had tended to your pony when we were boys. I asked for permission to write and seek your advice on the case, and Inspector Shotley was kind enough to say that

222

he would appreciate any insight you might have on how to untangle what happened. I enclose the inspector's address if you wish to wire him.

Wishing you the best of health and fortune, in remembrance of happy times in service at Mycroft, most sincerely yours,

Saml. Rudd, Esq.

This was the message that had roused my friend from his morose chagrin at his mistakes regarding the matter of Mrs. Munro and Lucy Hebron, [5] and set us on the next train north in search of spectral giants in the dim watery pre-dawn light of the Yorkshire moors.

The path we had been following diverted from the Carr Beck. That fast-flowing freshet ran deep and chill with mountain-snow melt-off, tumbling down too steeply to follow up further, but it was not so wide that we couldn't stride across. We traced left along the contour of the ridge. Below us all was white haze. The scattered houses of rural Burley Woodhead were less than a half-mile behind, but they were quite invisible now.

"Mr. Lister was said to be a fellow of regular habits," Holmes noted. "What route did he take for his morning walk?"

"Why, t' same path as we're on now," Slaithwaite answered. "There's a loop, along t' low ridge overlooking t' tarns as far as t' Grubstones, then back along t' 'igh ridge, coomin' past the Great Skirtful and t' broken barrow, and so back down t' way you coom up."

Holmes checked a sketch-map he had made of the local geography that showed the moor's footpaths and streams, along with some ground contours indicating the steep inclines up from the farm. I could easily trace the anti-clockwise route that Lister had walked his dog each day, a stroll of perhaps two-and-a-half miles.

"You were one of the people who found Mr. Lister up by the cairn ring," Holmes observed to Slaithwaite.

"By t' Great Skirtful, aye. Well, when they worked out e'd gone missing, there was three on us went up there looking for 'im, sent out by Mrs. Ophelia, 'is 'ousekeeper like. Me, an' Lister 'oo you knows, and George Sutton – that's a stable-'and. Some others went off towards Menston and Burley-in-Wharfedale, and a couple went agate [6] t'Ilkley Road a few miles.

"Wait," I interrupted. "Why search anywhere but where he took his daily walk?"

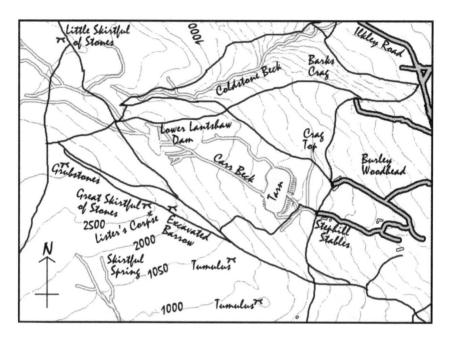

"'Cos none of us knew as 'ed gone out that day, 'til 'e were missed at breakfast. 'E'd been up in't night, chasing that moors-knocker round t'ouse and getting nowhere, so they jus' thought as 'e'd slept in. Besides, there'd been an unseasonal late snow, an' it weren't fit t' go a-hikin' up on't moors, not for someone on 'is years. But old Jack Widdison, 'e says, 'E taks gawm, lookee up't gill where 'e were so glottened before'."

"Ah . . . right," I responded

Our guide saw that he had lost us at last with his local patois and deigned to translate, "That is, sirs, 'e says 'Listen to me, look up on't 'ill where Mr. Lister 'ad 'is fright t'other time."

"Where he saw the giants," I supplied.

"Well aye. So's we coom on up and we 'ears 'is dog barking like a mad thing, an' there 'e is, poor feller, fallen down t'scar [7] wi' 'is ead all spretched – that is, cracked open." [8]

"How was he laid?" Holmes enquired.

"On 'is front, wi' one arm under 'im and t' other out t' 't side. And one leg bent right unnatural where it 'ad broken. And I said t' George Sutton, 'Well that's 'im gone, then,' and George Sutton says t'me, 'Well what d'y' expect when e' goes digging up that old barrow-like?' 'Cos them places was graves once, they do say, from the old days 'afore the churchyards."

Holmes ignored the commentary for now and continued his interrogation. "Was there blood? Was it dried?"

224

"There were plenty, all over t' glocken [9] snow – which were wet, o' course, so it 'adn't storkened. [10] 'Ee'd split 'is skull when 'e tumbled, I reckoned. But them perlice-men says no."

"There was snow. Were there tracks? Any prints but his?"

"Nobbut some sheep prints an' small game, either up on't ridge or down in t' scar, and 'is setter what 'ad morrised about all over t'place. It were t'devvil's own job getting down t' 'im where 'e'd tumbled. They 'ad t' fetch ropes to 'aul 'im out."

This testimony and Holmes's demands for additional details took us a hundred yards up the slippery track, to the *T*-junction onto the loop that was Lister's regular circuit. I had expected Holmes to take the left path, which would lead us past Lister's excavated barrow and bring us more quickly to the ruined ring of stones above where the body was discovered. Instead he set off right, following the dead man's customary route.

"Tell me about the moors-knockers, Mr. Slaithwaite," the great detective instructed our guide.

"Well, sirs, I don't 'old wi' boggarts and hobs," Slaithwaite insisted. "I was minded as the mischief were done by 'uman 'ands, and if I finds 'oo set a fire in the barn or let our 'orses out into the night or messed up my tack-room, then 'e'll feel the back o' my 'and! But I were on watch some nights per Mr. Lister's orders, and I nivver saw owt as explained them bangings an' goings on! So maybe George Sutton were right about t' mound being cursed."

"Did you suspect anyone of playing tricks?" I wondered.

"Aye, well, at first I thought it might be them Champions, young Alice's kin after she were dismissed for cheeking Mrs. Ophelia on t' matter of washing vegetables proper. 'Er brothers aren't above a bit of poachin' and roguery. And George Sutton, 'e's 'er cousin sometimes removed. But none o' them could 'ave got inside the Big 'Ouse t' do stuff."

Ezekiel Slaithwaite was not the first resident of Stephill that Holmes had interviewed on this topic. Indeed, I knew that beside Rudd's letter in Holmes's pocket were the notes I had compiled for him based on our interviews yesterday about the people and timings of the farm haunting:

> *Residents in the Big House at Stephill:*
> *Hogarth Lister, 61 (deceased) – Disliked owner,*
> *   since September 1887;*
> *Punch, his setter;*
> *Mrs. Mary Ophelia, 56, housekeeper, hired in York;*
> *Betty Coombe, 22, parlour maid, transferred from*
> *   Lister's York townhouse;*

Sukie Murgatroyd, 17, maid of all work, local, hired in November after previous local maid Alice Champion dismissed for impertinence;

Larry Tope, 16, page, local.

Residents of outbuildings at Stephill:
Ezekiel Slaithwaite, 48, head groom and stableman, local, 23 years service at Stephill;

Samuel Rudd, 53, groom, ostler, 12 years service at Stephill;

Carl Ophelia, 32, groom, son of housekeeper, hired in York;

George Sutton, 26, stable hand, local, hired in February after dismissal of previous local man Fred Clough after row with employer;

Jack Widdison, 67, general labourer, 38 years service at Stephill;

Lewis Wilson, 21, jockey, hired in York in December last after dismissal of previous local man Adam Boothe for row with Carl.

Day-Labourers: Up to fifteen local men hired as required for field and stables duties.

Principal disturbances at and around Stephill:
Monday 5th March – Cutting begins at the barrow; Row with protesting locals;

Tuesday 6th March – Landowner Mrs. Duexbury refuses to revoke permission for dig;

Wednesday 7th March – Dig concludes – Spear head, palstave, and several amber beads were found, tentatively dated to Bronze Age;

Also Wednesday 7th March – First night-time disturbances at Stephill, knocking on doors and shutters;

Thursday 8th March – Night-time knocking continues, Lister complains to police, sets watch;

Friday 9th March – First sounds of stones rattling off roof slates, No missiles found the following morning;

Saturday, 10th March – Knocks and bangs, more roof rattles; No prints in snowfall;

Monday 12th March – Knocks on shutters despite watch by Slaithwaite, Rudd, Ophelia;

Tuesday 13th March – Coal scuttle overturned in kitchen, More knocks;

Wednesday 14th March – Spoons moved to cupboard under sink (discovered by Mrs. Ophelia); Protest from domestic staff; Horses set loose in night;

Thursday 15th March – Jam jars in cellar broken across floor, "tappings in walls";

Friday 16th March – Betty Coombe finds maggots in her bed – hysterics;

Saturday 17th March – Small fire in hay-barn, discovered and doused by Rudd;

Monday 19th March – "Bad night", many knocks, rattles, bangs at Big House and in stables;

Tuesday 20th March – Lister's shaving kit moved from his dresser to the pantry, smeared with unidentified grease;

Wednesday 21st March – More roof noise, spoons again moved to cupboard under sink (Discovered there by Sukie); Several stable stalls opened, allowing horses to escape;

Thursday, 22nd March – Saturday 24th March – Lister on business in York; No disturbances;

Monday 26th March – Upper floor shutters and windows opened during snowfall; Betty accused, tearfully gives four weeks' notice;

Tuesday 27th March – Mrs. Lister's clock moved to head of main staircase, along with six spoons (Discovered by Lister himself);

Wednesday 28th March – Lister rages out of house at 11 p.m. to "chase the idiots throwing stones at his window"; Thinks he sees someone fleeing across the pasture field;

Thursday 29th March – Saddles and equipment in stables tack-room scattered over floor, some damaged (discovered by Widdison, 3:15 p.m.);

Saturday 31st March – Mrs. Lister's clock disappears; Lister's antiquarian notes and

227

> *finds scattered around his study (Door still locked, only Lister held key);*
>
> *Monday 2nd April – Lister walks dog, encounters spectral giants, returns home shocked, does not venture outside again until day of his demise;*
>
> *Tuesday 3rd April – Friday 6th April – More general disturbances, knocking, thumping;*
>
> *Friday 6th April – Lister writes to his man of business about quitting Stephill and returning to York;*
>
> *Saturday 7th April – Volume on local history loaned by Mrs. Duexbury found torn to pieces and thrown on dining room fire (Discovered by Tope);*
>
> *Monday 9th April, approx. 10:15 a.m. – Lister discovered dead below the Great Skirtful of Rocks.*

To this summary of our interviews Holmes had appended in his own cramped handwriting:

> *Of note:*
>
> *No disturbances on Sundays or on Friday 30th March (Good Friday).*
>
> *Possible romantic relationship between Carl Ophelia and Sukie Murgatroyd?*
>
> *Rudd says servants suspect occasional "irregular" relationship between Lister and his "town maid" Betty Coombe – but Betty has now given notice.*
>
> *Local estate owner Mrs. Claire Duexbury is a widow of considerable worth. She has been a frequent visitor at Stephill.*
>
> *The clock.*
>
> *The spoons.*

I reviewed our evidence so far, trying to see the case as Holmes would, but as usual the trick eluded me.

We left the ridge's shelter and were assailed by the bitter Yorkshire cold. It seemed unfair that we should suffer both chill wind on the high ground and freezing mist in the valley below.

Holmes led the way, setting the pace with his long gangly legs. He checked his pocketwatch, and then a compass. "Nine-twenty-five," he noted with satisfaction. "Almost the time that Mr. Lister observed his giants. We must hurry."

"You expect to see them also?" I asked, doubtfully.

"Only if we are fortunate, Watson. But if the spectres favour us with an appearance, then I guarantee that we shall encounter more of them than he did."

Slaithwaite was eager to take us up the remainder of the incline. Looming above to the left was the mist-smudged silhouette of the moor cairn where Lister had cut open the ancient tumulus and had experienced his extraordinary encounter. A short way beyond it, but not visible from our lower path, was the badly damaged Bronze Age cairn called the Great Skirtful, where the deceased had been discovered. [11]

"It's not far now, sirs," Slaithwaite assured us.

But Holmes halted and called our guide back. "I wish to remain here for the moment, Mr. Slaithwaite. We are approximately halfway to the fork that leads to the Grubstones or the reservoir, are we not, at an elevation of around one-thousand-and-fifty feet?"

"T' tarn, tha means? Aye, it's ovver there. That track teks y' above it, an if y' goes far enough y' find t' Little Skirtful. [12] There's cairns and Ne-o-lithic enclosures all 'cross these moors, and nobbut 'alf mile that way's t' Twelve Apostles stone circle." [13]

Holmes was not interested in any of those features for now. His attention was focussed on the crest west of us, the ridge where Lister's high return path ran. Behind and below us I could just glimpse the tarns, still partly iced over. In no direction was there any sign of civilisation, not even a house. With fog below and a cloud-heavy slow-dawning sky above, the bleak fields and ling were almost monochrome.

I confess to a moment's nervousness. There was on that lonely moor a sense of timeless mystery, of being close to things that were forgotten but not gone. Slaithwaite shifted uneasily.

Holmes checked his watch again. "By this time in Lister's regular routine, he would have reached the Great Skirtful," he judged. "It was evidently his custom to sit there on the old stones for five minutes and recover his breath. Then he would progress on towards the excavated barrow." He consulted his compass and watch again. "An understanding of the geography of the area is vital, quite vital."

Above us on the crest, something caught my eye. Something was moving in the mist by the cairn – something huge.

"Holmes!" I exclaimed, drawing the detective's attention to the thing.

"The giant," he whispered back to me, in fascinated tones.

What we saw was a mere silhouette, a darker shape in the obscuring mist, but it was unlike any outline I had ever seen. It loomed impossibly, supernaturally large. As well as a shadowy smudge in a vaguely humanoid form, the moving object was surrounded by a glowing aura. It shimmered with rainbow arcs and seemed to rise up higher even as we watched it. Then a second shape shimmered in beside it, and a third.

We had found the giants of Rombald's Moor.

The spectral titans loomed over the sundered barrow, looking towards us like primitive gods.

Slaithwaite muttered an oath. "Ah've not seen t' like o' that since I were a bairn," he whispered.

The central giant raised his arm and lifted his hat to us. I turned and saw that Holmes had raised his deerstalker cap in a similar fashion, as if greeting the apparitions.

My mind raced back to my friend's conversation yesterday on the train from King's Cross:

"The *Brockengespenst*, or Brocken Spectre, is named for the Brocken Mountain in Saxony-Anhalt, tallest of the Harz range," Holmes had lectured me. "It was originally described in the literature from first-hand observations by Lutheran pastor Johann Silberschlag in 1780. He was climbing the Brocken's slopes one morning when he saw ahead a vast shadowy giant looming from the mist, surrounded with a rainbow aura."

"And his account was believed?" I asked.

"Silberschlag was a man of science. He carefully observed and noted that the spectre mirrored his own motions. When he raised his hand so did it. As he approached, the apparition diminished in size. In this way he concluded that he had encountered an unusual and fascinating optical phenomenon. The dawn sun behind and below him was projecting his shadow onto low cloud in the mists about him. Air-moisture refracted the light to cause the fractal glow. In short, Watson, the spectre was not spectral, but of the spectrum." [14]

"That is a most remarkable weather condition," I owned. "You believe that this accounts for Lister's vision?"

"The so-called 'Brocken Giant' has been witnessed on other hillsides in similar conditions at dawn and dusk. I believe there are accounts of a Big Grey Man of Ben McDhui in Scotland, for example. [15] And you will note from Rudd's missive that the children of Burley brave the moors to view their local spectre often, which suggests a replicable event."

"Lister was rather affected by a mere optical illusion, Holmes!"

"By reputable accounts, the vision can be somewhat disturbing, Doctor. The shadow falls on water droplets at varying distances from the eye, confusing depth perception. Movements of the clouds can seem to impart the giant with independent motion. Running from the giant actually causes the shadow to swell in size and appear to be catching up. And of course, at the highest climes in thin oxygen, the mind is scarcely at its most acute. In Hogarth Lister's case, however, I suspect that it was the violence he witnessed between those shadows that disturbed him the most. He was convinced that one had murdered the other."

"But Holmes . . . if we accept that Lister saw human silhouettes projected onto cloud or fog, then perhaps he did witness an attack! Then the mortal murderer had strong reason to go for the sole observer of his crime."

But as usual, Holmes would not be lured into theorising without sufficient data. "We must wait our time, my friend – and then we must hunt our ghosts!"

And hunt them we had. As I peered through that cold wet miasma at the swollen apparitions that filled the sky before us, I felt the same prickle of superstitious awe that primitive man must have felt at such encounters in an age before scholarship or civilisation. Here on the edge of the Neolithic moor we seemed on the border between the settled realms of Britain and something from a lost and uncanny time.

As I turned to Holmes, so too one of the Spectres resorted to his companion.

"Remarkable," Holmes murmured. "All the accounts are verified. The shifting stratus clouds indeed produce an illusion of independent activity."

I thought of how carefully Holmes had positioned us. "We are almost exactly east of the barrow," I realised. "This is the only place that lines up the rising sun, the shadow-caster, and the monument."

"And the ridge-edge hides us from view from anyone further along the higher track. The drop acts like a *ha-ha* in a landscaped garden, [16] obscuring the persons whose shadows are projected whilst their silhouettes are shown large upon the mists."

"We coomed oop 'ere as lads," Slaithwaite reminisced, "if we durst. T' giants al'us appear in our likenesses. [17] My granny, she said that's 'ow's they shews themse'ns when they comes in judgement. Like as we're testing of ours'cn."

"They surely tested Mr. Lister," I admitted. "Holmes, if there were two people at this spot on the morn that Lister saw his Spectres, then surely what he apprehended was an act of violence between two mortal beings. One assaulted, perhaps murdered the other." I cast around the barren ridge-track for any sign of lethal deeds.

"Too much time and too many boots have passed since Easter Monday," the detective cautioned. He replaced his cap and strode on, dismissing the apparitions now they had offered their testimony. "Come, we must proceed to the monuments."

His Brocken Spectre turned away too and rippled into insubstantial cloud. The instant of primal awe faded and I felt like myself again.

We climbed out of the wet mist, along a left fork that led us up a steep edge until we were a hundred feet higher. Eventually we reached another junction where a spur track doubled back to the Grubstones. [18] There was little to see at the ancient site, save for a dozen stubby rocks in a circle in the heather and bracken. Some part of the ring may have been lost to a more recent grouse but. [19]

Another short brisk walk brought us to the Great Skirtful of Stones where the wrathful giantess had emptied her pinafore of gritstone slabs. The scatter of rocks was frost-rimed white, a low strand that appeared suddenly as the rising sun peered above it as we approached. The phantasmal mist melted away.

"Mr. Lister were ovver there," our guide told us, pointing beyond the low brow of the scattered monument. He brought us to a shallow drop that might have been dug out as a hunting hide. A steep bank dropped perhaps twenty feet and there were some protruding stones that might have caused serious injury to a falling man, but it was hardly the precipice that I had been expecting.

Holmes questioned Slaithwaite again on the detail of the scene as it had been discovered, but the head groom had absorbed little additional detail. "'E were just dead in't sike," [20] he shrugged.

We clambered down with difficulty to where Lister had lain guarded by his agitated setter. "Was the dog fierce?" Holmes wanted to know. "Might she have gone for a stranger who tried to harm her master?"

Slaithwaite shook his head. "Punch were a town dog," he revealed, as if he was confessing some terrible defect. "She's as timid as owt."

"Where is she now?" I wondered.

"Missus Duexbury's 'ouse at Crag Top. Poor thing were frit t' death," our guide reported, then added, "T' dog, I mean. Missus Duexbury din't seem mort [21] bothered when she 'eard about Mr. Lister."

"But the staff seem to feel there was some closeness between the lady and your employer," I noted.

Slaithwaite blew out his cheeks. "Some folks 'as too much time t' gossip on stuff that's now't of their concern," he disapproved. "May'ap as Missus Duexbury did take a shine to Mr. Lister. She's been a widderwoman these ten years an' more, and 'er a fine figure of a lady wi' lands and a fair income. If she saw Mr. Lister as a good prospect, then 'e 'ad no less a reason to court 'er. Though *I'd* look carefully if my daughter was to be walking out wi' that sour old fellow as 'er second."

"Why?" I wondered. Rudd's letter had not painted his employer in an entirely favourable light, but there was something in the head groom's tone that suggested more than a casual caution.

Slaithwaite paused, reluctant to speak ill of the dead. At last he ventured, "'E weren't alus kind t' lasses. That Betty Coombe for one."

"Miss Coombe denied any special relationship with Mr. Lister," Holmes mentioned.

"Aye, well, it's not my way t' repeat stories. I didn't see now't nor 'ear now't. But I'd'uv looked askance at my lassie stepping out wi' Mr. Lister. Nobbut that would be different from 'is courting a rich lady like Mrs. Duexbury."

Slaithwaite could not be drawn further on the subject. We trudged on along the high ridge path to the broken ground where Lister had cut open a barrow mound to such local consternation. The heather-topped tump was little more than a swelling out of the slope, scattered with more of the same stones that formed so many prehistoric relics on these moors. A wedge of newly-turned soil showed where diggers had broken into the cairn to seek for treasure.

"Who undertook the work?" Holmes enquired.

"Them as wanted Mr. Lister's brass more'n to drink quietly in any public 'ouse in these parts," our guide assured us. "Local fellers and some blokes 'ired in Ilkley and Burley-in-Middleton. You've no idea of the rows. George Sutton, 'e nearly clouted a bloke in't White 'Orse. But they was only 'ere for three days, for there were now't in't 'cairn but for a few scraps."

"Why was the dig so controversial?" I wondered.

Slaithwaite screwed his face up with thought as he tried to express his feeling. "T' mound . . . it's on Mrs. Duexbury's land alright, but . . . it's not 'ers. She's a newcomer, only been 'ere these twenty-five years. That mound, it's been ere for . . . well, since Moses were a lad. And it's . . . well, it shouldn't be maithered, [22] that all."

Holmes climbed atop the ruin and ascertained that the lower path was not quite visible because of the gradients between.

"This is close to where Lister must have witnessed the Brocken spectres," I judged.

Holmes agreed absently, but I could tell his attention was occupied by the scatter of dig debris. He squatted down and examined some of the overturned stones more carefully.

"These have been shifted twice," he determined, bringing out his magnifying lens to look more closely at a small cluster of rocks. "The first time was when they were disturbed by the excavation. You can see the ancient water-marks and lichen patterns on the side that was formerly exposed. But they have been moved again since they were put back into the hole. Note these much fainter traces of exposure, and the way that the frost coats this section differently?"

Holmes carefully lifted the stones away. Buried beneath them was a burlap bag no larger than a fist, tied up with a piece of twine. He carefully pulled it out and sniffed it. "Ah. Yes."

"What is it?" I enquired inevitably.

"*Pimpinella anisum*, if I am not mistaken," my friend answered. He carefully sliced the twine, leaving the knot intact for later inspection, and opened the bag to reveal sage-coloured dried ovoid fruits no larger than peanuts. "Aniseed," he verified triumphantly. "A carminative digestive and expectorant. The Romans attributed it with aphrodisiac qualities and used it regularly in cooking." [23]

"What's it doing a-buried there?" Slaithwaite puzzled. "Aniseed's not from these parts."

"From Egypt originally, Mr. Slaithwaite," Holmes instructed. "As for its placement and concealment, well . . . that was part of the plan to murder Hogarth Lister!"

Holmes interviewed the housekeeper.

"Why no," Mrs. Ophelia told us, "I didn't know Mr. Lister before we came to Stephill. My boy and I answered an advertisement for a cook and handyman at Mr. Lister's York house after his previous housekeeper had resigned. But before we ever moved in, Mr. Lister sold up and came out here to the wilds of the West Riding. The local people? Well some of 'em's all right, but there's others what wouldn't give you the time of day. The disturbances? Well, first I thought it were that Alice Champion's family a-causing trouble, but now I'm convinced it was the work of spirits. How else does you account for all them knockings and rappings of a night? It's a buried prince under that barrow that was disturbed, or I'll be bound. Betty Coombe? Well I'm not one to talk, but when you hears a quiet tread creeping to 'er room in the attic some nights, you 'as to wonder, don't you? And Mr. Lister the only fellow in the house? Mrs. Duexbury? Didn't see much of 'er except to serve up tea. She and Mr. Lister spent a fair bit of time getting excited about that there cairn, but I reckon that the bloom came of the rose a bit after they found nought much. I daresay she discovered the master's bad temper, like as not. And he had one."

Holmes questioned the maid of all work.

"Oh yes, this place is 'aunted, sirs, no question of that. Why, if you only 'eard t' knockings and bangings of an evening! Such a racket as you'd scarcely believe. It's just as old Jack Widdison warned." Sukie Murgatroyd leaned in confidentially. "*No* good comes of breaking into t' moors mounds. Just look at pore Mr. Lister! Yes, it was me as discovered t' spoons in the bucket under t' kitchen sink – and '*ow* they got there from their drawer with neither me nor Mrs. Ophelia seeing owt I cannot say. Me, I took service 'ere after Alice Champion went last November. Service is service in these times. But she warned me, like, to steer clear of old Lister's wanderin' 'ands, though. 'Don't you end up like that Betty Coombe from town,' she told me, and I've been careful. Yes, I 'ave sometimes taken a stroll with Carl Ophelia. Can't a lass chat with a fellow without there's nasty rumours? I'm a good chapel girl. No, I don't 'ave keys to the 'ouse. Only Mr. Lister and Mrs. Ophelia 'as them, and Mr. Lister was the only one with keys to 'is study."

Holmes spoke with Larry the page boy.

"It was me what found Mrs. Duexbury's book all tore up on't fire," he revealed proudly. "An' I was second one there when t' coal scuttle got pushed over, after Mrs. O. 'erself. And I saw all t' jam jars brokken i't cellar – 'ad to clean 'em up – *and* I saw Mr. Lister's study when it was all tore up. We all thought 'e'd go into a mighty rage at that, but instead 'e just went all quiet-like. Aye, I've know Sukie an' Alice all me life, played together as bairns. No, I stay away from't stables if I can. That Lewis Wilson clouted me round' t'ear-oil. Aye, I know t' giant. But you 'ave t' pick your morning and be lucky wi't weather. An it's not alus safe to go t' giants, 'cos sometimes they take a misliking t' you, like they did wi' Mr. Lister."

Holmes confronted the town maid.

"Like I told you before, it's nobody's business but mine if anybody tried to take liberties," Betty Coombe insisted. "Some people just 'as nasty minds. If there was any mischief then it was Mr. Lister 'oo started it and what's a pore girl to do what needs to keep 'er place? But I'd 'ad enough of the old miser and 'is grousing. And then Mr. Lister accuses me of opening all the upstairs shutters an' letting the snow in. No, it was the last straw. I gave my notice. I'm back to York and good riddance t' this place! Ghosties and knockers and fire-starters and giants! And what about them wriggly maggots in my bed, eh? Brr, I shudder to remember it! I'm leaving this accursed place an' never coming back. Mrs. Duexbury? Don't talk to me about Mrs. Duexbury. I 'ave nothing to say about Mrs. Duexbury."

"Gaw, it's not boggarts!" old Jack Widdison insisted. "Nor any other foolishness. 'Tis men as caused Mr. Lister's death and men as made mischief in't stables and big 'ouse. I said as opening t' mound 'ud bring trouble, but not 'cause of t' soo-per-natural. We 'as enough troubles wi'out t' divvil getting involved. But that dig as caused so much bad feeling in't village an' came t' nowt, that were t' start on it. 'There'll be trouble,' says I, and lo, we 'as fires and rackets and things gone astray, and then we 'as bloody murther! Aye, I found t' mess i' tack room, but that were no bogie or moors-knocker. That were a bloke as needs a thrashing."

"Hardly knew Mr. Lister," Carl Ophelia declared, "'cept that 'e gave me orders about the 'orses and yard. Saw and 'eard some of the strange events, and I was one of the men on guard some nights. Me mum thinks it was unquiet spirits. She's chapel but I'm not really a believer. 'Er and Sukie are both a bit gullible like that – too gullible. I've been watching to see 'oo's not about and 'oo is when trouble 'appens, not but what things 'aven't gone quiet since Mr. Lister turned up dead. I'm watching Lewis Wilson, the jockey, specially 'ard. There's something about 'im. I didn't get on with the fellow afore 'im, but Wilson . . . well, I don't like t' turn my back on the man."

"Carl Ophelia's a cheat and a liar," Lewis Wilson countered when we saw the jockey. "'E cheats at cards and I reckon as 'e's leading young Sukie on. 'E got the fellow before me sacked, an' I reckon it was 'cause Ophelia owned 'im money. Lister? Well, 'e 'ad a nasty temper. Beat that page lad something cruel when 'is clock vanished. Dismissed one of the maids on evidence as wouldn't hang a dog. But he got 'is comeuppance with the hill-spectres. 'E were a different man after that. I didn't think 'ed ever venture onto those moors again. Why would he? But 'e did – and that were the end of 'im!"

"I dunno," the groom George Sutton told us. It seemed to be his favourite word. "It's all a mickle mystery. I was there a-watching out all t' night and I 'ears the noises but I sees nowt. I dunno but it must be bogies. I've nivver known owt like it, sirs. I've been 'ere since Fred Clough were let go, an' it's not what you'd call an 'appy place. Fred? 'E's working over Manchester way now, pore soul. [24] As to why Mr. Lister went back oop t' 'ill, well . . . I reckon the giants must uv called 'im. No other reason, is there? Trick o' t' light? Aye, some says that, but I dunno . . . ."

"I 'ope y' don't mind me callin' you like this, sir," Samuel Rudd repeated to Holmes as he had when we had first arrived. "It's just that it's so murky, an' I bethought, 'Well, Sam, 'oo could ivver get to t' bottom o' this?' So I wrote."

"And right you were to bring me in," Sherlock Holmes assured the stableman. "The matter is hardly complex, but it offers a patina of interest that diverts me from a recent failure. You brought me my telegrams from Ilkley? Splendid. Now we shall progress towards a solution."

We arrived at Mrs. Duexbury's house in time for high tea. "Your recent opening of the cairn near the Great Skirtful has been rather controversial," Holmes began as he sipped his Oolong.

That was enough to set the lady into a long recitation of grievances about who had said what in the village, about the complaints from vicar and Methodist minister, about what some grouse-hunting colonel had demanded, about letters of protest from people who had never even been to the shire. That led her to discussion of Hogarth Lister, whom she described in a manner that suggested any affection she might have felt for him had significantly cooled. "I had thought him a gentleman," Mrs. Duexbury sniffed when I dared broach that topic, "but I was proved wrong."

"How did you come to this understanding?" I asked.

"I received a visit from . . . an individual who appraised me of some of Mr. Lister's personal failings. Then I felt rather foolish for supporting him in the matter of opening the tumulus in the face of local opposition. And for . . . considering any suit he may have brought."

"This individual informed you of an infidelity that brought Lister's character into disrepute," Holmes observed, telling rather than asking. "Did you inform Mr. Lister of what you had learned?"

"The information was confidential, but I was able to verify it. I merely told Hogarth – that is, Mr. Lister – that I was not minded to receive him on the same terms as before."

"This would be on or just before Saturday the 7th," Holmes supposed. To me he explained, "The date that Mrs. Duexbury's book was shredded and burned. May we assume that this particular event was not initiated by the ghost? Young Larry Tope discovered the volume in the hearth and drew an erroneous conclusion,"

"Mr. Lister was not pleased at my rejection," Mrs. Duexbury admitted.

"You took his dog in," I observed.

"I saw no need for Punch to suffer abandonment as well."

"Did you have any further communication with Lister after the 7th?" Holmes checked. "You sent no message?"

"I did not. I was done with him. I had not previously understood the viciousness and intensity of his temper, nor the core meanness of his personality. I consider myself fortunately warned."

Burley Woodhead not being large enough even to have its own constable, our last visit of the day was to the police house in Burley-in-Wharfdale. Inspector Shotley met us there to hear what progress Holmes had made in a case that seemed impenetrable to the rustic officer. "I'm not even sure but it's not a matter for the church rather than the constabulary," he confessed to us.

"I think we can avoid a liturgy of exorcism," Holmes assured him. "There were from the start a number of features that helped distinguish between diablerie and the merely diabolic. Any evil here comes from wholly mortal roots. I refer you to the following facts: That disturbances at Stephill took place both inside and beyond the big house, but never on a Sunday, that a bag of aniseed was buried where the barrow had been opened; that Burley Woodhead is a small insular village in a tightly-knit community; that Mrs. Duexbury turned down Mr. Lister on discovering something from a third party; that Mr. Lister's mother's clock was moved and then vanished; and that the ghost was attracted to Mr. Lister's spoons."

"How can any of that untangle this mess?" Shotley demanded in gruff frustration.

"Holmes can find sense where the rest of us founder in supposition and confusion," I warranted my friend.

The great detective responded modestly with an acknowledging bow. "There are a few more details I must confirm," he told us. "I am awaiting a message from Lister's man of business in York, and another from the County Registrar. Then I will tell you who murdered the Brocken Spectre and why, and we may bring Hogarth Lister's killers to justice."

We returned to Stephill Farm, and Holmes spoke to Sukie as she took our coats. "Let Mrs. Ophelia and Mr. Slaiththwaite know that all the staff must gather here at eight-thirty sharp tomorrow. I have an announcement and will be setting the ghosts of Burley Woodhead to rest." To me he added, "The information I expect from my long-range enquiries will be here by then, and I will have all the proof I require to offer you answers to this elementary little puzzle."

We retired to the parlour, where a fire had been set because of the unseasonal chill, and we watched the sun set over Rombald's Moor. "Whatever happened to old Rombald when his wife caught him?" I pondered. "Or is he still running?"

"We have seen spouses do dire things *in extremis*, Watson, and go to significant lengths to avoid being caught for it," Holmes reminded me. "Domestic disputes can raise the very devil. Ah, Betty, thank you." The parlour-maid had brought us our evening toddies.

"Are you able to tell me who and what you suspect yet, Holmes?" I ventured. "I know that you affect the showman's preference for the grand reveal, some habit from your days treading the boards, [25] but pity the poor fellow who has to write an account of this. At least tell me the significance of the spoons."

Betty left us alone watching the darkening Yorkshire wilds. Holmes offered me one piece of important advice, noting, "I am reminded of a case from 1716, recorded by none other than the founder of Methodism the Reverend John Wesley, who experienced events similar to those at Stephill as a boy growing up in his family home at Epworth, Lincolnshire. Wesley's father, the parish vicar, was unpopular in the neighbourhood because of his support of legislation that would drain the local fens, depriving many men of their lucrative smuggling side-trade. For two months the family endured a persecution of supposed knocking spirits, of petty mischiefs attributed to phantoms, and of all the trappings of a fine rural ghost story. The Wesleys' accounts are perhaps the most comprehensive study of such events ever to be committed to paper." [26]

"You draw parallels with the apparent hauntings here at Stephill?"

"Indeed. An unpopular 'outcomer' moves to a lonely pastoral setting and comes into conflict with the denizens. Attempts are made to frighten him, to drive him away. The question is why. In Samuel Wesley's case, it was almost certainly because of his political views. Here the matter is more personal: The assault upon the shaving kit, for example. Then there was the vanishing of Lister's mother's clock, an object which was precious to him – perhaps a caution that he was running out of time. The recurring tampering with the spoons is the key to the case, of course, and I have the advantage of having corresponded with Hogarth Lister's man of business regarding that matter."

"The man mentioned cutlery?"

"He was able to tell me that some thirty-three years ago, Lister acrimoniously dismissed a staff member for the theft of some silver spoons. She denied the allegations but was released without references, with a stain upon her character."

"Lister was a fellow prone to jumping to conclusions and punishing his domestics with little evidence," I noted. I doubt I would have got on with the man in life.

"At Epworth Rectory, I would have begun by reviewing where any perpetrator of the ghost's tricks must have been located to perform his hauntings. Since some things happened inside the house and others outside I would have begun with the hypothesis that at least two persons were involved, one with access to the family – or one of the family – and another able to approach the house in the darkness to work mischief outside."

"Here we have had events inside and others in the stables," I recognised. "And presumably someone rattling shutters and disturbing to roof. That speaks to more than one hoaxer."

"There was always likely to be more, Watson. It takes a pair to project two Brocken spectres."

"But one killed the other. Lister witnessed it."

"Did he? Think on the occasion. Lister was following his regular and fixed routine, walking his dog. He was delayed until the sun was right at the excavated barrow. Punch was fascinated by the dig and would not come away."

I puzzled as to how Holmes might deduce this, then remembered his discovery. "The aniseed bag! Dogs react to it as a cat does to catnip! She would have been hard to drag away from that spot. And that put Lister in the exact and only place where he might witness the cloud giants."

"Who is to say that the cairn was not put there those thousands of years ago to mark the precise place where such encounters occurred? But watch."

Holmes held his hands so that the lamp projected their shadows onto the parlour wall. He seemed in silhouette to stab two fingers of the right hand into the left, but I could see that his hands were six inches apart, one behind the other.

"Two actors might mime an assault, were they both lined up with the rising sun," I realised. "What Lister took for a vision of murder may have been another charade to scare him."

"Much of the pantomime here seems to have been intended as a message: 'Do the right thing at last', or 'Your sins will find you out'. Almost all the most distinctive hauntings were directed at the old man personally, right up to the ransacking of his study – though that may have had a secondary reason. Lister's will is missing."

"His will? Why would . . . ?"

"Murder was the final resort," Holmes suggested. "When ghostly raps would not suffice to make Lister relent, the phantoms became more imaginative. At last they deployed the giants of the moor to give their warning. When that failed to move the victim, they had to arrange his demise."

"But how would they lure Lister back to the moors after his previous fright?"

"There are several ways, but the most likely would be a simple ruse. Perhaps a message came, supposedly from Mrs. Duexbury, seeking a reconciliation – a secret dawn meeting at the Great Skirtful? There are other possibilities; I do not insist upon that interpretation."

"You sound to have already decided who the murderer is, Holmes."

"It was always only a matter of gathering evidence to prove a theory, Watson. But now we must retire. We may expect a long and interrupted night."

I smelled smoke around five in the morning. When I rose to investigate, I found the corridor and landing thick with fume.

Holmes appeared from his chamber. Like me, he was full dressed, ready for adventure.

240

"If you are right about our bedtime drinks," I told him, "then we have just survived a murder attempt. If we had been drugged insensible, then we would be smothered by smoke inhalation."

We wrapped scarves across our lower faces and plunged through the fumes to find the source of the fire. A blaze had been started in Lister's ground floor study, directly below the rooms where Holmes and I had been lodged. Some accelerant – Holmes believed it was stable paraffin – had been used to hasten and magnify the blaze.

I sounded the alarm, pounding on the dinner gong to warn the household of the danger. I judged that the fire was too well set to douse now. It would claim the big house.

Holmes counted out the bleary, surprised staff. Woken by my alarum, the stable crew began to appear, clamouring to see what could be done in the way of fire-fighting.

"We are missing Betty," Holmes alerted me. "Come, Watson, we must venture back upstairs. Rudd, it's too late for a bucket chain. Evacuate everybody to the stable tack room. Send Sutton to summon Inspector Shotley and the police fire-watch."

With these words he plunged back into the smoke, making for the attic where the parlour maid slept. I surged after him, trying to hold my breath as we passed through the worst of the fire-fumes.

We used the servant's steps to reach the attic. Flames were licking at the stair treads as we chased up them. Holmes quickly found the room where Betty Coombe was quartered.

I half-expected the girl not to be there. It was she who had brought us our toddies, the drink that Holmes had warned me not to consume. "Kitchen staff may add all kinds of things to their preparations," he had cautioned. "Who can now say what hallucinogen Lister had ingested on the day he encountered Brocken Spectres?"

But Betty lay there, unconscious, either from the thick vapours that now choked the upper floors of the house, or for more sinister reasons. She too had drunk a bedtime cup. I checked her pulse and found it, though it was thready.

Holmes hoisted her across his shoulder in a fireman's lift. We groped our way back along the passage, escaping down the main stair which had not yet been consumed by the spreading conflagration.

It felt icy cold outside the house, away from the flames. Rudd and Slaithwaite were watching in consternation as the building went up. They hastened forward to help us carry Betty to the distant tack room.

I did a quick check of who was there. Of the staff, George Sutton and Carl Ophelia had gone for aid but the others were all present.

"What 'appened to Betty?" Rudd asked urgently.

241

"She has been drugged," I opined. "The same narcotic was meant to sedate Holmes and I, so that we all died in that fire. Somebody heard Holmes announce that he was ready to reveal Lister's murderer, and therefore took decisive action."

"I might have preferred a less pyrotechnic way of dispatching me," the detective added. "I am sorry to have endangered the rest of you. I had not realised how damaged Mrs. Ophelia was."

The housekeeper startled as she was named. "Me? The fire never touched me."

"But Hogarth Lister did," Holmes revealed. "Thirty-three years ago, when you were in service to him under a different name. His man of business remembers it all. How you claimed he had married you, but the certificate was false, the wedding a sham. How you were with child. But then you were accused of theft and dismissed without reference – pregnant, disgraced, and forgotten."

"I don't know what you're on about," Mrs. Ophelia protested.

"Come, now," Holmes chided her. "A pious woman who would not allow the haunting to happen on Sundays and holy days should not resort to falsehoods. It is time for the truth – *Anna Siddle*."

Mrs. Ophelia blanched at the name. "You'd think a man would remember a woman 'oo's child 'e fathered, 'oo's life 'e ruined," she spat. "But I suppose I've changed a lot over thirty 'ard desperate years, doing as I 'ad to t' bring up a son."

Sukie's eyes went wide. "You can't tell 'un . . . !" she blurted.

"She need not. It is evident," Holmes declared. "When appeals for support and attempts at blackmail failed, Mrs. Ophelia and her lad took service in Lister's own household,. The previous housekeeper had resigned in protest at Lister's treatment of Betty, and Lister sought to escape the growing rumours of his behaviour by rusticating to the country."

I realised what had happened. "And Lister brought the Ophelias along! With the mother in the kitchen, preparing all food, and with access to keys, and the son in the stables able to roam freely at night, they were well set to go into the haunting business."

Holmes crooked a long finger at the housekeeper. "'*God has given you one face, and you make yourself another*,' [27] Mrs. Ophelia."

"It were you?" Slaithwaite demanded, pointing an accusing finger at the snarling woman.

"Not her and Carl alone. More agents make for better alibis and a far better ghost story. That's why Carl had to suborn Sukie, so that a young and inexperienced maid in her first service would add her efforts to the spookery. And why Alice Champion's aggrieved family were probably

242

engaged to avenge their kinwoman's dismissal. The Champions and the Murgatroyds are allied by marriage several times, I believe."

Sukie trembled, her eyes flicking from Mrs. Ophelia to Holmes. "I nivver thowt t' kill no-one!" she promised. "It were just t' skeer t' nasty owd man so's 'e'd do right by Carl. Nivver a penny's inheritance! Nivver an acknowledgement of 'is own lad! But . . . ." She cast an anguished, betrayed look at the housekeeper.

"Lister seems to have done a dirty trick on you long ago," I told Mrs. Ophelia. "But you have committed murder."

"Her and Carl, miming on the hill," Holmes agreed, "and then when even the Brocken Spectres did not move Lister to honesty, the message luring him onto the moors again, to make the prophetic vision come true."

Mrs. Ophelia was defiant, even venomous. "Saying it's one thing. Proving it's another!"

"The only other victims of your campaign were those whom you saw as rivals," Holmes went on. "The maggots in Betty's bed – were they to drive her away from an abusive employer or to punish her for succumbing to the same pressures as you once did? Did she suspect too much, living and working beside you these months, that she had to be disposed of as Watson and I were to have been? Did she know that you had sneaked a copy of Lister's study key so you might find, perhaps substitute, his last will and testament? And of course it was you, not Betty, who revealed the truth of Lister's character to Mrs. Duexbury."

"All supposition," Mrs. Ophelia crowed.

She was no match for Sherlock Holmes. "Your true identity can be verified. Watson and I have samples of the drinks you prepared for us. When she wakes, Betty can testify as to who prepared the toddies. And I doubt that Sukie here will withhold much once she is interviewed by Inspector Shotley."

"Carl Ophelia!" I cried. "He went to fetch the police!"

"Sutton went for't bobbies," Slaithwaite corrected me. "Ophelia went t' get 'elp from t' other farms."

"Or t' flee away ovver t' moors," Rudd added wrathfully.

"I hope he does," Mrs. Ophelia snarled. "I 'ope you never catch 'im."

There was more leg-work to be done, detail to verify, but that was routine that Inspector Shotley's investigation could pursue. Mrs. Ophelia – Anna Siddle as she had been when she was a young, naïve girl who had believed herself lawfully and fortunately wed to coal tycoon Hogarth Lister – had lived a difficult and disreputable life, as any woman cast out without reputation or family and with a child swelling her belly might suffer. Sukie Murgatroyd, her head turned by the glamour of an older city suitor, would quickly confess her misdeeds. The surly Champions would confess too. They had intended mischief, not murder.

But Carl Ophelia was gone. The man who had met Lister alone at the Skirtful of Stones and battered him to death for his mother's sake was fled over the moors.

"Ah doubt it," old Jack Widdison told us. "Not 'afore dawn coomes oop. It's not easy ta flit o'a t' moors by neet. It's not safe, all scars and sikes, an' t' boggarts dooan't like it!"

"It's not easy," I agreed. "Not when one is being pursued by Sherlock Holmes."

We set off at first light, when Shotley had brought men to douse the big house blaze and to begin the manhunt for Ophelia. Holmes led Rudd and one group up past the tarn to the low ridge track, while I took Shotley, Slaithwaite, and others by the high ridge. We climbed through the mist, aware that the damp clinging fog might obscure a fugitive only yards away from us.

As the sun rose before us, I saw for the second time that strange, eerie phenomenon of the Brocken Spectre surrounded by its rainbow glory. Holmes had achieved the same spot as we had occupied before, and it was the great detective's distinctive giant silhouette that loomed huge on the grey westward clouds. He rose vast and implacable, a titan of justice, and I felt a pang of pity for Carl Ophelia or any wrongdoer who saw him approaching.

I often wonder if that Spectre was the last thing that the hunted man ever saw. It was my search party who found him, fallen into one of the grouse buts not far from the Little Skirtful. His neck was broken.

To Slaithwaite, Widdison, and Sutton, the ancient giants of Rombald's Moor had claimed their vengeance.

NOTES

1 –   Frightened.

2 –   This remarkable Mesolithic and Neolithic landscape is well-described in *Prehistoric Rock Art of the West Riding: Cup-and-ring-marked Rocks of the Valleys of the Aire, Wharfe, Washburn and Nidd* (2003) by Boughey and Vickerman, (ISBN: 1870453328), but the volume is out of print so readers are advised to track down the CD version, or refer to the summary on Rombald's Moor at:
http://www.stone-circles.org.uk/stone/rombaldsmoor.htm

3 –   Pinafore.

4 –   According to W.S. Baring-Gould's biography *Sherlock Holmes of Baker Street* (1962), the great detective was born on January 6th, 1854 at Mycroft in the North Riding of Yorkshire. His older brother was named after the location. This same source records Holmes's parents as Siger and Violet (*née* Sherringford) Holmes and gives his full name as William Sherlock Scott Holmes.

5 –   Mr. Grant Munro consulted Holmes in the first week of April 1888 to discover why his wife was requesting significant sums of money and sneaking away to secret rendezvous at a rural cottage. Holmes concluded that Mrs. Munro's American first husband had returned to blackmail her. For once the great detective erred. The occupant of the Norbury cottage was actually Lucy, Mrs. Munro's daughter by her first marriage to the now-deceased lawyer John Hebron. Since Hebron was a black man and the child of mixed race, Effie Munro had been afraid to reveal Lucy's existence to her second husband. On learning the truth, Mr. Munro welcomed wife and step-daughter into his care, to Watson's approval.

The account is given in "The Adventure of the Yellow Face" in *The Memoirs of Sherlock Holmes* (1893), wherein Holmes ruefully says, *"Watson, if it should ever strike you that I am getting a little overconfident in my powers, or giving less pains to a case than it deserves, kindly whisper 'Norbury' in my ear, and I shall be infinitely obliged to you."*

The story is notable as a rare occasion where Holmes is proved wrong and does not solve the case – events work out despite not because of him – and of a sympathetic Victorian treatment of mixed-race marriages and children.

6 –   Yorkshire dialect of "off away", from the Danish *gata*, meaning "way or street". "Get agate!" is a brusque dismissal meaning "Be on your way."

7 – Yorkshire dialect for a steep rockface, from the Old Norse *skera*, meaning a cut.

8 – From the Norwegian *sprekk* and Swedish *sprikka*, meaning "to crack".

9 – Yorkshire dialect for "starting to thaw or clear", from the Icelandic *glöggur*.

10 – Stiffened, set, or coagulated, from the Old Norse *storkna*

11 – The Great Skirtful of Stones is found at *OS Map Ref SE141446*. (2300 B.C.– 700 B.C.). All that now remains of the badly damaged Bronze Age cairn is a low ring of stones about twenty-six yards in diameter and eighteen inches high. A larger stone that might be a boundary marker or milestone stands in the middle of the site. Previous unsympathetic digging has partially destroyed the site, rubbish has been dumped into the holes, and much of the original stone had been robbed away. A smaller 'barrow' cairn to the southeast has been reduced even more – by Mr. Hogarth Lister, according to Dr. Watson's account.

A 1901 article in the *Shipley Express* (reprinted in *A History of Menston and Hawksworth*, Alistair Laurence, 1991, ISBN-10: 1870071751), describes *"a huge cairn of small boulders, nearly a hundred tons on a heap, although for centuries loads have been taken away to mend the trackways across the moor . . . . The centre of the cairn is now hollow, as it was explored many years ago, and from the middle human bones were taken and submitted to Canon Greenwell and other archaeologists"*.

Near the centre of the giant cairn is a large once-upright stone of more recent centuries upon which is etched the words, *"This is Rumbles Law."* The *Shipley Express* article explains that *". . . 'law' was always used in the British sense for a hill, and Rumbles Hill, or cairn, was a conspicuous boundary mark for many centuries. [Historian Mr. Turner] found in the Burley Manor Rolls, two centuries back, that on Rogation Day, when the boundaries were beaten by the inhabitants, they met on this hill, and describing their boundaries, they concluded the nominy by joining in the words, "This is Rumbles Law.""*

12 – The Little Skirtful of Stones at *OS Map Ref SE138452* is another Bronze Age round cairn, rather better preserved than the Great Skirtful though its centre has been dug out.

13 – The Twelve Apostles at *OS Map Ref SE126452* is a stone circle of about twelve yards diameter with twelve remaiing stones up to four feet high. It has been "modified" in the last two centuries and unofficially "restored" in recent years, with fallen stones re-erected, making its original layout hard to

determine. From this site, the rising summer solstice sun appears exactly above the turf-cut White Horse at Kilburn.

14 – The Brocken Spectre was a known phenomenon in the 19th century, though its cause was perhaps not universally understood. It makes an early fictional appearance in James Hogg's 1824 novel *The Private Memoirs and Confessions of a Justified Sinner: Written by Himself: With a Detail of Curious Traditionary Facts and Other Evidence by the Editor*. Dickens mentions it in *Little Dorrit* (1855-7) Book II Chapter 23 wherein Flora Finching says, "... *'ere yet Mr. F appeared a misty shadow on the horizon paying attentions like the well-known spectre of some place in Germany beginning with a B . . . .*" Lewis Caroll's humorous 1869 poem "Phantasmagoria" includes a Spectre who "... *tried the Brocken business first/but caught a sort of chill.*"

Perhaps the most complete reference is in Coleridge's "Constancy To His Ideal Object" (*Poetical Works*, 1828), which also notes how often the phenomenon is interpreted as a supernatural encounter. The poem closes:

> *And art thou nothing? Such thou art, as when*
> *The woodman winding westward up the glen*
> *At wintry dawn, where o'er the sheep-track's maze*
> *The viewless snow-mist weaves a glist'ning haze,*
> *Sees full before him, gliding without tread,*
> *An image with a glory round its head;*
> *The enamoured rustic worships its fair hues,*
> *Nor knows he makes the shadow he pursues!*

15 – Holmes refers to the *Am Fear Liath Mòr* that is encountered on Ben Macdui, the highest peak of the Cairngorms and second-highest mountain in the British Isles. His source for the legend is unclear, since the first published account of the Big Grey Man is commonly held to be climber J. Norman Collie's 1925 report of an 1891 encounter. Collie's report includes auditory phenomenon also, though: "*I began to think I heard something else than merely the noise of my own footsteps. For every few steps I took I heard a crunch, and then another crunch as if someone was walking after me but taking steps three or four times the length of my own . . . [as] the eerie crunch, crunch, sounded behind me, I was seized with terror and took to my heels, staggering blindly among the boulders for four or five miles.*"

A Scottish Brocken Spectre at Bidean nam Bian in Glen Coe featured on the BBC news website as recently as November 2018. The page includes some amazing photographs of the phenomenon:
https://www.bbc.com/news/uk-scotland-highlands-islands-46277410

16 – The *ha-ha*, a visual garden feature that hides a dividing trench and makes a lawn terrace appear continuous despite a boundary ditch, originated in New France from 1686 (as in Saint-Louis-du-Ha! Ha!), and appeared in the gardens of the Château de Meudon around 1700. It was described in Dezallier d'Argenville's *La théorie et la pratique du jardinage* (1709) and translated into English in 1712 by architect John James. Thereafter the feature was made fashionable by influential landscapers Charles Bridgeman, William Kent, and Capability Brown.

17 – "In Search of the Brocken Spectre on Burley Moor," a *Guardian* picture essay by Rebecca Cole and Janise Elie in March 2019 includes excellent images of the local phantom giants, which are indeed a long-known feature of the terrain and weather.
https://www.theguardian.com/environment/2019/mar/04/search-brocken-spectre-burley-moor

18 – The site is located at OS Map Ref SE137447. It has been variously interpreted as a Bronze Age ring cairn, a robbed round cairn, or the foundation wall of an Iron Age hut. English Heritage notes it as a stone circle. Only twenty stones remain, some almost buried in the heather.

19 – A trench dug as a hide for grouse shooting. There are many of these on Ilkley Moor, some of which have been lined from stones "borrowed" from the cairns and circles nearby.

20 – Yorkshire dialect for gulley or small stream, possibly from the Icelandic *siki*, meaning a rill.

21 – Much.

22 – Bothered, disturbed.

23 – The spiced Roman aniseed cake *mustaceoe* was served as a final course at erotic feasts and is cited as the origin of the mediaeval tradition of a wedding cake.

24 – Manchester is in Lancashire, the neighbouring county and great rival to Yorkshire, which is why Fred, forced to work there, has George Sutton's sympathies.

25 – Baring-Gould's Holmes biography reveals Holmes's travels as part of Michael Sasanoff's theatre troupe in 1879-1880, including an American tour where "*Holmes's Malvolio offered the most adequate presentation of that character that America had ever seen up to that time.*" Baring-Gould attributes Holmes's predilection to quoting Shakespeare to this period of the great detective's life.

26 – Diaries and essays from several family members and visitors chronicle the poltergeist-like events witnessed by thirteen-year-old John Wesley in 1716.

John Wesley reported, *"My father was thrice pushed by an invisible power, once against the corner of his bed, then against the door of the matted chamber, a third time against his study door. His dog always gave warning by running whining towards him, though he no longer barked at it as he did the first time."*

John's mother Susannah Wesley wrote, *"One night it made such a noise in the room over our heads as if several people were walking; then run up and down the stairs, and was so outrageous that we thought the children would be frightened, so your father and I rose and went down in the dark to light a candle. Just as we came to the bottom of the broad stairs, having hold of each other, on my side there seemed as if somebody had emptied a bag of money at my feet and on his as if all the bottles under the stairs (which were many) had been dashed into a thousand pieces [. . .] Sometimes it would make a noise like the winding up of a jack; at other times, as that night Mr. Hoole was with us, like a carpenter planning deals; but mostly commonly it knocked three and stopped and then thrice again and so many hours together."*

There are several good summaries of the incidents. I.A. Watson's monograph on the topic appears in his essay book *Where Stories Dwell* (2014, Pro Se Press, ISBN 10: 1500666173).

27 – Holmes quotes *Hamlet, Prince of Denmark*, Act 1 Scene III, where Hamlet rages at Ophelia, accusing her of corruption. The maiden in the play has cause to feel betrayed and abandoned by the prince who had formerly courted her, and at his rejection she runs mad and eventually kills herself.

The Adventure of
Miss Anna Truegrace
by Arthur Hall

Despite the continuing rain, I had decided on a short walk after breakfast. Sherlock Holmes was in the blackest of moods, hardly consenting even to acknowledge my greeting as I descended from my room, and causing me to seek the open air in order to steel myself against his morose demeanour. After walking the wet pavements for half-an-hour, I resolved to return to Baker Street, and it was as I approached our lodgings that I saw two people beneath a large umbrella standing uncertainly nearby.

Folding down and shaking my own umbrella, I opened the door and stepped inside. I turned to face the couple, and it was indeed a man and a woman as I had supposed, now watching me with enquiring eyes. "Mr. Sherlock Holmes?" the man enquired.

"No, but this is his residence. I am his associate, Doctor John Watson, and I'm sure Mr. Holmes will see you. Please leave your umbrella in the hallstand there, and follow me."

They did so, the lady closing the front door before they climbed the stairs behind me. I stepped into our sitting room with something of a flourish, watching with relief and pleasure my friend's surprise on seeing that I was accompanied.

"Ah, Watson. You have bought me new clients, I perceive."

"Conceivably, though I have not yet enquired as to their difficulty."

Holmes smiled quickly and introduced himself, having shed his rueful expression. "I have high hopes that they will present me with an interesting problem. I saw them alight from a four-wheeler as I looked down from our window, and noted that it took fully four minutes of discussion before they decided to approach our door. Surely, a simple matter would have required less consultation." He gestured towards the armchairs near the fire. "Pray let Doctor Watson relieve you of your outer garments and come to sit near the fire while I call for tea. Then, when you are ready, you can tell me how I can assist you."

I saw relief in the faces of both our visitors as I hung up their coats. Holmes shouted down to Mrs. Hudson and closed the door, before we took our seats.

"I'm Mr. Cedric Truegrace," the young man began rather stiffly before either Holmes or I could speak, "and this is my sister, Miss Anna Truegrace."

"You work in a clerical capacity and your sister has great fear of you," Holmes finished.

Mr. Truegrace appeared shocked. I had seen Holmes perform this feat many times before, but on this occasion it held no mystery for me. Our visitors glanced at each other, astonishment written on their faces.

"How in the world . . . ?"

"Come now, Mr. Truegrace," my friend continued. "The ink on your shirt cuff tells its own story, also revealing that you are left-handed, and anxious glances from your sister have been directed at you since the moment you entered the room." His stare grew hard. "Do you beat this lady, sir?"

I half-rose from my chair, horrified at the prospect of this innocent-looking girl being subjected to such treatment.

"No, gentlemen," she said quickly. "That is not the situation at all."

"I swear that I would never do any such thing," her brother protested. As he spoke, I heard the rattle of teacups outside our door and immediately intercepted Mrs. Hudson and relieved her of the tray. I placed it on a side-table and poured for the four of us before Mr. Truegrace continued. "No, things have occurred differently. It is a strange story."

"We are quite used to those." Holmes assured him.

"Anna saw herself in a vision, as the victim of a murderer. She could not see his face, but heard herself call my name."

Holmes surprised me by not receiving this with incredulity. He looked at Miss Truegrace with a thoughtful expression on his face. "You could not be mistaken? For example, could it be that you were calling to your brother for assistance?"

"Truly, I cannot say, for the vision was no more than a blurred image. I only know that I have been in mortal terror since. It is only with the greatest effort that I can bear to be in the company of Cedric, such is the pain of my apprehension."

The next few moments were passed in silence as we drank. I spent the interval in observing our visitors' appearance.

Mr. Truegrace, I believed, was in his late twenties, while his sister was perhaps two years his junior. They were of average height, he with whiskers dark along his jawbone and almost reaching his chin, while her auburn tresses hung shining below her bonnet. From their speech, I formed the impression that their education had not been neglected.

251

Miss Truegrace spoke again suddenly. "Such things have happened to me before, over the years, but never like this. That Cedric would harm me I cannot believe, and yet it is what I saw."

At once disappointment crept into my friend's face, yet I also sensed that he was mildly amused. He had anticipated a confrontation with a problem of complexity or intrigue, only to be faced with what he would surely regard as little more than a fairy story.

"I have encountered a 'visionary' before," Holmes said in a slow voice of forced tolerance. "I accompanied a client of a few years ago to a meeting, where a woman who called herself 'The Enlightened One' would retire to a locked room and experience visions with messages for members of her audience without. She appeared to be remarkably successful and profited greatly, until I discovered that another onlooker left the chamber at the same time with the selection of each new subject. He turned out to be her accomplice, who disclosed to her information he had gleaned through overheard conversations while mingling with the spectators, communicated through a parallel window by mirror flashes using a pre-arranged code." He fixed our visitors with a stern gaze. "You will see then why I find the concept incredible, even humorous, in its way."

"Was this during your residence in Montague Street?" I asked, not having heard this account before.

"It was well before your time, Watson. I had almost forgotten the affair. It was a ridiculously simple matter, which I solved quite quickly. The woman's stipulation that she was open to these experiences only on fine days, gave it away at once."

"My experiences are not rooted in trickery!' Miss Truegrace retorted. "They have troubled me all of my life."

"She speaks the truth," her brother confirmed. "There have been many instances during our childhood when such happenings have caused her distress, especially when our parents and other adults in whom she placed her confidence humoured her or responded with mockery. She informed a neighbour that his horse would run off, never to be seen again, and that very thing occurred within a week. A child disappeared and was found alive and well, exactly as Anna had described. As with all the other instances, her ability was never acknowledged."

"And recently? I cannot think that you would be here today, were there nothing more."

"There is indeed, Mr. Holmes. Two weeks ago our elderly maid, Ellen, collapsed and died while in our village on an errand. Four days before, Anna told me that this would happen. We confided in no one, not wishing to attract again the ridicule of years before. One of the reasons

252

that we gave up our home in the centre of Worcester to move to Courtney Dale was to escape this."

"And when did your latest experience occur?"

"This morning," Miss Truegrace said in a subdued voice. "During the early hours."

"But no crime has actually been committed?"

Her brother looked suddenly uncomfortable. "None, which is why we cannot avail ourselves of the protection of the official force. We have heard however, that you specialise in throwing light on the inexplicable."

"I have said before that I have no belief in the supernatural, and you must surely realise that even if that were not so and such things were a reality, I would have no power against them. Perhaps a priest would be of more use to you than I."

There was a long silence, during which our visitors took on a look of despair. Doubtlessly, I reflected, Sherlock Holmes was their last hope of preventing a crime that had yet to happen. I reviewed the words of Mr. Truegrace, and the fate of the maid, Ellen, troubled me. An incident from long ago came into my mind.

"Holmes, I have to tell you that I, also, have met something like this before." He turned his head towards me, as I continued. "I once had a patient, a most down-to-earth young woman whose honesty I would have staked my life upon, who often professed to have visions. She also had some success with her predictions, although she never attempted to profit from them. Neither were any of her revelations harmful."

From his expression, I saw that my interruption had not been welcomed. It was clear to me, because I knew my friend, that a conflict was raging in his mind. Despite his rejection of the mystical, he was reluctant to return to the stagnation that had been upon him before the appearance of this curious affair.

A succession of hansoms passed along Baker Street as he collected his thoughts. The cries of the coachmen, urging their horses to greater speed, and the occasional crack of a whip floated up to us through the half-open window. The hiss of metal-rimmed wheels on the wet road surface told me that the rain had resumed.

"I will look into this," Holmes said then, "but not from a supernatural aspect. I accept that you, Miss Truegrace, could possess an ability that we do not fully understand. The demise of your maid gives an element of truth to your fears, and if I can prevent you suffering the fate that you have witnessed then I'm bound to do so. Tell me, was Ellen's death accepted as by natural causes?"

"Doctor Caulfield examined her thoroughly. The death certificate states that she died from heart failure, and we have since discovered that she had a history of such affliction."

"No doubt she failed to inform you of this for fear of losing her position," I ventured, "although I'm sure she need not have feared on that score."

Mr. Truegrace nodded. "Not at all. She served us well."

"I take it that you are employed within the village, Mr. Truegrace." Holmes enquired.

"As you correctly deduced, I earn my living as a clerk. I work for our local solicitors, Craven and Hibberdson. Mr. Craven has been dead for some years, but the name has been retained. There is just Mr. Fyffe Hibberdson and myself, and a secretary that attends when required."

"And you reside not far away?"

"Tregothan Farm, the name by which it is still called, although it has not functioned as such for many years, is situated about a half-mile further on from the village of Courtney Dale. It isn't difficult to find, since the drive leads directly from the main Worcester Road."

Holmes nodded. "The local inns provide fair accommodation, I trust."

"Most certainly. There are several of good reputation."

"Excellent." My friend rose and we all did the same. "I don't think that there is much else that I need to know, at this point. You may expect us on the early afternoon train tomorrow. We will visit you at your residence after some preliminary enquiries. Also," he looked directly at Miss Truegrace, "I would reassure you as to your brother's intentions. There can be no doubt that something is amiss here, or that some crime has been committed or will be committed, but the perpetrator will, I'm sure, not be he. We will see what comes of a few enquiries thereabouts."

Our visitors then thanked us both and left.

"What was it that convinced you of Mr. Truegrace's lack of malice towards his sister?" I asked Holmes as we watched from our window our clients hailing a cab.

"Did you not see the pain in his eyes as she recounted the vision and her interpretation of it?" He shook his head. "No man could manufacture such deep grief as the accusation caused him."

"I confess that I did not, but I detected a tremor in his voice."

He took his *Bradshaw* from the bookshelf. "Watson, have you sufficient time to accompany me on a brief visit to Worcestershire?"

"You do not anticipate a lengthy investigation, then?"

"I believe I have assimilated a fair idea of what we may be dealing with here. I find this result disturbing though, as I'm at a loss to explain Miss Truegrace's vision. There are, however, several gaps in my understanding of the likely sequence of events. We will clear those up in a day or two, I think."

"I am with you, Holmes, as ever."

"I thought that I knew my Watson," he smiled.

The following morning found us at Paddington Station in time for the early train. I recall little of the journey, other than Holmes's observations concerning the countryside and, occasionally, of the waiting passengers at the various stations through which we passed. Eventually he lapsed into silence as he became lost in his own thoughts, and I think I would have fallen asleep had he not suddenly peered through the window as the train came to a halt.\

"We have arrived I think, Watson. This is Shrub Hill Station."

We retrieved our scant luggage and were among the first to alight. No trap or cart awaited us, but Holmes quickly selected and engaged a burly, red-haired fellow from the half-dozen drivers who lined the platform. We learned that Courtney Dale was three miles distant, and Tregothan Farm a further half-mile.

We passed through leafy countryside, fresh from recent rains, and a lake in a field of uncut grass before the straight road led us to Courtney Dale. The village appeared to comprise mostly of the shops along this thoroughfare, which began and ended with a church of striking architecture. I noticed that several side streets branched off to our left, some containing warehouses and further trading establishments, while others boasted long rows of villas of local stone. Holmes instructed our driver to halt as he caught sight of an inn of impressive appearance, and proceeded to carry both his bag and my own through its door. He returned within ten minutes.

"I have secured us two good, clean rooms," he informed me, "and in deference to you I have ascertained that the cuisine is quite edible."

"Thank you for your consideration."

"But now," he said, standing beside the cart, "I think we should explore this charming village before we go about our business. I will pay this good fellow what we owe and we can visit Tregothan Farm later."

After we had watched our driver turn his cart around and set off back to the town, I asked my friend about his sudden change of objective.

"I noticed the office of the solicitors, Craven and Hibberdson, a short way along the street," he replied, "and thought it as well to interview Mr. Fyffe Hibberdson, if he is available, immediately as a possible way to bring this enquiry to a more speedy conclusion."

We sat across his desk from the solicitor in a wood-panelled office that smelled faintly of cigar-smoke.

Mr. Fyffe Hibberdson had little of the appearance that one associates with members of his profession. From above the spotless winged collar a weather-beaten face, such as old sailors often have, held a critical expression. He was of no more than average height, but of stocky build with thick hair that was prematurely grey. I would have placed him in his middle years, but his gaze was of one much older. Probably, I concluded, as a result of much time spent unravelling the legal problems of others.

"I have heard much about you, Mr. Holmes," he said with surprising friendliness. "Tell me, what has brought you to this office today?"

Holmes answered before I could speak. "I'm conducting an enquiry in which someone of your acquaintance is loosely concerned. It is not a serious matter, but it is always as well to learn something of those on the fringe of the situation in order to obtain a more complete appreciation of the circumstances. Knowing of your connection, it occurred to me that you might be prepared to furnish some basic information."

"I understand." Something of what might have been relief crossed Mr. Hibberdson's face. "I will, of course, help if I can. That is to say, provided that no aspect of confidentiality is breached."

"Capital. I understand that you have in your employment Mr. Cedric Truegrace."

"My clerk? It is he about whom you wish to enquire?"

"To be more precise, it is his sister. Presumably you will have met her on social occasions, or perhaps she has called here from time to time."

Mr. Hibberdson nodded. "That is so. They were among my guests for an informal evening no more than two weeks past. I had met her previously of course, and I must confess that she struck me as – how shall I put it? – a rather nervous girl. She appeared to me as the sort of person who is powerless to prevent her imagination running away with her, so to speak."

"As a medical man, I can confirm that," I commented, more as an encouragement of him to elaborate than from my observations.

"What, in particular, caused you to draw such a conclusion?" Holmes asked.

"I'm uncertain. After all, I am a solicitor and not a doctor, but probably it was my impression that she was possessed of a state of constant unease. As I have said, I'm totally unqualified to judge, but I sensed that she is to some extent neurotic, or even in the grip of the early stages of brain fever."

"An extensive diagnosis, nevertheless," I observed.

"Not as such," Mr. Hibberdson's expression lightened. "I say this only because I have seen similar symptoms in others before now."

Holmes rose to his feet, and I did the same. "You have been most helpful, Mr. Hibberdson, in enhancing my investigation. I will now wish you good day sir, with my thanks."

The solicitor accompanied us to the door and showed us out courteously. As we left, I noticed that his eyes now held a quite different expression, perhaps a hint of uncertainty or fear. It crossed my mind that, should this affair conclude with Mr. Cedric Truegrace facing some sort of criminal charges after all, then a replacement clerk might, in a country village, be difficult to come by. This possibility, I imagined, would cause a degree of concern to Mr. Hibberdson.

After a scant lunch in a nearby tea-house, we secured one of the few hansoms in the village, all of which were operated by a single company, for the half-mile to Tregothan Farm. The outhouses spread across the wide yard revealed at once the previous purpose of the place, before Mr. Truegrace and his sister adopted it as their residence. I had imagined it to boast a thatched roof, but in fact the house was adorned with purple slate. The walls, I could see, were once white, but now a creeping green moss discoloured the upper floors. As our conveyance left us, Holmes strode to the door with me in his wake. It opened before he could knock, and Miss Anna Truegrace admitted us.

We were conducted to a tastefully-decorated parlour, where Mr. Cedric Truegrace rose from his armchair as we entered. Greetings were exchanged and glasses of sherry bought and consumed, before our host cautiously asked whether our enquiries had yet yielded anything of significance.

"It would be true to say that I have made some progress," Holmes answered.

"From what source?" Mr. Truegrace asked.

"Less than an hour ago I interviewed your employer, Mr. Fyffe Hibberdson."

Our host's uncertain expression deepened. "But how is he involved in this?"

"He is not, as yet. He has provided information about the general situation here, which I consider essential if I'm to arrive at the solution to this most unusual case. I must now make of you a request, to the same end."

"What is it that you wish?" Miss Truegrace enquired.

My friend turned in his chair, so that he faced them both. "I would like you to conduct me on a tour of this house, especially the room where you experienced the 'vision'."

Mr. Truegrace sprang to his feet instantly. "That is a condition which is easily satisfied." He beckoned in a way that encompassed both Holmes and myself. "Come."

We followed him throughout the building, Holmes making examinations of the walls in all rooms. There seemed nothing remarkable anywhere, but he ensured most of all that the room of Miss Gracechurch's experience, the master bedroom, was sound.

"Well, Mr. Holmes," our host said when we were all settled again, "can I take it that you discovered something that will throw some light on the situation?"

"You may take it that I found exactly what I expected to find."

"And what is that, pray?"

"I found nothing. That is to say, I found nothing to either substantiate or dismiss the theory that I have formed."

"How disappointing," Miss Truegrace commented.

"May I ask how long it is since you took up residence here?" I asked.

Mr. Truegrace considered for a moment. "Why, it must be almost three years, by now. We hoped the change would somehow see an end to Anna's visions."

"Was the experience concerning the maid the first since then?" Holmes enquired.

"It was. Until that occurrence, we believed we had been successful in leaving them behind."

"Can you recall from whom you bought the property?"

"I cannot, but that information is easily obtainable. The papers are in my study."

He made to rise, but his sister precluded the action. "There is no need, Cedric. I remember that the previous owner was Mr. Gareth Sternwell. He had lived here but a short while, when an inheritance enabled him to move to grander accommodation on the far side of the village. I believe that he mentioned his former profession to be that of a professional gambler, in Worcester."

"Most interesting," Holmes remarked.

"Mr. Holmes, are we not clutching at straws here?" Mr. Truegrace asked in a puzzled voice. "After all, it was the strange vision and the resulting dread of my sister that drove us to consult you. I do not see how our history can reveal anything."

My friend regarded him with an expression that gave away nothing. After a moment of silence he spoke quietly. "Due to the singular nature of this case, for it is one the like of which I haven't had placed before me until now, I must approach it in a befitting fashion. From the first I had formulated several theories, most of which have been disproved by subsequent events, but I'm determined to establish whether your sister's vision, as you refer to it, has any substance or is merely fanciful. Be content to let me proceed in my own way. Humour me if you will, for I have high expectations that the truth of this matter will be evident before long." He rose and picked up his hat. "But as for now, I think a late afternoon walk back to the village will provide sufficient stimulation for me to consider at length the information that you have furnished. Come, Watson."

We left Tregothan Farm then, I with the feeling that Holmes considered himself the subject of a mild insult. He was silent, staring at the grassy slope underfoot, while we walked parallel to the road for much of the way. Only once did he vary his posture, just before we came upon the outskirts of the village and then the inn, glancing suddenly towards a group of trees while a hansom and two four-wheelers passed us. He acted as if he suspected that we were observed.

Later, after changing our clothes, we enjoyed an excellent meal of roast pork, and then spent some time in conversation over pints of good ale before retiring a little earlier than was our custom.

At breakfast, Holmes asked the landlord about the whereabouts of Mr. Gareth Sternwell. Having served us bacon, eggs, and toast, the fellow scratched his head before the answer came to him.

"Ah, I know who you mean sir, now that I've thought about it. He was a gambler or a betting man in Worcester, I think. These days he lives in a place called Parkfield Heights, on a hill leading out of the village as you pass the old miller's pond and the livery stable. I'm told the house looks like as Greek temple, so you can't miss it. I say, most of the gamblers I've known end up as beggars, but this one must have done well for himself, wouldn't you say?"

"Indeed, it would seem so," Holmes acknowledged. "My thanks to you, landlord."

Shortly afterwards, we were fortunate in procuring a hansom that had dropped its fare at the inn as we were about to leave. It left us near the brow of a hill covered in tall elms and flowering shrubs, within sight of a structure that did indeed resemble the abode of the Olympian gods.

"This man surely did well at the tables," I remarked.

Holmes opened the wrought-iron gate to allow us to pass onto the steep drive. "Possibly, but from the description of our clients, I would say that his inheritance most likely determined his future."

We were rather breathless after the short climb. Holmes lifted the heavy door-knocker, shaped like the head of a tiger, and released it. The impact echoed among the pillars that stood to each side of us, before a liveried footman opened the door and asked us our business. Holmes produced his card and we waited until the fellow returned. With a little bow, he informed us that Mr. Sternwell would see us in the breakfast room.

I confess to being overawed by the splendour of the place. Mr. Sternwell must have inherited a vast sum, I thought, to possess such a home. The footman led us along a short corridor, into a large airy room that reminded me of a hothouse such as tropical plants require to flourish in our country. I saw aspidistras and tall flowers, surrounding a large table on which the remains of a meal awaited removal. A short distance away stood several armchairs, upholstered in a garish pattern, and a matching settee where a man lounged as he watched us.

"Good morning, gentlemen," he said without rising. "Tell me, what possible reason could there be for me to receive a visit from a consulting detective? I assure you, my gambling debts have long since been settled."

We returned his greeting. I could tell that Holmes was slightly put out by the man's lack of courtesy. Mr. Sternwell struck me as rather eccentric, reclining in a turquoise-patterned dressing gown as the time approached mid-morning. His thin face bore a moustache as red as his hair, and his eyes were filled with suspicion as much as any I have ever seen. I could well imagine facing his shifty gaze across a spinning roulette wheel or in the midst of a hand of *chemin-de-fer*.

"I see that you are anxious," Holmes observed. "Pray calm yourself, for we are not the official force and have no interest in your past activities."

Mr. Sternwell adjusted his position. "I was curious as to your intentions. That is why you were admitted."

"We are here merely to ask questions, if you will permit us, concerning your previous ownership of Tregothan Farm," I enlightened him.

"Ah, that place," the wariness left his expression at once. "I lived there for but a short while, it could not have been more than a month or two, before this place became vacant and I bought it. I fear that I can tell you little about my former home. I found it to be rather uninteresting. The country life, I think, is not for me."

"We have been aware of some unusual happenings there," Holmes said. "The current owners are quite alarmed."

"Happenings? Ghosts, do you mean? Hauntings? I saw or heard not the slightest suggestion of such occurrences at any time. Look, Mr. Holmes, if your clients are set on getting their money back from me, you can tell them that I won't have it! I did warn them, when they approached me to buy, that the place was old. They should have taken notice."

"That is not the case at all. They have no desire to live elsewhere, or to relinquish their home. It is simply that strange, or *seemingly* strange, events have caused some confusion which I'm attempting to clear up."

Mr. Sternwell nodded. "Then I repeat, I cannot assist you."

Holmes bent his thin frame in a slight bow. "You have already done so, sir. I thank you for seeing us."

We turned and moved towards the door, where the footman had appeared, apparently without being summoned. Just as we passed a tall flowering plant that clung to the wall, Mr. Sternwell called to us.

"I am sure that the man I bought the farm from would have been bound to mention anything out of the ordinary in the house. Mr. Fyffe Hibberdson is an honourable man."

"You bought the farm from him? The solicitor?" Holmes turned and retraced his steps.

"I did. After his wife disappeared, he seemed to be eager to change his residence. Probably he wished to be rid of unpleasant memories." He leaned forward in a conspiratorial fashion. "There were rumours, you see. It was said that she was seen around the village with Albert Ridden. Very indiscreet I'm sure, but she couldn't hope for secrecy – the walls in Courtney Dale have eyes."

"Was Mr. Hibberdson aware of this?"

"Who knows? If he had become so, I doubt if his behaviour towards her would have changed. It is well-known that he took much pleasure in beating the poor woman, long before then."

"She disappeared, I think you said?"

Mr. Sternwell shrugged. "So it is assumed. One morning Mr. Hibberdson reported that his wife had been away all night, and expressed deep concern. Inspector Carew of the local force interviewed Albert Ridden, who seemed as puzzled as anyone else. Enquiries were made as far away as Worcester, without result, after the farms and woods hereabouts had been thoroughly searched. As I understand it, Ridden was suspected for a while, until the case was abandoned because of lack of evidence."

"What was the official verdict?" Holmes enquired.

"It came to be believed that Elizabeth Hibberdson had grown weary of her situation here and left to make a new start in life. There was once some talk of her being seen as far away as Bristol, but the description was so vague that no one took it seriously."

"Most interesting. If I may trouble you once more, pray tell me about this man Albert Ridden."

Mr. Sternwell lay back on well-stuffed cushions, as if the effort of these revelations had been too much for him. "In truth, I have never met the man, so I can say little other than what is considered common knowledge."

"Nevertheless, please continue."

"According to local gossip, he was always something of a tearaway. Elizabeth Hibberdson was not his first conquest by far. At the time, he was employed as a labourer at Elleston Farm, five miles or so north of the village, but he suffered some sort of injury and now lives in the alms houses along Cardinal Way. I think there is no more that I can tell you, Mr. Holmes. As I said, I have never set eyes on Ridden."

"Again, my thanks to you, sir," my friend said. "You have been of immense help, after all."

Having taken our leave, we set off down the hill. By the time we regained the inn, we had become breathless and a little weary. The landlord had already begun to serve luncheon and I had no hesitation in ordering a portion of what turned out to be an excellent fish pie, while Holmes would take only a small amount of bread and cheese.

We were surprised when the landlord served wine.

"My good sir, we did not order this," Holmes remarked.

"It was delivered by a boy who is not known to me," the fellow replied. He searched in a pocket of his apron. "It was accompanied by this card."

My friend glanced at it before showing it to me: *From a grateful client.*

"From Mr. Truegrace and his sister," I concluded.

"I think not. At no time did we inform them as to where we are staying."

"Who, then?"

Holmes scrutinized the bottle carefully, before pouring some of the contents into a glass. He swirled the liquid around. Smelled it and observed the sheen that had formed upon the surface.

"Landlord, there has been some negligence here. This wine, I can tell you for a certainty, was exposed to the air too soon. Pray dispose of it, but on no account let anyone drink, since the result would doubtlessly be a severe illness of the stomach."

The astonished man removed the bottle and glasses and withdrew.

"A pity, Holmes," I said. "A glass would have been welcome, before we set out."

He glanced at me with an amused expression. "I doubt you would have enjoyed it for long, Watson. I wished to avoid alarming our friend the landlord, but unless I'm much mistaken it was laced with a deadly poison, probably some easily dissolved alkaloid."

262

"Good heavens! Who would do this?"

"We will discover that soon, I think."

Afterwards, my friend again consulted the landlord regarding local knowledge, to discover that Cardinal Way was within easy walking distance. We set off shortly after receiving directions.

"It is the next street on the right," I said as we strode past the Post Office, "if the landlord is to be relied upon."

"I have no doubt that he is," Holmes replied, "for I can see the sign already."

"Why are we seeking out this man Ridden? What has he to do with the vision experienced by Miss Anna Truegrace?"

"Unless I'm mistaken, this case has taken a different path, quite unlike its apparent nature at the outset. At the root of it is a very real crime."

He said no more until we were confronted by a row of identical brick-terraced houses, in a long and narrow street. These, I knew, were inhabited by people who were, for various reasons, unable to support themselves. They were maintained by charitable donations, and tenants were expected to do what work they were able towards their upkeep.

Holmes rapped upon the first door with his cane. He bowed courteously to the elderly lady who answered his summons and asked if she knew the address of Albert Ridden. She nodded and pointed further along the street, giving elaborate directions. He thanked her and we continued for perhaps fifty yards until we came upon a wide arch which we entered. After a sloping path with high walls, we found ourselves in an enclosure. I saw a small patch of ground to the right, evidently used for growing vegetables, with a small brick structure nearer to the path. Its door hung open to reveal a deep copper bowl set atop a low wall, which I presumed was for the communal washing of clothes. To our left were three houses, two with drawn curtains, and no sign of life. Holmes approached the third and again rapped with his cane.

At first there was no response, and Holmes was about to repeat his action when we heard trudging footsteps from within. The door opened, barely an inch.

"Who is it?" A hoarse voice, no more than a whisper.

"My name is Sherlock Holmes. My friend is Doctor John Watson."

"What do you want?"

"I am a consulting detective. I wish to speak to you concerning Mrs. Elizabeth Hibberdson."

A long silence intervened, and then a breathless croak. "She is gone."

"That is why I'm here."

"She disappeared. No one knows where."

Holmes paused, as if deciding how to proceed. Then: "My investigation has brought me close to discovering the truth. I'm hoping you will assist me."

"That is unlikely. What can I tell you?"

Mr. Ridden, let me make it clear that I know what transpired between you and this lady. I'm not here to judge you or Mrs. Hibberdson, only to bring her murderer to justice."

The door opened a few inches wider. "You are certain that she was murdered, then?"

"I'm in no doubt of it."

There was silence again for some moments, before a faint murmur. "You had better come in."

The door swung fully open and the meagre light from within framed a slightly stooped figure. As we entered, the man's features were revealed to us and I sensed Holmes grow tense, as I fought to prevent myself from recoiling with horror and revulsion.

Mr. Ridden's face was distorted. Along the left side of his head was a wrinkled brown patch that ran from above the ear, past the jawbone, and across part of the throat. The affected eye seemed to be set deeper than its companion, and was covered with a milky sheen. I understood at once his reason for living behind closed curtains: He wished to spare the world from the sight of him.

"We will not disturb you for long," Holmes assured him.

Mr. Ridden gestured that we should all sit down on the worn armchairs. "That is unimportant, sirs. I see few people these days. If I can throw any light on the fate of Elizabeth, I will be pleased to do so."

"You no longer work at Elleston farm," I presumed, "because of your injuries?"

He shook his head. "I cannot work, although God knows I have tried. What you see of me is but part of the burden I bear, for I'm in constant pain and cannot abide the pity or the gaze of others."

"I'm truly sorry for you predicament. We were not aware of it."

"This is my punishment, my judgement for taking the wife of another man, despicable though he is. You say you know of my friendship with Elizabeth as, I dare say, do many others by now. None of it would ever have happened had not Fyffe Hibberdson driven her away with his cruelty. His appearance does not betray it, but that man is a monster. I saw the marks of his excesses on her flesh and heard the pain in her voice, many times. The condition I'm in now was brought about by a fellow who concealed his face behind a mask as he splashed me with vitriol. I have always suspected that this was Hibbertson's revenge, taken personally or by means of an agent, but I cannot prove it. Even if I could, his position in the community and my poverty would keep the case from the courts." He lowered his head, lost for a moment in recollection and regret. "But I digress. Please ask what you will."

"You have already answered most of my questions by means of your most interesting narrative," said Holmes. "But there is one more issue on which I remain uncertain."

Mr. Ridden leaned forward to catch my friend's enquiry, then squirmed at the painful result of his movement. "I'm at your disposal."

"Please do think I am making light of this, when I ask: What was the colour of Mrs. Hibberdson's hair?"

Astonishment crossed the disfigured face, but the answer was immediately forthcoming. "Why, Elizabeth had long tresses of a rich brown lustre."

Holmes rose from his chair and I followed.

"That is all I wish to know. My thanks to you, sir. And I apologise again for the intrusion."

Holmes said nothing until we had left Cardinal Way. "We will take the long route back to the inn, I think. The exercise will be beneficial as I review my findings."

"I cannot help but feel sorry for that poor fellow, Holmes. He has paid a terrible price for his indiscretion."

"And continues to do so, since he now has little choice but to live the life of a hermit."

"You are sure that Mrs. Hibberdson was murdered, and did not simply flee from her husband's cruelty?"

"Yes. It seems certain that she and Mr. Ridden had come to have considerable affection for each other. I cannot imagine her leaving the village without asking him to accompany her, or at least informing him of her destination."

Little else was said between us until we reached the inn. Because of our longer walk, it was now almost time for dinner. At my friend's suggestion, we each enjoyed a pint of good ale as the landlord and his wife made their preparations, and then sat down to a meal of braised steak. For once, Holmes ate with relish.

"Your appetite has improved," I observed. "A sure and certain sign that you have arrived at the solution of a case."

"I had not realized that I'm so predictable, Watson," he smiled. "But you are not quite correct. There is a final piece to be fitted to the puzzle, and then my case will be complete."

"That is for tomorrow, then?"

"Not at all. What do you say to another, but much shorter, walk after dinner? If I'm right about what I expect to see, this affair will be cleared up before mid-day tomorrow, and when we will be on the late morning train to London."

When our plates had been cleared away, I indulged myself with a thick slice of the landlord's wife's apple pie, while Holmes looked on with some amusement as he sipped a cup of strong coffee. At the moment I finished my own coffee, he got to his feet and we emerged into the street as the light faded.

Holmes was as good as his word. The work was indeed short, to the extent that we passed but a few shops and paused outside the closed establishment of Mr. Fyffe Hibberdson. Holmes bent to peer at something displayed in the window and turned abruptly.

"That is sufficient. If you wish, Watson, we can now return to the inn to sit and reminisce about our past experiences together over a glass of brandy. I'm quite sure that you will derive something to over-dramatize and add to your journals.

I was surprised that our excursion was of such short duration, but the opportunity to discuss our previous adventures was a rarity with Holmes. I readily agreed to his suggestion and we retraced our steps.

"You are now satisfied then, that you have solved this curious affair?"

"It is now all clear to me," was all that he would say.

Holmes entered the inn as I sat down to breakfast, seating himself opposite me as I awaited the landlord's attention.

"There is a slight tinge of colour in your face, Holmes. Clearly, you have enjoyed a bracing walk."

"I have been to the local police station to see Inspector Carew, who seems to be a most agreeable fellow. Doubtless, we will see something of him later."

I was served a hearty meal, and Holmes contented himself with coffee and a single slice of toast. Already I had noticed the glitter of anticipation in his eyes, which betrayed his eagerness to savour the last act of this affair and bring it to a successful conclusion. Indeed, I had hardly consumed the final mouthful of food before he rose abruptly.

"Come, Watson, let us complete our work here."

I stood up and hesitated. "There is much about this that I fail to understand. Before we proceed, perhaps you could enlighten me."

"I have come to realise that there is much that I, myself, failed to comprehend at its beginning, but all is now plain to me. As for explanations, see what you can make of this morning's activity and I will furnish a full account as we return to Baker Street."

I knew that he would say nothing more until then, so I followed him out into the morning sunshine. We walked the short distance to the office of the solicitors, Craven and Hibberdson, and paused before entering.

"You are armed, I take it?" my friend whispered.

"My service revolver is never far from me."

"Excellent."

He pushed open the door, to reveal Mr. Fyffe Hibberdson speaking to a young woman, presumably his secretary.

"Mr. Holmes. Doctor Watson!" His surprise was evident, and a hint of wariness crept into his face. "I had not expected to see you again. Is there something new?"

"We have made some progress," said Holmes. "But one question remains before we return to London."

Mr. Hibberdson said something to the young woman, who nodded. He gave us a suspicious glance before ushering us into his office.

When we were all seated, he looked at us uncertainly. His weather-beaten face held a rather fixed smile.

"And so, Mr. Holmes, you have reached the end of your investigation. May I ask, have you achieved your objective?"

"It would be more accurate, I think, to say that events took an unexpected turn. As I said, one aspect is still unresolved."

Mr. Hibberdson nodded. "It is something that you believe I'm able to assist with, or you would not be here."

"It is indeed."

"Then what is it, pray?"

Holmes stood up quickly. "We wish to know where you have hidden your wife's body."

All expression left Mr. Hibberdson's face, and as he rose from his chair his breathing became laboured. A stray lock of grey hair fell across his forehead.

"What do you mean?" he stammered.

"Pretence is useless. We know all."

Fury crossed Mr. Hibberdson's face then, and desperation. He quickly pulled out a drawer and produced a pistol, which he lowered immediately as he saw that my own was pointed at his heart. He dropped his weapon and slumped into his seat, leaning across his desk with his head in his hands.

"I was desperate," he looked up at us for understanding or sympathy, and found none. "My wife had taken up with another man, a filthy farm worker."

"She found your cruelty repugnant," I told him.

"A small measure of the whip now and then does no harm, but reminds a woman of her place. I'm not an evil man, gentlemen."

Holmes fixed him with a steely stare. "Then it would be interesting to hear your explanation as to why you lay in wait for us as we returned from the Truegrace's residence. I was aware that we were followed as we left, but not that it was by yourself. The sun glinted on the barrel of your pistol, but the passing of several vehicles obscured your line of fire. Subsequently, you attempted to murder Doctor Watson and myself by sending poisoned wine to the inn."

Hibberdson hammered on his desk with his fists, completely distraught now. "Do you not see? I had to protect myself! I knew of your reputation, and it was certain that you would soon uncover what I had so carefully concealed. The risk was too great."

I let my eyes stray to a portrait above him. A stern figure, possibly the late Mr. Craven, looked down.

"And it was you, of course, who disfigured Mr. Ridden?"

"I could not bear to think of him escaping unscathed after affecting my life so."

"I ask you again," Holmes said harshly, "where is the body of Elizabeth Hibberdson?"

Hibbersdon went very still. "She is at the bottom of Merren Lake, near the county border," he said in a quiet voice. "I could bear the humiliation she brought upon me no longer."

"Your confession solves an old mystery," said the tall sharp-faced man who had quietly entered the room. "I must now ask you to accompany me to Grovell Police Station, where you will be formally charged."

"Ah, Inspector Carew," Holmes said lightly, "arriving exactly as we arranged. I trust that what you have just witnessed, together with the full report I supplied earlier, will suffice for your purposes?"

The inspector smiled briefly, the expression appearing out of place on that harsh countenance, before replying. "It will be more than adequate, I am sure. My thanks to you and Doctor Watson for your timely assistance on this unsolved case."

My friend, looking away from Hibberdson, inclined his head in acknowledgement. "We are pleased to have been of service." He consulted his pocket-watch. "But now I see that we scarcely have time to return to Worcester for the morning train. We wish you good morning, Inspector."

We departed after sending a short message to your clients, as Holmes felt that there was no need to explain in person. The return journey was without mention of the case. As was sometimes his custom, Sherlock Holmes expounded on several unrelated subjects, so that my frustration had reached unbearable heights by the time we were but a few miles from London.

I turned from the window, as the train plunged into the heavy fog that had quickly settled. "Holmes, I must say that you surprised me by taking the brother and sister Truegrace seriously."

"I wondered whether you would be able to restrain your curiosity as far as Baker Street," he laughed. "I found it amusing to watch your expressions as I spoke of other things."

"Am I so obvious?"

"Not always, old fellow, and never, I would think, to the untrained eye."

"Thank you for your reassurance. Perhaps you will now furnish me with an explanation."

The train came to a halt at the last rural station before approaching the capital. On the single platform, passengers and porters moved about like grey ghosts. The fog showed no signs of lifting.

"You were surprised that I agreed to take the case, because of my aversion to the belief in the supernatural," he began. "In fact, I started with the assumption that no such thing was involved here. At first I thought, quite wrongly, that there was something sinister about the predicted demise of the maid, and that either or both of the Truegraces were somehow responsible. I was only certain of the identity of the murderer of Mrs. Hibberson when I saw the injuries inflicted on Mr. Albert Ridden."

As the train began to move again, I thought about this. "I can see no connection."

"That is because you failed to notice the old burns on Hibberdson's hands when we first encountered him. They meant nothing to me at the time, but on seeing the vitriol burns on Mr. Ridden, it became apparent that Hibberdson had accidentally spilled some on himself as he transferred the chemical from a large container to a portable-sized jar. At the same time, a possibility occurred to me. What if this vision of Miss Truegrace's were not of herself and her brother, but of two other people? I then asked myself who else it could have been, and recalled that we had learned of the disappearance of Hibberdson's wife after many violent clashes with her husband. I then looked for similarities between Miss Truegrace and Mrs. Hibberdson – you will recall my asking Mr. Ridden about the colour of Mrs. Hibberdson's hair – and discovered that my theory was sound."

I could follow his reasoning, but detected a flaw.

"Holmes, are you forgetting that the woman in the vision actually named her murderer?"

"That was the final confirmation. You will recall our short walk, last evening?"

I nodded. "As far as Hibberdson's office."

"Precisely. Displayed in the window was his certificate of qualification to practice in the legal profession. It bore the name '*Fyffe Jonathan Peter Cedric Hibberdson*'."

Suddenly, it was all clear to me. "So Hibberdson also had the name 'Cedric', as did Mr. Truegrace."

"I doubted our client's guilt when I saw the genuine fear in the sister's eyes, and the hurt at being thought of as a likely murderer in those of her brother. That something was amiss was a certainty, and curiosity impelled me to investigate."

"But none of this," I observed with a curious satisfaction, "explains the vision of Miss Anna Truegrace. Since it was that which led to this affair, may I take it that you now acknowledge such occurrences as reality?"

The train slid to a gentle halt at Paddington Station and passengers, soon made indistinct by the smoke from the engine and the fog, streamed out onto the platform. My friend rose steadily, retrieving his bag and handing mine to me.

"No," he said then. "The supernatural, if it exists, remains as much a mystery as ever. But you can take it, Watson, that I am truly amazed when new capabilities of the infinitely complicated human mind reveal themselves."

The Haunting of Bottomly's Grandmother
by Tim Gambrell

Chapter I

It had been a dashed foul day. The thick, foggy atmosphere clogged the lungs, clung to the clothes, and persistently lingered, despite an almost constant drizzling rain. I returned home to Baker Street miserable, as sodden as a fish and reeking like a careless mortuary attendant. As I removed my hat and overcoat, poor Mrs. Hudson endeavoured to conceal the effect of the stench upon her, but to little avail. She promised to draw me a bath at the soonest opportunity, for which I was grateful.

Holmes was waiting for me in our rooms. The intensity of his eyes and the downward curl of his almost-smile told me he had information to impart. It was a singular honour of mine to be his *confidante*, his sounding board at times such as this. No matter how hellish the day had been, I always had time for my friend.

"Come, Watson, sit. Have a drink. Revitalise while I tell you an incredible – " He paused and flexed his nose. "You have a new cologne?"

I sighed and threw open the sash window. The merest second was more than sufficient to enlighten Holmes as to my particular aroma.

"I see."

"Mrs. Hudson is drawing me a bath. And I suspect my laundry man will be overrun following a day such as today. It'll be some time before I see these clothes again."

Holmes laughed at my chagrin, which undercut my mood.

"What was it you wished to impart?" I enquired.

"Ah yes. I received, today, the most extraordinary telegram from an acquaintance at the Diogenes Club. One Sir Rodney Phipps-Willis." Here Holmes produced the paper from his desk and referred to its wording at times. "Sir Rodney reports that his secretary has, once again, been woken by the spectral visage of a hag, appearing in his chamber in the dead of night and demanding five pounds in sterling for 'deeds untold' by Sir Rodney. This has now happened twice, and his secretary has had to be given a month's convalescence in Eastbourne, which has put Sir Rodney to considerable trouble – not to mention the cost. Then he signs off with some derogatory comments about the weather of late. What do you think?"

I told Holmes it sounded like a ridiculous load of tosh, and Sir Rodney's secretary ought to consider changing his tobacconist.

Any further discussion was curtailed by Mrs. Hudson advising that my bath was ready.

Chapter II

Some days after this, Holmes and I were visited by Inspector Lestrade. He seemed rather awkward in his demeanour and had a young constable in tow. The youth was introduced as Charlie Bottomly. His grandmother, Lestrade told us, had fairly recently died. She was a profligate drinker and gambler who worked up plenty of debts. Bottomly confirmed that this was so, and what a strain and embarrassment she'd been to the family.

"Tell the gentlemen your story," Lestrade ordered.

Bottomly saluted, stood as if to attention, cleared his throat and began.

"Well, sirs," he said. "It's like this, really. Granny lived with me Ma, me sister, and me. We don't 'ave no dad, see."

"Stick to the story, lad. And don't drop yer aitches."

He looked at Lestrade apologetically. "Sorry, sir. *H*anyway – "

Here Holmes interrupted and asked Bottomly to simply speak as he would normally. This seemed to relax the constable, a little. He continued. He had the lively accent of one brought up on London's East End streets.

"It was her heart what gave out. Ma always said running from her enemies would do her in one day. So, off she went, up to Heaven – we hope – "

"Some hope, lad, from what I've heard of her," added Lestrade with a forced chuckle. Holmes glared at the inspector and asked if he was telling the story or his subordinate. Lestrade indicated for Bottomly to continue and then strolled over to the mantelpiece to admire our ornaments.

"So we was worried that her creditors would come looking for us to settle old debts. And one or two did make enquiries out and about. But, the last week or so, they've started coming to the family home, claiming that Granny is haunting them, and then they write off their debts. Some of them have even given us money instead."

"Sounds ideal," I commented.

"Does it, Doctor Watson?" Bottomly had a look of desperation in his eyes. "I may be poor, but I'm a clean-living lad, what says his prayers and does the best he can. That's why I joined the Force, see. I don't like the thought of my old Granny's ghost haunting them who she probably wronged in the first place."

For shame, I could see the lad's point, and apologised. I noted that Holmes rolled his eyes at me. Bottomly continued.

"Me Ma's the same. It's upsetting her more now we're freed of them debts than it did when we feared we'd have to pay. Cos of the unholy scandal, like."

"I can understand that," observed Holmes. "Neither situation is enviable. And what of your sister?"

"Oh, she thinks it's all fine, not being saddled with debts. But she's engaged to be married soon. All she thinks about, to be honest. Be different if Granny starts haunting us, too."

Holmes nodded. "Indeed. She's only seen at night, you say?"

"That's what they all say. A spectral hag, they call her, appearing when they're asleep."

The words "spectral hag" immediately resonated with me. I recalled Holmes's letter from Rodney Phipps-Willis. It was clear from Holmes's expression that he had too.

"What do you expect us to do about this, then, Inspector? Do you not consider this a police matter?"

Lestrade turned back to us. "How can I, Mr. Holmes? They'd think we were wasting police time trying to follow up on Penny Dreadful tales like this."

"But you clearly believe Constable Bottomly."

"Like he said, sir, he's honest, clean-living – the best sort we've got coming through the ranks. I look him in the eye, and I can see he's telling the truth."

"Fair enough," said Holmes. "That's reasonable. So, Constable, tell me something: Do you believe your Grandmother is truly dead, or could this be some scheme she cooked up to get out of her debts."

"Oh, Lord, sir!" said Bottomly. "Not in a million years. She's dead all right. Found her *meself*, I did. In the gutter, near my home. And I maybe should have said before, but the witnesses, when they tell us what they've seen, they all say the same thing. She's not actually a ghost, or a wraith, or whatever they're called. She has physical form. She's there, in the room, with them. Her face, it has the pallor of death. Her mouth is sewn up, as the undertaker does, and her eyes – Her eyes, Mr. Holmes, are like the black pits of hell."

Lestrade was right. There was no doubting Bottomly's conviction. I couldn't suppress a shiver.

"Then one final question for now: Has anyone checked to see if the body is still in the coffin?"

No one had.

Chapter III

The following day, I was at my surgery when a constable arrived and requested that I accompany him. I assumed he had been sent by Holmes.

"Indirectly, sir," he said. "Inspector Lestrade wishes to see you both. Mr. Holmes advised me you would be here."

I obliged the constable and hastily made arrangements to cover the remainder of the day. We travelled as fast as the heavy midday traffic would permit. Upon arrival at Scotland Yard, I found Holmes waiting impatiently in Lestrade's office.

"About time," Holmes snapped. "Were you in a problematic consultation?"

I explained about the traffic. So as to assuage my frustration at Holmes's somewhat high-handed attitude, I asked Lestrade the reason for the summons. I had been at my work, after all.

"Follow me, gentlemen," he said, enigmatically, and led us down to the cells.

I abhorred the cells beneath New Scotland Yard. They gave the impression that the relatively new building above had been constructed on top of some ancient medieval dungeon.

Holmes remained like a tightly wound spring. "I am no fan of parlour games, Inspector. Surely a few words about what we are to expect is not out of the question?

Lestrade turned suddenly. The periodic wall lamps cast his face in a macabre fashion.

"The hauntings," he hissed. "I need to be careful what I say. Walls have ears."

"You've made an arrest?" called Holmes, after Lestrade's retreating form.

We followed, eagerly. Rather than assuage our curiosity, Lestrade had very much whetted it. *Whatever could be waiting for us?* I wondered.

The cells were like a labyrinth. The air was dank and foul. The stone block walls cold and moist, and the lighting pitiful at best. I had visited mortuaries with less feeling of decay than here. We followed Lestrade through the maze to what he termed the high security area. He unlocked a large metal door, not dissimilar to that of a bank vault. As soon as the door started opening, we heard the screams.

The light inside this section was even worse than that in the main cells area. Lestrade closed and locked the heavy door.

"Sorry, again, gentlemen, for the secrecy, but I feel obliged to try to protect the lad."

"Lad?" I asked.

Lestrade indicated for us to approach the cell at the far end. The screaming came from there. A cursory glance to either side showed me that no other cells were currently occupied. A face appeared at the bars in the cell door. It was manic and pained, as if possessed – puffy and swollen, with a froth of blood and saliva around its clenched jaws.

"Constable Bottomly?" I hissed in shock.

"You've had your moment, then, Inspector," Holmes said, darkly. "Now tell us what we need to know to assist you."

"We were called to an affray at Bottomly's address last night. Lucky I was still on duty, otherwise he'd be the talk of the Yard by now. When we arrived, the lad was going mad – pretty much as you see him now, to be honest, except he was raving about his grandmother. Took all of us to hold him down so we could take him away. His poor mother and sister were beside themselves."

"I can imagine," I said. "And he's been like this ever since?"

"Yes, Doctor."

"You fool!" I spat with anger. "You should have called for me immediately. Goodness knows what damage he's done to himself down here all this time." I sifted around in my professional bag. "Let me in there, please. I need to give the poor lad a sedative at the very least."

"I'll need your help with this, Mr. Holmes," grumbled Lestrade, clearly not relishing the prospect.

It was an effort, indeed, but between Lestrade and Holmes, they managed to hold Bottomly down on the cell bed sufficiently for me to apply the needle. It was a heavy dose and the sedative started to take effect almost immediately. The sudden silence was chilling.

"He will sleep for some time, now, Inspector," I said. "We should be able to tell after he wakes if there is much in the way of permanent damage to his reason. Possibly we'll even be able to learn what caused it."

"We know that much already," replied Lestrade. "Kept screaming, 'Don't let her get me down here!' when we locked him up. Seems he was visited by the ghost of his grandmother."

We were sitting, quietly, in the cab as it trundled along. The window had been lowered, and I breathed deeply and regularly in an effort to calm myself. Although the London air was never fresh, it was sweeter by far than the depraved atmosphere of the cells where Bottomly was kept.

After a while, I looked at Holmes. He was leaning forward, deep in thought, his fingers steepled. I cleared my throat and tried to speak.

"Surely, Holmes . . . Ghosts aren't – " I was struggling to find the words to express myself properly. "The supernatural. It's the realm of the fantasist. Holmes, you don't believe – ?"

He interrupted me, putting me out of my floundering misery.

"We are rational men, Watson," he confirmed, with a sideways glance. "I've no doubt that the answer will lie in whatever evidence is placed before our eyes."

"But the evidence so far," I said, again not managing to finish the sentence. "First the telegram, and now the broken-minded constable."

"Merely scratching the surface, my friend," Holmes replied. "We have many avenues yet to search. For example, we have not been informed that any other recipients of a visit from Bottomly's grandmother have reacted as wildly as the poor constable, have we?"

"Well, no, but – ?"

"Then, we must assume that something else happened, along with the visitation, to break his mind like that. Assuming he wasn't already in a fragile state."

"He didn't seem in a fragile state when he came to Baker Street. Very sure of himself, I thought."

"Precisely, Watson. So . . . ?"

"Indeed," I pondered. "What the deuce could have happened to set him off like that?"

"Unless he's faking it."

"Why would he do that, pray?"

"To avoid suspicion, if he's masterminded the whole scheme."

"Never." I was adamant. "No man could fake that, and for that long. I could see it in his eyes, and I would stake my reputation on it."

"In which case, my friend, we must wait until the poor fellow wakes and hope that he can remember enough to satisfy our curiosity."

And on we journeyed towards Whitechapel, the slums, and the Bottomly family home.

Chapter IV

Maude Bottomly was a plump, steadfast woman who had clearly done her best to make up for her husband's abscondment many years previously and was happy to tell as much to anyone who asked. She was cut from a different cloth to her mother, Bottomly's grandmother, who had never been the same, she told us, since the resurgent gin craze, back at mid-century. Maude was a woman used to hardship and looking out for herself and her own – and, unfortunately, used to being let down by those close to her. I could only admire her for what she'd been through. And, it seemed, her mother was continuing to provide her with trouble from beyond the grave.

When we arrived, Maude was berating her daughter, Maisie, who was wearing perfume. Never mind that Maisie being upwards of twenty years old, she was having her ears boxed good and proper and being accused of theft. Maisie looked at us with relief as we knocked and entered. Maude released her daughter and straightened her cap.

"This one thinks she's some French tart," grumbled Maude in her East London drawl, as Maisie curtsied and left the room. "What business have two gentlemen got, calling round here, then?"

We told her that we'd been to see her son, and that was sufficient for her to invite us in. She told us how proud they'd all been of Charlie, joining the police, trying to better himself, and how typical it would be of her life if his mind was now broken and he'd have to live out his years as a raving simpleton. Maisie, too, was trying to better herself, we were told, though not by wearing perfume. She was to be married, although her fiancé's family had spoken about Teddy, Maisie's intended, calling it off in light of the scandal over Maude's mother. This, also, was classified as being typical of Maude's luck in life.

"Got people coming at me in the street, now, all the time," she said. "Telling me more of mother's *to-do*s, giving me their sixpence-worth when I never asked. Bleeding liberty."

"I see," I said, trying to offer some condolences. "How very upsetting for you."

"I had all that when *he* walked out years ago. I'll tell you this, if she comes haunting me around here, I'll give her what for, ghost or no ghost."

"Well, quite." I looked at Holmes, who appeared to be thoroughly charmed by the whole conversation.

Maisie returned. "We'll show them, Ma. You can live with me and Teddy after the wedding. Somewhere nice, up town."

"See this, Mr. Holmes? Airs and graces, I ask you."

"Well, why not, Ma? Teddy promised. Get us away from here, at least."

"That's if he marries you, my girl."

"He will, too. He loves me. Said so, and all."

"Loves you smelling like some tart, does he? Well he won't love you if you go down for thieving."

"I didn't steal nothing, Ma. I bought the perfume. For the wedding. I saved some money. Treated myself. Fed up with smelling like a chamber pot. I was just testing it out."

Maude shook her head.

"Do you believe it's really your mother's ghost haunting these people, Mrs. Bottomly?" I asked.

"What else can it be, sir?" she replied. "Plenty's seen her. Plenty more claim it. She came here last night and broke poor Charlie's reason."

Holmes suddenly spoke up. "Yet you yourself did not see the apparition, Mrs. Bottomly?"

"Appar – *what*?"

"The ghost. Your mother."

"No, I was asleep. First I knew was when Charlie started screaming. Maisie was there afore me. Next I knew someone had called in the peelers, and they took him away. How is he, by the way? They putting him away for a stretch?"

I couldn't help but smile. Her concern was genuine, but her scattergun approach to all aspects of her life made it seem like poor Charlie was only an afterthought. I told her that he was sleeping under sedation, which she assumed was a judicial term and started weeping. I corrected her and told her I would be better able to judge his condition after he'd woken. She kept insisting he was a good lad, until Maisie asked us if we wanted to see Charlie's bedchamber, to which Holmes willingly agreed.

As things turned out, Holmes didn't spend very long examining the room. It was very basic and not particularly clean, although it had been tidied and swept after the struggle in the night when Bottomly was taken away. A faint aroma of vomit hung on the air – doubtless from Bottomly. I mentioned as much to Holmes.

A small pane of glass was broken and had been boarded up, but Maisie informed us that this was from some years ago, during childhood. There was only one door in and out. The window didn't open due to the boarded pane. There was nothing suspicious under the bed, under the rug, in or under the chest of drawers, or on or around the sole chair which stood in the corner. Similarly with the ceiling, beyond some stains which spoke of a leaking roof above.

I sensed Holmes's frustration, but truly there was nothing out of place or out of the ordinary there – even the floorboards. Unless the very fact of it being ordinary was of importance, there was nothing else the room could tell us.

Holmes begged indulgence to look around the rest of the house, which was granted. He tasked me with checking downstairs while he remained up. As I descended, I became aware of an altercation at the front door.

"Not another one! I tell you, I'm no witch! Ain't got no control over her. She's been dead and buried this last month!"

"For all that's Holy, Mrs. Bottomly, here, take this. And please, whatever you can do, I don't care, just don't let her visit me again."

The voice belonged to a man of roughly my own age. He was well-dressed, and certainly didn't belong in these parts.

"I say!" I called to him. "Do excuse the intrusion, but I'm here to assist Mrs. Bottomly. May I ask what the problem is?"

"I'll tell you what the problem is," Mrs. Bottomly said, turning and holding out her hand. "He's given me ten bob to stop my mother from haunting him again. Like I have any control over her. Like I *ever* had any control over her."

I beckoned the man aside and spoke to him more confidentially. He was a Mr. Taylor. He'd recently taken possession of rooms in Stepney Green. Two nights previously, he'd been disturbed by a figure in the night. The grandmother. She must have mistaken him for a former resident, a gambler. She told him she'd been good to him in life and now he had to be good to her family in her death and give them money to stop her visiting him. He didn't have his spectacles to hand, so he couldn't see her clearly, but the spectre had the aroma of death and decay and it had taken him until now to find the courage to leave his room and seek out Mrs. Bottomly.

"So, the ghost provided you with an address?" asked Holmes, descending the stairs and clearly having overheard the whole conversation.

"My landlady provided the detail, sir. And you are – ?"

"Sherlock Holmes, Mr. Taylor. Consulting detective, at your service."

"Consulting detective?" Taylor looked at Mrs. Bottomly. "You don't need a consulting detective, woman. You need a priest!" And with that, he turned and hastily left.

I raised my brows at Holmes.

"What am I gonna do with this?" bleated Maude, holding her hand open.

Maisie bounced down the stairs, jingling a linen bag. "Add it to the rest, Ma," she said, counting in each of the ten shilling pieces.

"Have all the callers been like that?" Holmes asked, pressing the front door to.

"Pretty much," confirmed Maisie.

Holmes pursed his lips and paused, before continuing.

"Mrs. Bottomly. I'm afraid the best way to prove whether or not the hauntings are fake is to exhume the body."

Maude was sceptical. "What will that prove?"

"Well, if the body isn't there, then we can presume that either she's not dead after all, or she's being used in some macabre way to enact these hauntings."

"And if it *is* still there?" Maude and Maisie asked, simultaneously.

"Then, we'll have to consider that perhaps there *are* more things in heaven and earth than are dreamed of in our philosophy, Mrs. Bottomly."

"Eh?"

"Well, I think he's right, Ma. We should dig Granny up."

But Maude was having none of it. "It's against God and nature, Maisie. There's already enough of that we've been accused of as it is, without inviting more. Sorry, Mr. Holmes, but I won't have it. Let her lie until she rots or until she rests again." Then, picking up a large basket of clothes from near the hearth, she moved to the doorway herself. "Now, you'll have to excuse me, gents, but I gotta deliver this *laundery*. Maisie'll see you out when you're done."

And with that, she was gone.

Chapter V

It was a full twenty-four hours before we received word from Lestrade that Bottomly had woken. As he led us back down to the cells, I was again convinced this was no place for many a human, least of all a broken lad like Bottomly. No screaming greeted us this time, which I found immediately encouraging.

"Has he spoken?" I asked.

"A few words, not much. Said his head hurt."

I was not surprised by that in the slightest. "Eaten or drunk anything?"

"A quart of water, Doctor, that's all."

"His body will be exhausted, Inspector. He'll need a good meal after we've seen him."

"A good meal?" grumbled Lestrade. "We're hardly the Ritz."

"The best that prisoner rations will allow, then," I snapped, somewhat exasperated.

"Fine. Do you wish to enter?" Lestrade dangled the key.

"Of course, we do," stated Holmes, as if this was the most obvious thing in the world.

Bottomly was dozing on the bench. I wished they could have provided a mattress for his comfort, at least, but Lestrade was already showing frustration at my demands.

"Constable Bottomly?" I spoke gently. No response. "Charlie?"

280

He stirred and sat up. When he registered who we were in the half-light, he tried to stand, but I made him remain on the bench. I asked if he minded me giving him a quick examination, to which he willingly acquiesced.

"Can we do anything about this abominable light?" I asked.

Some clattering followed, outside the cell, then Lestrade came forward with a musty paraffin lamp, which he informed us was kept down there for this very purpose. Holmes lit it and held it up for me while I performed my tasks. The physical and mental strain had left their marks on the poor lad, that was clear. A good meal, some fresh air, and a period of rest at home would, I had every confidence, see Bottomly back to health.

I said as much to Lestrade, who thanked me in such a way as to make it patently clear that Bottomly would not be released from his cell.

Having done my part, I took the lamp from Holmes so he could perform his.

"Constable, do you feel able to describe for me, please, what exactly happened two nights ago?"

Bottomly paused. I briefly worried that the recollection might send him back into a fit, but he remained calm and after a few deep breaths he commenced his story.

"I was sleeping, Mr. Holmes. I was woken by a noise, and a draught. I sat up to see what was going on, ready to scold whoever had disturbed me. And there she was, standing at the end of my bed, large as life. Granny. In her nightgown and bonnet, and carrying a lamp, just as the others had said."

"Did she speak?"

Bottomly nodded. "She did, sir."

"With the voice you recognised as hers?"

"No," he replied. "Her voice was croaky – dry, like death. And her mouth didn't really move, on account of her lips being sewn together."

"What did she say," I asked. "Do you recall?"

"She told me to keep my nose out of her business."

"Did she now? Fascinating!" Holmes's eyes shone in the light of the lamp.

"Yeah. And then she said she's just trying to clear things up to make it better for us all, now she's dead."

"That's very noble of her."

Bottomly nodded. "She's cleared us of her debt, and now she's going to start making us some money instead. Then God will let her into Heaven."

281

I couldn't help but interrupt again. "She said that? Those very words?"

Bottomly nodded. "I told her that Ma won't spend the money we've been given. Says it's dirty. Unholy. She told me that we should take it and spend it. I said I didn't think I could do that either, on account of how I was working for the Law now. She called me ungrateful. I pleaded that I was just trying to make things better for the family. She told me I had to do as I was told, just like she always did in life. Well, Mr Holmes, I'd had enough of that anyway. I told her to get back to her grave, or sling her hook and go haunt someone else, and to leave me alone. Next thing I knew, she jumped on me."

"She jumped on you?' I repeated. 'The ghost jumped on you?"

"Like everyone's said, Doctor Watson – she has physical form, yes. She jumped on top of me on the bed and started to throttle me. I was horrified, but I struggled back as best I could. I pushed at her face. There was a cry and then, and then, this . . . foul liquid spewed out all over me. Didn't come from her sewn-up mouth. No. Came from her nose, the pits of her eyes, from – I dunno – seemed like it sprayed at me from everywhere. Some kind of ghostly vomit."

I recalled the aroma of vomit in the bedchamber, which I'd assumed had come from Bottomly himself.

"Then,: Bottomly concluded, "she jumped off me and flew out through the door. That's all that I recall."

My eyes popped. "She flew out through the door?"

Bottomly frowned. "Yes. Next thing I remember was waking up here."

"Your boarded-up window," said Holmes. "Does it cause a draught, at all?"

"Only when the local children push at it with sticks."

"But you hadn't noticed such an occurrence before you retired to bed?"

"No, sir."

"And at what time did you go to bed that night?"

"Gone eleven, I shouldn't wonder, sir. Life round our way starts to get a bit quieter, then, you . . . see."

I noticed Bottomly start to waver and wobble and I knew we'd extracted as much as we could, or should, from him for now. I returned the lamp to Holmes (doubtless somewhat unceremoniously) and helped the poor lad to lie down. I removed my overcoat and rolled it up to use as a pillow.

"Why is this happening to me?" he asked, suddenly fragile again. "I've lived a good, honest life. I was a good lad to her. Why is she punishing me?"

I had no answers to these questions. The best I could do was to give him another sedative. Just a light one, this time, enough for only a few hours rest. Then he'd need to eat, or his body would start to waste.

"We will try to find out," I said. "Give you and your family some peace. In the meantime, rest again, and when you wake, the inspector will have a good meal ready for you."

As before, he'd lost consciousness almost before I could remove the needle. I returned my affairs to my bag, and we left Bottomly to his fragile slumbers.

Chapter VI

We reached Derby Gate before we were able to hail a hansom. The lack of an overcoat had left me somewhat exposed to the elements, although it was hardly any warmer inside the cab than outside. But at least the journey passed by more quickly. Holmes silently brooded, and I passed the time explaining to him (whether he was listening or not) why I was confident of a full recovery from Bottomly.

Upon our return to Baker Street, Holmes finally broke his silence and asked me my view of the case. I took a few moments to gather my thoughts before speaking.

"A half-glimpsed spectre, or a note written in the old lady's hand I could pass off as a deception. But they have seen *her* – very specifically her, and in her death mask too. And she actually attacked her grandson. It troubles me deeply, Holmes, that we have no rational explanation for it. And, as we have observed before now, we are both rational men."

"It troubles me, also," Holmes admitted. "But it troubles me most that we don't yet have enough pieces of the puzzle. We are still trailing in the wake of this mystery, reliant solely on gossip and reported instances. I am slowly beginning to get a better idea of what's possibly been going on, but we need to take control and lead, not follow."

"Holmes," I said, "you're not suggesting we should be there waiting when Bottomly's Grandmother strikes next?"

"No, my friend," he reassured me. "We know she has already covered all her creditors, at least, and I think we'd have to be fortunate indeed to guess correctly any future targets."

"Then, what are you thinking?"

Here he slapped his hand on the desk. "By hook or by crook, we need to exhume that corpse." He punctuated the final few words with further slaps of his hand.

I offered him a constitutional whisky, but he declined. However, I had a need. It went down very smoothly, so I had another. Holmes was staring out through the window when his enigmatic silhouette spoke next.

"Watson, I have a mission for you."

I swiftly finished my drink. "Do I have time to find my other overcoat first?" My primary coat had been laundered following the recent fog, and the other was still at Scotland Yard.

"Of course," he agreed with a nod. "I need you to pay another visit to Maude Bottomly. We must obtain her permission. She has to see that checking the contents of the coffin is the best course of action, and you, my dear Watson, you, are the very man to charm that acquiescence from her."

I doubted that very much, but I wasn't going to decline his request.

"I would come too, but I note there was a summons from Mycroft while we were out. I had better attend and discover what ails him."

I understood. Discussions between Holmes and his brother was one area of his life into which I was rarely invited.

As I feared, Maude Bottomly was a woman with whom charm held no sway. Less so her daughter. After some reasoned and impassioned discussion, I felt I was getting some way to convincing Maisie that an exhumation was the best course of action. But Maude remained rigid.

"It's against nature, against the Word of the Lord, and against the sanctity of death," she repeated over and over.

"Against the sanctity of death? Mrs. Bottomly," I expostulated, "surely these accusations of your dear departed mother haunting and extorting is further in breach of the sanctity of death than checking if she's still in her coffin?" Yet, still she was having none of it.

I had just reached the end of my tether when there was a sharp rap at the door. Before anyone could get to it, the latch was forced and a twisted, cloaked figure entered. He walked with the aid of a stick and his stench reminded me if the cells under New Scotland Yard. In short, he reeked of evil and depravity.

I stood. "What is the meaning of this intrusion?" I asked. "Explain yourself, sir."

"Got gentlefolks helping ye, have ye now, Biddy Bottomly?" he sneered. His voice held no charm, and Maude hardly looked pleased at his use of the familiar epithet, biddy.

"Never you mind who he is, friend," Maude replied. "You keep a civil tongue in your head. Account for yourself and be on your way. We're respectful, clean living folk, here. Don't want no trouble."

"Never used to be, though, ah?" The figure gave a chuckle.

I was having none of this. "You heard the lady, sir. Mind your manners and get to the point, or, by Jove, you'll taste the end of my cane."

"As you wish," he said, indicating neither fear nor remorse. "I've come to tell you, Biddy, I've been haunted by your mother every night this last se'ennight."

Maude shook her head, resigned. Maisie looked surprised.

"Have you come to clear a debt or make a donation to the family upkeep?" I asked.

"Neither," the man grunted. "I'm getting fed up with it, oh, my puff! Every night, always the same. Takes more than a ghoulish old hag to frighten Elias Turpentine, but she don't take no for an answer, does she? So, I've had enough. Come here today to demand to see her body dug up." He swept a gnarled, cautionary finger around the room. "Prove to me she's not still alive and playing games."

"That's not possible!" burst Maisie.

I turned to her, such was her vehemence. "Why not possible, my dear?"

Maisie seemed to stutter over her thoughts. "Well, err, Ma won't hear of it. And we know all of Granny's creditors, by now. Met them all. No creature like this was one of them."

"Appeared to many, has she?" Turpentine asked.

"Yes she has! So we're told," Maisie replied.

"The rest were all *frighted* out of their wits, and out of pocket, I'll wager?"

Maisie nodded. The creature chuckled again.

"I was cut from a different cloth, me dear." Turpentine's hook nose and unpleasant face, partially concealed within its grey cloak, turned to Maude and he pointed an accusatory finger. "I won't be the last, you know that. Come along, Biddy, let's get the old woman dug up."

"Ma?" Maisie asked. "I don't trust him. We don't know who he is. And we don't need to help him. I say we tell him to sling his hook."

But two tears could be seen cutting grooves through the grime down Maude's cheeks. "No, Maisie. It's the only way. And, as he says, like as much he won't be the last."

"No, Ma We don't know that."

But Maude was firm. "Come, I've had enough now. Let's go and see the parson."

With Maisie's hand for comfort, Maude Bottomly sadly left her cottage. The cloaked, hunched figure of Turpentine followed. I didn't trust him, but he'd achieved what had escaped me, so for that, at least, I was thankful.

If only Holmes were there, too. This was exactly what he wanted, but he would miss it all unless I could get word to him very shortly. I wondered if I should go myself. I could hardly send a street urchin off to Whitehall or the Diogenes Club. That was part of the problem. Holmes hadn't indicated where he was meeting Mycroft. I'd assumed he'd join me here as soon as he was able, unless I'd already been back at Baker Street, licking my wounds.

That, then, was my best option. I would remain here with Maude and Maisie and watch over proceedings. I would send a local lad off to Baker Street with a message for Mrs. Hudson. She could then inform Holmes as to my actions and pass on instructions for him to join me with all haste upon his return.

Chapter VII

In my, thankfully limited, experience with exhumations, negotiations with the Church have always been the most delicate, not to say thorny, part of the process – even when armed with a Court Order. We had no such official sanction this time, but, truly, there was not a single brow raised in objection. It was surely a mark of the effect that the hauntings were having on the local community that, when we arrived at St. Mary's, Whitechapel, to seek permission, the parson already had his gravediggers on standby. No questions asked, save for a cursory "Are you certain?" to Maude Bottomly. There was a sense of "About time, too," in the attitude of the gravediggers, as they set off to do their work. Clearly this action had long been expected, either from the family or from the police.

It was another day under a blanket of oppressive grey cloud. The terrible fog had not yet returned, but the blanket of cloud was oppressive enough. Added to this, Whitechapel had an atmosphere all of its own. Even the open spaces around St. Mary's were hung with the grime and the tang of the East London slums – so much suffering and degradation. And then, within all of that, there was a certain positivity, as exemplified by the Bottomly family. Maude was a strong matriarch, who knew the world and how to survive in it. Maisie was clearly marrying someone a little better than her, socially – a step up the ladder that the next generation might take further again. And then there was Charlie – Good, honest, willing young Constable Bottomly. It took nerve to be a police officer and still live in these areas – I knew that much.

A hacking cough from Elias Turpentine dragged me back to the very worst that these areas had to offer. A hard life had clearly turned him into something very different to Maude Bottomly. I watched him watching everyone else. He was like a hawk, with that beak of a nose and beady, piercing eyes. Worst still, he appeared to be very much at home in the cemetery. His hunched, grey-cloaked body seemed somehow at one with the mouldering gravestones, as if he had emerged from them, fully formed.

I paused and rubbed my brow. All this recent talk of the supernatural was clearly having an effect on my reason. Turpentine may be a fiend, but he was no wraith. I noted, however, that everyone instinctively treated him with caution and reserve – the parson included. A gap remained around him at all times, even when we reached the graveside.

As they began their work, Turpentine urged the diggers on from the graveside. His East London accent had never sounded stronger. The ground hadn't yet compacted fully, which made it easier for the diggers, but it was still hard work and slow going. After several objections to the sort of enthusiastic encouragement they were receiving from the twisted, cloaked figure, he threw them a large coin each and they suddenly found more joy in their task. All this time I kept an eye out for Holmes to arrive.

Maude and Maisie were standing to one side. Maude looked shocked, like she'd suddenly lost touch with the world. Doubtless the presence of her son would have been a great help now. Maisie only appeared to be able to offer her very limited comforts. She was more focussed on what was happening at the grave and watching Turpentine like a hawk. The parson was there, too, doing all that he could, but as far as I could hear, mainly offering platitudes that did little to settle Maude's concerns.

The coffin was finally revealed and, with some effort, hoisted up to ground level. The grave diggers asked if we wanted the other one, too. It was then that I realised Bottomly's Grandmother had been buried in a shared plot, next to her husband, Maude's father, who had died several years previously. The parson declined on her behalf, and so we gathered around to see what the inside of the casket would reveal. Turpentine eagerly reached out for it, but the parson remonstrated that he hadn't yet prayed for the soul held within.

"Amen," we all intoned at the end of the Parson's prayer, except for Turpentine who just kept grumbling, "Come on!"

With a creak of wood, the nails holding the lid down were forced out and the top removed. I found myself instinctively holding my breath. A body was revealed, within. Dead some weeks, only. The stomach was bloated with gas and the skin blue with the progressive stages of putrefaction setting in. I wasn't convinced that the mortuary had done a very thorough job in preparing the body, to be honest. I was noting as much as I could to pass on to Holmes. Turpentine's stick suddenly reached out and prodded the corpse.

"Have a care," I snapped. "And show some respect, you fiend."

"Just checking," he said.

I wiped the back of my hand across my mouth. "Assuming that's her body, she is dead, then. Can anyone confirm?"

Maude indicated that she couldn't look. Maisie drew strength from somewhere and joined me.

"That's Granny," she said. "She's all there. Can we put her back now please?"

Behind us, Maude heaved a sigh of relief.

Maisie turned to Turpentine. "Satisfied, now, wretch?" she spat, vehemently.

"I perceive, gentlemen, that this presents us with something of a mystery, now," said the parson, quietly.

"Indeed," I agreed. I was, however, franker in my own thoughts. *If the body is there, then it truly must have been the spirit who was visiting everyone. Including her own grandson, and this unpleasant Turpentine creature, too.*

As if he heard my thoughts, the fiend hobbled over to me. I managed to contain the urge to back away.

The gravediggers were about to replace the coffin lid, but Turpentine held out a hand to stay their actions.

"What now?" pleaded Maisie.

"One moment, please, my dear," he sneered. "I would like the views of the Good Doctor, here." At this he stroked my arm. I shuddered.

"How do you know my profession?" I demanded. I had never, to the best of my knowledge, had any dealings with this creature before.

"I knows everyone, Doctor Watson," said Turpentine, somewhat enigmatically. "What do you make of the face?"

The face of the corpse was a mess, it was true. Far more advanced in its decay than the rest of the body. The flesh glistened in the dull afternoon light. I realised something was amiss. Clearly Turpentine had, too. The face should be blue, like the hands and the neck. And now I looked more closely, there were no lips, only the toothless gums beneath. Things could be seen writhing in the slightly open mouth, as nature took its course.

"Please. Put Granny back now," said Maisie. "It's causing Ma terrible upset."

'One moment more," called Turpentine. "Go on, Doctor Watson. I feel you were about to say something."

I nodded. "Only that it looks to me like the face has been skilfully skinned, as a Red Indian would scalp a victim."

"That's just her rotting, though, ain't it?" Maisie pleaded. "Happens to dead people, we knows that. Parson, can't you say something?"

"Not this quickly, Maisie, no," I said. The parson looked torn. I continued. "The top layers of skin and lips have been removed, revealing the flesh and muscles underneath."

"Good Heavens!" said the parson, looking more closely. "But . . . but who would do such a thing, and when?"

"Someone close to the deceased, or someone who worked at the undertakers, I'd imagine."

Maude spoke, remaining behind us. "The undertakers? That was Maisie's Teddy. Works in the family business, he does."

"Don't listen to them, Ma."

Turpentine nodded beneath his cloak. "Interesting. And what could you do with the face of a dead old woman, eh? Particularly if you still had access to her clothes, too."

"They're doing it deliberately, to upset you, Ma." Maisie was sounding increasingly upset herself.

Ghoulish thoughts began to spin through my head. A death mask. An *actual* mask. All I could mutter was how dreadful the stench would be, after a while.

Turpentine continued, gesturing with his hands. "Indeed, it would be a formidable disguise that someone could wear. And they could use that disguise to frighten people, perhaps? People like creditors, perhaps? Or to extort money from wealthy businessmen? Perhaps to be able to afford to move out of an area such as Whitechapel, into somewhere more prosperous? Maybe provide a dowry for a bride, who might otherwise have nothing?"

Maude Bottomly now stepped forward to join us. Her hard edge had returned. Her eyes fumed as the tears instantly dried.

"What was all that?"

Maisie was close behind her. "He's making stuff up, Ma. He's not one of Granny's creditors. I said before, I know all of them. They've been dealt with. They'll leave us alone now."

Suddenly, Turpentine, the twisted creditor, stood upright and threw off his cloak and disguise.

"Good Lord!" I ejaculated. "Holmes! It was you all along." For it was truly him.

"Indeed, my friend. And I must apologise to you, Mrs. Bottomly, and to you, Parson, and your stout, hard-working men, here. But I knew that I had to force the situation with a little character play to get people to reveal their true hands."

"Come on, Ma," said Maisie, hurriedly. "These posh folk are playing games with us. Let's get home, quick."

She turned, only to be met by the surprising figure of Inspector Lestrade, who had crept up on us after the agreed signal of Holmes's revealing himself.

"It was an enterprising idea, Maisie," Holmes said, "wearing the clothes and the face of your deceased grandmother to scare off the creditors like that. Complete with blacked out eyes and the sewn-together lips."

I was shocked and sickened at such a horrific, macabre crime. I listened as Holmes continued.

"But it was more successful than you thought it might be, wasn't it? You got carried away, got greedy. Not only clearing the family debts but trying to make money as well, with a bit of extortion."

"Maisie!"

"Ma! I'm – "

She tried to make a run for it, but two of Lestrade's men intercepted her easily.

"You already have her accomplice?" Holmes asked.

Lestrade nodded.

"Not – not the Constable?" I asked.

"Good Lord, no, Watson. Her intended, Teddy."

"Taken earlier today," confirmed Lestrade. "Complete with his lock-picking kit."

"No wonder you had to wear that strong perfume," continued Holmes. "Paid for from your extortions, no doubt. I imagine the mask is becoming quite putrid by now. Wearing it the other night when you visited your poor brother, it made you sick, didn't it? Ghosts don't vomit, but you couldn't help it. You made a good effort at cleaning it all up, but there was always going to be the stench. Perfume can't hide everything."

"Why, Maisie?" her mother asked, clearly heartbroken.

"I did it for us, Ma," Maisie said through her own tears. "We've always struggled, what with granny how she was, and dad long gone. I'm fed up with us being the lowest of the low. I wanted to be comfortable for once. More so than we could be with Charlie on his peeler wage."

"Maisie. How could you?"

We all knew the voice, even before Constable Bottomly appeared.

"So, you tried to kill me instead."

"I dunno what happened there. I panicked cos of what you said. I – I'm sorry, Charlie. Truly I am."

Inspector Lestrade indicated to the constables holding Maisie. "I think it's time you came along with us, Miss. And we'll need to rebury the . . . mask."

The escorted the tearful Maisie away.

"How are you feeling, Constable?" I asked Bottomly.

"Fine, Doctor, thanking you," he replied.

"Charlie," his mother called him to him. "Go with them, my lovely boy. Make sure Maisie's all right, won't you? She's still your sister."

Bottomly nodded and followed his colleagues.

"I'm sorry, Mrs. Bottomly," I said.

"Like I said to you the other day, Doctor, I'm used to such things in my life."

Indeed, I truly felt for the poor woman.

"Come," said Holmes. "We'll see you safely home."

Maude agreed. "And there's something you gents can do for me when we're there, and all."

Chapter VIII

Upon returning to Baker Street, we found Mrs. Hudson had smoked some mackerel for us, which we soundly polished off. Afterwards, we retired to our usual seats in order to enjoy a brandy. I had a few unanswered queries regarding the ghostly case.

"Elias Turpentine?" I guffawed. "Really, Holmes. You and your disguises."

My friend appeared to take much joy from my amusement. "You must forgive me on that front, Watson. I was arranging the pieces of the puzzle in my head, and I knew the key move had to be exhuming the corpse. I was also certain that Mrs. Bottomly would never agree to it. So I had to send you there, as my innocent dupe, while I disguised myself in order to push the point home further."

"So, your message from Mycroft – ?"

"Was a ruse, yes indeed."

"You must have already suspected Maisie, then?" I surmised.

"Maisie, or possibly Maude, yes. Maisie seemed the more likely candidate once I'd mapped out in my head what we already knew. When Constable Bottomly said that the ghost of his grandmother had spewed forth something vile when she attacked him and he pushed a hand into her face, I knew it had to be someone wearing the dead woman's putrefying face. You recall how badly you smelled when you returned home recently, in that cloying, thick fog? That's what brought it to my mind. That was enough to turn people's stomachs on its own. Maisie was known to wear strong perfume. This would have become a necessity as the decay of the mask increased. Also, she was engaged to one of the sons of Butcher, Rowe, and Sons, the undertakers, which would have provided her with an opportunity to access the corpse before burial. That her fiancé was her co-conspirator and accomplice started out as a common-sense hunch. She'd need someone to help apply the mask and disguise, open and close doors, pick locks, and be on hand to help out in tricky situations. They were breaking and entering, after all. That person was unlikely to be Maude, and it was clear that Charlie's mental condition was not an act by your professional reaction and the way he responded to your treatment. If I wasn't already certain about Maisie, the way she reacted to Turpentine was sufficient persuasion, too. Maude took me at face value at the house – as did you, Watson. Maisie treated me with suspicion from the start. She probably thought that I was a chancer out to get what I could at first. Then, when Maude conceded to the exhumation, she was so desperate to have her granny put back immediately, it was like a beacon alerting me to her guilt."

"At the time, I just thought she was trying to ease the pain for her poor mother," I said, with a nod. "Her intended being in on it, though – the use of an accomplice would help explain why the 'ghost' was able to fly out through the door, as Constable Bottomly reported."

"Alas, Watson, you are too credulous at times. That was a turn of phrase. He'd already reported a draught, which couldn't have come from the window, so it must have come from his door, carelessly left open, it being his own home. Even near the end, there, you were still convinced that the body in the coffin meant that an actual ghost had done the haunting."

"Yes, well," I huffed a little, eager to change the subject if I could. "At least the parson and gravediggers got something for their efforts."

"Indeed. That was a saintly gesture by Mrs. Bottomly. She never approved of the money that had been given to the family in that gruesome way, to begin with. Best to donate it to the church and allow it to do its charitable best there. Which reminds me," Holmes said, downing the remainder of his drink, standing suddenly and moving to the desk. "I must write back to Sir Rodney, care of the Club, and tell him that the night-time manifestations should be no more. He's desperate to recall his secretary from Eastbourne.

While Holmes settled down to fashion his communication, I satisfied myself that I had garnered all the salient points for the successful recording of this, one of our seemingly macabre and more gruesome tales.

The Adventure of the
Intrusive Spirit
by Shane Simmons

Word came to me, as it often did, that Mr. Holmes demanded an audience at Baker Street. When I came up to his rooms, I found the detective alone, leaning against the mantel of the fireplace, and gazing deeply into a letter in his hand. He wasn't reading it so much as staring it down, and I was sure it was telling him all sorts of things that weren't written on the page.

"Wiggins, have a look at this and give me your thoughts," he said, holding it out for me to take.

I weren't so literate then as I am now. Picking my way through the entire letter would have taken me hours, so I set about trying to make some deductions like Mr. Holmes would.

"A rich fellow sent this," I concluded. "Nice paper, good quality."

I held it up to the light.

"It even has a watermark. Looks like a family crest. Very snooty stuff."

"Indeed," Mr. Holmes agreed.

I could see he was waiting for me to read it. I gave it a go, but could see it was going to be a hard slog much past "*Dear Mr. Holmes*". I stalled for time with more deducing.

"Um, the penmanship suggests a well-educated man, and the ink is – Well, it's black India ink with, er . . . ."

I was about to put my nose to the page to smell it when Mr. Holmes snatched it away.

"Allow me, Wiggins," he said, and I guess he must have known I'd already stretched my reading and deducing to their limits.

Mr. Holmes read me the whole thing, back to front. I can't remember all of what it said, and the original is probably lost at the bottom of one of his many files, never to resurface. But I remember the gist of it.

The story was a sad one, written by the brother of a woman who had lost her young daughter in a drowning accident a year earlier. This happened at a time that was already difficult for the woman. Her husband – a liar, a cheat, and a habitual gambler – had all but left her, visiting only occasionally to see his child, who was the one person in the family he ever had any real love for. It was during one of his visits that tragedy struck.

On a walk across the property with her father, the girl, only five-years-old, wandered off and drowned in a marsh. Upon hearing the news, the mother fell into a deep funk that persisted for months. She refused to leave the house, hardly ate, and spoke to no one. That is, she spoke to no one until her brother started to hear her chatting away to somebody in the middle of the night. He was worried his sister had gone mad with grief and loneliness. They lived together in the countryside, miles from the nearest village, and her estranged husband hadn't been seen since the funeral. When he finally asked her who she spoke to at night, the sister said it was her daughter, returned from the dead. Obviously, the brother thought this was nothing more than a delusion, but then he saw this ghost for himself one night.

It was past midnight when he happened to look out a window at the side of the house and saw a tiny figure approaching through the open field. She carried a lantern in her little hand, which lit her deathly white face, and he recognised his niece at once. He lost sight of her for only a moment before hearing voices in his sister's room. Racing up the stairs at once, he flung open the door and found his sister alone, sitting at her vanity, clutching a string of pearls like they were worry beads. The child – if she had ever been there at all – was gone, but his sister wept inconsolably, insisting that her brother had frightened off the spirit of her dear deceased daughter. Whether there had been an actual spirit in the room or not, the brother couldn't say for certain, but he did find an extinguished lantern tipped over on the floor that remained warm to the touch.

Since that night, the visitations continued, and the brother stayed up late several times, managing to spot the ghost's approach on more than one occasion. His poor mad sister, however, had taken to locking her bedroom door at night, to keep him from interrupting another mother-daughter reunion. He listened to these nocturnal exchanges as best he could through the old house's thick walls, and thought he could distinguish two different voices inside the sealed room, but couldn't make out what was said. His sister refused to elaborate beyond saying that her daughter returns to her several times a week, comforting her until she falls asleep, and is always gone again by the time she wakes.

The letter ended with a plea for Mr. Holmes's assistance in getting to the truth of the matter. I figured there was no hope in that, since Mr. Holmes weren't one for ghost stories, phantoms, or folklore. That's why I was so surprised when he said he was catching the next train out to Saxilby to investigate.

"Ain't Dr. Watson coming to help you solve this mystery like he usually does?" I asked, noting his absence.

"The doctor, I am informed, is currently unavailable to lend his friend assistance with the intrigue currently before us," said Mr. Holmes in an irritable tone.

"One of his patients take a heart attack or something?"

"Unfortunately, no, Wiggins. Watson has been recruited by his good lady wife into the pressing business of purchasing a new settee. One that *matches*. Matches what, I have no idea, nor do I wish to be illuminated."

"I expect such things seem awfully important when you have a new home," I considered.

"The banality of the entire affair does not bear consideration," said Mr. Holmes, turning up his lip.

"What, shopping with the missus?"

"Marriage."

"Well if there's anything I might do to fill in . . . ." I began, not for a moment actually assuming Mr. Holmes would have me on.

"In fact, Wiggins," he said, "I have summoned you for the very purpose. It occurs to me that you may have some special expertise in this field, and I have already anticipated a need for talents you possess which I cannot match."

If there was anything under the sun I could accomplish that Mr. Holmes, for all his abilities, could not, it was beyond my figuring. But you take your compliments where you can get them, regardless of whether you understand them or not. I didn't argue the point. I merely tipped my hat and clicked my heels together.

"Anything you need, sir," I submitted.

We were on the way out to hail a cab to the train station not more than a few minutes later. As if summoned by the mention of his name, we ran into a familiar face before we were even as far as the entry hall of 221b.

"Holmes!" said Dr. Watson as he caught us on the stairs, "Good news! I have been able to extract myself from the day's chores in order to accompany you on your case."

I expected to be sacked then and there. Holmes and Watson always had a better ring to it than Holmes and Wiggins.

"Out in the countryside, eh?" said Dr. Watson, observing Mr. Holmes's deerstalker, which was hardly fitting city apparel. "Count me game for some fresh air and rolling hills."

"My dear Watson," said Mr. Holmes, "I am touched by your gesture of excusing yourself from your husbandly duties, but I am afraid your attendance on this – *adventure* – is quite unnecessary and, indeed, superfluous. I have, as you can see, recruited elsewhere."

"Wiggins?" exclaimed the doctor with such incredulity that I might have been insulted if I ever let that sort of thing get to me.

295

"The same," confirmed Mr. Holmes, as though the decision were final and unshakable.

"If you're quite sure, Holmes," said Dr. Watson who, it has to be said, had the look of a reprimanded dog about him.

"I am," answered Mr. Holmes, and passed him on his way down the stairs to the street. I followed closely and said nothing, not wanting to get in the middle of this awkward exchange between friends. Dr. Watson wasn't quite done with us, however, and called after Mr. Holmes.

"Well, if there's anything I can do to assist you on your current – "

"Nothing at all Watson," said Mr. Holmes, without ever looking back.

I tipped my hat to the doctor and joined the detective outside as his replacement right-hand man for the day.

"I had expected Dr. Watson to be in your company."

This from Maynard Highmore, the author of the letter, several hours later, once we arrived from the Saxilby station by a carriage hired to take us to the remote house.

"So did Dr. Watson," I muttered.

"Watson," said Mr. Holmes, "for all his uses, is ill-fitted to the task. It is my trusted associate, Wiggins, who will be filling in on this occasion."

"As you see fit, Mr. Holmes. It is only a resolution to this dreadful affair I seek. Your means of accomplishing this are entirely at your discretion."

Having successfully lured Mr. Holmes and his deductive skills to his family home and troubles, Highmore showed us inside.

"I place all blame firmly at the feet of Ellis Baldwin, the scoundrel," Highmore sneered once we were in the great house. "My sister was of sound mind – stable, pragmatic, and never prone to flights of fancy – until he spoiled her life and visited nothing but despair and heartache upon so good a woman."

"He lived here, with you and your sister?" Mr. Holmes asked.

"For as long as the marriage lasted. And when he wasn't off on one of his binges of cards and dice and horses!"

"Free with his money, was he not?"

"When he'd had a winning streak."

"But there came a losing streak," Mr. Holmes surmised. "A long, dark one."

"It strained his relations with everyone. Eleanor, most of all.

"It must have stung him, to go from being a country gentleman, living in a fine house, married into a fine family, to whatever circumstances he finds himself in now."

"Good riddance to bad rubbish!" spat Highmore. "I never cared for him, and his behaviour after the loss of his daughter was inexcusable."

"Grief manifests itself in different ways with different people."

"In this case, it manifested itself as even more belligerence, even more thoughtlessness. I was glad when he left, though it put poor Eleanor in an even worse state."

"Show me the window from which you observe these nightly visitations," said Mr. Holmes.

Highmore directed us to an east-facing window that offered a view of a broad field, ridged with a line of trees and woods beyond.

"She . . . ." began Highmore, and corrected himself at once. "The figure, as it were, approaches across the field there, usually with a lamp or candle to guide the way."

"Have you observed footprints indicating a more tangible visitor than some spirit?"

Highmore shook his head.

"I have been out to look, more than once, but the grass is high, and there is no mud to capture prints. If the grass were ever pressed down by the passage of a person, the wind blows away any evidence of it by morning."

"And you say that scarcely more than a few moments pass between seeing the figure outside and hearing your sister interact with someone upstairs."

"It is, I'll admit, as though an incorporeal ghost has passed straight through our walls."

"No window is found opened? No door ajar?"

"This window I watch from is the only one on this side of the house. It is locked at night, as are all other conceivable entries."

The impossibility of the intrusion didn't give Mr. Holmes any pause. It's like he expected as much.

"Tell me about the building itself," he prompted. "Its history."

"The house has been in the Highmore family for generations. It was built by my great-grandfather, Thomas Highmore, late last century."

"A home to many secrets, no doubt," commented Mr. Holmes.

"How so, sir?"

"As you might imagine, criminology interests me, both personally and professionally. I study a great many histories for both work and relaxation. The criminals may change, but crime is ever consistent, lurking always beneath the veneer of human civilisation. One should know of past misdeeds to better anticipate future acts of ill-intent. The name Thomas Highmore is not unknown to me. He was a bent man, as I recall, twisted and small, but of great stature in the criminal underworld. A notorious smuggler, he moved goods across the kingdom, using his hideout in Saxilby as a pivotal waypoint. Perhaps, it has been surmised, this very house."

"As I said, Mr. Holmes," bristled Highmore, offense brewing, "that was generations ago, and I'll thank you not to tarnish my family name with spurious rumours of how my great-grandfather made his fortune. He was never convicted, nor even charged with a single crime."

"Yet the police did make enquiries routinely. Walked these very halls on more than one occasion."

"And found nothing."

"Rest assured, Mr. Highmore, I do not judge sons for the crimes of their fathers. Nor great-grandsons for accusations levelled against family members long dead. It is merely a point of personal interest."

"With no bearing on our family's current misfortune," added Highmore.

"Of course not," agreed Mr. Holmes civilly. "Perhaps now would be a good time to introduce us to your sister, if she is well enough to receive guests."

We were shown upstairs to Eleanor Baldwin's room. Before we entered, her brother cautioned us, "Please do not tax her with too many questions. She has been in a delicate state."

"A few words and some simple observations should suffice," Mr. Holmes assured him.

After a gentle knock on the door from Highmore, he carefully cracked it open and asked, "Ellie, are you good to greet a couple of visitors?"

Eleanor Baldwin sat quietly in the corner of her room, like another bit of furniture, immobile. She didn't seem grieved by the fate of her daughter, or elated by her apparent return. Rather, she came across as distant – barely aware we were there, barely there herself, like we were all ghosts less substantial than the one who haunted her by night.

After introductions were made, to which Mrs. Baldwin had no response, Mr. Holmes stepped forward to begin his interview. Even so, he seemed less interested in anything the woman had to say, and more interested in the room itself. His eyes flicked back and forth, up and down, to every corner, taking in facts and making calculations, as was his way.

"I was grieved to hear of your loss," said Mr. Holmes, remembering his manners as an afterthought.

This penetrated Eleanor Baldwin's haze. Her lips turned up in a faint smile and she softly replied, "Oh, but Mr. Holmes, it was no loss at all. My daughter, Julia, visits me most nights without fail."

"Is that so?"

"I sleep irregularly, fitfully, when she is not with me. But of late, when I wake in the middle of the night, as I so often do, she is in the room, playing with my things, wanting to dress up just as her mother does. She says little, but I talk to her, sing to her, tell her stories. I brush her hair and let her wear my finery. She stays with me until I drift off again. It saddens me to awake in the morning and find her gone. But I am consoled that I shall see her again later. My brother thinks her a spirit, but she feels real enough to me – in my arms as I embrace her, and in my heart as I feel her presence."

Items on Mrs. Baldwin's vanity seemed to catch Mr. Holmes's attention for a fleeting moment. What conclusion he drew from an open jewellery box, a single pearl necklace, and a brush, I couldn't say. By the time I even spotted him looking at them, his eyes had shifted elsewhere. If these things were important at all, they didn't warrant him taking a closer look with the magnifying glass I knew that he always kept in his pocket.

Eleanor Baldwin was back to staring at nothing in particular, waiting for sleep to take her again, and either her dreams or her insomnia to deliver her daughter once more.

"It was a pleasure meeting you, madam," said Mr. Holmes, calling the encounter short. "We shan't disturb you further."

Having excused ourselves, we reconvened in the hall as Maynard Highmore silently shut the door behind us.

"As you can see, she is not well," he said. "Had I not seen this figure approaching in the night myself, I would think she had gone insane. Even so, I remain unconvinced Eleanor has been host to this spirit in her room, behind locked doors. Witness as I have been, I have never seen the child inside the house, nor is there a way she could have infiltrated. Not unless she truly is a ghost, capable of manifesting herself at will."

"That is the master bedroom of the house?" Mr. Holmes asked, to which Highmore nodded a confirmation the detective expected.

There was the soft click of a key turning in a lock. Apparently Mrs. Baldwin had risen from her seat to bar the door against intrusion, so as not to disturb her next visitation.

"Evening approaches," noted Mr. Holmes. "The sun will set in another hour, and I expect we have an eventful night ahead of us."

"Can anything be done to untangle this puzzle?" Highmore asked.

"Possibly," said Mr. Holmes, tapping his lip in thought. "I fear we have but one chance to apprehend this ghost. Unless I am very much mistaken, these emotional reunions are about to end once and for all, and the departed soul of Julia Baldwin shall be forever departed and beyond our reach."

"What can I do to assist you?"

"Nothing at all," replied Mr. Holmes. "Seal the doors and lock the windows as per usual once we leave. My assistant and I shall do our utmost to resolve this issue before the sun rises again. With luck, the new dawn will usher in a solution and a much-changed state of affairs."

We left Maynard Highmore behind, taking the stairs down to the front hall. But we didn't leave right away. Mr. Holmes instead led me into largest room of the lower level. It stretched from one end of the house to the other, and featured the east-facing window from which Mr. Highmore kept spotting these strange nocturnal activities.

"What do you make of it, Wiggins?" asked the detective.

"Me, sir? I don't think nothing about nothing. Not without your say-so. You're the sleuth."

"Nevertheless, I wish to know how the story strikes you. What can you deduce about this ghost?"

I considered my words carefully.

"Well, it ain't no ghost."

"A bold conclusion," laughed Mr. Holmes. "And how did you come upon it?"

"There ain't no such thing," I said, adding, less certain. "Is there?"

"I should say not," said Mr. Holmes. "Just as there are no real mind readers, psychics, or gypsies capable to foreseeing your future in the lines of your palm. This you well know."

"So it's a trick?"

"Perhaps," was all he would say in conclusion.

"If it's no ghost, does that mean the girl is still alive?"

"So it would appear. Surely Mrs. Baldwin would recognise her own daughter."

"Unless she's truly gone funny in the head."

I could tell the possibility had crossed Mr. Holmes's mind, but he must have dismissed it. We wouldn't be there at all if it was just a matter of some rich lady who'd gone looney over her dead child.

"Assuming it's a trick," said Mr. Holmes, "how would you go about performing it?"

"I'd use a double," I said after only a moment's consideration. "One kid inside, one outside, dressed the same. Simple."

"It would have to be a very close match indeed to fool anyone, considering the light shining directly upon both faces."

"Twins then."

"I expect Mrs. Baldwin would recall birthing a second daughter."

I'd seen plenty of parents who seemed to have lost track of how many children they had. The ranks of The Irregulars were full of forgotten children, uncounted and abandoned. But then I don't suppose the upper crust ever forget how many mouths they have to feed when they have so much to eat.

I stopped throwing out quick answers to questions that needed more thought.

"So one ghost," I wondered, "who ain't no ghost, but can still walk through walls."

"Let us contemplate that," said Mr. Holmes, pacing back and forth across the room like he was having hisself a good hard think.

"The trick," I ventured after a long period of silence, "isn't the ghost. It's the wall."

"First rate, Wiggins! My trust in bringing you along was not misplaced."

For a moment I let myself believe I had helped lead Mr. Holmes to some conclusion he might not have come to otherwise. But then, on his final pace of the room, he stopped right at the wall, his nose almost touching the wood panelling.

"It's short," he announced. "By approximately one pace – at least a pace made by a man of my height. I could tell you how short down to the inch with a surveyor's theodolite, but we have no need to be as precise as that."

"What do you mean, it's short?" I asked.

"The dimensions of this room, indeed the entire house, are smaller than the exterior should allow."

"You already knew," I said, disappointed.

"Only once I saw the house for myself. I might not have noticed even then, but I already had my suspicions when the story was first related to me in Maynard Highmore's correspondence. It merely took some rudimentary measurements to confirm the hypothesis."

It was just like Mr. Holmes to get halfway to a solution from only a letter that came in the morning mail.

"Come, Wiggins! There are no more answers for us inside. It is the grounds that must next be examined."

Outside, we started to take a tour around the house, but Mr. Holmes stopped near the carriage shed that sat back some distance from the east end.

"Oh, I see," I said, "You think there's a tunnel from the shed to the house."

I thought it was a pretty good deduction as deductions go, but Mr. Holmes wasn't having it.

"A tunnel cannot account for the rapidity of the apparition's reappearance inside," he said. "Assuming a flesh-and-blood spectre, she would have to climb down into a tunnel, cross to the house, and ascend back up through not one but two levels. Even factoring great haste, there is not enough time to accomplish this feat and be consistent with the account we have heard. No, Wiggins, our ghost has to be taking a more direct route."

With that, Mr. Holmes walked right past the shed – what I thought was our most promising starting point – and went straight to a waist-high fence that ran directly behind it, bridging a gap between it at the house. He leaned on it and stared at the white-washed bricks of the mostly featureless side of the Baldwin home.

"What do we observe here, Wiggins?" asked Mr. Holmes, like he was testing me.

"The side of a house. A wall. Bricks," I answered, because that's all there was.

"Nothing more?"

"It's just a brick wall."

"So it appears. Yet there is something more vital to our observation of that wall. Can you not see it?"

I couldn't, and my exaggerated shrug said as much.

"Our vantage point," said Mr. Holmes.

I looked around, but couldn't see anything special about where we stood. It wasn't much of a view. It truth, it was dull and ordinary. Mr. Holmes spelled it out for me.

"We find ourselves in the countryside, with open land all about. And yet here, in this one spot, we are boxed in by a shed, a wing of the house, and a fence. This segment of the wall can only be viewed from the single small patch of ground we find ourselves upon, with any other view of it made either impossible or highly inconvenient."

"Seems a bad design," I noted of the cramped passage at the back of the house.

"Or a brilliant one."

"How do you mean?"

"The art of observation relies heavily on perspective, Wiggins. Should one find that perspective contrived or forced, one must always seek a new perspective from which to view the problem."

With that, Mr. Holmes swung one of his long legs over the low fence that held us back from the wall of the house. His foot planted on the other side, he drew his other leg over and took a few paces towards the brickwork.

Halfway there, he stopped and turned around.

"Keep your eyes on me, Wiggins," he said, and took a step back.

"How do I look?" he asked.

"Like a madman walking backwards for no good reason," I replied.

302

"And now?" he said, taking another long step back.

"The same."

Mr. Holmes took one more step back, putting his back to the wall.

"And now?"

I merely shrugged in response.

With that, Mr. Holmes took another step – this one to the side – and vanished before my very eyes.

I couldn't comprehend what I had just seen. One moment he was there, the next he was gone like he had fallen through a thin slit cut into our world from the beyond. A second later, Mr. Holmes reappeared. Or at least a part of him did. I could see his face, tilted drastically to one side, but no body to go with it.

"Mr. Holmes!" I exclaimed, "It looks like your head's come off!"

But then an arm joined his floating head and beckoned me.

"Come," he ordered, and his head and arm vanished again.

The fence was little more than a wooden rail, supported at intervals by posts. Being so much shorter than Mr. Holmes, it was quicker and easier for me to duck under than to climb over. The short walk across the grass quickly went from peculiar to strange. The closer I got, the odder the wall appeared, until I realised I wasn't looking at one wall, but two. The second one was pushed back into the house, two feet deeper than the outer wall. I found Mr. Holmes tucked around the corner, squeezed into a space between them.

"Well, that's a neat trick," I whistled.

"Simple in effect, complex in design," said Mr. Holmes, stepping back out.

He pointed out some of the highlights of the masonry to me, marvelling at the craftsmanship.

"Larger bricks on the backdrop, precisely aligned with the smaller bricks on the front. As one wing of the house shelters the spot from sunlight at all times of the day, and all seasons of the year, no shadow can be cast to spoil the illusion. A magnificent bit of architectural illusion, meant to obscure the fact that it is not a plain brick wall, but a recessed doorway, allowing access to the interior around one of the corners."

"But what was so much effort for?" I wondered. "Who could even fit through there?"

"Of late, it is little Julie Baldwin who finds her way through the narrow gap. Did you not observe the house is being burgled nightly in these hauntings? The girl has been absconding with her mother's jewellery, one or two pieces at a time. Eleanor Baldwin's jewellery box has been picked clean, with but one necklace left to be pilfered."

"Are you so sure it's a living person we're talking about?"

"The long blonde hairs on Mrs. Baldwin's brush do not match their owner, and ghosts can scarcely be expected to shed."

"That Ellis Baldwin fellow must be behind this!" I said, starting to catch up with Mr. Holmes at last.

"An acrimonious separation, with a child declared dead out of spite, and then used as an instrument of recompense," he agreed. "The thief is an unwitting one, acting on the instructions of her lamentable father. As far as that poor manipulated girl grasps, she's merely visiting her mother – sick with grief for reasons she doesn't understand. A nightly game of dress-up with a mentally broken woman, and the child comes away with another few baubles to help feed Baldwin's gambling debts."

"Why doesn't the blighter do his own dirty work?" I asked bitterly.

"The passage is too small for him or any man of moderate height," said Mr. Holmes. "The infamous Thomas Highmore was a stunted fellow, of both body and soul. But not of intellect! Doubtless he designed his own house and hideout with features to serve his criminal enterprises. The space behind this windowless wall saw the passage of much contraband over his years here, I suspect, with the added benefit of being an avenue of escape for him should the police ever arrive with a warrant he couldn't wriggle out of. Ellis Baldwin must have discovered a hidden entry point inside while snooping about, sometime before the failure of his marriage. He may have been too large to fully explore it, but not his young daughter. Nor, I expect, you, Wiggins."

"You say you had me along on this mystery instead of Dr. Watson because I'm short?" I barked indignantly.

"Yes," replied Mr. Holmes.

"Fair enough," I agreed after a moment's reflection.

We spent the next few hours huddled out in the field, low in the tall grass, watching the house from a distance. By the time the sun was all the way down, we were quite invisible in the dark. Only a few lights from the house shone out as any sort of beacon until one additional spot of light appeared at the edge of the woods. Tiny, flickering, it appeared to be a single candle, bobbing its way towards the Highmore residence.

As the new light came closer to our position, I could see a spectral face aglow behind it. It was white as a sheet, with black hollow eyes like you'd see in a fleshless skull. If it weren't no ghost, it surely didn't look alive!

"What's that?" I whispered at Mr. Holmes.

"That, my dear Wiggins, is your cue," he said, and gave me a push towards the creeping figure.

"Follow her!" he hissed. "Keep close, make no noise, and do not be seen!"

I didn't much fancy chasing after a spectre through tight spaces in the middle of the night, even if Mr. Holmes had reliably deduced that there was nothing supernatural in the works. Still, I did as he demanded, and shuffled through the weeds quick enough to see the tiny figure duck under the fence and disappear around the concealed corner in the wall of the house.

A mirror image of the same motions, I brought up the rear and squeezed into the secret passage, letting myself in through a small hatch that kept the weather out. Inside, I found myself in the narrow space between walls interior and exterior. It was a hazardous journey through studs and beams as I shuffled my way along in the dark, following the faintest hint of light shining off the candle somewhere ahead of me. A ladder allowed access to the next leg of the passage on the second level. By the time I was up it, the light was gone completely, and I had to feel my way on hands and knees until I came upon another hatch.

I passed from one tiny space and into another. At least this one had a regular-sized door. I tried it, and found myself inside Eleanor Baldwin's room. The woman herself was asleep in bed, breathing uneasily, hardly at rest. The only light on was the candle I'd been following. By its faint flicker, I could see a little girl in a long white burial robe, standing over the vanity, trying on the pearl necklace that had so far escaped her sticky fingers. What I could see of her face was a horror – something born straight from the grave, and it made me quake in my boots. She must have heard me because she turned her awful vacant eyes my way, grabbing her candle so she might better spot the third person in the room.

The girl gasped when she saw a stranger and bolted, shoving right past me and into the closet I had just emerged from.

Mrs. Baldwin stirred in her sleep and opened her eyes.

"Julia?" she asked me.

"Not as such, no," I admitted. "The name's Wiggins. We met earlier."

"What are you doing here?" she asked, no doubt baffled by my presence in her locked bed chamber, especially considering I hadn't arrived from the hereafter.

"Beggin' your pardon, ma'am," I said, tipping my hat. "I'm off to nab your ghost and drag her back to the land of the living."

With that, I dove back into the closet and through the open hatch door concealed in the rear. Only a few feet in, I spotted the candle light not far ahead of me, and crawled towards it as fast as I could, bruising my knees on the uneven flooring in an effort to make haste.

When I arrived at the candle light, I found it was no longer being carried by the retreating ghost. It had been set down on the boards, guttering in the drafty space, dripping wax down the squat iron candle stick that held it in place. I was still staring into the flame when an eerie visage closed in right in front of me. It was the face of Julia Baldwin, pale and expressionless, with those giant staring eyes as black as coal.

I screamed in the dark. And if the whole household wasn't awake before, they were by the time that holler died in my throat.

Julia Baldwin didn't react at all. She only kept staring at me by the dim light as I recoiled from her, panting. Then she drew a short, sharp breath and blew out the candle, plunging me into total pitch.

And I screamed again, I'm ashamed to admit.

It took me a while to gather my nerve and feel my way back out of that tight maze. Julia Baldwin was long gone, and I had to admit as much to Mr. Holmes when I found him again by the carriage shed.

"She gave me the slip in the dark. Or passed straight through me if she's a real ghost after all."

"Spare me any excuses, Wiggins. There's no time to waste! If she's taken that last morsel of value from Mrs. Baldwin's jewellery box, her wayward husband will be gone for good and their daughter with him."

"We don't even know where they got to," I said.

"There's nothing for it but to try to pick up the trail at the edge of the woods – at the very spot where we first saw the girl's light emerge! Surely she will rendezvous with her father close by."

Together we ran across the field, hoping to make up the distance faster than Julia's little legs could remove her from the scene. There was no sign of her once we arrived at the tree line, but by the glimmer of the rising moon we could see it was not all wilderness ahead of us. A high gate blocked off a stretch of cleared land that bordered the marshy wastes beyond the short tangle of woods. It was the mostly likely meeting spot for miles.

Slipping through the gate, we found ourselves in the local cemetery. Graves from nearby Saxilby dotted the grounds. Mostly they were modest headstones, but there were also a few crypts of wealthier families jutting above the rest. Atop one of them was a clearly chiselled name: *Highmore*.

Hushed voices spoke to each other inside, through the stone vault that stood ajar.

"And what did you bring your daddy this night?" I heard one say.

Mr. Holmes and I approached, one on either side of the door, and peered inside. The chamber within was well-lit by a lantern, and I could see the stacked sarcophagi and niches containing past generations of Highmores, going all the way back to Thomas Highmore hisself.

Two more relations stood in the centre of that family tomb, and I saw a man who could only be Ellis Baldwin accepting an offered gift from the girl who was barely half his height.

"Is that the last of it?" he asked, holding the string of pearls up to better assess what they might be pawned for.

"It is certainly the final bit of profit you'll ever see out of your unfortunate wife," said Mr. Holmes, stepping into the crypt. I was right behind him, ready to back him in any way I could.

"Who in the blazes – ?" Baldwin began, but Mr. Holmes cut him off with a wave of his hand. There wasn't a single fact he could offer as to what had been going on that the detective hadn't already figured out. He was more interested in the child, who turned towards us and looked just as frightened as someone who had seen a genuine ghost – something she obviously wasn't.

"Not so unnerving a vision in better lighting, is she Wiggins?"

The makeup and costume seemed rather more obvious once I had a better look at it.

"I don't know who you think you are, sir, but I am – "

And again Mr. Holmes cut Baldwin off.

"A thief and a degenerate," he said. "One so morally bankrupt as to use your own daughter in a cruel and inhuman trick to bleed your long-suffering wife of a few final pounds. Say no more! If you wish to speak, save your lies for the inspectors."

"Mr. Holmes?" said someone outside. "Is that you in there?"

"Join us, Mr. Highmore," replied the detective. "We are having a family reunion. Many remain dead. Others, it turns out, are rather more lively than has been assumed."

Maynard Highmore, bearing a lantern of his own, joined us in the tomb.

"There were terrible screams at the house," he said. "Like the braying of some wild animal. I leapt from my bed immediately and followed you here when I saw you and your associate dashing across the field."

I didn't have to confess to being that braying animal before Highmore spotted his niece.

"Julia? Alive? How?" he said, flabbergasted. "I saw the death certificate myself!"

"Are coroners immune from bribery or coercion?" said Mr. Holmes. "Writing that someone has died has no bearing on reality if a body cannot be produced."

"So who's buried in here then?" I asked of a small set of stone slabs that encased an undersized coffin.

"Not a *who*," said Mr. Holmes. "A *what*. Some simple weights to convince the pallbearers that their burden from the cart to the crypt was a young child."

"Stones?" I suggested.

"No. I will venture sacks of flour," he said. Mr. Holmes locked eyes with Ellis Baldwin and judged. "Two of them."

"The devil you say, sir!" Baldwin roared at the detective's conclusion.

Mr. Holmes didn't have to argue with him. The man's rage was as good as a confession.

"No need to open the vault," said Mr. Holmes. "The look on your face suggests my surmise is accurate. Sacks of flour would not easily shift and spoil the illusion as the coffin was set in place. And there is a handy mill nearby. You still patronise it in your schemes, if only to dust the girl's face to make it appear more ghostly."

I ran a finger down Julia's cheek and the tip came back gritty and white. It was flour all right, with dashes of charcoal around her eyes to make them seem sunken. From a distance, she was quite haunting. Up close, she looked like a child on her way to a costume party, which was close to the truth.

"Baldwin, you vile, duplicitous . . . ." began Highmore.

But he didn't stop there. The litany of foul language that poured out of him wasn't fit for a proper gentleman – nor for the ears of a young girl, or even the dearly departed resting in sacred ground. Given the circumstances, though, I can't blame him for giving the dirty bugger both barrels.

Ellis Baldwin didn't care to hear much if it. Before his former brother-in-law could even unload half of what he had to say to the villain, he dashed straight through us like a bull. So quick and violent was the run he made, none of us were able to slow him down or trip him up before he was outside in the field of headstones.

Within moments, he was scrambling over the nearest length of cemetery fence, trying to get clear of us and justice. In his haste, Baldwin chose the side nearest the marsh, and the land under the fence had suffered much erosion. With his weight on the iron posts, they gave way and threw him into the muck beyond with a sickening report of filthy water and decay. In the dark, we could hear Baldwin's cries as he splashed around, trying to get a firm foothold in the slippery mess, only it sounded like he was losing himself farther into the marsh with each passing moment.

Before long, the bog burbled, settled, and no more could be heard of Ellis Baldwin.

"Good riddance to him!" growled Highmore. "He was gone from our lives once, now he is truly gone for good."

Julia came out of the crypt and joined us, no doubt looking to see where her father had got to. It was just as well she'd been spared the dim view of his even dimmer fate.

"Return the child to her mother," Mr. Holmes instructed Highmore. "Perhaps it will help restore your sister to a more sound frame of mind. Wiggins and I will see to informing the authorities about these strange events."

"How would you like to come back home and live with your mother again?" Highmore asked his niece gently. "She's waiting for you at the house, and there will be no more brief visits late at night, past your bedtime."

As Maynard Highmore took Julia's hand and began to lead her home again, Mr. Holmes dug into his pocket and produced his favourite travelling pipe. Lighting it and taking a well-deserved puff, he stared out into the desolation – the wasted land that had just swallowed a wasted life.

"Claimed by the very marsh he said took his child," noted Sherlock Holmes. "The local constabulary will have the unenviable task of dredging for his body tomorrow. I hope they will at least be met with agreeable weather."

The Paddington Poltergeist
by Bob Bishop

It can be somewhat painful to look back on the brief years encompassing the all-too-short time of my marriage to dear Mary, but an article in *The Times* today brought back the memory of an odd case I have not previously recorded which took place during that time. A family living in Leeds, according to today's *Times* correspondent, claim to have been forced from their home by the actions of a malevolent spirit. This mischievous entity had become so disruptive that continued habitation of their property became next to impossible. "*The final straw came last Thursday,*" claimed the poor mother of the household, "*when my littlest was lifted from his bed by unseen hands, and thrown across the room.*" No one was actually hauled from their bed in the case that Holmes and I investigated back then, but a series of odd things happened, and we filed it away under the heading of *The Paddington Poltergeist*.

It was the autumn of '89. In the months since my marriage I had seen little of my friend, whose attentions were almost entirely being taken up by unravelling the many strings of the criminal empire of James Moriarty – the investigation which so nearly cost him his life. I had built up a small but promising private practice in the Paddington district of the city. One afternoon I returned home at around three o'clock, having completed my rounds rather earlier than usual. I spent a short time making brief notes of my calls, then took myself to the sitting room, intending to read more of the novel that I was currently enjoying. I found Mary already in possession of the room, in the company of a lady who was unfamiliar to me. A tray of tea and selection of fancy cakes had been brought in, and Mary's guest was occupying my favourite chair, deep in conversation with her. The ladies ceased talking as I entered.

"I beg your pardon, my dear," said I. "Pray excuse my precipitant entry. I did not realise that you were entertaining this afternoon." I turned on my heel, intending to leave them alone, but Mary called me back.

"No, John, don't go," she said. "This is Mrs. Alicia Marten. We know each other from the Ladies' Political Union." I took the lady's proffered gloved hand and murmured that I was pleased to make her acquaintance.

"Alicia has been telling me of some rather singular occurrences in her house which have given her cause for concern of late."

"Indeed?" I said, adding, "Well, I have no wish to disturb your *tête-a-tête*. If you have no objection, I will just take one of these excellent cakes and leave you in peace to continue your discourse."

"Please stay, Doctor," said the visitor. "Your wife has been telling me that you are something of an expert in the solving of teasing mysteries."

"Hardly that," I responded, "though I have had the privilege, on a number of occasions, to assist one who is certainly gifted in that respect."

"Mr. Sherlock Holmes, I believe, is the expert to whom you allude. I have heard others speak of him. I understand he is establishing quite a reputation as an investigator."

"He has had many notable successes in recent years," I said. "I truly believe there is no one in London with more acute observational and deductive skills than my friend, Holmes."

"That is what I have been told, also. I am glad to hear you confirm it."

"Might I ask if you have been the victim of some criminal activity?" I asked.

"Not criminal, no," she replied. "Do you know what a poltergeist is, Doctor?"

"I know what a poltergeist is *alleged* to be," I said. "Some sort of noisy spirit which makes a nuisance of itself in people's homes. I must tell you, however, Mrs. Marten, that Sherlock Holmes is a criminal investigator, not a psychic one. Indeed, I believe he is not a believer in any branch of the paranormal."

"Then he and I should get along famously," the lady said, "for neither am I. I am certain that there is a rational explanation for the recent goings-on in my house, but for the life of me I cannot think what that explanation might be."

"Why don't you tell John what you told me?" Mary suggested. "Perhaps he could offer some suggestions?" She stood, and busied herself ringing for an extra cup and some more hot water so that I could take tea while I listened. I sat in the seat that Mary had vacated and received her friend's description of the occurrences in her house over recent weeks. It amounted chiefly to unexplained noises, and objects being moved from their usual places, sometimes repeatedly – minor annoyances that I believe people often report at the start of what is popularly referred to as poltergeist activity. I try to keep an open mind on such subjects, but Holmes, I knew, would dismiss them out of hand. There is no room in his philosophy for anything that cannot be explained away rationally. Certainly, the minor events which Mrs. Marten was describing to me could each individually be explained without any need to bring in supernatural forces, but taken altogether, did they amount to something more significant?

"Do you think your friend would call round to put my mind at rest?" concluded the lady when she was done reciting the incidents which were disturbing her. I was quite certain that Holmes would not. I shuddered at the thought of the scorn he would pour upon any suggestion that such trivial matters were worthy of his valued time and consideration. I could hardly say that to Mary's friend, however, so I told her that I would talk to him about it when next we met.

Mary came over to me with my fresh cup of tea at this point and said, "John, why don't you call round yourself first and see what you think? You might be able to spot straight away what is happening."

I was about to demur when our guest seized upon the suggestion with the greatest enthusiasm. "What an excellent idea, Mary! Even better, you must *both* call upon me. A visit is long overdue. I insist upon it! Shall we say next Thursday, in the afternoon?"

"I am not certain if I shall be able to make it, Mrs. Marten," I said, hastily. "My patients may need me at short notice . . . ."

"I am sure John will be able to work around his patients," overruled my wife, shooting me a sharp glance. "We would love to see your house in any case, wouldn't we, dearest?"

And so the visit was agreed upon – at least to the satisfaction of both ladies.

Mrs. Alicia Marten lived alone in one end of a once-elegant terrace of houses on the fashionable side of the district. Her husband, my wife informed me the following Thursday as we walked the short distance between our houses, had been taken from her some eight or nine months previously, following a short but distressing illness. She kept a single servant who lived in, and had been wondering of late whether a slightly smaller property might be better suited to her current situation. The recent distressing occurrences she had just described were helping to stiffen her resolve in this direction.

The servant who answered the door to us looked young enough still to be attending school. Her hair was awry. She wore a rather grubby apron over a shapeless grey day-dress, and had a feather duster held aloft in her free hand as though she might be considering the merits of beating us back from the door-step with it. It was not quite the reception that I had anticipated.

"Doctor and Mrs. Watson to see Mrs. Marten," said my wife, calmly. "We are expected."

The girl said nothing, but shifted her weight from one foot to the other and lowered the duster to point at the floor.

"Shall we come inside?" asked Mary. "Or would you prefer us to wait here on the door-mat?"

"You'd better come in," said the girl, opening the door more fully and flattening herself against the wall to allow us to pass. We duly entered the hallway, which was plunged into semi-darkness when the door was closed behind us. The only light now came from a small fanlight over the top. In the gloom I could make out a flight of stairs ascending into even more gloom, and a narrow passage extending forward, pierced by several closed doors. The hallway was further restricted by being somewhat over-furnished. A side-table, a noisy long-case clock, a porter's chair, and an over-sized glass display cabinet featuring what looked like stuffed tropical birds all fought each other for the available wall space. The maid was obliged to squeeze past us with a muttered "'Scuse me," in order to alert her mistress of our arrival. Before she could do so, however, a door at the end of the passage opened, admitting some illumination from the other side of the house. The silhouette of Alicia Marten could be seen framed in the oblong of light. The servant girl all but collided with her.

"Visitors, ma'am," she said. "Mr. and Mrs, er . . . ."

"I can see who it is," said the lady of the house. "Mary! Dr. Watson! So glad that you were able to come." She turned upon the maid-servant with a curt, "What do you mean by answering the door with that thing in your hand, Matilda? And in that filthy apron? Go and smarten yourself up at once, and bring us some tea in the parlour." Adding, as the child rushed away, "And wash your hands first!" As the maid scuttled off, Mrs. Marten advanced down the hallway, kissed my wife warmly on the cheek, and offered me her hand. She threw open one of the doors close to where we all stood and ushered us into the room. The parlour was as brightly illuminated as the hallway was dark. Tall windows let in shafts of sunlight to reveal a spacious, roughly square room, extravagantly furnished in a fussy style no longer strictly fashionable. The wallpaper was an elaborate trellis-work of bamboo, behind which were inter-twined fronds of greenery in which brightly-coloured exotic birds frolicked. I was reminded, a little painfully, of India. It seemed that Mrs. Marten was inordinately fond of birds.

She ushered us towards a vast sofa, into whose folds we both sank, deeply. Unfashionable it might have been, but is was extremely comfortable. The ladies talked for a while about their club activities, and I had to fight off the temptation to fall asleep, until I was saved by the door being thrown open and the entry of the maid, pushing before her a wheeled tea-trolley. Matilda had made a commendable effort to smarten herself up, although her hair still escaped in all directions from the bun in which it was supposedly tied. In keeping with our surroundings, the tea was Indian. An occasional table under the window was carved in an unmistakably Indian fashion. A photograph over the mantel showed a well-dressed white

313

family of mother, father, and mature daughter on the lawns of a large, low house with a glass veranda. They were surrounded by impeccably-dressed dark-skinned attendants. It did not require Holmes's deductive skills to tell me that Mrs. Marten had spent some time on the sub-continent. Perhaps she might even be the younger woman in the photograph?

When she had served us tea and home-made madeira cake, Matilda stood back respectfully whilst we refreshed ourselves. As soon as someone's cup was empty, she rushed to refill it. When Mary finished her slice of cake, she scuttled over to offer more, all her words tumbling out in a rush. "Another slice of cake, Mrs. Watson?" I think was what she asked. Mary evidently thought so too, for she fixed the maid with her most charming smile and said, "No thank you, my dear, but it was delicious."

Once it became obvious that the tea ceremony was completed, Matilda wheeled the used crockery away, presumably to wash it up in the scullery. Now was surely the appropriate time to turn our attention to the primary reason for today's invitation. Who was to broach the subject first, I wondered? I decided it should be me, before the two ladies were tempted to return to their former conversation.

"Would this be a good time to talk of the matters that have been troubling you, Mrs. Marten?" I asked.

"Alicia, please, Doctor."

"And you must call my husband 'John'," Mary returned.

Must she? I never feel very comfortable calling people by their given names unless we have become very close. I cannot, for example, even once recall calling my best friend and colleague "Sherlock", and I would, I am sure, be startled if I heard him refer to me as "John". It is, I suppose, a hangover from school days, when everyone was known to everyone else by surname alone – unless, of course, they had been given a nickname which stuck. I had a chum whom we all called "Sniffy" because he was suffering from a bad cold when he first joined the school. To this day I am uncertain what his actual surname was. Even the masters used to call him Sniffy. I think it might have been "Johnson". His surname, I mean.

I realised that the lady who had been invited to refer to me by my first name was speaking. "It is difficult to know where to begin, John," she said. I believe I might have winced ever so slightly. I would like to think that I did not.

"You suggested that the disturbances took several different forms?" I began. "Noises, and objects moved about, for example. Anything at all outside these categories?"

"Yes, indeed. There are the little things that keep appearing in the house – things, I know, that I have not placed somewhere appear there as if from nowhere."

My wife and I exchanged glances. I am sure we were both thinking the same thing – *Matilda*.

"What sort of things?" Mary asked.

"I can show you," said the lady. (I suppose that I must come to think of her as Alicia.) Crossing to the fireplace, she took from the mantelshelf a small wooden box, shaped like a casket. She brought it over to us and, opening its lid, shook out upon the vacant seat cushion between us a collection of small objects. They were an odd assortment: A child's silver rattle, a pine cone, a butterfly broach, an American silver dollar, several mis-matched buttons, and other small items I can no longer bring to mind. I asked if any belonged to her. She said they did not. She had never seen them before they made their appearance in the house.

It was Mary who asked her the obvious question. "Could they all have belonged to Matilda?"

"I asked her that question in every case," replied our hostess. "And she has assured me that she had never seen any of them before either."

"And do you believe her?" I felt compelled to ask.

"I do, yes. She is young, and has a lot to learn about being in service, but there has never been a single moment when I have had occasion to question her honesty."

"How long has she been with you?" Mary asked.

"That would be last November. The Major and I had only recently returned from a lengthy spell in India, and dear Bertram's system was quite unprepared for the germs which are so prevalent in England's damp, chilly climate. He caught influenza and passed away before we had even time to appoint any servants. I was quite unable to cope, I'm afraid. It was a very difficult time, as you might imagine. Fortunately, a friend of mine – you might know her, Mary – Elizabeth Grantley? She lives on Garden Crescent?"

"I am afraid not," my wife replied.

"No? She is on a great many committees. Anyway, Elizabeth had a housekeeper whose niece had just finished schooling and was looking for employment, and I was happy to take her on. Because she was inexperienced, she did not expect high wages, and I was, at the time, uncertain of how far my suddenly reduced income was going to stretch. In any case, everyone has to start somewhere, do they not? Matilda is learning slowly, and her heart is in the right place, I am certain."

"Are these things which your late husband might have collected, I wonder?" I asked, indicating the little collection of objects.

"I am sure they are not. I forced myself to sort through everything he had when he died, you see. I would have remembered seeing some of them at that time, I'm sure. In any case, even if they had belonged to Bertram,

315

that would not explain why they keep appearing in odd places around the house, would it?"

I was forced to concede that it would not. I asked next where the items were found deposited.

"All manner of places: On shelves, tables, window-ledges . . . This one . . . ." she picked up the silver dollar, "I found in the middle of the hall carpet."

"Tell me about the noises," I said. Although Mrs. Marten – I am sorry, I really cannot think of her as Alicia – felt that the appearance of the small objects was mystifying, I could not help but think of the many times I had discovered things in my own house that I could not for the life of me remember having put there, or even realised that I owned. "What sort of noises are they?" I persisted.

"All sorts of noises – creaks, bangs, scrapes, groans – "

"Groans?" interrupted my wife. "Do you mean people groaning, as in pain?"

"I cannot say for certain they were made by people. But the whispers were."

"You have heard whispering?"

"Oh yes. When the house is very silent. Matilda and I have both heard the whispers."

"When you were together? In the same room, at the same time?" I asked.

"Oh yes. Almost always. Matilda's young ears are so much more sensitive than mine. She usually hears them first. The poor girl becomes quite distressed when the whispers start."

"What do the whisperers say?" I demanded, trying to ignore the creeping feeling of hairs on the back of my neck beginning to stand erect.

"It is never possible to make out the words. The voices are too low."

"You say 'voices'. Is it the voice of one person, or does it seem like a conversation between two or more?"

"I'm sorry, John. I really couldn't say. It was just whispering."

"On several occasions?"

"Oh yes."

"I see."

I did not see at all. One person might conceivably imagine whispering in an empty house, but two? In the same room? "What of the things that you say were moved around?" I asked. "What sort of things were moved? How far?"

"Chairs, usually. And ornaments. Once a small table. Usually only a foot or two."

"Whilst you are in the room? Or overnight, say?"

316

"Both. Only last week I was rinsing a glass under the scullery tap – Matilda was out, running an errand. I turned around with the glass in my hand and walked straight into a high-backed chair I'm certain I had left tucked under the table only moments before. I dropped the glass and broke it."

"Anything else you have not mentioned?"

"Pictures fall off the wall. Yesterday one dropped to the floor whilst I was in the room. The glass smashed and the frame was broken. It was one of poor Bertie's favourite scenes."

Mary and I asked a few more questions, but I was having to admit to myself that I had no explanations to offer.

Next, we were shown over the house. There was nothing to see, really – it was just an ordinary house, with ordinary rooms and ordinary furniture. Some chairs were pointed out to us as the ones that had moved at some point. They were stationary enough while we looked at them.

The time came for us to take our leave, On the way out, I found myself believing that the porter's chair was further out from the wall than it had been when we arrived. I had been no help to the poor woman at all, but I promised to give some careful thought to all that I had been told. As we started to walk away, to underline my uselessness, Alicia Marten called after us. "I do hope your friend, Mr. Holmes, will agree to call on me, once you have talked to him."

"There might be a new profession opening up for you, old chap," Holmes said with a smile. It was the following morning, and I had called 'round to Baker Street after a light morning surgery, in the off-chance that he might be at home and prepared to listen to my adventure of the day before. He was, and he did, before coming out with the above observation. I could tell by his attitude that he found the whole affair amusing.

"There are not enough trustworthy psychic investigators around, you know," he added. "Most of them are complete charlatans. There is a real niche to be filled here by an honest man like yourself, Watson. I should be surprised if you are not in great demand once you have successfully banished Mrs. Whatshername's ghost."

"Mrs. Marten. She asked me to call her Alicia."

Holmes laughed. "And did you?"

"Once or twice. Mary got her to call me John. It was awful!"

"I almost wish I had been there."

"Well, I wish you had as well. I had no explanations to offer the poor woman at all. It was you she really wanted to consult."

"I am honoured. But she is in safe hands with you, Watson. I have every confidence in my pupil. I know that you will apply my methods and reach a speedy and satisfactory conclusion."

"I don't suppose you could just pop round and . . . ?"

"No."

"You don't seem too pressed for time. You were reading a book when I arrived."

"*Advanced Accounting Systems.* I have to find a weak point somewhere in Moriarty's meticulously constructed empire."

"You told me Moriarty is a mathematical genius."

"And so he is. A professor of the subject, no less."

"Then I don't see how reading that book will make you his superior in that regard."

"I don't need to outsmart the Master. I just need to be better than one of the weaker links in his chain. I am *that* close to closing the net, Watson, and rather fear he knows it. If I allow myself to be distracted at this stage it could prove fatal. The Professor would like nothing better than to see me out of the way, you know – preferably on a permanent basis."

"Permanent? You mean dead? He would really go that far?"

"Of course he would. There is too much at stake for him not to have me removed from the equation, once he knows how close I am getting to the centre of his web. I am under no illusions on that score, and neither should you be."

His words chilled me. "For goodness sake, Holmes!" I cried, "Do you value your life so lightly? I implore you to hand your collected material to the police and let them finish the job!"

"And a fine mess they would make of it! A few lesser villains behind bars, and Moriarty and his top men free to carry on as before. Do you believe my life would be any safer under those circumstances?"

"Probably not, since you put it like that."

"I am too far down the line, Watson. In the end, I fear, it is going to have to be him, or me."

Little did either of us know at that time quite how accurate this gloomy prophesy would turn out to be. Chastened somewhat by the turn our conversation had taken, I rose from my chair and took up my hat, determined not to distract my dear friend by any further discussion of my own trivial little puzzle.

"You are not leaving already, are you?" he said. "You have only just arrived."

"I had not quite realised the dangers you are facing at this time," I said. "I would not for worlds be the cause of any loss of focus on your part."

"Come, man. Sit down again. We are safe enough in these chambers. Mrs. Hudson would take her rolling-pin to any assassin who tried to cross her threshold, I promise you." We both smiled at the thought.

"Whilst you are on your feet, be so good as to ring the bell. Mrs. Hudson can take time out from disarming ruffians long enough to make us some light refreshment, I dare say." I rang the bell as instructed, and before long we were sipping tea and enjoying some of my former landlady's home-made macaroons. It was quite like old times. As I was discretely wiping the final crumbs from my moustache, Holmes returned to the subject of Alicia Marten's domestic disturbances, though I had determined not to bring the subject up again myself.

"So, Watson," said he, stretching out his feet a little closer to the fire, "Tell me how far you have come with your psychic investigation. Any preliminary conclusions? Any promising lines of enquiry?"

"I really don't know where to start," I confessed.

"Of course you do. You will at least have made a mental list of all the possible explanations, both plausible and implausible.

"No."

"Really? Then let us do so now. Starting at the beginning. Mrs . . . Martin, was it?"

"Mart*en*. With an *E*."

"Mrs. Mart*en* approaches your wife with a story of her house possibly harbouring a poltergeist . . . ."

"She claims not to believe in poltergeists."

"Sensible woman. Let us say, then, *poltergeist-like* disturbances. What possible reasons can we ascribe to her actions so far?"

"*Her* actions? I don't understand."

"Why has she asked you and your wife for help? What could be her motivation?

"Because she is worried and wants help from someone else."

"Good. The most obvious first. Any others?"

"None that I can think of."

"Then you need to exercise your imagination more. I can think of several, and I have never met the woman."

"Indeed? Would you like to suggest some?"

"By all means. She might be an attention-seeking individual. Nothing interests others more than a good ghost story."

"Fair enough. Carry on."

"She could be confused in her mind. How old is she?"

"Around my age. She seems sharp enough to talk to. Anything else?"

"She is quite recently widowed, you said. Perhaps she has invented these mysterious happenings as an excuse to bring a man into the house and enjoy some male company."

"That is quite ridiculous, Holmes! I am a happily married man! How would it benefit her to invite *me* to her house? She could hardly have designs upon me as a replacement husband!"

"Ah, but it was not really *you* whom she wanted to pay a call upon her, was it? You said she first asked for an introduction to *me*."

"You are saying she might have set her hat at *you*, as an eligible bachelor?"

"Is that so ridiculous?"

"But you have never shown any interest in . . . affairs of the heart!"

"Only because I cannot afford any distraction from my work, as long as it keeps coming in. Women, though delightful as companions, are a terrible distraction, you know. They expect to have first call upon a man's attention. You must have noticed it, surely? In any case, my attitude to women is irrelevant. It is how *they* might regard *me* which is the critical factor. You are not saying, I hope, that with all my accomplishments and physical attributes, I might not represent what I believe is sometimes called 'a good catch' to ladies of a certain situation in life?"

"Are you seriously saying that Mrs. Marten made up this whole story just to get you to pay her a visit?"

"Of course not! I am saying that, at the start of any investigation, you should think up as many explanations as you can to account for a client's motivation in consulting you. Some will be obvious, some improbable, some possibly fantastical. Later, you hope that the facts, as they emerge, fit one explanation better than all the others. The same process goes for any aspect of the case which is not immediately crystal clear. How many possible explanations can you think of? Rank them in order of probability – there is no point at all in wasting a disproportionate amount of time in consideration of unlikely scenarios, unless future developments render it a necessity. You hope, as each new piece of evidence is added, to rule the original possibilities out, one by one, until just a single explanation remains, which must represent the truth."

"I see what you mean."

"Good. Now apply the method to the apports in your case."

"To the what?"

"The apports. It is, I believe, what spiritualists call objects appearing to be produced out of nowhere by members of the spirit world – in your case, the box of small, apparently random objects, collected from around the house. Give me every explanation you can think of to account for their mysterious appearance. Come along, Watson – you can do this."

"Very well. Let me see . . . One: Mrs. Marten put them there herself and afterwards forgot."

"Excellent. Go on."

"Two: The servant girl, Matilda, put them there."

"Very good. Three?"

"Three . . . A third party is responsible – a visitor, say, or a tradesman."

"Now you are thinking like a detective, Watson! Anything else?"

"Well, I suppose, for completeness, we should add Four: It really was a poltergeist who materialized them from nowhere."

"Well done! You have covered, I think, all possibilities. Mrs. Marten put them there, someone else did, or it was, indeed, a poltergeist. Which of these seems least likely as an explanation?"

"The poltergeist," I said, at once.

"I agree, so we can leave that as a very last resort. Suppose Mrs. Marten put them there. Either she is telling the truth, or she is lying to you. If the truth, what can you deduce?"

"Well, if she put them in odd places and neither recognises them again nor remembers doing so, then she must be suffering from early senility, or other form of mental aberration, for it to have happened so often."

"Exactly. So, to rule out this possibility, you look for any other signs that her mind might be failing. The maid would be a primary source of information. What does she have to say about the whole affair, by the way?"

"I have not spoken to her about it."

"T-cha! Watson! You have a great deal to learn if you are going to become a successful psychic investigator!"

"I don't want to become a psychic investigator, Holmes, successful or otherwise! But I do see now the way to go if I am to be any assistance at all to Mrs. Marten."

"Alicia, to you, surely?"

"That is not even remotely amusing, Holmes."

"I apologise, John. Why don't you have another macaroon?"

I was tempted to shy the last ones on the plate in his direction.

It was a curious fact that, though I had worked closely alongside Sherlock Holmes on innumerable occasions, I had never really asked myself what thought processes were going on in his head as he worked through a case. I knew his deductions were based upon logic, that he observed and recalled with the greatest precision, but I had not realised how he must have been constantly asking himself questions and generating theoretical answers – how he had been mentally ranking those answers in

321

terms of probability, and how he had been crossing off and discarding from start to finish until he was left with one straight path through the labyrinth. That he could sustain so many thoughts in his head at once, and continue to hold conversations and contend with the demands of everyday life with at least a semblance of normality, became a matter of great wonderment.

As I sat in my consulting room the day after our Baker Street conversation, attempting to ask myself all the right questions about Mrs. Marten's infestation, I found it quite impossible to cope with all the possibilities which sprung from each step along the path without resorting to pen and paper. Even then I had to keep starting afresh as each possibility generated fresh branches of new possibilities and there was insufficient room on the page to display them all. Nevertheless, the mental exercise was at times exhilarating, and I began to understand a small fraction of the frisson which Holmes experiences when a new and challenging conundrum is presented to him. It did not take so very much paper-shuffling to note that all the facts of the case revolved around two key points: Was Mrs. Marten confused, lying, or deceived? And if deceived, by whom? Of course, Matilda, the maid, had to be suspect number one if her employer were of sound mind and telling the truth. No wonder Holmes was shocked that I had not even questioned the girl. No person other than Matilda was in the house all the time and in such a good position to comment on her employer's mental state – or, alternatively, to initiate the mischief herself. But why would she do that? What possible reason could she have for playing such pointless tricks upon her mistress? I scribbled down a list of possible motives, in order of probability, as I saw it:

1.   *It is in her nature to cause mischief, and she gets pleasure from vexing others;*
2.   *She feels she is treated harshly by her mistress and is fighting back in her own way;*
3.   *She is being rewarded by some third party (unknown) to act in this way; or*
4.   *She is mentally unbalanced and does not behave rationally.*

I was uncertain about the correct ranking of motives one and two in the list, but felt that, overall, Holmes would be appreciative of my progress in mastering his method. I determined to plan my questioning of the maid well in advance, assuming I intended to take the investigation further. Was I not sufficiently occupied as a medical practitioner and occasional detective's assistant, without taking on any fresh roles in life?

The third day after my consultation with Holmes, everything changed.

About an hour into my morning surgery, I followed my usual practice of asking a departing patient to invite the next patient in line to enter the surgery, while I went to scrub my hands at the sink. I heard the patient enter, and the consulting room door close, so called over my shoulder, "I shall be with you in a moment. Please take a seat."

A familiar voice replied, "That is very genial of you, Watson." I turned in surprise, hands still dripping, to see Sherlock Holmes already seated in the patients' chair at my desk.

"My goodness, Holmes!" I exclaimed. "Are you unwell?"

"I should not be at all surprised," he replied. "I have been sitting next to an elderly person out there who has been coughing all over me for the past quarter-of-an-hour." I finished drying my hands and went to sit on my own side of the desk.

"So," I said, "if you have not come to consult me on medical grounds, to what do I owe this pleasure? If it is a social call, I really should ask you to wait until I have seen my last patient, as you will appreciate that they have to take precedence during surgery hours."

"I stand admonished," replied Holmes. "But I shall not take up much of your valuable time, Doctor. I wished only to say that I have been giving more thought to your Paddington Poltergeist affair, and have decided that I should, after all, appreciate some personal involvement."

"You mean, you are prepared, now, to meet with Mrs. Marten?"

"Exactly so – as long as you promise to dissuade her from calling me by my first name."

I was more than a little taken a-back. "But you said it would be a dangerous distraction from your current investigation," I reminded him.

"It is just possible that I might have overstated the current degree of risk to my person. To my certain knowledge, Moriarty and his second-in-command are both out of the country as of yesterday, and I think a little light relief might give my tired brain some welcome respite."

"Well, Holmes," I said, "you are quite the enigma. I as good as told her that you would not be available."

"Then she will be in for a pleasant surprise when you introduce me. Shall we call upon her next Wednesday, late afternoon? I will leave you to make the appointment. You may telegraph to confirm." So saying, he rose to his feet and made for the door, turning only to add, "I'll ask the next patient to enter, shall I? Before he infects everyone else in your waiting room."

My wife made the necessary arrangements when she met Alicia Marten at their next Ladies' Political Union session. Wednesday, late afternoon, would suit her perfectly for a second visit, she reported back. I had asked Mary not to mention that Holmes would be present. I was not sure how I felt about his taking an interest. I think it is possible that, after all the preparatory notes I had made, and the long hours of introspection, part of me would have liked to have seen the job through without him. But I tried to put such selfish thoughts aside, for I knew, from my client's viewpoint, a satisfactory outcome was now virtually assured.

On the appointed afternoon, I was fortunate not to have any emergency cases to delay me. Holmes arrived by cab and retained it for the short distance between my house and Alicia Marten's, where we travelled together.

"We could easily have walked from here," I told him, as we commenced the ride.

"Far better to take a cab," Holmes said. "It might rain. Also, to arrive on foot looks both impoverished and amateurish. Not the sort of impression one wishes to make upon a client. Besides," he added, impishly, "as lead investigator in the case, you will no doubt be paying the cabbie in this instance, so I did not have to count the cost." I had not thought of that.

"When we arrive," Holmes said a short while later, "introduce me, then leave me alone with Mrs. Marten for a while. We will see if she tells her story to me exactly as you have reported it. Talk to the maid, meanwhile, and try to put her at her ease. Be careful not to let her think you suspect her at all. Just ask for her personal account of the goings-on."

"We *have* arrived," I said, as the vehicle clattered to a stop. "And that was my plan, as well."

Once again, the door was answered by Matilda, this time *sans* feather duster or grubby apron. Even her hair looked quite tidy. She recognised me, but gave Holmes a quick, suspicious glance. He smiled at her, and she softened.

"Hello, Matilda," I said. "This is my colleague, Mr. Sherlock Holmes. Can you tell your mistress we are here?"

We had to wait in the cramped hallway for the very shortest time before Mrs. Marten made her appearance. She beamed when she saw Holmes and offered her hand at once. "Oh, it *is* Mr. Holmes, isn't it? Matilda didn't get the name quite right, but I was *sure* it would be you! How good of you to find the time to come and see me!" She did appear remarkably excited to see Holmes, and quite forgot to welcome me at all. I began to wonder whether the previously low probability theory of the whole story being an excuse to tempt Holmes to visit might have to be elevated somewhat in the rankings. The plan we had agreed upon worked smoothly at first. Whilst Holmes listened to Mrs. Marten's story in the parlour, I made the excuse of wanting to see around the house again. Matilda was deputed to accompany me. As the door closed to the parlour, we stood together in the gloomy hallway. Matilda, when inactive, appeared to droop, head lowered, arms by her sides, waiting to be activated by an instruction. Light conversation between us suddenly seemed unlikely. What would Holmes do? He had said to make her feel at ease, but not mentioned how that was to be achieved.

"Do you think." I said, when remaining where we were in silence was no longer an option, "you could possibly make me a cup of tea before we start?" Without a word, she set off down the shadowy passage towards the back of the house. I followed. We entered the kitchen, where sunlight played from windows facing a long garden plot. I sat at the table and watched as she busied herself with the task. "How long have you worked for Mrs. Marten, Matilda?" I began.

"Not sure, sir. Not long, sir."

"And do you enjoy working here?"

"Enjoy it?"

"I mean, do you have any complaints about the way you are treated?"

"Oh, no, sir!" She disappeared into the scullery, and I heard water flow. I mentally struck through one of the possibilities on my list of motives. Matilda came back in and placed the kettle upon the range. She took the lid off the teapot and reached a box of tea down from a low shelf.

"Better make enough for the others," I suggested. She looked confused. "In the parlour," I amplified, "Mr. Holmes and Mrs. Marten. They might like tea, too, don't you think?" More tea went into the pot, but no words came from her mouth. Small talk seemed to be off the menu. I decided I should get straight to the point.

"Mrs. Marten thinks that strange things have been happening in the house, doesn't she?"

"Yessir."

"What do you think?"

"What do I think?"

"Yes. What do you think?"

"'Bout what, sir?"

"Do you think strange things have been happening?" She nodded, vigorously.

"Can you tell me about them?"

"There's noises," she said, after a moment's consideration. The kettle on the stove began to hiss, filling the long gaps in our faltering dialogue.

"Can you tell me about the noises? What strange noises have you heard?"

"All sorts. Bangs. And thumps. And clangs." We seemed to be making progress.

"Where do they appear to come from?"

"Don't know, sir. All around."

"And when do you usually hear the noises? In the daytime, or at night?"

"Day *and* night," she said, nodding as though to confirm her assessment.

"Can you remember the last time you heard something?" I asked. Before she could answer there was a loud bang from the direction of the range. We both jumped. It was just a trapped water droplet under the kettle exploding. I laughed.

"Just the kettle, that time," I said. Matilda smiled, then she laughed, too. Conversation became easier after that. She told me how she had found a scatter of buttons on the floor of her attic bedroom once, buttons that had come off no garment that she owned. She told me of chairs that crossed the floor when one's back was turned, and paintings that fell from walls for no obvious reason.

The kettle boiled. She made the tea, and took a freshly-baked cake from a rack and put it on a large plate, commenting as she did so, "Oops, Doily first, Matilda!" in a fair impersonation of her mistress. It was something else for us to laugh at together. I felt very conspiratorial. As she was wheeling the trolley out of the kitchen, I felt our rapport had become strong enough to ask, "Matilda, do you think there is any chance at all that Mrs. Marten might be doing all these weird things herself?" She seemed to give the question serious consideration, before replying "I'm sure she isn't doing it, sir. I mean – why would she?"

Why, indeed?

Matilda wheeled herself off down the shadowy hallway, and I sat back in my chair. At the same moment, I heard a light bump-bump-bump sound from out in the hallway. I rushed to the door in time to see a rubber ball bounce from the bottom step of the stairs to the tiled floor of the hall. Matilda was standing at the parlour door, knob in hand, about to enter the room with her trolley. The rubber ball bounced a few times on the hall floor, then settled. Matilda picked it up, and brought it to me. It was just a child's small rubber ball, in a faded red colour.

"Definitely not Mrs. Marten," I said, more to myself than to her, and put the ball in my pocket. My first piece of direct evidence. I had become my own witness.

Matilda delivered the tea to the parlour, and stayed to serve it. I took the opportunity to walk round the house, lingering wherever I wanted without having to explain myself or make conversation. The houses in the terrace comprised four floors: A lower ground, built no doubt as kitchens and servant quarters. The stairs in Alicia Marten's house led down to rooms used to store old furniture and items that might come in useful one day, all covered in a thick layer of dust, and dimly illuminated by window-wells, all much encrusted on the outside by greenery. In one of the rooms stood a wood-worker's bench, plus a neat collection of tools on hooks and nails above and around it – the property, I assumed, of the late Major Marten. Nothing of great significance down here. On the next floor up were the main reception rooms, the entrance hall, the kitchen, and scullery. The floor above that contained bedrooms – three of them, all furnished, but only one – Mrs. Marten's – in regular use. Also on this floor was a vast bathroom, which must have been the pride of the house when first constructed. The large cast-iron and enamelled bath had a hood over one end, pieced by rusty and corroded shower spouts. There was a water closet built into a wooden box, with a capacious cistern over it, and, against one wall, the largest hand wash-basin I have seen anywhere. A copper cylinder over the bath hissed at me. Was this a possible culprit for the generation of strange knocking noises?

A narrower set of stairs led upwards to the top floor, a floor which had not been included in my tour of the property the week before. On this floor the ceilings were lower, the windows smaller, and the furnishings minimal. Only two of the rooms had beds, two were completely empty, one held a store of pictures in gilt frames, some smashed, and several heaps of very dusty books and old magazines. Of all the six rooms, only the last that I looked into showed evidence of habitation – clearly the room occupied by Matilda. It was at the end of the corridor, larger than the others, and furnished by a single bed, a dressing table and chair, a small chest of drawers, and a very large wardrobe.

I felt uncomfortable as I looked at the little maid's sorry collection of personal belongings, including her hair-brush and scatter of pins and grips on the dressing table, and yesterday's soiled, grey dress in a crumpled heap at the foot of the bed. I left the room after a cursory glance, and made my way back down to the entrance hall, where I encountered Matilda herself, just coming out of the parlour with the trolley of used crockery. I held the door open for her, and she gave me a friendly smile. On seeing me, Mrs. Marten called out, "There you are, John. Come and join us!" I thought I detected the corner of Holmes's mouth twitch slightly. I decided to brave it out. "Thank you, Alicia," I said. There was definitely a twitch this time.

I came fully into the room, refused any more refreshment, and sat in a vacant armchair. I noted that the little box of apports had been emptied once again, this time onto the top of the Indian side table, which had been brought up close to the sofa. I wondered whether to mention the rubber ball – and decided against it, for the moment. Mrs. Marten spoke up. "I have told your friend everything that I told you, John. If he has no further questions for the moment, I will leave the two of you to share your thoughts and opinions for a short while, if you will both excuse me?" We were happy to do so. As soon as the door had closed behind her, Holmes rose from his seat and crossed to one of the windows, where he stood, hands behind his back, looking out into the street. I kept silent, assuming he was assembling his thoughts. After a moment he turned back to face me.

"Well, Watson," he said, "I do not think I have heard anything from Mrs. Marten today which need cause me to modify any of my fundamental beliefs on the subject of the supernatural. How did you fare with the maid?"

"She is a shy, timid little thing. She opened up to me eventually. Enough to convince me that she is not mischievous enough, nor even imaginative enough, to be the instigator of these disturbances. I really don't think she has it in her. I liked her, actually."

"Hmm," mused the detective. "Well, some human agency is responsible for these annoyances. One of these two women is almost certainly behind it and, notwithstanding your good opinion of her, I am afraid, of the two, it has to be the maid preying upon the mistress in this case."

"Why should she do that? What possible profit would there be in it for her?"

"Why, indeed? It is always the 'why'? at the root of every conundrum. And there is always profit to be gained for someone from every human undertaking, criminal or otherwise."

"You do not suspect any criminal activity in this case, surely?"

"Certainly I do. Why else would I have involved myself?"

"I thought to help me."

"Well, that too, Watson, of course. That too."

"You cannot seriously expect me to believe that that timid little child out there is some kind of criminal mastermind? The idea is preposterous!"

"Did I use the term 'mastermind'?"

"Also – you need to hear this, Holmes – whilst you were in here, listening to Mrs. Marten's account of the matter, I was out there, in the hall, with Matilda. She was occupied with the tea-trolley and at the same moment a rubber ball came bouncing down the stairs. I saw it with my own eyes!"

"A rubber ball? From the floor above?"

"Yes. This one!" I fished in my pocket and handed the little red ball to him. "And mark this," I said. "I searched every room in the house immediately afterwards, while all three of you were here in the parlour, and there is nobody else in the house at all, I can promise you that. Nobody!" I spoke with perhaps more passion than was strictly appropriate, perhaps, because I was still riled that Holmes had not been fully open with me regarding the true reasons for his suddenly taking an active interest in my little investigation – an investigation which he had previously been quick to ridicule.

As I was speaking, my companion had on his face the sort of smile which made me suspect that he was humouring me, which, of course, only served to increase my annoyance further. "So, you are saying what, then, my dear fellow?" he asked, calmly. "That it is your considered opinion that a ghost threw this ball downstairs?"

"I don't know what I'm saying," I said. "I just think that it's unusual."

Suddenly Holmes stiffened, and held up a hand to silence me. "Quiet a moment!" he hissed.

"What is it? Have you heard something?"

"Quiet, man! Listen!" I listened. I heard nothing. Holmes had on his face an expression of intense concentration, an expression I have seen so many times in the past when he is hot upon some scent. I still heard nothing. "What is it?" I whispered, eventually. "What am I listening for?"

"The whispering!" Holmes replied, in a whisper of his own. "Surely you can hear the whispering?"

I strained my ears, and suddenly, coming from the air around me I seemed to hear the faintest of human voices, murmuring at the very lowest intensity. Holmes's own hearing must be very acute indeed to have picked out such faint sounds whilst we were talking. I concentrated as hard as I could, but could not make out any individual words at all, although the sounds my ears were now straining to pick up were unmistakably human whispers, on the very fringe of audibility. I lowered my own voice to say, "I can hear them now, Holmes! What are they saying? Can you pick out any of the words?"

Holmes concentrated expression melted into a smile, as he replied, in quite normal tones, "I cannot pick out any words, because I can hear nothing at all." He opened his hands in an expansive gesture. "Can you hear anything, Watson? Really? Can you still hear whispering?" I listened. I heard nothing.

"Well no," I replied. "It has stopped now."

"You really heard it though?"

"Why, yes. So did you."

"I heard nothing at all."

"But you said – !"

"I was making a demonstration."

"A demonstration? A demonstration of what?"

"Suggestibility. You believed that I heard something, because you trust me not to lie to you. At first you heard nothing. Then, when I so obviously did, your brain told you that there was something to hear, and, presto! You heard the very sounds you expected to hear."

"Are you trying to make a fool of me, Holmes?"

"By no means. You are no more or less suggestible than the rest of us. I might be just as easily fooled in a similar situation. Suggestibility explains so many of the phenomena people ascribe to the spirit world, and Mesmerism absolutely relies upon it. I think we can say with certainty that many of the seemingly inexplicable events in this enquiry can be accounted for by the very process I have just demonstrated to you."

"And does suggestibility also account for the ball I saw bouncing down the stairs?"

"No," he replied, "something else accounts for that. Come." He opened the parlour door and we went out into the hallway. I followed.

"Where was Matilda and her trolley when you heard the first bounce?"

"I should say about here," I said, indicating a spot about half-way down the narrow passage.

"And where were you?"

"In the kitchen doorway, about to sit down," I said, turning to indicate the exact spot. Instantly I heard the sound of the ball bouncing downstairs again. I turned back in time to see Holmes catch it on its final bounce.

"You threw that when I looked away!" I accused him.

"Of course I did," said Holmes. "And so did Matilda."

Before I could argue, the air was split by a series of terrible screams, emanating from somewhere above our heads. Alicia Marten came hurrying out from the dining room across the passage. The screams continued, echoing down the stairwell from high up in the building. Holmes took the stairs two at a time. I was not far behind him. Matilda (for it was, of course, she) had stopped screaming by the time we reached her attic room. She was sitting on her bed, head in hands, trembling all over. There was no need to ask the reason for her distress, for on the wall of her room in large, scratchy black letters was written:

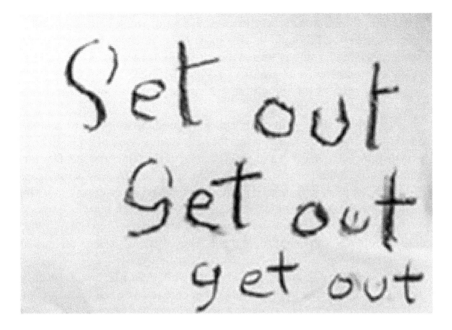

At first my brain was slow to cope. I had seen this wall only a few short minutes ago, and there had been no writing on it then. I also failed to read the message correctly at first. "*Set out?*" I questioned. "What does it mean, 'set out'?"

"Those are not *S*'s," said Holmes, "They are lower-case *G*'s, written large. Look at the bottom line – that couldn't be clearer."

"That writing was not there a few minutes ago, Holmes, I can swear it. I was in here myself, and there was no writing on the wall then!" I exclaimed. At once, Matilda took her hands from her face and gave me a chilling look. I realised that I had inadvertently admitted to snooping in her room. At the same moment, Alicia Marten entered, panting from her scramble up the stairs to the top of the house. She took in the situation at once – the scribbled message on the wall, the terrified maid on the bed, and, I dare say, the disconcerted look on my own face. She sat herself beside Matilda and, hesitating only briefly, placed a motherly hand around her servant's back, drawing her in close. The girl turned thankfully to press her head against the shoulder of her protectress, and fell to sobbing uncontrollably.

"It is all right, Matilda, dear," said her mistress, patting her back gently. "This is too much to bear for either of us. Spirits who throw things and make noises are one thing, but when they start to write warnings upon the walls it is too much. We will leave this house. I shall put it up for sale today."

331

Holmes took a step across the room. He gently took both of Matilda's hands into his own. I thought he was showing an uncharacteristic moment of tenderness, but he slowly turned the girl's hands face up, and we all saw very clearly the black, sooty marks all over the fingers of one of them.

Holmes said, "I think the time has come, Matilda, for you to tell us all why you are doing these things."

The sobbing stopped at once, and for a moment only, Matilda stared around the room, as though looking for help from some unknown quarter. Then she jumped to her feet and pointed an accusing finger at me. Her face became distorted with rage. "*He* did it!" she spat out. "*He* was in my room! *He* did it!" The change from terrified victim to angry accuser was shocking to behold. "Ask him why he wrote that on my wall! Ask him!"

"Why don't you show her your hands, Watson?" asked Holmes, quietly. I held up both hands, palms out. They were, of course, unmarked.

"He's just washed 'em!" she retorted, instantly.

"Dr. Watson did not write on your wall, Matilda," said Holmes, sternly. "*You* did – as your hands prove. Where did you put the charcoal? Shall we look in here?" He strode to the little chest and reached out to open the top drawer. At once, Matilda fell upon him, spitting, snarling and snatching away his hand. I noticed that her clawing grasp had drawn blood on the back of Holmes's hand. He made no reaction at all. Turning to Mrs. Marten, who was now standing, her face showing both shock and concern, he said, "Mrs. Marten, if you will instruct your maid to open the contents of her room for inspection, I think we may hope to lay your poltergeist to rest once and for all.

"Matilda!" Mrs. Marten said, sternly, "You will allow us to inspect your room. I insist upon it." Matilda looked terrified. She took in each of our faces, desperate to see some hint of sympathy. She settled upon me. "Doctor Watson," she said, her voice once again that of the helpless victim, "You believe me, don't you? Tell them it wasn't me. Tell them it was the ghost! It was the ghost what done it!" Here she pointed at the scrawled message on the wall. "The ghost done everything!" Tears began to flow again, and she adopted that stoop-shouldered, limp-armed stance I had taken to be that of her natural, down-trodden self. What a little actress! I had been taken in completely!

"You need to let us search your room, Matilda," I said. "If you have nothing to hide, you have nothing to fear."

Instead of replying, she suddenly darted for the door. I tried to bar her way, but she pushed me violently aside. Her strength was remarkable for one so slight of build. I made to follow her, but Holmes called me back. "Let her go, Watson," he said. "She is younger, fitter, faster, and has a head start on you. Let us see what secrets she has hidden in here." He pulled open the top drawer, and inside was a collection of small objects that would have gone very well with the diverse collection in the little box in the parlour. There was a green ball, a partner to the red one Holmes now had back in his pocket. Also two more foreign coins of small denomination. We found a thick stick of charcoal, tossed on top of the other things. I looked again at the wall-writing.

"Why would she write upon the wall of her own room?" I wondered out loud. "Why not somewhere more public?"

"An intelligent choice, I should say," Alicia Marten replied. "She would think me less likely to suspect her if she also appeared to be under attack."

"I agree," said Holmes.

"I have never seen her like this before," Mrs. Marten said. "Why has she been doing this to me? What have I done to deserve it?"

"Somewhere in this house, I am sure, is the answer to that question," Holmes said.

Under the householder's supervision, we continued to look through the other drawers in the chest, but found nothing but clothes. Once again, I felt very uncomfortable rifling through Matilda's private possessions, even though I now knew her to be someone quite different from the timid, tongue-tied little servant she had been portraying so convincingly. We found nothing more in the way of equipment for a haunting, other than a small hammer, which could, I suppose, have created knocking noises. Such mischief as the girl had performed had been largely by means of her own ingenuity.

We looked over the house again, Holmes spending a long time examining every inch of the basement rooms. He did not find what he was looking for. Finally, he turned to Mrs. Marten. "Does this house have any attics?" he asked.

"My husband used to sometimes attend to water pipes in the roof-space," she replied. "But do not ask me how he got up there – I never needed to ask." Once again, we all went up to the top floor. There was no sign of concealed attic stairs, or even trapdoors let into any of the ceilings. Matilda's room, at the end of the corridor, was the final room to re-visit. At once, Holmes gave a sigh of exasperation. "Of course!" he exclaimed. "Watson, give me a hand to move this wardrobe."

Sure enough, the heavy press concealed a low doorway, and behind that, a narrow, steep flight of stairs. The attic at the top was lofty and extensive, stretching across all four of the properties in the terrace, with no dividing walls between them. Daylight came in through roof-lights spaced at intervals. Packing cases lined the walls, there was a long work-bench at the far end, and in pride of place, dead centre, stood a gleaming machine on a wooden plinth, fairly bristling with wheels, handles, and rollers. I went over to examine it. Holmes called out at once, "Don't touch it! Don't touch anything!" I halted in my tracks. He moved from crate to crate along the back wall, touching nothing, but looking intently at details. Finally, he found a crate that pleased him and beckoned me over. This one had not been sealed up, as it was only half-filled. It contained pile upon pile of crisp, green, freshly-minted banknotes – American dollar bills, all of them!

"Counterfeit?" I whispered.

"Freshly made on the premises," confirmed Holmes.

"Why dollars? Why not pounds?"

"Pounds are a good choice throughout the Empire, but dollars are desirable across the whole world," he said. "If I were a counterfeiter, I would print dollars, too." He carefully lifted one of the bills with delicate finger-tips, and folding it into his wallet said, "I think we have seen enough, Watson. Let us go, quickly, before our forger comes up and surprises us."

It was almost a week later. I was sitting with Holmes in his sitting room, in my old place by the fire. Holmes had delayed any conversation until he had a pipe going to his satisfaction. Finally, he indicated he was ready to give me his attention.

"Before you ask," he said, waving tobacco-smoke clouds towards the fire, "as I very much feared, the police were too slow to act. By the time they raided the place, there was not a single dollar bill remaining, other than the sole example of which I was able to provide them."

"What of the press itself? Surely that was still there?"

"Oh yes, but none of the plates. There is no crime committed by the simple possession of a printing press. You or I could own one."

"So, who was the forger? Do you know?"

"No. The other three houses in the row are owned by a businessman called Miles Jallop. He has been quietly acquiring them over several years. It must have been very annoying when the Martens took up residence in the end house after it had stood empty for so many years. Jallop is merely the facilitator, I am certain. Even he might not know the name of the master forger who uses his attics."

"And you already knew of this man, Jallop?"

"Oh yes. He is one of Moriarty's three money-men. When you told me where your friend Alicia Marten lived, I thought her address rang a bell. The next day I looked through my notes and realised why it was familiar."

"Which is why you suddenly offered to help me out, of course."

"I feel bad about that."

"You should. I have not yet forgiven you.

"At least you were able to conclude your case to the satisfaction of your client. My own remains wide open."

"Why did they rely upon that girl to scare her mistress into selling the house? It seems an amateurish ploy. If Moriarty is as ruthless as you claim, he could just have had the poor woman taken out – is that the right expression?"

"This way would have been cheaper, and much less risky, if it had worked. And it very nearly did, remember. Now I expect that Moriarty will resent my meddling in his affairs again, and I shall have to watch my back even more carefully now that he has been so inconvenienced. That property will be of no further use to them, now that the police have taken an interest, however clumsily. They will have to start up all over again somewhere else, at great trouble and expense."

"Will Moriarty know you had a hand in it?"

"That depends upon how carefully Matilda was listening when you introduced me. She seems very resourceful. I shall assume the worst."

"What will become of her?" I asked, wondering why I cared.

"I am sure the Organisation will find another niche for her. She certainly will not be getting a very good reference if she intends to remain in service."

"No indeed. She could get a job in the acting profession, I suppose. I would write her a reference for that!"

Holmes smiled. "It is certainly not the case that all the best actors are to be found on stage – which makes our job all the more interesting, don't you think?"

"Your job, not mine," I said. "I am very content to be a simple G.P."

"Not a Psychic Investigator on the side, after all, then?"

"Definitely not. It left me out of pocket. I had to pay for your wretched cab fare."

Holmes laughed out loud, and stooped to rebuild the fire, remarking as he did so, "Well, if you should change your mind, Watson, I know where you can get some business cards printed at a very good discount."

We both laughed at that, and I decided that I had forgiven him, after all.

The Spectral Pterosaur
by Mark Mower

Compared to many of his police colleagues, Inspector Stephen Maddocks was an infrequent visitor to Baker Street. Seldom would he admit to being stumped or outwitted on a case. When he needed help within Scotland Yard, it was usually to his old school chum, Sergeant Vincent Fulton, that he deferred. But on the very rare occasions he required external assistance, it was always to Sherlock Holmes that he turned. So it was that on a cold Friday evening in the October of 1889 the dutiful inspector called in at 221b to consult with my friend and was shown up to the first floor study.

"An unexpected pleasure, Maddocks. Please take a seat. Would you like a cup of tea, or something a tad stronger?"

The detective ambled slowly and uneasily towards one of the armchairs, removing his brown Derby and long black overcoat. I stepped forward to take both from him which elicited only a weary and somewhat absent-minded, "Thank you, Doctor." He sat heavily, and I noticed that he had gained some weight since we last met. "A large brandy would be much appreciated."

I declined the offer of a glass myself, while Holmes poured a small measure of his own and then sat in a chair close to the hearth. "Now, how can we assist you?"

The poor fellow looked dog-tired, his eyes bloodshot and the skin beneath them dark and puffy. There was a distinct wheeziness in his breathing and a slight rasp to his voice. His face was flushed with pink. Having downed the spirit in one swallow, he placed the glass upon the side table to his right and responded, "Sergeant Fulton and I have been investigating the theft of some rare museum artefacts, mainly preserved animal bones. *Fossils*, I believed they're called. A number of private collections have also been raided, so we have been told to leave no stone unturned in catching those responsible. Apparently, these old bones are irreplaceable and worth a lot of money . . . ."

He coughed deeply and brought his fist up to his mouth. An uncomfortable silence followed which I felt obliged to fill. "Yes, Inspector. Paleontology is a relatively new science, but interest in it has grown since Charles Darwin first published his book, *On the Origin of Species*, in 1859. Since that time, men of science have been scouring the planet to unearth the preserved remains of prehistoric creatures to confirm or refute his theories about *evolutionary biology*."

Maddocks spluttered once more and interjected. "Well, that's as may be, Doctor. All I know is it's a terrifying business I've experienced – an unearthly vision – and I find myself completely baffled. In all the years of my service, I cannot recall seeing anything remotely like it . . . ."

Holmes waited for him to elaborate, scrutinising the face of the police officer with evident intent. But there were no further words. Maddocks sat rigidly in the armchair, his eyes wide, his gaze fixed, and his mouth poised to continue. Whatever inexplicable narrative he had planned to relate was not forthcoming.

I was quick to spring into action, recognising before my colleague that all was not well. Maddocks had stopped breathing and I could detect no pulse in his left wrist. For the next few minutes I tried in vain to resuscitate him, but eventually conceded that nothing more could be done. Already I could see that the skin on his face had taken on a deep crimson hue. Added to the rigid contortion of his body, it was clear to me that he had suffered an immediate and fatal heart attack. Having undertaken his own brief examination, Holmes concurred.

We sat for some time in silence, both overwhelmed by the drama we had witnessed. While he could be detached and methodical in times of heightened tension, I could tell that Holmes was deeply troubled by Maddocks's departure. The unsettling emotion prompted him within minutes to focus instead on the cold comfort of the logical, and the facts at hand.

"I think we had both noted that the inspector was not in the best of health on arriving here this evening, but I would not have expected such a rapid deterioration and expiration. Perhaps this 'unearthly vision' he referred to has sent him to his death." He stared into his brandy glass. "Although, of course, we should not rule out poison at this stage."

I stared at him incredulously, "You cannot mean that the brandy is poisoned?"

Despite the solemnity of the occasion, Holmes smiled. "No, Watson. As you can see, I am perfectly fine, having drunk from the same bottle as the inspector. I suggest only that we must be sure of our facts and eliminate all of the possibilities with a few toxicology tests. Procedurally, of course, we must contact Scotland Yard and let them handle all of this. But we must impress upon the doctor called to undertake the *post mortem* that this may not be a straightforward death."

Holmes wasted no time in despatching a short telegram to Scotland Yard's "*B*" Division explaining what had happened and requesting that a pathologist be asked to accompany any investigating officers. It was a good two hours later when the heavy footfall of boots could be heard ascending the seventeen stairs to the first floor. Holmes opened the door of the study and ushered in three tall gentlemen in heavy overcoats.

"Ah! Inspector Bradstreet and Sergeant West. Good evening, gentleman." He nodded towards the last of the trio. "And this must be our medical man."

The police surgeon had no time to answer before I stepped forward and interrupted, offering him my hand. "Doctor Lorimer, it is a pleasure to meet you again. Doctor John Watson, formerly of the Fifth Northumberland Fusiliers. You may remember that we worked together briefly some ten years ago before I made the passage to India."

His face lit up in recognition and he extended his hand towards me. "Indeed I do, sir. I spent a year at the Royal Victoria Hospital. And I remember that while you were with us at Netley for just a few months, you made a great impression." He looked towards Holmes. "Of course, your life has taken a distinctly different course since that time."

I was unsure what he meant by this but let the matter rest. When we were all seated, Holmes explained briefly what had occurred earlier in the evening, although I noted that he failed to mention the inspector's reference to the "unearthly vision". Dr. Lorimer took his leave and went across to examine the body, which we had laid out beside Holmes's chemical apparatus. I felt obliged to go with him, but continued to listen carefully to the conversation behind me.

"A glass of brandy, you say, Mr. Holmes?"

"Yes, Inspector. I poured Maddocks a large measure at his request."

"I see. Well I think we'd best take the bottle with us. Not that I'm setting hares coursing, you'll understand. We just need to be thorough."

"Of course," replied Holmes. There was more than a hint of sarcasm in his tone.

Sergeant West had evidently risen from his chair to retrieve the bottle from the table near the window. "How can we be sure that no one has tampered with this, sir?"

It was my turn to pour scorn on the proceedings. I spun around to face the group. "I can assure you, Sergeant, that Holmes and I have acted with the utmost professionalism in reporting this matter and laying the facts before you. Are you suggesting that we had a reason to want Maddocks dead and have sought to cover something up?"

West looked sheepish but remained silent. Bradstreet then intervened to restore some accord. "No one is saying that, Doctor. But we must follow procedures. The death of a police officer while on duty is always considered a very serious matter."

Holmes interposed. "You say that Maddocks was still *on duty* when he visited here this evening? I had assumed that he had completed his shift, for I have never known him to accept any form of alcoholic beverage while working."

Bradstreet looked bemused. "Yes, he and Sergeant Fulton had been sent to the British Museum's Natural History building to ensure that its collection of fossils and dinosaur bones remained secure. After all the recent raids, the curator at the museum feared they might be targeted next."

"And is Fulton still at the museum?"

"As far as I know." He pulled his fob watch from his waistcoat and glanced at the time. "They were due to finish their shift at ten o'clock, so Sergeant Fulton still has well over an hour until he stands down."

"In that case, could I suggest we make our way to the museum and quiz Fulton about events earlier this evening?"

Bradstreet nodded. "Certainly. I had hoped to speak to Fulton when he returned to the station, for he will be unaware that Maddocks has passed away. The two have always been close. I think it best if I break the news first, before we all descend on him."

There was general agreement to this. Lorrimer, West, and I then attended to the body, struggling to manoeuvre the corpse from the study and down the stairs. Inspector Bradstreet had clearly thought ahead, for a covered police wagon was sat outside the house, fronted by two large horses. Its driver jumped down on seeing us and helped to carry the body to the rear of the vehicle. Lorrimer and West climbed into the back of the wagon to accompany the cadaver back to the police morgue, the doctor inviting me to attend the *post mortem* the following morning. When the wagon had departed, Bradstreet, Holmes, and I set off to walk the three miles to Cromwell Road.

It was a chilly night and a thin layer of mist hung in the air. By the time we reached Hyde Park it was difficult to see for more than a few yards in any direction. For the most part we walked in silence, with Bradstreet making occasional remarks about the quickest route to the museum. I could sense Holmes's annoyance at this, for no one knew the streets and geography of the capital better than he.

We arrived at the museum a little before ten. Knocking at the main entrance, we were greeted by a night watchman, who explained that Sergeant Fulton had been on duty for some hours and could be found in the vaulted central hall. As agreed, we let Inspector Bradstreet go ahead of us to inform Fulton about his colleague's demise. Some minutes later the inspector returned and said that Fulton had taken the news as well as could be expected and was comfortable to talk to the three of us about events earlier that evening.

Holmes and I had met the muscular Vincent Fulton on only one previous occasion. Some months earlier, the Yorkshireman had accompanied Inspector Maddocks to Baker Street when the pair had been seeking information about Gabrielle Cavellaro, a volatile Italian anarchist, whose notoriety as a bomb maker had made him the toast of the London underworld. Shortly after getting involved in the case, Holmes had surprised me one day by announcing that Cavellaro no longer posed a threat. Pressing him for further information, my colleague had added only five words: "He had a short fuse."

The police officer that stood before us now looked to have none of the self-confidence that he had displayed on his visit to 221b. It was clear that Fulton had taken the news of the death badly. His face was ashen and his eyes betrayed the deep shock he had experienced. It was all he could do to nod and acknowledge our arrival as we joined him in the main hall and shook him by the hand.

We stood at the foot of the magnificent stone staircase, surrounded by the most incredible exhibits I had ever set eyes upon. With more than a passing interest in recent discoveries, I could see the preserved remains of various species, including *Iguanodon*, *Hylaeosaurus*, and *Megalosaurus*. In a long glass case to my right was the preserved skull of an *Ichthyosaur*. I remembered that the renowned anatomist Sir Richard Owen, the first director of the British Museum, had first coined the term *Dinosaurus* from the Greek words for *terrible* and *lizard*. And in a lecture I had attended only one year earlier, I recalled that the British paleontologist Harry Seeley had argued that the dinosaurs fell into two distinct groups, largely defined by differences in the pelvis. There were the "bird-hipped" *Ornithischians* and the "lizard-hipped" *Saurischians*. The exhibition had clearly been arranged along those lines.

Bradstreet appeared disinterested in the displays and got straight down to business. He asked Fulton to explain why Maddocks had deserted him at the museum when both men had been instructed to guard the building during their shift. Holmes interrupted before the perplexed sergeant could answer.

"I am sorry to interject, Inspector, but I would be keen to know what had happened prior to that. I think we need to build up a complete picture of the events earlier. We may then be in possession of all the relevant facts."

Bradstreet did not seem to be offended and merely nodded for Fulton to respond.

"We began work at ten this morning and spent the first hour at the station being briefed about the recent raids and the significance of these paleontology collections. Stephen had no great interest in the work and

340

was content for me to take notes and decide how best to arrange things once we got to the museum. Before making our way here, he accepted my suggestion that we have a quick meal at my house. We thought it would be a long night and didn't think we'd get the chance to eat again."

"And where is it you live, Sergeant?" enquired Holmes.

"Gloucester Road, South Kensington. It's less than half-a-mile from here."

"I see. And what did you eat?"

The question prompted a bemused look from Bradstreet.

"I had a pie in the pantry that I'd baked the previous evening. We ate some of that with a few potatoes. I live on my own, you see, as my wife died three years back. Stephen often stayed for dinner. We've been pals since our days at the Giggleswick School near Settle."

"You both had a good education, then," I stated, somewhat surprised to hear him say this. "Giggleswick is a public school, is it not?"

"Yes. Stephen's father was a barrister and could afford the fees. I received a scholarship to attend. I can't say that I enjoyed my time there, but it helped me to get this job."

Holmes then enquired, "Did you both join the Metropolitan Force at the same time?"

Fulton snorted unexpectedly. "No. I joined some years earlier than Stephen and put in a good word for him at the time he applied." He looked towards Bradstreet in a somewhat contemptable manner. "His upbringing was clearly better than mine, for he made it to *Inspector* three years ago. I've been told that I'll never progress beyond *Sergeant*."

Inspector Bradstreet was not immune to the gibe. "All right, that's enough, Fulton. Just tell us what happened after you'd had the meal."

"We walked to Cromwell Road and arrived here at about twelve-thirty. We were shown around the main exhibition area by Mr. Flower, the Director of the Museum."

"William Henry Flower?" I enquired, knowing something of the man's history.

"Yes. He replaced the previous director, Sir Richard Owen. Both share a devotion to natural history although, interestingly, the two have never got on. You might remember that they fell out in various scientific circles while debating theories of evolution. Flower is a devotee of Charles Darwin, but also believes that religion and paleontology are not incompatible." He pointed towards a white statue on one wall of the central hall. "It was he who commissioned the seated marble statue of Darwin that sits over there."

Holmes appeared to be greatly impressed by Fulton's display of knowledge. "Did Mr. Flower tell you all of this?"

"No. I take a great interest in such matters. I am something of an amateur rock collector and enjoy reading about all the new discoveries."

Bradstreet was clearly irritated by the deviation. "Can we get back to the matter at hand? What happened after you'd been *shown around* by Mr. Flower?"

"Stephen was content to wander around the hall scrutinising all of the exhibits. He seemed distracted, acting oddly, and occasionally mumbling to himself. He appeared oblivious to the fact that the building was now full of large numbers of visitors. I left him to it and began to do a tour of the museum, noting down all of the security arrangements and trying to spot the most likely areas where a break-in might occur. I suppose I might have been gone for a couple of hours. When I returned to the hall I was lambasted by an irate curator whom I had met but briefly while in the company of Mr. Flower. He said that my colleague had been causing quite a disturbance in front of the visitors and, in the interests of everyone's safety, he had been manhandled into the office of one of the academic staff."

Inspector Bradstreet expressed his dismay at the revelation. "Had he been drinking, Fulton?"

"No, sir. Not to my knowledge. Well, not before we came here. I found him in the company of a geologist by the name of Phelps. He had managed to calm Stephen down and was busy administering what he said was the inspector's third glass of brandy. Phelps explained that the dinosaur bones often scared some of the younger visitors, but he had never known a grown man – let alone a senior police officer – to exhibit such terror."

The word did not escape Holmes's attention. "*Terror*? Did he really say that?"

"Yes. And I soon understood why. Stephen had apparently become fixated with a fossilised Pterodactyl. The display contains a detailed drawing showing what the creature would have looked like when it was alive in the Jurassic period. He had been staring at this for some time under the watchful eye of the museum staff, before becoming convinced that the *Pterosaur* had . . . come to life."

The narrative was too much for Bradstreet, who exploded with apoplexy. "Clearly the man was intoxicated, as you know only too well, Sergeant! I have no idea what this *Ter . . . o . . . whatsit* is, but can tell you that this will not sit well with the Commissioner when he hears about it! Did you not challenge Maddocks?"

Fulton stood his ground. "I tried to talk to him, sir, but for an hour or more he spoke nothing but nonsense. For periods he would sit quietly, but would then act manically, for no particular reason, convinced that there were dinosaurs in the room with us. He kept pointing upwards, saying that he could see 'the flying reptile' and 'the Devil's own bird'."

"And yet *you* saw nothing, so he was clearly delusional." It was more of an observation than a question. One upon which I then felt obliged to elaborate: "If we accept that Maddocks had *not* been drinking before arriving at the museum, and the episodes began *before* he was ushered in Phelps's room, it is quite possible that he was experiencing some form of temporary *mania*. It is not uncommon in times of acute anxiety."

Holmes was amenable to the suggestion. "I agree, Watson. And you are right to point out that this was in all likelihood a *temporary aberration* on his part, for he displayed none of these behaviours later at 221b. And yet it seems hard to imagine that the one of the exhibits would trigger such a reaction . . . ."

Bradstreet remained unconvinced. "Dress it up anyway you wish, Mr. Holmes, but my instincts tell me he'd just had one too many. So having humiliated himself and disgraced the honour of the Yard, how did he manage to find his way to Baker Street?"

It was convenient that Bradstreet focused his attention on Fulton at that point, for both Holmes and I exchanged a look at the mention of the Yard's "honour".

"I sat with Stephen for a short while longer, until he began to display signs of weariness. At that point he was laid out on a bench along one wall of Phelps's office. Convinced that he would sleep off whatever illness he was suffering from, I thought it best to leave him and continue with the work we had been asked to do.

"I went back to my earlier duties, continuing to examine all of the doors, windows, and others points of access in the museum and recording these in my notebook. It was some time beyond five o'clock when I returned to the office and found it to be empty. I couldn't locate Phelps, learning later that he had left for the day. And enquiring about the whereabouts of my colleague, I was then told by the staff at the public entrance that Stephen had departed from the museum without saying anything and leaving no message. While concerned, I felt it was my duty to stay put as I had been instructed to do."

"Quite right," opined Bradstreet, "although you might have seen fit to send a short telegram to the station explaining what had occurred. Heaven knows how we are going to resolve this with the museum's director."

Fulton looked suitably admonished and asked if he might be relieved of his duty. There was the sound of footsteps away to our left, and I could see that the night watchman had re-entered the hall, this time in the company of two more police officers whom I imagined to be the men sent to replace Maddocks and Fulton. Inspector Bradstreet confirmed that this was indeed the case and, while releasing Fulton, made it quite clear that he expected the sergeant to make a full statement of what he had told us first thing the next morning.

Holmes had been walking among the exhibits while all of this was going on and, having re-joined us, said that we would also take our leave, as it had been a long day. He suggested that we might call on the inspector at one o'clock the following day. Bradstreet seemed content with this, and I confirmed that the timing would be good for me also, given the planned *post mortem*. We left the main hall alongside a weary-looking Sergeant Fulton.

The temperature outside had continued to drop, although the fog had lifted somewhat making visibility that much easier. Holmes fell in with Fulton, explaining that we would walk with him as far as Gloucester Road and then try to catch a cab. I knew this to be a ruse, as our route back to Baker Street was in the opposite direction, but the sergeant appeared to be none the wiser.

When we reached the left turn into Gloucester Road, Holmes announced suddenly that he felt weak and feared he might pass out. Feigning weariness and acting like he was about to collapse, he grabbed for my arm and steadied himself with his walking cane. Fulton was taken in completely, while I played along with the charade. I explained that Holmes was susceptible to such attacks when he had not eaten for some hours. The concerned sergeant said that his house was but a short walk away and he would be glad to furnish the great detective with a morsel or two to speed his recovery.

The gas lamp across the street cast a warm glow on the red-brick terraced house that Fulton occupied. It was a neatly-proportioned property with a solid front door, single downstairs window and three upper windows. Stepping inside the front room it was easy to see the feminine touches of Fulton's late wife – the neatly crocheted antimacassars on the armchairs and an elaborate fabric lambrequin running along the top and sides of the window frame. It was to Fulton's credit that he had maintained the interior to an immaculate standard.

Our unwitting host invited us to make ourselves comfortable and offered to prepare some bread and cheese for our late supper.

"Splendid!" said Holmes. "That would be most agreeable. But please do not go to any particular trouble – a thin slice of bread and a small wedge of Cheddar would be quite sufficient." He winked at me slyly as Fulton exited the room.

We sat in silence until the police officer returned from the kitchen, not daring to exchange any words in case we were overheard. Fulton had prepared a small plate for each of us, on which sat a sharp knife, a sizeable chunk of cheese, some pickled onions, a wholesome round of bread, and a drop of homemade pickle. In spite of the obfuscation, Holmes and I enjoyed every mouthful of the repast.

With our supper consumed, Holmes insisted on collecting the empty plates and said that he would return them to the kitchen. I followed my colleague's lead and immediately engaged Fulton in conversation, asking him about the rock collection he had referred to earlier. The enquiry brought the sergeant to life as he talked effusively about his fascination with geology. Holmes returned some minutes later, a light smile playing around his lips.

We bid our farewells to Fulton, thanking him once more for the supper and making our way back out onto the street. The light fog had all but disappeared as we headed onto Cromwell Road and hailed the first empty hansom that we saw. It was only when we were seated in the cab and on our way to Baker Street that Holmes began to talk about the case.

"Fulton is our man, Watson! I felt it from the very beginning when we first approached him at the museum. I was convinced that his shocked reaction had little to do with the news about Maddocks. It was more the surprise of learning that his colleague had approached us after leaving the museum. He knows our reputation for ferreting out the truth."

I was stunned by the revelation but did not fully comprehend what he meant. "Are you saying that Fulton set out to murder Maddocks?"

"No, I don't think he did, but his actions have inadvertently led to the inspector's demise. All should become clearer when we meet with Bradstreet tomorrow lunchtime. I have some work to complete while you are attending the autopsy with Dr. Lorrimer. We should then be a position to present our case to Scotland Yard. Maddocks did indeed see a *Pterosaur*, but like the limited vision we experienced in the fog earlier, his perception was not all it should have been.

With this cryptic allusion he fell silent and refused to be drawn further, adding only that he required "further data" to confirm his suspicions.

I rose early the next morning in order to attend the *post mortem* with Dr. Lorrimer. Arriving at his surgery in Harrington Road a few minutes before nine o'clock, I found he was already well advanced in his preparations for the examination. Suitably attired, I began to assist him with the dissection.

It was fascinating to see a fellow surgeon work with such dexterity. We exchanged few words at first, and I fell in with his preferred ways of operating. When he had examined all of the major organs and had begun to remove tissue samples for the toxicology tests he planned, he began to talk more freely and openly.

"Do you find it easy to work with Holmes?" he enquired, somewhat out of the blue.

I paused before responding, trying to imagine why he might have asked such a question. "I have heard others say that they find his approach somewhat brusque, but I have to say that whatever shortcomings he might possess, I have always found Holmes to be both loyal and inspirational. He is the finest man I have ever had the fortune to associate with. Why do you ask?"

The question took him by surprise. "I must apologise. I did not intend to offend you, Watson. It's just that when I'm working with some of the detectives from Scotland Yard, they seem to have few positive things to say about him. Of course, they recognise his uncanny skills and abilities, but their overwhelming view seems to be that he is a destabilising force."

"*Destabilising*? Now there's a euphemism I can imagine coming from the likes of Bradstreet. They're content to ask for his help when all else fails. Far from being a subversive force, I would say that he helps to protect the reputation of their profession!"

Lorrimer tried to play Devil's Advocate. "Yes, but imagine your colleague decided to stray into your professional domain, telling you how to perform surgery or tend to your patients. You cannot tell me that you would willingly accept his *amateur interventions*."

I could feel my hackles rising but sought to keep things civil. "There is one thing you must realise about the man, Lorrimer. He is uniquely placed to conduct the work that he does as a consulting detective. In the same way that every generation produces scientists, barristers, or engineers who are at the pinnacle of their profession, Holmes is the cream of the crop when it comes to detective work. He does not claim to know everything. In fact, he is most honest about his limitations. In short, there is nothing *amateur* about his work."

To his credit, Lorrimer did not pursue the matter – realising, I suspect, that further protestations would be futile. For my part, I settled back into the routine of assisting him. Within a couple of hours we had completed the autopsy and concluded all of the tests Lorrimer felt necessary. We were agreed on the conclusions, but I could not help but think that both Bradstreet and Holmes would be disappointed with what Lorrimer had to tell them.

With the meeting at Bow Street Police Station scheduled for one o'clock, we began to clean ourselves up and ensure that we had recorded the results of all our work. Lorrimer had two mortuary assistants on standby who agreed to take over at that point, enabling us to catch a cab and arrive at the station with just a few minutes to spare.

We were shown up to the first floor of the building and into the spacious office which Inspector Bradstreet occupied. Holmes was already there, sitting to one side of Bradstreet's desk and clutching what looked look a small glass vial. He smiled at me enigmatically as I took a seat beside him.

Bradstreet welcomed us and talked through a few developments in the investigation. Sergeant Fulton had come into work earlier that morning to make a full statement. He had apologised for his actions the day before, but had requested that he be allowed to continue his patrol duties at the museum. Bradstreet had consented to the request. Beyond that, there had been no further reports of raids or thefts in the case. The inspector then invited Dr. Lorrimer to give an account of what had been discovered during the *post mortem*.

"Doctor Watson and I conducted a thorough examination and also completed a large number of laboratory tests. We confirmed that the death had been the result of an acute heart attack. However, Maddocks looked to have been in very good health and there were no obvious signs of liver, heart, lung, or arterial damage which might have led to such rapid heart failure. In such a case, I would have expected to find some evidence within the blood or tissue samples of an agent which had triggered the attack. We tested for the full range of toxins which can kill with such speed – including mercury, strychnine, cyanide, and arsenic – but found no traces. We then tried to ascertain the presence of other poisons, such as prussic acid, hemlock, and digitalis, all without success. At this stage, we are forced to conclude that the death remains unexplained and foul play cannot be ruled out."

I nodded in agreement. Bradstreet said he was surprised to hear this and turned towards Holmes, who had yet to voice any opinion. My colleague then took a curious line of questioning. "Doctor Lorrimer, did you test for any chemical deliriants?"

Lorrimer stiffened. "Meaning what, exactly?"

"I was curious to know whether you had tested for any chemicals which might have induced Maddocks to see an extinct flying reptile at the museum yesterday. It was, after all, the most singular and fascinating aspect of this whole affair."

The surgeon bristled even more. "Maddocks was clearly delusional, and I must say that I tend to agree with Inspector Bradstreet that his condition was most likely the result of too much alcohol."

Holmes was polite, but direct. "I cannot agree, as I believe it was only after seeing the *Pterosaur* that Maddocks began to drink. It is well known that certain chemicals can trigger hallucinations, perceptual anomalies, and other substantial subjective changes in human thoughts, emotions, and consciousness. I believe that someone administered such a deliriant deliberately."

It was Bradstreet's turn to raise a query: "To kill Maddocks?"

"No. To put him into a delusional state in which his judgement – and ability to do his job – would be hampered.

The inspector confessed to being more than a little confused. "Mr. Holmes. As entertaining as your theories often are, I find myself at a loss with this one. Can you get to the point and explain exactly what it is you are asserting?"

"Certainly, Inspector. Sergeant Fulton set out to undermine Maddocks's position as the senior officer on this case. I cannot be certain, but imagine he has held a deep-seated hatred for Maddocks since his colleague was promoted to inspector and he was overlooked for promotion. The fact that all of this occurred at the same time as Fulton lost his beloved wife is probably a contributory factor. I met Fulton for the first time some three months back in the company of Maddocks. It was clear to me then that he had an intense dislike of the other man and was trying very hard to conceal it. I noted the fact at the time, but did not imagine it would ever prove to be relevant in a criminal case. Eager to learn more about their so-called friendship, I sent a telegram to the Giggleswick School this morning. The headmaster replied, saying that he remembered both boys and confirmed that they were fiercely competitive, often coming to blows, with Fulton almost always the underdog."

Bradstreet looked at him askance. "The pair could be bull-headed certainly, but I find this hard to believe. How exactly did he put Maddocks in this *delusional state* and, more importantly, what reason did he have for going to such extraordinary lengths?"

Holmes nodded. "Let me answer the first of those questions, as it will set the scene for the second. I have known Maddocks for some time and always believed him to be a sober, level-headed man not given to flights of fancy. His practical, hard-nosed approach to policing had much to commend it. Now, he said that he saw an extinct reptile, and ordinarily I would be inclined to take his account at face value. And yet . . . clearly such a sighting would be improbable – unless he had truly discovered a lost world *.

"Having heard Fulton's testimony, I was convinced that Maddocks had seen what he believed to be a flying reptile. Now, had he been completely delusional, the symptoms would have manifested themselves sometime earlier and would have persisted later when he arrived at Baker Street. I concluded therefore, that he must have ingested something just before the walk to the museum which prompted these temporary hallucinations. And it was Fulton's account which gave me the first clue. You may remember that he said they'd eaten *a pie* which he had baked the previous evening.

"Watson and I walked with Fulton to his home when he left the museum last night. It was a deliberate tactic on my part. We had some supper with him and, just before I left the house, I was able to gain access to the pantry without the man's knowledge. There was evidence in the kitchen that he and Maddocks had eaten a meal exactly as he had suggested. I would have expected nothing less, for there had been no opportunity to clear up as the pair had gone straight to the museum after their lunch. And yet, I discovered that he had been somewhat economical with the truth when he said he had baked *a pie*. In fact, there were the remains of *two pies* in the pantry. One had been baked especially for Maddocks."

Dr. Lorrimer huffed. "How could you know that?"

Holmes smiled and raised the glass vial. "Because of this. I took samples from both pies and tested them myself this morning. Both contained a variety of edible fungi, but one contained a recognisable deliriant. A bucket in the pantry also contained some of the discarded remains of the mushrooms used in the pies. Having gathered some of those as well, I was able to identify the fungus responsible for Maddocks's condition. The distinctive brown, conical-shaped mushroom is known as the 'liberty cap'. The German mycologist Paul Kummer gave it the scientific name of *Psilocybe semilanceata* in 1871."

I recollected an article in *The Lancet* some years earlier which had detailed an account of poisoning by liberty cap mushrooms. In 1799, a family picked some of the fungus in London's Green Park and ate them in a meal. It was documented that the father and children had experienced pupil dilation, delirium, and uncontrollable laughter. I knew that Holmes had hit upon the agent responsible for the officer's malaise. Lorrimer, however, remained unconvinced.

"I'm aware that liberty cap mushrooms can induce hallucinations, but have never known them to cause death."

Holmes's jaw was set hard. "I did not suggest that the fungus killed him, merely that it gave rise to the mental state in which he was able to see a living creature which has been extinct for some considerable time."

Bradstreet intervened. "I think you may be on to something there, Mr. Holmes. I have known Fulton to talk about his forays into the countryside to collect mushrooms and the like. He's very knowledgeable about the natural world. In fact, he asked to work with Maddocks on this investigation because of his interest in old rocks and bones."

"That is most telling."

"In what sense?"

"Because Fulton had a material interest in being *on the inside* of this investigation. In fact, it is the reason he has gone to the *extraordinary lengths* you enquired about earlier. He has been supplying information to the gang responsible for all of the recent raids and break-ins. That is why he worked so diligently to assess the security arrangements at the museum. The information will be used by his criminal associates who plan to raid the dinosaur collection this very evening."

I was astonished to learn this. Bradstreet also appeared stunned. Even Lorrimer looked as if he had been knocked off his perch.

"How do you know all of this?" Bradstreet asked.

"Observation, deduction, and legwork," replied Holmes, "the essence of our craft. It was clear from Fulton's talk at the museum that he knows a great deal about paleontology – the casual references to '*Ichthyosaur*', '*Jurassic Period*', and '*Pterosaur*'. He is also likely to know which exhibits are the rarest and most likely to fetch the highest price when sold illegally to fossil collectors around the world.

"When we first entered the exhibition hall, Fulton looked shocked. This was not because he had learned of Maddocks's death, but because he realised that Watson and I had been visited by his colleague. How could he be sure that Maddocks had not become aware of his scheme to deceive everyone? So he played it cautiously, emphasising Maddocks's bizarre behaviour as a smokescreen for what he was really been up to.

"When we greeted Fulton, Dr. Watson and I shook him by the hand. I noted that he had a chalky residue on the tips of his fingers. There had to be a reason. Taking the time to wander among the exhibits, I observed the explanation. Visibly, but discreetly, Fulton had chalked a small '*M*' on the floor to the side of a number of the displays. A direction to the thieves, showing which fossils should be stolen."

"Why '*M*'?" interrupted Lorrimer.

"A recognised gang symbol or somebody's initial, I suspect. In any case, he had done a very comprehensive job of working out how best to get in and out of the museum without the need to spend time deciding which fossils to steal."

I cut in. "I see. And feeding Maddocks the mushrooms was a ruse to keep him out of the way, while Fulton did his work."

"Exactly. Maddocks was a solid detective, who would have known that his colleague was up to something. And the more Maddocks acted strangely, the more he was likely to distract the museum workers and visitors from what Fulton was doing. That would also explain why Fulton was in no hurry to let the station know of Maddocks's condition, just in case further officers arrived to stop him completing his reconnaissance."

"Why are you so sure that this break-in will be tonight?" asked Bradstreet, reaching for a cigarette from a small wooden box to the side of the desk. He offered the box around, although no one took up the offer.

"This is where the legwork came in," Holmes responded. "Having returned to Baker Street last night, I was convinced that Fulton was working with the criminals behind the fossil raids. Even at that late hour, I was able to despatch some trusted associates of my own to watch Fulton's house. I have a small band of loyal street urchins who are willing to carry out such work. Just before I set off to come here today, I received word from Wiggins, their designated leader. Fulton had left Gloucester Road at around five o'clock this morning, heading into the city. One of my young allies by the name of Remblance was able to follow the sergeant at a safe distance.

"Fulton's destination was a brewer's yard close to Brick Lane. Remblance was able to slip into the yard unseen. Following the sound of two voices, he positioned himself behind some barrels and heard most of the conversation which followed. The excellent information he was later to relay to Wiggins has earned the boys a Guinea prize.

"In short, Fulton confirmed that the break-in is set for eight o'clock this evening. A stolen key will enable the raiders to gain entry through a large oak door at the back of the museum. Six men will be involved, travelling to the raid aboard a brewery dray containing large oak barrels and long wooden boxes. From their conversation, Remblance formed the impression that the gang had used this method to steal fossils on previous occasions. He heard Fulton say that only one night watchman will be on duty and that he would be 'taken care of, by eight o'clock'. When the raiders have lifted all of the marked exhibits, they will rough Fulton up and leave him bound and gagged on the floor of the museum to give every impression that he was overwhelmed by the gang."

"Extraordinary!" roared Bradstreet. "That is a remarkable piece of detective work, Mr. Holmes. And it is some credit to your young accomplices that they have been so adept at outwitting Fulton, who is clearly no fool. This duplicity by one of our own will not go down well with the Commissioner, but if we can intervene early, prevent the night watchman from being hurt, and catch these thieves red-handed, I believe we should be able to snatch victory from the jaws of defeat!"

I had never known Bradstreet to be so complimentary. We had first encountered the inspector in 1882 on a case I had recorded as "The Manila Envelope". At that stage he was serving in Scotland Yard's "*E*" Division and still retained some enthusiasm for the role. Seven years later, he had been transferred to "*B*" Division to serve out his remaining years as a detective. From what I had gathered, it had not been a move he had welcomed.

There was little more to discuss at that stage. Bradstreet thanked Dr. Lorrimer for his work and asked him if he would liaise with the local coroner in enabling the inquest into Maddocks's death to be completed. The doctor confirmed that he would, but expressed some concern about the likely verdict given what we now knew about the liberty cap mushrooms. In reply, Bradstreet said that he also thought it unlikely that Fulton would face a charge of either "murder" or "attempted murder" for what he had done.

To that point, I had imagined that Holmes would want to be in on the subsequent arrest and detention of Fulton and the fossil thieves. Bradstreet also seemed surprised when my colleague announced that he was content to let Scotland Yard conclude the business and was not seeking any recognition for our involvement in the case. I wanted to voice my objection, but knew that Holmes would not welcome such a challenge in front of the others.

It was only when we were sat before a warm fire in the cosy surrounds of the Baker Street apartment that he shared his real reason for not wishing to see the case through.

"There are times, Watson, when it is better to leave Scotland Yard in ignorance of certain facts. It seems quite clear to me that in the rush to bring Fulton to justice and the eagerness to thwart a gang of high-profile fossil thieves, the death of poor Maddocks has been largely obscured. Lorrimer was not wrong to suggest that the deliriant mushrooms were unlikely to have been the cause of his demise. You see, I took a walk through Green Park this morning before making my way to Bow Street. It is only two miles from Fulton's house. I found liberty cap mushrooms growing in abundance, alongside all of the other fungi that had been baked in the pie fed to Maddocks."

"Is that not a confirmation of everything you expected?" I asked, unsure where he was heading with his narrative.

"Indeed. But it was only when I chanced upon some of the browny-grey edible mushrooms that I had also seen in Fulton's pantry, that I realised what had killed Maddocks. The common ink cap was first recorded by the French naturalist Pierre Bulliard in 1786. He named it *Agaricus atramentarious* from the Latin *atramentum*, meaning 'ink'. In the middle ages, the fungus had been used to produce a cheap supply of the writing fluid. While palatable, the mushroom has an unusual property. When mixed with alcohol, it produces a toxin which can lead to symptoms such as flushing, malaise, agitation, palpitations – "

352

" – and occasionally, heart failure!" I exclaimed. "That's it, Holmes! At the museum, Phelps had already and unknowingly plied Maddocks with at least three glasses of brandy to calm him down. When he arrived here he downed a further large glass, increasing the intensity of the poison. It was the spirits that killed him, rather than the sight of the Pterodactyl!"

Holmes nodded. "Yes, and you might know that the traditional name of the ink cap is 'Tippler's Bane'."

It was some months before Sergeant Fulton was to face trial, alongside a dozen of his criminal associates. The gang had been responsible for fossil thefts across length and breadth of Europe, selling the scientific rarities to collectors for sizeable sums of money. Most of the men received sentences of between seven and fifteen years. But the judicial system reserved the largest sentence for the corrupt police officer – Fulton being incarcerated for a minimum of twenty years.

Bradstreet's only disappointment was Scotland Yard's failure to detain the one person who had apparently orchestrated the enterprise. All of the convicted men received their sentences without divulging his name or whereabouts. They referred to him simply as "*M*".

Holmes rarely talked about the case in the years that followed. When he did, it was often with a faraway look in his eye which accompanied the words: "Like the spectral *Pterosaur*, we will all be extinct one day."

NOTE

* Readers may be aware that my literary agent, Sir Arthur Conan Doyle, is credited with having written a wholly fictional account of just such a world. – *JHW*

The Weird of Caxton
by Kelvin Jones

One cold November morning in 1890, I had called upon my friend, Sherlock Holmes, to find his landlady, Mrs Hudson, in a state of considerable anxiety. It seemed that she had entered the sitting room at nine o'clock to find him sitting bolt upright on the floor, a position that he had apparently occupied for most of the night.

"I fear that it may be apoplexy," the poor woman cried, wringing her hands and speaking in that slow, halting fashion which is the mark of a Scot, "though I am not surprised, frankly. Such peculiar hours he keeps and his meals are often half-finished."

Allaying her fears as best I could, I made my way up the narrow stairs to the cosy sitting room that had been the scene of so many of our past adventures. Mrs Hudson had not exaggerated, it seemed, for, as I opened the door, I was confronted by my friend's lean form, squatting cross-legged in the centre of the room, his keen eyes fixed steadily in front of him. Fearing that he had fallen into some kind of catatonic trance, I knelt down and hit his face with the flat of my hand. Suddenly he turned his head and laughed loudly.

"Well, Watson," he exclaimed, "it may be a bizarre way to greet one's friend, but it does wonders for the nerve endings."

I asked him what on earth he meant by this peculiar practice of sitting on floors.

"Perhaps you have not heard of *Hatha Yoga*," he replied, rising from his position. "It is a system of relaxation and meditation practised by the Tibetan monks. I first encountered it during my investigation into the affairs Madame Blavatsky. No doubt you will recall that episode?"

I nodded. The story of his exposure of the notoriously fraudulent madame is a subject I hope eventually to reveal to my readers when the controversy has ceased to trouble the occult world. For now I have kept detailed notes of the affair, and since my colleague has allowed me unlimited access to the records, no doubt the public will one day be enlightened.

"What do you make of this, Doctor?" Holmes exclaimed. He handed me a small brown envelope containing a telegram. The message inside read: *Must See. Urgent re Weird Gresham. 11 a.m. Today.*

"Hardly coherent," I remarked.

354

"At first glance, no. It would indicate that the person who dictated it was certainly in a great hurry. Or maybe the Post Office clerk was half asleep. Either way, it presents something of a conundrum."

"But it makes no sense at all!" I objected.

"Now look again. That phrase: *Weird Gresham*", for example . . . ."

"Gresham is a name, weird an adjective."

"Or is it? *Weird* can also be taken to mean a *curse*. In which case we can proceed to: *Must see you urgently re the curse at eleven a.m. today.*"

"And Gresham is the name of the sender?"

"Precisely. Now, Watson, behind you is a volume of Burke's *Peerage*. If you would be so kind . . . ."

I handed him the book.

"Green . . . Greer – Ah, here we are. '*Gresham, Lord. Born ninth October, 1868. M.Sc. Cantab., D. Litt. Married, Twenty-ninth descendant of Lord Arthur Gresham. Residence, Caxton Mote, Suffolk,* etc., etc.' Hmm. Brief, but to the point. Vintage Burke."

As he spoke, there was a prolonged ring on the doorbell, followed by a woman's voice. The door to the sitting room opened to reveal a woman of exceptional beauty. She was richly attired in a black velvet dress and she wore a wide hat from which a veil half-concealed her face. Her pale but aristocratic face was marred only by the pallor of her cheeks.

"Mr. Holmes?"

"This is Mr. Holmes, madam. I am Dr. John Watson, his associate."

I ushered her to an easy chair and as she sat, the rich velvet of the dress clung to her figure, revealing a tight waist and ample bosom.

"Mr. Holmes, you must help me . . . ." she began, in a strained and tearful voice. "I am at my wits' end."

Homes placed a reassuring hand on her arm. "Madam, compose yourself. Whatever it is that vexes you, we shall do our best to put matters right. However, I cannot assist you unless you first tell me who you are and the reason for your visit."

The woman blushed and smiled slightly, revealing pearl-white teeth. Again, I was struck by the fineness of her complexion and the softness of her skin.

"You are right of course. But since yesterday morning, you must understand that my world has been shattered."

"I take it then that you are Lord Gresham's wife?"

"Yes. We have been married now for over five years."

"And that some tragedy has befallen your husband."

Lady Gresham shook her head wearily.

"Come, come," said Holmes after a slight pause. "If you expect to help me, you must be more forthcoming. Tell me what has happened."

Lady Gresham removed her hat and veil to reveal a fine head of hair, jet black, lustrous, and arranged in the Grecian style that was at that time fashionable among the wealthy. The dark eyes and somewhat swarthy complexion, I conjectured, suggested someone of either Italian or South American origin.

"Very well then," she began, as I poured coffee for the three of us. "As you may be aware, my husband and I live in an isolated area some miles east of Dundwych. Yesterday, at about two in the morning, I think it was, I was suddenly awakened by the sound of cries. You probably do not know that Caxton Mote, the family residence, is a moated castle of considerable proportions, and that beyond the moat itself lie a number of trees and laurel bushes. I immediately went to look, for my room overlooks the moat itself, and was appalled, for the cries I heard were of a man in terrible torment. They did not cease for some while but went on, each time becoming more prolonged and more harrowing. At last I could stand it no longer and, putting on my robe, I immediately went down to investigate, thinking it might be a poacher who had caught himself in one of our mantraps. However, when I arrived at the spot . . . ."

Our speaker paused and lowered her head, unable to continue.

"Go on, Lady Gresham," said Holmes, calm and reassuring.

"When I arrived I found that it was my brother-in-law. He had been attacked and savaged about the throat by a dog which I suspected had run loose from one of the three farms which adjoin our property. The farmers in these parts are lawless folk, and there have been several disagreements between my brother-in-law and a farmer known as Loxley who owns three powerful mastiffs that are allowed to roam the perimeter of his property after dark. On one occasion I had to put down one of our horses – a fine gelding – who had been savagely attacked during the night. I could not prove that the dogs had done it, of course, but I had my suspicions. Anyway, I did what I could for Michael and made a tourniquet from a section of my nightdress, but he had already lost a great deal of blood. By the time my husband and I had carried him back to the castle, he was already dead."

There was a long pause while Lady Gresham sipped her coffee, and Holmes reached up to the mantelpiece for the curved briar that he often chose to smoke whilst in a reflective mood. I observed Lady Gresham's face, profiled in the gaslight, the finely drawn features stained by tears. I noticed that Holmes was also observing her closely, a circumstance which surprised me, considering that usually he displayed no interest in the fair sex.

"Lady Gresham," he said at last, twisting the strands of tobacco into the bowl of the pipe, "why have you come to consult me?" He drew a spill from the fireplace and lowered it gently into the flames.

"Really, Holmes," I objected, annoyed by my friend's insensitivity, "I would have thought, under the circumstances – "

"Not at all, Watson," he snapped back. "I stand by what I said. There is nothing so far in this case that the police could not have handled – unless of course you have knowingly concealed something from me, Lady Gresham? You mentioned, for example, in your telegram, something about a curse . . . ?"

She looked at Holmes fixedly.

"That is why I have come to you, sir, for I understand that you are something of an expert."

"I claim no special powers in supposedly supernatural matters, although I have enjoyed some success, in an investigatory capacity, in debunking a number of them."

"My husband believes that his family is cursed."

"Cursed? Cursed by what?"

"By a wolf."

Holmes lit a match and drew it across the bowl of his pipe.

"A wolf you say? That is most unusual, though I have come across the tradition in certain parts of Eastern Europe. I take it that this is no ordinary wolf?"

"Perhaps I should explain."

"I wish you would."

"The original Lord Gresham who built Caxton Mote was said to have made a pact with the Devil around the year 1435. He was given the power to turn base metal into gold in exchange for his soul. He manufactured the gold in great quantities and exchanged it in the nearby town of Ipswich. But it was soon discovered that what he had made was fool's gold. When he realised that he had been tricked, he tried to break the pact, but it is said that the Devil sent a creature to him in the likeness of a wolf, which then devoured him. The wolf was eventually trapped and shot by the town's inhabitants, but not before it had killed several women and children. The body of Lord Gresham was never discovered."

Holmes smiled.

"An amusing legend. I have come across similar tales in parts of the West Country and in Herefordshire, but not as yet in the eastern counties. But why should your husband believe that the curse applies to him?"

"Because every male descendant of the Gresham family has suffered a violent fate."

"Without exception? Surely not."

"Absolutely without exception. And all have died alone."

"And you believe, I suppose, that your brother-in-law was also a victim of this curse?"

"I cannot believe it to be otherwise."

"Then if what you say is true – and we have yet to verify it – there is very little that I can do to help you. Evil from such an ancient and corrupted source has ways and means of overcoming the most stout defences. But that would only apply in the material world."

The woman before us raised her head in an imploring fashion and placed her gloved hand on Holmes's arm.

"Mr. Holmes, I beg of you, come with me to Caxton and at least talk to my husband."

"Very well, then, but I can promise nothing," he replied.

Lady Gresham rose, the velvet dress rustling about her ankles. "I am relying on you. May we see you soon?"

"Dr. Watson and I will catch the evening train."

"I am most grateful to you for this."

She turned to go, her tall, elegant figure framed against the fire. I have never seen such anxiety in a woman's face.

When Mrs Hudson had seen our visitor to the door, Holmes turned to me. "Well, what did you make of her?"

"A most attractive woman."

"Yes, yes," he said impatiently, "but there is more to her than meets the eye. That is why I have agreed to make the journey."

I should have known that my friend's reasons for complying with her request were based, not on common humanity, but on suspicion and curiosity. Even so, I was glad of the opportunity to get away from a wintry London into the countryside. It was not long, therefore, before we were sitting snugly inside a first-class railway carriage, foot warmers tucked beneath our tartan blankets, watching the endless rows of suburban streets stretch away on either side of us.

"See, Doctor, the drones have not been idle," Holmes remarked. His loathing for the provincial architecture of his own age was profound. I said nothing but sank back into my seat and observed the blotched terrain of North London give way to the broad flat fields of Essex. Here and there the skyline would be broken by a cluster of thatched cottages, each with its own distinctly Norman church. As dusk slowly fell and Holmes began to fill the carriage with his acrid pipe smoke, we passed into an altogether lonelier terrain where there were few hedgerows and even fewer hamlets to break up the monotony of the journey. There was a great eeriness and loneliness about this countryside as I watched it slipping into the darkness.

358

It was like a face on which all the creases had been removed and one was left staring at a flat, level skin.

As the train drew in to a succession of small stations, then lurched once more upon its way, I was struck by the lack of human figures in the landscape. Only once was the pattern broken when we drew level to a small group of travellers on the road, which lay parallel to the track. The driver of the fly was a man probably in his mid-twenties, yet the harshness of his existence, visible even from my vantage, had lined his face and drawn crows' feet around his eyes. His wife and child sat huddled in the back of the vehicle, their eyes dull and tinged with melancholy. After such a sight, I began to hanker again after the gaudy London streets.

At last the train juddered to a halt and we emerged amid a cloud of acrid steam onto the platform at Ipswich. Fortunately, a cob and four-wheeler had been provided for our convenience, and we were whisked out of the ancient town and onto a series of rough, uneven roads where clusters of oak trees predominated. Eventually we passed over a low bridge and down a narrow dirt track. There ahead of us stood the tall, imposing towers of Caxton Mote, outlined against the darkening sky.

"A fifteenth-century extravagance, by all accounts," remarked Holmes "Certainly it was built as a home rather than a castle."

He was correct, for the Mote lay surrounded by a steep-sided valley and was narrow in proportions. As we drew closer, I could see that the limestone walls bore rich carvings and designs of all manner of birds and animals. On each tower the head of a large wolf predominated, which looked strangely life-like in the gloom of the valley.

As I got out of the four-wheeler, the sun, which had followed us from Ipswich, sank behind a bank of inky-black cloud. Already the distant hills had turned to a dirty dun colour. The building before me seemed unreal as if a giant hand had placed it there. The spiralling towers and narrow, shuttered windows gave expression to its pale walls and ivy-covered gateway.

Holmes paid the driver and we made our way over the narrow drawbridge.

"Let us hope that it is a more friendly place within than without," he remarked to me as he pulled on the bell. There was a sound of footsteps and the great studded door opened to reveal Lady Gresham. She looked even more pale and drawn than at our previous meeting, an effect that was highlighted by the sombre gown that she was wearing.

"I am so glad that you have come," she said. "Please, you will join us for dinner."

A manservant appeared at her side and took our valises upstairs. Lady Gresham conducted us through a narrow hall into a large room containing a long oak table at the head of which sat a bearded man who regarded us intently. He stood as we entered and nodded grimly.

"And who is this?" he enquired, looking sharply at Lady Gresham.

"Sherlock Holmes, the investigator . . . ." the woman began, but she did not finish, for the man pushed his plate across the table and walked past us out of the room.

"It seems that we are not entirely welcome," observed Holmes.

"Pay him no regard," said Lady Gresham. "He has been greatly overcome by his brother's death. I suggested that you come here, but it was not his wish."

"I see. However, I trust that this will in no way impede the investigation?"

Lady Gresham did her best to reassure him, then rang for the maid, who brought us a selection of cold meats and salad. As she was clearing away the remains of Lord Gresham's supper, Holmes turned to her.

"I see your master disdains to eat the fowl."

"Why no sir, he eats no meat. He doesn't care for it. Never has, and there's a fact."

After supper had been concluded, Holmes asked if he might see the body of Lord Gresham's brother.

"I'm afraid that won't be possible," our hostess replied. "The body has been removed and is with the coroner at present."

"You have kept the clothes he was wearing?"

"Yes, of course. You may see them if you wish."

We ascended the stairs into a small bedroom, where Lady Gresham pointed to a sack containing the bloodstained clothing.

"When you discovered him, he was wearing this jacket as well?" Holmes asked, going through the garments.

"Yes, he was."

"Thank you. And now I should like to see the spot where the incident took place."

Lady Gresham called for three lanterns and we made our way over the moat and into a clump of bushes where a clearing was revealed to us.

"Hold the lamp for me," Holmes instructed in his usual peremptory manner while he began to crawl about on all fours, pausing every so often to inspect the soil. Then he stood up and examined the leaves of the surrounding bushes by the light of the lamp. Suddenly he brushed his hands and smiled enigmatically.

"Does your husband smoke, Lady Gresham?"

"Why, no."

"But your brother-in-law did?"

"Yes – "

"Thank you. I think that I have all the information I now require. And now, if you will excuse me, it has been a long day and I would like greatly to retire."

"Then you have proved the cause of death?" Lady Gresham asked, apprehensively.

"There is really little I can do to throw additional light upon the matter, though I believe I may be able to assist you in some small way. Now Lady Gresham, I must say goodnight to you." And picking up his lamp, he strode past us in the direction of the drawbridge.

After I had apologised to Lady Gresham for my friend's abruptness, we walked back together to the house. Then, after taking my leave, I too announced my decision to retire, and made my way into the house and up the ornate staircase to our rooms. At the end of a broad landing a pointed window reflected the last rays of light of the setting sun. Elsewhere the passageway lay swathed in muted browns and greys. I found that I could see through a transparent pane of glass at the head of the stair which gave me a panoramic view of the house and its surroundings. Past the courtyard, over an oval lake, the view, illuminated by the powerful Edison lamps, swept into the vast expanse of wood and brush and then on to the high ridge now concealing the sun. Thick ivy covered this side of the Mote, and on either side lancet windows peered like tiny eyes over the murky waters. I reached out and drew my hand over the coloured panes. Their touch was cold and unwelcoming. An heraldic sign, inlaid with thorns and briars and executed in pre-Raphaelite fashion, lay there. The motif was one I had never seen before, a wolf's head mounted on a pole, the mouth bloody and gaping. Through the lower jaw a broad sword had been thrust upwards. The oddness of the design was reinforced by the creature's eyes, which seemed particularly human in intent. The colours were violent, the patterns intricate.

"Admiring the view, Watson?" came a familiar voice from behind me.

"Admiring the window actually. Whose arms are these?"

"A distant ancestor of Lord Gresham, no doubt."

I looked round to find Holmes winding a stout rope about his arm.

"What on earth is that for?"

"It is a net for the butterfly. You need not undress, for we have a night's work ahead of us."

He would say nothing further than that we were to leave the castle in one hour's time and conceal ourselves in the shrubbery at the perimeter of the Mote. Accordingly, we made our way downstairs and out across the narrow drawbridge, Holmes insisting that the lamps be lit only when we had reached the safety of the undergrowth. I sat, shivering in the intense

361

cold, warming my hands by the wick of the lamp. At length, overcome by fatigue (for the journey had been a long and tedious one) I must have drifted off into a fitful doze, for I recall dreaming of a wide lake adjoining a ruined castle whose encrusted battlements were lined with ravens. Their glassy eyes shone luminously above me as I waded into the cold waters. Trapped in a cataleptic trance, I felt the cold waters lapping over my face and filling my mouth until I began to choke for dear life. When I awoke, I found Holmes staring down at me with a sardonic grin.

"Come, Watson. Think how Our Lord must have felt in The Garden of Gesthemene," he whispered. From then on I returned to my vigil.

It seemed that we had waited there in the cold for an eternity when suddenly, at about two o'clock, a light flickered at one of the windows of the castle.

"There's our man," whispered Holmes

Sure enough, there was to be seen a slight movement at the door, attended by a succession of odd sounds. As I watched, the moon passed from behind a cloud into the open and I saw what curiously appeared to be a loping figure, padding its way cautiously along the drawbridge like a dog. But this was no dog. Every so often it would pause and look upwards, as if sniffing the air for its prey.

As the man reached the end of the drawbridge, he tensed himself and began to growl. I caught a glimpse in the moonlight of a coarse lined face, the eyes flashing angrily, the teeth bared in a grotesque rictus. The fingers were stretched in a semblance of claws, whilst the hair on his head was uncombed and wild. However, what disturbed me most about the awful vision on the bridge was the demonic intent behind those eyes and the quick determination as the figure bounded towards us, its arms outstretched, the hands twisting in an odd, spasmodic fashion as if its owner were the victim of epilepsy. Then suddenly it froze, twisting its head sideways, as if again sniffing the night air.

Holmes leapt from behind the bush and shouted to me to bring the rope, but I think he hadn't accounted for the crazed man's agility. He was on Holmes in a second, his mouth biting and flashing at my friend's throat. I knew then that if I delayed a moment longer the madman would tear Holmes to ribbons. I drew my service revolver and fired at his torso. There was a howl of pain that was terrifying in the extreme, and then he rolled over to one side, shaking.

I brought the rope over to Holmes, who by this time was kneeling by the writhing body of his attacker.

"Is he badly injured?" I asked.

"Possibly. I must fetch Lady Gresham. Stay here and see what can be done for him."

I applied a pad made from my pocket handkerchief to staunch the bleeding from the abdomen and waited for my friend's return, too shocked at what had transpired even to speak to the poor man next to me.

"Lycanthropy is an ancient belief," remarked Holmes, when we were once more ensconced within his cosy Baker Street sitting room, "with records of it found even among the ancients. The term, as you probably know, is derived from the Greek words, *lukos*, a wolf and *anthropos*, a man, but is frequently employed regarding a transformation into any animal shape. It is chiefly in those countries where wolves are numerous that we find such tales concerning them, a fact which makes the madness of Lord Gresham even more curious."

"I am well aware of the divided nature of some personalities, but I must confess I've never seen anything quite so remarkable."

"And yet you must agree that the belief that every human possesses an animal form into which he enters at death, or at will, is still popular with certain tribes."

"Agreed. Yet this is something radically different. I've seen patients in an advanced state of schizophrenia imbued with great strength, but nothing so bizarre as this."

"Yes, it was truly remarkable."

"But what made you suspect that it was Lord Gresham who murdered his brother?"

"Because all the evidence pointed to it. My suspicions were first aroused by the fact that Lady Gresham herself had come to see me. Why not her husband who, after all, had more to fear? Then there was the story of the pact. You will remember that, according to what Lady Gresham said, the body of the original Lord Gresham was never discovered. Now that is odd, for it is rare for a lone wolf to devour an entire body. It seemed more likely to me that the original Lord Gresham himself created the legend of the family werewolf for his own dark purposes.

"Let me tell you, Watson, that before I met you at the upstairs window, I managed to gain access to Lord Gresham's private library, after some discussion with the manservant. It is a large collection consisting of mainly classical works, but at the far end of the room lies a great safe. I had but limited time at my disposal and, fearing an intrusion, I looked in several drawers, for I felt instinctively that in that safe I would find confirmation of my suspicions about Lord Gresham. At last I found the safe key. Inside, among a collection of letters, I discovered this."

He reached into his pocket and then handed me a scroll of thick vellum. I untied the ribbon and saw that it was a lengthy narrative written in faded black ink and headed "*The Gresham Werewolf, The Year of Our Lord 1643*",

"I think that this will explain," commented my friend, as he rose to draw the blinds.

A true Discourse (the document read) *Declaring the Damnable life and death of one Lord Peter Gresham, A most wicked man, who, in the guise of a wolf, committed many murders, killing many women and children. Who, for the same fact was taken and executed on the 31ˢᵗ October 1547, in the Towne of Ipswich.*

Those whome the Lord doth leaue to followe the Imagination of their owne hartes, dispising his proffered grace, in the end through the hardnes of hart and contempt of his fatherly mercy, they enter the right path of perdicion and destruction of the body and sole for euer. Such a one was the bloody and murderous Lord Gresham who, from his youth, was greatly inclined to euil and the practising of wicked Artes euen from twelue yeers of age till twentye, and so forwards till his dying day. The Deuill who hath a readye ear to listen to the lewde motions of cursed men, promised to give vnto him whatsoeuer his hart desired during his mortall life, whereupon this vile wretch desired great riches and that at his pressure he might work his lust and malice on men, women and children, in the shape of a beast. So the Deuill who sawe in him a fit instrument to perfourm mischeefe as a wicked feend, gaue unto him a girdle which, being put about him, disguised him into the likeness of a greedy deuouring Woolf, strong and mighty, with eyes great and large, which in the night sparkeled like vnto brandes of fire, a mouth great and wide, with most sharp and cruell teeth. A huge body and mighty pawes.

Lord Gresham was heerwith exceedingly pleased. And he grew rich by the transforming of base metal into gold, being known to all and sundrey as a most respectable citizen, whilst at night in Woolfish likeness, he would indulge his filthy luste, walking abroad in the fields and laying holde of maidens and children alike, and after his luste was fulfilled, he would murder them presentlye. Thus within the compass of a few yeeres he had murdered thirteene yong children and two yong women bigge with child, tearing the children out of their wombes in most bloody and sauage sorte and after eate their

364

hearts panting hotte and rawe, which he accounted dainty morsells and best agreeing to his appetite.

Thus this damnable Lord Gresham liued the tearme of fiue and twenty yeeres, unsuspected to be author of so many cruell and vnaturall murders, in which time he had destroyed and spoyled an vnknown number of men, women, and children, sheepe, lambes, and goates. And although they had practised all the meanes that men could deuise to take this rauenous beast, yet until the Lord had determined his fall, the inhabitants of Ipswich could not in any wise preuaille. Notwithstanding, they daylye continued their purpose, and dayly sought to entrap him, and for that intent continually maintained great mastyes and Dogges of much strength to hunt and chase the beast wheresoeer they could finde him. At length it pleased God that they shoulde find him in a field, tearing the vitals from a sheep and presently he slipped his girdle from him whereby the shape of a Woolfe cleaune auoided, and he appeared presently in his true shape & likeness. This wrought a wonderfull amazement in their mindes and they came unto him and talking with him they brought him home to his owne house and finding him to be the man indeede, they had him incontinent before the maiestrates to be examined.

Thus being apprehended, he was shortly after put to the racke in the Town of Ipswich, but fearing torture he voluntarily confessed his whole life and made known the villanies which he had committed for the space of XXV yeares.

After he had some space beene imprisoned, the maiestrates found him guilty of these abominable acts and Lord Gresham was iudged first to have his body laide on a wheel, and with red hotte pincers in ten seueral places to haue the flesh puld off from the bones, after that, his legges and arms to be broken with a wooden axe or hatchet, afterwards his head strook from his body, then to haue his carcase burnde to ashes.

Thus Gentle Reeder haue I set down the true discourse of this wicked man Lord Gresham, which I desire to be a warning to all Sorcerers and Witches which unlawfully followe their own diuellish imagination to the utter ruine and destruction of their soules eternally. Amen.

I finished reading and handed the scroll back to Holmes.

"Fascinating. So Lady Gresham lied about the legend?"

"Indeed she did."

"Then how did the other descendants die? Did she also lie about that?"

"Well, that is open to verification, though for my own part I believe that they probably murdered each other, rather in the manner that the present Lord Gresham killed his brother. What I do know is that Lord Gresham killed his brother for a very good reason."

"Why are you so certain of that?"

"An examination of the location of the murder provided me with evidence. I discovered three sets of footprints on the ground. Fortunately the soil was soft, so I was able to distinguish them. There were no dog prints to be seen, Watson. That ruled out the possibility of a canine – or wolf – attack. But what struck me was that in addition to the footprints there were also impressions made by hands, knees, and the toes of shoes. No one who intends to kill his brother does so on his hands and knees. This was evidently the work of a man who believed that he had the power of a lycanthrope. My examination of the dead man's clothes led me to the motive. You will have observed that whilst the shirt and trousers were drenched in blood, the jacket itself was clean."

"Which would indicate that the dead man took off the jacket before he was murdered?"

"Good, Watson! That fact, coupled with the large quantity of ash from a cigar that I discovered lying on a leaf nearby, indicated that the man had stayed there some considerable time before he was attacked. Now why should a man walk out into the country in the middle of the night and then remove his jacket?"

"I really cannot imagine."

"One of the sets of footprints belonged to a woman."

"You mean . . . ."

"That the two had thought their secret safe. Lord Gresham obviously found out and the matter preyed upon his already unbalanced mind. But he took no immediate action, hoping, I would imagine, that the relationship would eventually cease. But when the conscious mind attempts to bury the burden of family guilt, it is invariably the subconscious that suffers. In this case, it took the most unusual form of atavism I have witnessed for a long while. You will have noticed that Lord Gresham had renounced the practice of eating meat?"

I nodded.

"That, Doctor, provided me with my second clue. He had started to believe that he actually *was* a wolf, and was fighting the notion."

"Do you think he will ever recover?"

"I very much doubt it. After all, what sort of a future does he face incarcerated in Broadmoor? No, Watson, the world is full of tragedy, but when it strikes at the heart of the family, there does it strike its most deadly blow."

And, leaning forward in the chair, he reached for the poker and began to stir the dying embers of the fire. For my own part, I turned up the lamp and soon the shadows of the room abated and I was glad of the yellow glow of the coals and the calm light of reason offered by my companion.

The Adventure of the
Obsessive Ghost
by Jayantika Ganguly

It was a few weeks after the affair of the red-headed men that I received an urgent telegram from an old army friend in Scotland, rather dramatically requesting the aid of Mr. Sherlock Holmes. I had known Captain James Morgan for a long time – since we had joined the army together – and I remembered him to be rational man, if a little stubborn, with no inclination for drama or hysterics. Perhaps that was the reason I found myself in Baker Street within a few hours of receiving Morgan's message.

Holmes was at home when I arrived, looking rather dull-eyed and bored. Mrs. Hudson had greeted me with a relieved smile and, before sending me upstairs, uttered a warning that the detective had been unusually quiet and lax for several days.

Holmes brightened visibly when he saw me. "You have a case for me," he said without preamble.

"And it is good to see you, too, Holmes," I replied mildly, handing him the telegram. I had known of his methods long enough not to be surprised that he knew why I was visiting him.

He chuckled at my sarcasm. "Ah, my dear Watson," he murmured absently, opening the telegram. "I really have missed you."

I ignored the pang of sentiment that his words caused.

The telegram read thus:

> *Watson old friend – for heaven's sake bring your detective Holmes – Estate haunted – In grave danger – Will die in a week unless you save me.*
>
> *Morgan*

"Morgan is . . . ." I began, only to be interrupted by Holmes.

"I presume this is the same Captain Morgan you spoke of a few years ago, when you were planning to invest in that South African scam?" he asked.

With slight irritation at the reminder, I nodded. It was thanks to Holmes that neither Morgan nor I ended up investing our hard-earned pounds in that particular mine. Though they had never met, Morgan had been very impressed with Holmes at the time. Since Holmes's fame had only grown since then, I was certain Morgan's admiration for my friend would only have increased further.

Holmes, on the other hand, thought of Morgan and myself as gullible ex-army men who naively fell prey to the lure of easy money by clever salesmen. Hence my annoyance.

"It appears Captain Morgan is terrified," Holmes remarked. "What do you think, Watson?"

I nodded. "Morgan is not prone to flights of fancy, and he most certainly does not believe in the supernatural. It is rather uncharacteristic of him to write something like this."

"I see," Holmes said. He tossed the telegram at me.

"Holmes!" I exclaimed, shocked at his nonchalance. "Won't you help my friend?"

"How can 'your detective Holmes' refuse you, my dear Watson?" Holmes retorted, a mischievous glint in his grey eyes that would please Mrs. Hudson for sure. "Shall we pay a visit to the Scottish Highlands?"

I couldn't help my smile.

After a long train journey, with Holmes sleeping through most of it, we found ourselves at St. Enoch Station. I had sent a telegram to Morgan before we left London, so I wasn't particularly surprised to find him waiting for us.

"I have reserved rooms for us at the station hotel," he told us after we exchanged greetings. "It is quite a ways back to the estate."

Morgan looked rather pale and wan, quite contrary to the large, florid man I remembered. I didn't remark on the change. He was clearly in turmoil.

The three of us made our way to the grand St. Enoch Railway Station Hotel, which was more luxurious than I imagined.

"Mycroft recommends their steak-and-kidney pie," Holmes remarked as we walked past the restaurant. At my surprised expression, Holmes chuckled and said, "No, Watson, he has never visited the place. However, he knows everything, as usual."

Morgan glanced at me enquiringly.

"His brother," I told him. "Works for the British government."

"Oh!" Morgan said. "I didn't know you had a brother, Mr. Holmes! Is he as clever as you?"

Holmes chuckled and replied, "Mycroft is much cleverer than I."

Morgan's eyes went comically wide. "Impossible!" he cried. "Watson swears that you are the cleverest man that he has ever known!"

369

Holmes laughed heartily and turned to me. "Is that so? That must have been before you met Mycroft."

Holmes was certainly in good spirits, I thought to myself, as I watched him interact with Morgan. He could be extremely charming when he wanted to be, and it seemed he had decided to be nice to Morgan. Perhaps Holmes felt that Morgan would be unable to relay a coherent story about his troubles until his mind was at ease. Sure enough, by the time the three of us sat down for a meal (steak-and-kidney pie, naturally), a little colour had returned to Morgan's cheeks, and his dark eyes looked less haunted.

The pie really was excellent, and the liquor even more so. After our hearty meal, we sat down with tumblers of an excellent whisky in our hands and Holmes finally asked Morgan about the matter.

Colour leeched from Morgan's face again, but he smiled bravely. "Watson must have told you, Mr. Holmes, that I am an average fellow with very little imagination. I absolutely do not believe in ghosts. However, I am at my wits' end, and I can find no other explanation for what has been happening at the estate for the last few weeks!"

Holmes pressed his fingertips together and leaned forward, his raptor-like gaze sharp and focused. "I have yet to meet a ghost," he said quietly, his voice deep and reassuring.

Morgan seemed a little relieved. "I will start from the beginning. Several years ago, I returned to my family estate after serving in the army. My father had already passed away by then, and my eldest brother had been looking after the estate – we run a modest brewery. Our production is not very big, but our Highland whisky is considered one of the best in the region," he said proudly.

Holmes smiled slightly, raising his glass in a salute. "Indeed," he said. "This is remarkable."

Morgan grinned, reminding me of the boyish charm he'd exuded when we were fresh recruits in the army quite a few years ago. He had been even more popular with the ladies than I, and had broken many a tender heart when he had returned home to marry his childhood sweetheart.

"I see that Watson really wasn't exaggerating your talents," Morgan said. "How did you know?"

Holmes's eyes gleamed. "I have my methods."

Morgan laughed. "I shall not pry into your trade secrets, then," he said jovially. He took a sip of his whisky and his expression turned serious. "I have five siblings, Mr. Holmes. My mother passed away when I was five, and my father never remarried. We had an aunt – my father's widowed sister – who brought us up. She died just a few months before

370

Father, while I was still serving overseas. As I said, my eldest brother looked after the estate until I returned, and since then, I have been helping him. My second brother lives in India, and has made it clear that he has no intention of ever returning to Britain. I am the third child. My younger sisters, both twins, are both married. One lives in South Africa with her husband, who works in a solicitor firm there, and the other, Jane, the youngest of the children, is married, and she and her husband own another brewery in the region, about twenty miles from ours. Jane and my wife, Maria, used to go to school together, actually, and that is how I met my wife." He smiled fondly. "We are expecting our first child soon."

"Congratulations, my friend," I said heartily. Holmes echoed the sentiment.

Morgan turned bashful for a moment before returning to his tale. "There are innumerable tales of ghosts and monsters and supernatural beings in these Highlands. We've never taken any of them seriously. When we were young, our aunt used to tell us about a thousand-year-old female ghost that haunted our estate and tried to kill young men when their wives were about to give birth, because her own husband abandoned her when she was with child, and she was so heartbroken that she burnt herself and her unborn child to death. My father never believed in such a superstition, and refused to budge when my aunt tried to send him away from the house for his own safety. However, my mother was a tad gullible, and she was so afraid of the ghost that she fell ill, so that my father took her to her parents' house and stayed there with her until we were born.

"All five of us were born at our maternal grandparents' estate. My eldest brother – Thomas – never married, and the rest of my siblings don't live at the estate anymore, so we all had forgotten about the tale. Now, however, strange things are taking place there, and Thomas insists that I travel to London and stay there until Maria has delivered the baby safely. But you see, Maria is delicate and it has been a difficult pregnancy for her. I absolutely can't leave her alone, and we definitely can't make her travel. Our doctor says even a slightly bumpy ride to Jane and Edward's place might be dangerous. Jane visits us often, and it was she who originally remembered Auntie Flora's tale and gave Thomas the idea. My Maria is generally level-headed, but recent events have taken a toll on her as well."

"How long since these strange occurrences began?" I asked.

"Exactly six weeks ago," Morgan replied. "I remember the day because Jane and Edward had visited us that day, and she suddenly spoke of this old curse and haunting. We all had a good laugh and Jane suggested jokingly that I move out for a while. However, when I went outside to see them off, a huge chunk of wood came flying at my head out of nowhere. I have fast reflexes thanks to my army training, so I had a narrow escape. It was then that I spotted a figure in the distance. It was white and floating at least ten feet above the ground! And then it burst into fire with a bang! Jane and Edward saw it, too. They refused to leave that night and escorted me back to the house. I wanted to go out and investigate, but everyone else refused to let me go out in the dark. We went to look the next morning, but there was nothing at the spot where we had seen the floating figure. Since then, every few days, unusual accidents have been happening around me. I have luckily escaped every time, and Maria is terrified." He gave us a wan smile and his hands shook slightly. "And so am I. The day I sent that telegram to you, I was nearly crushed to death by a falling boulder while out walking the dogs . . . and I saw that floating figure again – and it burst into flames again! In fact, it is thanks to the dogs that I have made it unscathed this far."

"Do all the incidents involve a projectile aimed at you?" Holmes asked.

"Mostly," Morgan replied, shaking his head. "But there have been other incidents as well. I have had six narrow escapes from heavy objects falling on me – a chunk of wood and boulder of which I spoke. A shelf in the library, a broken branch, an old statue in the garden, and an oak barrel that I managed to avoid, but I still ended up being drenched in half-made liquor – such a waste. Thomas had his hunting gun misfire and almost shot me accidentally. He now refuses to touch a gun again until the baby has been safely born. He is an excellent hunter, Mr. Holmes, so you can imagine how scared that he is to hang up his weapon! Once, I slipped and fell down the stairs to the cellar. I would have thought someone dropped a bit of oil on the stairs by mistake, but I saw that floating figure and its fire as I fell. Thankfully, Thomas had rolled up one of the carpets that needed cleaning and stored it by the staircase. I grabbed the carpet and managed to escape with a couple of minor bruises. Then there was the time when Jane's carriage horses suddenly went wild and nearly ran over me. The dogs saved me that time – we have three large wolfhounds, and each of them can easily push a man over. One of them pushed me over and the other two growled menacingly at the horses until they ran off. We found the horses wandering in the woods a few hours later, and they were back to normal by then, nuzzling my palm and demanding sugar cubes!"

"And this floating figure appeared each time?" I asked.

"Yes," Morgan said. "All of us have seen it by now, even some of the servants. One of our maids was telling Maria about a druid or a shaman the other day that would grant me protection from this evil ghost before it ended up killing me."

"It must be a rather incompetent ghost that has failed to kill you despite so many attempts," Holmes said dryly.

Morgan chuckled nervously. "Or I have the devil's own luck."

Holmes tapped his chin thoughtfully. "The figure bursts into fire every time, does it?"

"Yes," Morgan says. "And it makes a loud noise – similar to a gunshot, but different."

"I see," Holmes said. "Does it burn with a slightly reddish flame?"

Morgan blinked. "How did you know?"

Holmes smiled enigmatically.

"You said you would die in a week in your telegram," I said to Morgan. "Did something specific happen?"

Morgan nodded. "After escaping the falling boulder, I climbed up to investigate as soon as the floating figure disappeared. And there, on the ground, written in bright red, were the words '*You have one week to live*'. I returned to the house immediately and told Thomas, but it was all clean by the time we came back. I did, however, save a sample, because I had been intending to write to Watson by then."

Morgan handed a little vial to Holmes, who opened it gingerly and sniffed at it. "Blood," he said.

"That is pretty much all I had to say, Mr. Holmes," Morgan said.

Holmes leaned back in his seat and drummed his fingers on the armrest. "I have a few questions, if you do not mind."

Morgan nodded eagerly. "Of course."

"Has this ghost ever killed anyone in the past?"

Morgan and I both gave a start, and I glanced at Holmes, wondering if he was jesting. But he appeared perfectly serious.

Morgan rubbed his chin thoughtfully. "From what Jane remembered of Aunt Flora's tale the other day, two of our ancestors actually did die by her hand. You see, the girl was a servant, and the man who heartlessly abandoned her was a squire from our family."

"Were they burnt to death?"

"Er, I'm afraid I don't know, Mr. Holmes. Perhaps Jane could tell you the whole story tomorrow. Thomas and I don't really remember too well."

"And how many people are aware that you have called in a detective from London?"

"Just the family. Maria was nearly hysterical worrying over me, and Thomas and Jane were yet again trying to convince me to leave, so I told them that my friend was friends with Britain's greatest detective, and I had already invited you here. They didn't really believe me until Watson's telegram arrived." Morgan chuckled. "After that, everyone was excited. It was Thomas who suggested that I reserve rooms at this hotel and stay over, since the two of you would be exhausted after your long train journey."

"That was kind of your brother," I said.

Morgan smiled brightly, his affection for his brother apparent. "Thomas is more or less the one who brought us up. Father was always busy, and after Mother passed away, he was hardly around. Aunt Flora looked after us, but Thomas took on the paternal role. He is twelve years my senior. He was the only child for nearly a decade before the rest of us came along. There is only a year-and-a-half between me and my second brother, and the girls are twins, three years my junior."

"I see," Holmes said, standing up. "Well then, Watson, I can tell that you wish to catch up with your friend, so I shall retire to my room and let the two of you reminisce about the old days."

I blinked at Holmes, surprised, only to be met by sharp grey eyes and a silent warning. I understood that he suspected something might happen tonight. His instincts were usually correct, so I nodded. Holmes bade us a good night and retired.

"He's nicer and kinder than I would have thought," Morgan said to me after Holmes disappeared from our sight.

"He doesn't like being called 'nice and kind'," I grumbled. "He considers sentiment to be a grit in the lens. A fly in the ointment."

Morgan laughed heartily. We remained in the lounge for another hour or so, speaking of our army days and what our acquaintances from then were doing now. Morgan, it seemed, was in touch with quite a few. It wasn't particularly surprising, as he had always been a gregarious sort of fellow.

It was late when we finally stood and made our way upstairs. As we passed by Holmes's room – it was a corridor away from my room – we heard a loud crash. Alarmed, we tried the door and found it unlocked. We rushed in to see a broken window and Holmes picking up something from the carpeted floor.

"Ah, Watson, excellent timing," Holmes said.

And then Morgan whimpered beside me, and I looked out of the window to see a whitish figure in the distance that couldn't possibly be human. It floated amidst the high branches of tall trees.

I sucked in a sharp breath. "Holmes!" I hissed. "Look!"

Holmes straightened and glanced outside. "Ah, yes, the ghost. I saw it, Watson. There is no need to fret."

I pulled out my gun immediately and started to take aim at the white figure, but Holmes lay a gentle hand upon my wrist. "No need to waste a bullet," he said.

As if on cue, there was a noise – not very loud, perhaps due to the distance – and the ghost burst into reddish flames and then disappeared quickly without a trace.

I stared at Holmes in shock, and his lips curled up at the edges. He turned to Morgan, who was white as a sheet. "Captain," he said gently. "I assure you that you will not lose your life to a supernatural being."

"But . . . that . . . ." Morgan stuttered.

Holmes opened his palm to show us a stone. There was a note tied to it. He quickly unrolled it.

Beware! Do not return home if you wish to live.

Holmes chuckled. "Apparently your ghost has confused which of us is in which room," he remarked, "mistaking mine for yours, Captain." He studied the note more closely. "Most certainly written by a male hand. Yet your ghost is supposedly female, yes?"

Morgan nodded weakly. "How do you know? About the writing?"

"He has written monographs on handwriting analysis," I told Morgan before Holmes could reply. "If he says it is a male hand, then it has to be."

Morgan brightened a little.

I glanced at Holmes. He seemed excited. Clearly, he had deduced something that we didn't know.

"Shall we head to your estate tomorrow?" I asked.

Morgan nodded, his colour improving. "Certainly."

"Excellent," Holmes said, rubbing his hands. "Let us depart early in the morning."

Holmes seemed to have taken a stroll through the woods by the time Morgan and I were ready and went downstairs for breakfast. The detective was in a good mood, so I surmised that his early morning investigation had yielded some results. He greeted us cheerfully as we took our seats.

We chatted pleasantly for some time.

"Do any of your siblings have children?" I asked Morgan.

He shook his head. "Mine will be the first. We have a strange custom in the family, you know. The oldest son of each generation is supposed to inherit everything, even if his father is not the previous owner. That is how my grandfather got the place. He was the son of the fourth daughter, but still the eldest amongst his generation. My father was also the oldest, and he had only one sister and some younger cousins. Thomas is the first-born amongst us, and we have no more paternal cousins left. If Maria and I have a son, he will be the next owner . . . but I hope to convince Thomas to change this custom. I don't want my child to be tied to the estate. He should be free to do as he pleases. Thomas is very talented, you know. He could have been a great chemist, if he hadn't been bogged down by his responsibilities."

"Are your siblings aware?" Holmes asked.

"Not yet," Morgan replied. "I intended to tell them before the baby was born, but all this ghost business really made a mess. Perhaps it is better this way. If I have a daughter, there will be no problem for a while."

We finished breakfast in reasonable spirits, with Morgan telling us more about his estate in general. Then he led us to a large, comfortable-looking carriage and muttered, "I am afraid it will a few hours before we reach our destination."

I assured him that we didn't mind and boarded the carriage. It was a long, slightly bumpy ride, and Morgan continued to regale us with tales from his estate. Finally, we arrived.

I was flabbergasted at the sight that greeted me when I stepped out of the carriage. I had vaguely known that Morgan came from an affluent background, but I had no idea of the scale. The magnificent estate that stood before us would be worthy of a peer of the realm.

Morgan appeared embarrassed at my shock. "Watson, old man, don't look like that. I did tell you my family was well-to-do, didn't I?"

I shook my head and chuckled. "Do you have a title as well?" I asked.

Morgan rubbed the back of his neck, flushing. "Not really. I mean, Thomas does – but he doesn't use it. It isn't really a grand title or anything . . . ."

"A feudal baron, then?" Holmes asked.

"Indeed," came another voice, rich and warm – similar to Morgan's but deeper. It was accompanied by the arrival of a tall gentleman who bore a striking resemblance to Morgan.

"Sir Thomas, I presume?" Holmes asked politely, greeting him.

Morgan quickly introduced us to his brother, and the two of them led us into the house to meet Maria, Morgan's wife, as well as sister Jane and her husband Edward McKinney.

"So you are the famous Mr. Sherlock Holmes," Jane sneered, eyeing Holmes disdainfully. "You don't look like much."

"Jane!" Morgan cried, outraged. He turned to Holmes, clearly intending to apologise, but Holmes waved a casual hand and flashed Jane a charming smile.

The woman flushed slightly and looked away.

"Mr. Holmes is far cleverer than any of us," Morgan said sternly. "Jane, Mr. Holmes wanted to know if our two ancestors who were killed by this ghost were burnt to death?"

Jane frowned. "No," she said. "Why would they be? It was the ghost girl that burnt herself to death. I think one died of a knife wound and one fell down and broke his neck."

376

"Those could have been accidents," I muttered. "How did you know that they were supposedly killed by the ghost?"

"Aunt Flora said so," she replied, frowning at me.

"Are there no records?" I persisted.

"Of course not," Jane shot back, looking at me as if I were an idiot.

"Watson is right," Morgan said. "There should be records. There will at least be a footnote about the ghost and the people she killed, and how they knew that it was her and not some random accident."

"Well," Jane snapped, "your guests are welcome to scour the library, then,"

"No need," Holmes said. "There is no ghost. Captain Morgan's troubles were very much man-made."

"You don't know anything!" Jane snapped and glared at her brother. "There would be no need for any of this nonsense, James, if you simply went to London for a while!"

"I am not leaving my Maria alone here during the birth!" Morgan protested. "And you know Dr. Rhodes said she can't travel at all!" He took his wife's hand and sat down next to her. "Don't worry, darling. Mr. Holmes and Watson will find the truth. And I am not that easy to kill!" He frowned at his sister. "Besides, how do you know the ghost won't follow me to London? It followed me to St. Enoch!"

His family gasped and stared at him in horror. He told what had happened the previous night.

Maria turned to Holmes and pleaded, "Do you really think that James will be safe?"

Holmes smiled gently at her. "Rest assured, Mrs. Morgan. The ghost shall be exorcised today."

"How?" Edward McKinney demanded, speaking up for the first time.

"Trade secret," Holmes said cheekily, borrowing Morgan's words from the previous evening. "Have any of you heard of J.G. Ingram?"

"The balloon-maker, Holmes? What has he . . . ?" I asked, but stopped midway at the strange expressions of Morgan's siblings.

"It is a simple trick, Watson," Holmes continued. "A rubber balloon filled with hydrogen will float in the air, and will explode in a burst of reddish flames if lit. That is the ghost here."

"But . . . but what about the attempts to kill Morgan?" I asked.

"They were not attempts to kill. They were meant to scare him away and steal his child," Holmes said.

"What? Why?" Morgan demanded, jumping up from his seat in anger. "Tell me who it is, Mr. Holmes! I shall wring his neck!"

"This is not the work of a single person, Captain Morgan," Holmes replied.

Everyone stared at Holmes with varying degrees of confusion.

Holmes turned to the other couple in the room. "Oh, Mr. and Mrs. McKinney, I believe congratulations are in order."

The couple flushed.

"How the deuce did you know? We haven't told anyone yet!" Edward cried.

"Trade secret," Holmes repeated.

Morgan and his brother stared at their youngest sister in shock for a moment before hugs and good wishes were exchanged amongst the family members.

When the family finally quieted down, Holmes turned to Maria. "Mrs. Morgan," he asked quietly. "Do you, too, wish for a daughter so that your child will not have to inherit this estate and be bound to it?"

Maria Morgan gasped in shock. "James, you told him?" she asked her husband.

Sir Thomas Morgan, on the other hand, had gone rather pale. So had Jane and Edward McKinney.

"James, what is the meaning of this?" Thomas demanded. "You don't want your child to inherit our estate?"

Morgan smiled sheepishly. "Sorry, Thomas. I wanted to wait until the baby was born to tell you. It is true. I want my child to be free to choose what he or she wants to do. I don't want anyone else to have to make the sacrifices you were forced to . . . Not that I'm not grateful for everything you have done for us, but . . . ." He hesitated for a moment, and then lifted his chin and spoke firmly. "I would rather that the estate go to someone in the next generation who actually wants to look after it, rather than someone who happened to be born first."

Sir Thomas let out a shuddering breath and buried his face in his hands. "Dear Lord," he murmured. "What have we done?"

"Thomas!" Jane cried. "Don't listen to him! He's going to sell off the estate as soon as he can!"

Morgan frowned. "Why on earth would I sell off the estate?" he asked his sister.

She ignored him.

Morgan turned to Holmes and raised an eyebrow. Holmes shook his head slightly and said loudly, "Sir Thomas, would you prefer to explain the matter to Captain Morgan, or should I?"

Sir Thomas sighed and stood up. "James," he said quietly. "We have wronged you greatly. Mr. Holmes is right, there is no ghost. We set it up – Jane and Edward and myself."

Morgan staggered back. "Why?" he asked hoarsely.

"Because . . . because Jane convinced us that you intended to sell off the estate once your child became the heir."

"And so you wanted to steal my baby?" Morgan asked in an eerily calm voice. "Were you going to kill it?" Behind him, his wife was pale and held trembling arms protectively over her stomach, as if to shield her unborn child.

Sir Thomas blinked, aghast. "Kill it . . . ? What sort of monsters do you think we are? We only wanted you to leave for a while. Then, if the baby was a boy, we would have taken the infant to an orphanage and . . . and told Maria that he was stillborn. Then we would have visited the orphanage in secret and adopted the child back into the family. He wouldn't have been raised by strangers . . . ." He said this as if it were perfectly reasonable.

After a long silence, where Morgan simply stared into the distance, he simply said, "I see." Then he turned to Holmes and bowed. "Mr. Holmes, Watson – thank you very much solving the matter. That will be all."

Holmes nodded silently and turned to leave. I followed after him, still shocked at this turn of events.

"How did you know?" I asked Holmes as soon as we took our seats on the train. Morgan had ordered a servant to return us to St. Enoch Station, after telling us that he would depart from the manor permanently with his wife and child as soon as the doctor permitted them to travel. He, too, like his two other siblings, would seek his fortunes abroad.

"I shall make a ghost balloon and show you sometime," Holmes said lightly. "Your friend wasn't wrong. His brother would have made a first-rate chemist."

"Not that," I grumbled. "How did you know who it was?"

"It was a simple deduction. Every time Morgan was attacked, only two of the three perpetrators were in his company, while the third was managing the ghost – that by itself was suspicious. Then there was a convenient ghost story that fit in a little too perfectly. Also, none of the attempts were fatal, so they clearly didn't wish to injure Morgan seriously or kill him – that show's affection for him, does it not? Besides, if there was a stranger around, wouldn't the animals have made some noise?"

"I see," I muttered. It always sounds so simple when Holmes explains. However, no one but him can perform so perfectly in this particular art.

Several weeks later, Morgan visited us with his wife and his new-born son. They could travel now, and they left for South Africa soon after.

He never returned to Britain again, but he prospered and brought up his son (and his daughter who was born a few years later) just the way he wanted, leaving them free to choose their own path. He used to send us letters sometimes.

Sir Thomas and the McKinneys did not fare too badly, either. Sir Thomas never married. The estate was ultimately inherited by Jane's third son.

Holmes rolled his eyes when, years later, I referred to the matter as an unpleasant episode but with a happy ending, and said, "Perhaps you can write about it and odd 'family drama' to your repertoire of our cases, my dear Watson."

About the Contributors

The following contributors appear in this volume:
The MX Book of New Sherlock Holmes Stories
Part XVI – Whatever Remains . . .
Must Be the Truth (1881-1890)

Kareem Abdul-Jabbar is a huge Holmesian, the National Basketball Association's all-time leading scorer, a Basketball Hall of Fame inductee, and a *New York Times* bestselling author. In 2016, he received the Presidential Medal of Freedom, the USA's highest civilian honor, from former President Barack Obama. Currently he is chairman of the Skyhook Foundation, which "gives kids a shot that can't be blocked", a columnist for *The Guardian* newspaper, and a cultural critic for *The Hollywood Reporter.* He has written a number of books, and is a two-time NAACP aware-winning writer and producer. With Anna Waterhouse, he is the author of *Mycroft Holmes* (2015), *Mycroft and Sherlock* (2018), and *Mycroft and Sherlock: The Empty Birdcage* (2019).

Josh Anderson is twenty-four and lives in Wales, UK. He enjoys running, tennis, video games, and reading, and is currently training to be an English teacher. His favourite Sherlock Holmes author is James Lovegrove. This is his first story.

Brian Belanger is a publisher and editor, but is best known for his freelance illustration and cover design work. His distinctive style can be seen on several MX Publishing covers, including *Silent Meridian* by Elizabeth Crowen, *Sherlock Holmes and the Menacing Melbournian* by Allan Mitchell, *Sherlock Holmes and A Quantity of Debt* by David Marcum, *Welcome to Undershaw* by Luke Benjamen Kuhns, and many more. Brian is the co-founder of Belanger Books LLC, where he illustrates the popular *MacDougall Twins with Sherlock Holmes* young reader series (#1 bestsellers on Amazon.com UK). A prolific creator, he also designs t-shirts, mugs, stickers, and other merchandise on his personal art site: *www.redbubble.com/people/zhahadun.*

Derrick Belanger is an educator and also the author of the #1 bestselling book in its category, *Sherlock Holmes: The Adventure of the Peculiar Provenance*, which was in the top 200 bestselling books on Amazon. He also is the author of *The MacDougall Twins with Sherlock Holmes* books, and he edited the Sir Arthur Conan Doyle horror anthology *A Study in Terror: Sir Arthur Conan Doyle's Revolutionary Stories of Fear and the Supernatural*. Mr. Belanger co-owns the publishing company Belanger Books, which released the Sherlock Holmes anthologies *Beyond Watson, Holmes Away From Home: Adventures from the Great Hiatus* Volumes 1 and 2, *Sherlock Holmes: Before Baker Street*, and *Sherlock Holmes: Adventures in the Realms of H.G. Wells* Volumes I and 2. Derrick resides in Colorado and continues compiling unpublished works by Dr. John H. Watson.

Bob Bishop is the author of over twenty stage plays, musicals, and pantomimes, several written in collaboration with Norfolk composer, Bob McNeil Watson. Many of these theatrical works were first performed by the fringe theatre company of which he was principal director, The Fossick Valley Fumblers, at the Edinburgh Festival Fringe between 1982 and 2000. Amongst these works were four Sherlock Holmes plays, inspired by the playwright's lifelong affection for the works of Sir Arthur Conan Doyle. Bob's other works include the comic novel, *A Tickle Amongst the Cornstalks*, an anthology of short stories,

Shadows on the Blind, and a number of Sherlock Holmes pastiche novellas. He currently lives with his wife and three poodles in North Norfolk.

Andrew Bryant was born in Bridgend, Wales, and now lives in Burlington, Ontario, Canada. His previous publications include *Prism International, Existere, On Spec, The Dalhousie Review*, and second place in the 2015 *Toronto Star* short story contest. His first Holmes story, "The Shackled Man", was published in *The MX Book of New Sherlock Holmes Stories – Part XIII*. The story in this collection, "The Blue Lady of Dunraven", is situated at Dunraven Castle, a few miles from where he was born, and he remembers walking the house and grounds as a child. Tragically, the Castle was demolished in 1963, robbing the nation of a fascinating and mysterious historic landmark. Hopefully, The Blue Lady wanders the ruins still.

Sir Arthur Conan Doyle (1859-1930) *Holmes Chronicler Emeritus.* If not for him, this anthology would not exist. Author, physician, patriot, sportsman, spiritualist, husband and father, and advocate for the oppressed. He is remembered and honored for the purposes of this collection by being the man who introduced Sherlock Holmes to the world. Through fifty-six Holmes short stories, four novels, and additional Apocryphal entries, Doyle revolutionized mystery stories and also greatly influenced and improved police forensic methods and techniques for the betterment of all. *Steel True Blade Straight.*

Steve Emecz's main field is technology, in which he has been working for more than twenty years. Following multiple senior roles at Xerox, where he grew their European eCommerce from $6m to $200m. Steve worked for eCommerce provider Venda, mobile commerce platform Powa, collectAI in Hamburg (Artificial Intelligence) and is now back in London with CloudTrade. Steve is a regular trade show speaker on the subject of eCommerce, and his tech career has taken him to more than fifty countries – so he's no stranger to planes and airports. He wrote two mystery novels (one a bestseller) in the 1990's, and a screenplay in 2001. Shortly after, he set up MX Publishing, specialising in NLP books. In 2008, MX published its first Sherlock Holmes book (Alistair Duncan's wonderful *Eliminate the Impossible*), and MX has gone on to become the largest specialist Holmes publisher in the world. MX is a social enterprise and supports two main causes. The first is Happy Life Children's Home, a baby rescue project in Nairobi, Kenya, where he and his wife, Sharon, spend every Christmas at the rescue centre in Kasarani. In 2014, they wrote a short book about the project, *The Happy Life Story*, with a second edition in 2017. The second is the Stepping Stones School, of which Steve is a patron. Stepping Stones is located at Undershaw, Sir Arthur Conan Doyle's former home.

David Friend lives in Wales, Great Britain, where he divides his time between watching old detective films and thinking about old detective films. Now thirty, he's been scribbling out stories for twenty years and hopes, some day, to write something half-decent. Most of what he pens is set in an old-timey world of non-stop adventure with debonair sleuths, kick-ass damsels, criminal masterminds, and narrow escapes, and he wishes he could live there.

Mark A. Gagen BSI is co-founder of Wessex Press, sponsor of the popular *From Gillette to Brett* conferences, and publisher of *The Sherlock Holmes Reference Library* and many other fine Sherlockian titles. A life-long Holmes enthusiast, he is a member of *The Baker Street Irregulars* and *The Illustrious Clients of Indianapolis*. A graphic artist by profession, his work is often seen on the covers of *The Baker Street Journal* and various BSI books.

Tim Gambrell lives in Exeter, Devon, with his wife, two young sons, two cats, and seven chickens. He contributed "The Yellow Star of Cairo" to *Part XIII* of *The MX Book of New Sherlock Holmes Stories*, and has a story in the forthcoming collection *The Early Adventures of Sherlock Holmes* from Belanger Books. Outside of The World of Holmes, Tim has written extensively for Doctor Who spin-off ranges. He has recently had two linked novels published by Candy Jar Books: *Lethbridge-Stewart: The Laughing Gnome – Lucy Wilson & The Bledoe Cadets*, and *The Lucy Wilson Mysteries: The Brigadier and The Bledoe Cadets* (both Summer 2019). He also has a novella, *The Way of The Bry'hunee*, for the Erimem range from Thebes Publishing, which is due out in late 2019. Tim's short fiction includes stories *in Lethbridge-Stewart: The HAVOC Files* 3 (Candy Jar, 2017), *Bernice Summerfield: True Stories* (Big Finish, 2017), and *Relics . . . An Anthology* (Red Ted Books, 2018). Further short fiction will feature in the forthcoming collections *Lethbridge-Stewart: The HAVOC Files – The Laughing Gnome*, and *Lethbridge-Stewart: The HAVOC Files – Loose Ends* (both due later in 2019).

Jayantika Ganguly BSI is the General Secretary and Editor of the *Sherlock Holmes Society of India*, a member of the *Sherlock Holmes Society of London*, and the *Czech Sherlock Holmes Society*. She is the author of *The Holmes Sutra* (MX 2014). She is a corporate lawyer working with one of the Big Six law firms.

John Atkinson Grimshaw (1836-1893) was born in Leeds, England. His amazing paintings, usually featuring twilight or night scenes illuminated by gas-lamps or moonlight, are easily recognizable, and are often used on the covers of books about The Great Detective to set the mood, as shadowy figures move in the distance through misty mysterious settings and over rain-slicked streets.

Arthur Hall, who also has stories in Parts XVII and XVIII, was born in Aston, Birmingham, UK, in 1944. His interest in writing began during his schooldays and served as a growing ambition to become an author. Years later, his first novel *Sole Contact* was an espionage story about an ultra-secret government department known as "Sector Three" and has been followed, to date, by four sequels. The sixth in the series, *The Suicide Chase*, is currently in the course of preparation. Other works include five "rediscovered" cases from the files of Sherlock Holmes, two collections of bizarre short stories, and two novels about an adventurer called "Bernard Kramer", as well as several contributions to the ongoing anthology, *The MX Book of New Sherlock Holmes Stories*. His only ambition, apart from being published more widely, is to attend the premier of a film based on one of his novels, ideally at The Odeon, Leicester Square. He lives in the West Midlands, United Kingdom, where he often walks other people's dogs as he attempts to formulate new plots. His work can be seen at *arthurhallsbooksite.blogspot.com*, and the author can be contacted at *arthurhall7777@aol.co.uk*

Roger Johnson BSI, ASH is a retired librarian, now working as a volunteer assistant at the Essex Police Museum. In his spare time, he is commissioning editor of *The Sherlock Holmes Journal*, an occasional lecturer, and a frequent contributor to The Writings About the Writings. His sole work of Holmesian pastiche was published in 1997 in Mike Ashley's anthology *The Mammoth Book of New Sherlock Holmes Adventures*, and he has the greatest respect for the many authors who have contributed new tales to the present mighty trilogy. Like his wife, Jean Upton, he is a member of both *The Baker Street Irregulars* and *The Adventuresses of Sherlock Holmes*.

Kelvin I. Jones, who also has a story in Part XVIII, is the author of six books about Sherlock Holmes and the definitive biography of Conan Doyle as a spiritualist, *Conan Doyle and The Spirits*. A member of *The Sherlock Holmes Society of London*, he has published numerous short occult and ghost stories in British anthologies over the last thirty years. His work has appeared on BBC Radio, and in 1984 he won the Mason Hall Literary Award for his poem cycle about the survivors of Hiroshima and Nagasaki, recently reprinted as "Omega". (Oakmagic Publications) A one-time teacher of creative writing at the University of East Anglia, he is also the author of four crime novels featuring his ex-Met sleuth John Bottrell, who first appeared in *Stone Dead*. He has over fifty titles on Kindle, and is also the author of several novellas and short story collections featuring a Norwich-based detective, DCI Ketch, an intrepid sleuth who investigates East Anglian murder cases. He also published a series of short stories about an Edwardian psychic detective, Dr. John Carter (*Carter's Occult Casebook*). Ramsey Campbell, the British horror writer, and Francis King, the renowned novelist, have both compared his supernatural stories to those of M. R. James. He has also published children's fiction, namely *Odin's Eye*, and, in collaboration with his wife Debbie, *The Dark Entry*. Since 1995, he has been the proprietor of Oakmagic Publications, publishers of British folklore and of his fiction titles. He lives in Norfolk. (See *www.oakmagicpublications.co.uk*)

David Marcum, who also has stories in Parts XVII and XVIII, plays *The Game* with deadly seriousness. He first discovered Sherlock Holmes in 1975 at the age of ten, and since that time, he has collected, read, and chronologicized literally thousands of traditional Holmes pastiches in the form of novels, short stories, radio and television episodes, movies and scripts, comics, fan-fiction, and unpublished manuscripts. He is the author of over fifty Sherlockian pastiches, some published in anthologies and others collected in his own books, *The Papers of Sherlock Holmes*, *Sherlock Holmes and A Quantity of Debt*, and *Sherlock Holmes – Tangled Skeins*. He has edited nearly fifty books, including several dozen traditional Sherlockian anthologies, including the ongoing series *The MX Book of New Sherlock Holmes Stories*, which he created in 2015. This collection is now up to 18 volumes, with several more in preparation. He was responsible for bringing back August Derleth's Solar Pons for a new generation, first with his collection of authorized Pons stories, *The Papers of Solar Pons*, and then by editing the reissued authorized versions of the original Pons books. He is now doing the same for the adventures of Dr. Thorndyke. He has contributed numerous essays to various publications, and is a member of a number of Sherlockian groups and Scions. He is a licensed Civil Engineer, living in Tennessee with his wife and son. His irregular Sherlockian blog, *A Seventeen Step Program*, addresses various topics related to his favorite book friends (as his son used to call them when he was small), and can be found at *http://17stepprogram.blogspot.com/* Since the age of nineteen, he has worn a deerstalker as his regular-and-only hat from autumn to spring, and often summer as well. In 2013, he and his deerstalker were finally able make his first trip-of-a-lifetime Holmes Pilgrimage to England, with return Pilgrimages in 2015 and 2016, where you may have spotted him. If you ever run into him and his deerstalker out and about, feel free to say hello!

Mark Mower is a member of the *Crime Writers' Association, The Sherlock Holmes Society of London* and *The Solar Pons Society of London*. He writes true crime stories and fictional mysteries. His volumes of Holmes pastiches include *A Farewell to Baker Street, Sherlock Holmes: The Baker Street Case-Files*, and *Sherlock Holmes: The Baker Street Legacy* (all with MX Publishing) and, to date, he has contributed many stories to the ongoing series *The MX Book of New Sherlock Holmes Stories*. He has also had stories in two anthologies by Belanger Books: *Holmes Away From Home: Adventures from the Great*

386

Hiatus – Volume II – 1893-1894 (2016) and *Sherlock Holmes: Before Baker Street* (2017). More are bound to follow. Mark's non-fiction works include *Bloody British History: Norwich* (The History Press, 2014), *Suffolk Murders* (The History Press, 2011) and *Zeppelin Over Suffolk* (Pen & Sword Books, 2008).

Josh Pachter (1951-   ) is a writer, editor, and translator. His short fiction has appeared in *Ellery Queen Mystery Magazine, Alfred Hitchcock Mystery Magazine,* and many other periodicals, anthologies, and year's-best collections. *The Tree of Life* (Wildside Press, 2015) collected all ten of his Mahboob Chaudri stories. He edited *The Man Who Read Mysteries: The Short Fiction of William Brittain* (Crippen & Landru, 2018) and *The Misadventures of Nero Wolfe* (Mysterious Press, 2020), and co-edited *The Misadventures of Ellery Queen* (Wildside, 2018) and *Amsterdam Noir* (Akashic, 2019). His translations of stories by Dutch and Belgian authors appear regularly in *Ellery Queen Mystery Magazine's* "Passport to Crime" Department. In his day job, he teaches interpersonal communication and film history at Northern Virginia Community College's Loudoun Campus.

Sidney Paget (1860-1908), a few of whose illustrations are used within this anthology, was born in London, and like his two older brothers, became a famed illustrator and painter. He completed over three-hundred-and-fifty drawings for the Sherlock Holmes stories that were first published in *The Strand* magazine, defining Holmes's image forever after in the public mind.

Tracy J. Revels, who also has stories in Parts XVII and XVIII, has been a Sherlockian from the age of eleven. She is a professor of history at Wofford College in Spartanburg, South Carolina. She is a member of *The Survivors of the Gloria Scott* and *The Studious Scarlets Society,* and is a past recipient of the Beacon Society Award. Almost every semester, she teaches a class that covers The Canon, either to college students or to senior citizens. She is also the author of three supernatural Sherlockian pastiches with MX (*Shadowfall, Shadowblood,* and *Shadowwraith*), and a regular contributor to her scion's newsletter. She also has some notoriety as an author of very silly skits: For proof, see "The Adventure of the Adversarial Adventuress" and "Occupy Baker Street" on YouTube. When not studying Sherlock, she can be found researching the history of her native state, and has written books on Florida in the Civil War and on the development of Florida's tourism industry.

Brenda Seabrooke's stories have been published in sixteen reviews, journals, and anthologies. She has received grants from the National Endowment for the Arts and Emerson College's Robbie Macauley Award. She is the author of twenty-three books for young readers including *Scones and Bones on Baker Street: Sherlock's (maybe!) Dog and the Dirt Dilemma,* and *The Rascal in the Castle: Sherlock's (possible!) Dog and the Queen's Revenge.* Brenda states: "It was fun to write from Dr. Watson's point of view and not have to worry about fleas, smelly pits, ralphing, or scratching at inopportune times."

Shane Simmons is the author of the occult detective novels *Necropolis* and *Epitaph,* and the crime collection *Raw and Other Stories.* An award-winning screenwriter and graphic novelist, his work has appeared in international film festivals, museums, and lectures about design and structure. He was born in Lachine, a suburb of Montreal best known for being massacred in 1689 and having a joke name. Visit Shane's homepage at *eyestrainproductions.com* for more.

Mark Sohn was born in Brighton, England in 1967. After a hectic life and many dubious and varied careers, he settled down in Sussex with his wife, Angie. His first novel, *Sherlock Holmes and the Whitechapel Murders* was published in 2017. His second, *The Absentee Detective* is out now. Both are available from Amazon.com.
https://sherlockholmesof221b.blogspot.co.uk/
https://volcanocat.blogspot.co.uk/

Kevin P. Thornton has experienced a Taliban rocket attack in Kabul and a terrorist bombing in Johannesburg. He lives in Fort McMurray, Alberta, the town that burnt down in 2016. He has been shortlisted for the *Crime Writers of Canada* Unhanged writing award six times. He's never won. He was also a finalist for best short story in 2014 – the year Margaret Atwood entered. We're not saying he has luck issues, but don't bet on his stock tips. Born in Kenya, Kevin was a child in New Zealand, a student and soldier in Africa, a military contractor in Afghanistan, a forklift driver in Ontario, and an oilfield worker in North Western Canada. He writes poems that start out just fine, but turn ruder and cruder over time. From limerick to doggerel, they earn less than bugger-all, even though they all manage to rhyme. He also likes writing about Sherlock Holmes and dislikes writing about himself in the third person.

I.A. Watson is a novelist and jobbing writer from Yorkshire who cut his teeth on writing Sherlock Holmes stories and has even won an award for one. His works include *Holmes and Houdini*, *Labours of Hercules*, *St. George and the Dragon* Volumes 1 and 2, and *Women of Myth*, and the non-fiction essay book *Where Stories Dwell*. He pens short detective stories as a means of avoiding writing things that pay better. A full list of his sixty-plus published works appears at:
http://www.chillwater.org.uk/writing/iawatsonhome.htm

388

The MX Book of New Sherlock Holmes Stories
Whatever Remains . . .
Must Be the Truth
Part XVII – (1891-1898)
and
Part XVIII – (1899-1925)

Hugh Ashton was born in the U.K., and moved to Japan in 1988, where he remained until 2016, living with his wife Yoshiko in the historic city of Kamakura, a little to the south of Yokohama. He and Yoshiko have now moved to Lichfield, a small cathedral city in the Midlands of the U.K., the birthplace of Samuel Johnson, and one-time home of Erasmus Darwin. In the past, he has worked in the technology and financial services industries, which have provided him with material for some of his books set in the 21st century. He currently works as a writer: Novelist, freelance editor, and copywriter, (his work for large Japanese corporations has appeared in international business journals), and journalist, as well as producing industry reports on various aspects of the financial services industry. Recently, however, his lifelong interest in Sherlock Holmes has developed into an acclaimed series of adventures featuring the world's most famous detective, written in the style of the originals, and published by Inknbeans Press. In addition to these, he has also published historical and alternate historical novels, short stories, and thrillers. Together with artist Andy Boerger, he has produced the *Sherlock Ferret* series of stories for children, featuring the world's cutest detective.

S.F. Bennett has, at various times, been an actor, a lecturer, a journalist, a historian, an author and a potter. Whilst some of those things still apply, she has always been an avid collector, concentrating mainly on ephemera and other related items concerning Sherlock Holmes and British science-fiction of the 1970's. To date, she has written articles on aspects of The Canon for *The Baker Street Journal*, *The Sherlock Holmes Journal*, and *The Torr*, the journal of *The Sherlock Holmes Society of the West Country*. When not collecting, she can be found writing science-fiction and mystery stories, and has contributed to several anthologies of new Sherlock Holmes pastiches. Her first novel was *The Secret Diary of Mycroft Holmes: The Thoughts and Reminiscences of Sherlock Holmes's Elder Brother, 1880-1888* (2017). She is also the author of *A Study In Postcards: Sherlock Holmes in the Golden Age of the Picture Postcard* (*Sherlock Holmes Society of London*, 2019).

Thomas A. Burns, Jr. is the author of the *Natalie McMasters Mysteries*. He was born and grew up in New Jersey, attended Xavier High School in Manhattan, earned B.S degrees in Zoology and Microbiology at Michigan State University, and a M.S. in Microbiology at North Carolina State University. He currently resides in Wendell, North Carolina. As a kid, Tom started reading mysteries with The Hardy Boys, Ken Holt and Rick Brant, and graduated to the classic stories by authors such as A. Conan Doyle, Dorothy Sayers, John Dickson Carr, Erle Stanley Gardner, and Rex Stout, to name a few. Tom has written fiction as a hobby all of his life, starting with The Man from U.N.C.L.E. stories in marble-backed copybooks in grade school. He built a career as technical, science, and medical writer and editor for nearly thirty years in industry and government. Now that he's truly on his own as a novelist, he's excited to publish his own mystery series, as well as to contribute stories about his second-most-favorite detective, Sherlock Holmes, to *The MX anthology of New Sherlock Holmes Stories*.

Nick Cardillo has been a devotee of Sherlock Holmes since the age of six. His first published short story, "The Adventure of the Traveling Corpse" appeared in *The MX Book of New Sherlock Holmes Stories – Part VI: 2017 Annual*, and he has written subsequent stories for both MX Publishing and Belanger Books. In 2018, Nick completed his first anthology of new Sherlock Holmes adventures entitled *The Feats of Sherlock Holmes*. Nick is a fan of The Golden Age of Detective Fiction, Hammer Horror, and Doctor Who. He writes film reviews and analyses at *Sacred-Celluloid.blogspot.com*. He is a student at Susquehanna University in Selinsgrove, PA.

Chris Chan is a writer, educator, and historian. He works as a researcher and "International Goodwill Ambassador" for Agatha Christie Ltd. His true crime articles, reviews, and short fiction have appeared (or will soon appear) in *The Strand*, *The Wisconsin Magazine of History*, *Mystery Weekly*, *Gilbert!*, *Nerd HQ*, Akashic Books' *Mondays are Murder* web series, *The Baker Street Journal*, and *Sherlock Holmes Mystery Magazine*.

Bert Coules BSI wandered through a succession of jobs from fringe opera company manager to BBC radio drama producer-director before becoming a full-time writer at the beginning of 1989. Bert works in a wide range of genres, including science fiction, horror, comedy, romance and action-adventure but he is especially associated with crime and detective stories: he was the head writer on the BBC's unique project to dramatise the entire Sherlock Holmes canon, and went on to script four further series of original Holmes and Watson mysteries. As well as radio, he also writes for TV and the stage.

Harry DeMaio is a *nom de plume* of Harry B. DeMaio, successful author of several books on Information Security and Business Networks, as well as the ten-volume *Casebooks of Octavius Bear – Alternative Universe Mysteries for Adult Animal Lovers*. Octavius Bear is loosely based on Sherlock Holmes and Nero Wolfe in a world in which *homo sapiens* died out long ago in a global disaster, but most animals have advanced to a twenty-first century anthropomorphic state. "It's Time" is Harry's first offering treating Holmes and Watson in their original human condition. A retired business executive, consultant, information security specialist, former pilot, and graduate school adjunct professor, he whiles away his time traveling and writing preposterous articles and stories. He has appeared on many radio and TV shows and is an accomplished, frequent public speaker. Former New York City natives, he and his extremely patient and helpful wife, Virginia, and their Bichon Frisé, Woof, live in Cincinnati (and several other parallel universes.) They have two sons living in Scottsdale, Arizona and Cortlandt Manor, New York, both of whom are quite successful and quite normal – thus putting the lie to the theory that insanity is hereditary.

Anna Elliott is an author of historical fiction and fantasy. Her first series, the *Twilight of Avalon* trilogy, is a retelling of the Trystan & Isolde legend. She wrote her second series, *The Pride & Prejudice Chronicles*, chiefly to satisfy her own curiosity about what might have happened to Elizabeth Bennet, Mr. Darcy, and all the other wonderful cast of characters after the official end of Jane Austen's classic work. She enjoys stories about strong women and loves exploring the multitude of ways women can find their unique strengths. She was delighted to lend a hand with the Sherlock & Lucy series, and this story, firstly because she loves Sherlock Holmes as much as her father does, and second because it almost never happens that someone with a dilemma shouts, "Quick, we need an author of historical fiction!" Anna lives in Pennsylvania with her husband and their four children. Learn more about the Sherlock and Lucy series at *www.sherlockandlucy.com*

Matthew J. Elliott is the author of *Big Trouble in Mother Russia* (2016), the official sequel to the cult movie *Big Trouble in Little China*, *Lost in Time and Space: An Unofficial Guide to the Uncharted Journeys of Doctor Who* (2014), *Sherlock Holmes on the Air* (2012), *Sherlock Holmes in Pursuit* (2013), *The Immortals: An Unauthorized Guide to* Sherlock *and* Elementary (2013), and *The Throne Eternal* (2014). His articles, fiction, and reviews have appeared in the magazines *Scarlet Street, Total DVD, SHERLOCK*, and *Sherlock Holmes Mystery Magazine*, and the collections *The Game's Afoot, Curious Incidents 2, Gaslight Grimoire, The Mammoth Book of Best British Crime 8*, and *The MX Book of New Sherlock Holmes Stories – Part III: 1896-1929*. He has scripted over 260 radio plays, including episodes of *Doctor Who, The Further Adventures of Sherlock Holmes, The Twilight Zone, The New Adventures of Mickey Spillane's Mike Hammer, Fangoria's Dreadtime Stories*, and award-winning adaptations of *The Hound of the Baskervilles* and *The War of the Worlds*. He is the only radio dramatist to adapt all sixty original stories from The Canon for the series *The Classic Adventures of Sherlock Holmes*. Matthew is a writer and performer on *RiffTrax.com*, the online comedy experience from the creators of cult sci-fi TV series *Mystery Science Theater 3000* (*MST3K* to the initiated). He's also written a few comic books.

Paul D. Gilbert was born in 1954 and has lived in and around London all of his life. He has been married to Jackie for thirty-nine years, and she is a Holmes expert who keeps him on the straight and narrow! He has two sons, one of whom now lives in Spain. His interests include literature, ancient history, all religions, most sports, and movies. He is currently employed full-time as a funeral director. His books so far include *The Lost Files of Sherlock Holmes* (2007), *The Chronicles of Sherlock Holmes* (2008), *Sherlock Holmes and the Giant Rat of Sumatra* (2010), *The Annals of Sherlock Holmes* (2012), *Sherlock Holmes and the Unholy Trinity* (2015), *Sherlock Holmes: The Four Handed Game* (2017), and *The Illumination of Sherlock Holmes*, to be published 2019.

Dick Gillman is an English writer and acrylic artist living in Brittany, France with his wife Alex, Truffle, their Black Labrador, and Jean-Claude, their Breton cat. During his retirement from teaching, he has written over twenty Sherlock Holmes short stories which are published as both e-books and paperbacks. His contribution to the superb MX Sherlock Holmes collection, published in October 2015, was entitled "The Man on Westminster Bridge" and had the privilege of being chosen as the anchor story in *The MX Book of New Sherlock Holmes Stories – Part II (1890-1895)*.

Arthur Hall also has stories in the companion volumes, Parts XVII and XVIII.

Stephen Herczeg is an IT Geek, writer, actor, and film-maker based in Canberra Australia. He has been writing for over twenty years and has completed a couple of dodgy novels, sixteen feature length screenplays, and numerous short stories and scripts. Stephen was very successful in 2017's International Horror Hotel screenplay competition, with his scripts *TITAN* winning the Sci-Fi category and *Dark are the Woods* placing second in the horror category. His work has featured in *Sproutlings – A Compendium of Little Fictions* from Hunter Anthologies, the *Hells Bells* Christmas horror anthology published by the Australasian Horror Writers Association, and the *Below the Stairs, Trickster's Treats, Shades of Santa, Behind the Mask*, and *Beyond the Infinite* anthologies from *OzHorror.Con, The Body Horror Book, Anemone Enemy*, and *Petrified Punks* from Oscillate Wildly Press, and *Sherlock Holmes In the Realms of H.G. Wells* and *Sherlock Holmes: Adventures Beyond the Canon* from Belanger Books.

Paul Hiscock is an author of crime, fantasy, and science fiction tales. His short stories have appeared in several anthologies and include a seventeenth century whodunnit, a science fiction western, and a steampunk Sherlock Holmes story. Paul lives with his family in Kent, England, and spends his days chasing a toddler with more energy than the Duracell Bunny. He mainly does his writing in coffee shops with members of the local NaNoWriMo group, or in the middle of the night when his family has gone to sleep. Consequently, his stories tend to be fuelled by large amounts of black coffee. You can find out more about his writing at *www.detectivesanddragons.uk.*

Christopher James was born in 1975 in Paisley, Scotland. Educated at Newcastle and UEA, he was a winner of the UK's National Poetry Competition in 2008. He has written two full length Sherlock Holmes novels, *The Adventure of the Ruby Elephant* and *The Jeweller of Florence*, both published by MX, and is working on a third.

In the year 1998, **Craig Janacek** took his degree of Doctor of Medicine at Vanderbilt University, and proceeded to Stanford to go through the training prescribed for pediatricians in practice. Having completed his studies there, he was duly attached to the University of California, San Francisco as Associate Professor. The author of over seventy medical monographs upon a variety of obscure lesions, his travel-worn and battered tin dispatch-box is crammed with papers, nearly all of which are records of his fictional works. To date, these have been published solely in electronic format, including two non-Holmes novels (*The Oxford Deception* and *The Anger of Achilles Peterson*), the trio of holiday adventures collected as *The Midwinter Mysteries of Sherlock Holmes*, the Holmes story collections *The First of Criminals*, *The Assassination of Sherlock Holmes*, *The Treasury of Sherlock Holmes*, *The Schoolroom of Sorrow*, *An East Wind*, and the Watsonian novels *The Isle of Devils* and *The Gate of Gold*. Craig Janacek is a *nom de plume*.

Kelvin I. Jones also has a story in the companion volume Part XVIII.

Steven Philip Jones has written over sixty graphic novels and comic books including the horror series *Lovecraftian, Curious Cases of Sherlock Holmes*, the original series *Nightlinger, Street Heroes 2005*, adaptations of *Dracula*, several H. P. Lovecraft stories, and the 1985 film *Re-animator*. Steven is also the author of several novels and nonfiction books including *The Clive Cussler Adventures: A Critical Review, Comics Writing: Communicating With Comic Book* , *King of Harlem, Bushwackers, The House With the Witch's Hat, Talisman: The Knightmare Knife*, and *Henrietta Hex: Shadows From the Past.* Steven's other writing credits include a number of scripts for radio dramas that have been broadcast internationally. A graduate of the University of Iowa, Steven has a Bachelor of Arts in Journalism and Religion, and was accepted into Iowa's Writer's Workshop - M.F.A. program.

Michael Mallory is the Derringer-winning author of the "Amelia Watson" (The Second Mrs. Watson) series and "Dave Beauchamp" mystery series, and more than one-hundred-twenty-five short stories. An entertainment journalist by day, he has written eight nonfiction books on pop culture and more than six-hundred newspaper and magazine articles. Based in Los Angeles, Mike is also an occasional actor on television.

David Marcum also has stories in the companion volumes, Parts XVII and XVIII.

Will Murray is the author of over seventy novels, including forty *Destroyer* novels and seven posthumous *Doc Savage* collaborations with Lester Dent, under the name Kenneth

Robeson, for Bantam Books in the 1990's. Since 2011, he has written fourteen additional Doc Savage adventures for Altus Press, two of which co-starred The Shadow, as well as a solo Pat Savage novel. His 2015 Tarzan novel, *Return to Pal-Ul-Don*, was followed by *King Kong vs. Tarzan* in 2016. Murray has written short stories featuring such classic characters as Batman, Superman, Wonder Woman, Spider-Man, Ant-Man, the Hulk, Honey West, the Spider, the Avenger, the Green Hornet, the Phantom, and Cthulhu. A previous Murray Sherlock Holmes story appeared in Moonstone's *Sherlock Holmes: The Crossovers Casebook*, and another is forthcoming in *Sherlock Holmes and Doctor Was Not*, involving H. P. Lovecraft's Dr. Herbert West. Additionally, a number of his Sherlock Holmes stories have appeared in various volumes of *The MX Book of New Sherlock Holmes Stories*.

Tracy J. Revels also has stories in the companion volumes, Parts XVII and XVIII

Roger Riccard of Los Angeles, California, U.S.A., is a descendant of the Roses of Kilravock in Highland Scotland. He is the author of two previous Sherlock Holmes novels, *The Case of the Poisoned Lilly* and *The Case of the Twain Papers*, a series of short stories in two volumes, *Sherlock Holmes: Adventures for the Twelve Days of Christmas* and *Further Adventures for the Twelve Days of Christmas*, and the new series *A Sherlock Holmes Alphabet of Cases*, all of which are published by Baker Street Studios. He has another novel and a non-fiction Holmes reference work in various stages of completion. He became a Sherlock Holmes enthusiast as a teenager (many, many years ago), and, like all fans of The Great Detective, yearned for more stories after reading The Canon over and over. It was the Granada Television performances of Jeremy Brett and Edward Hardwicke, and the encouragement of his wife, Rosilyn, that at last inspired him to write his own Holmes adventures, using the Granada actor portrayals as his guide. He has been called *"The best pastiche writer since Val Andrews"* by the *Sherlockian E-Times*.

Jane Rubino is the author of A Jersey Shore mystery series, featuring a Jane Austen-loving amateur sleuth and a Sherlock Holmes-quoting detective; *Knight Errant, Lady Vernon and Her Daughter*, (a novel-length adaptation of Jane Austen's novella *Lady Susan*, co-authored with her daughter Caitlen Rubino-Bradway, *What Would Austen Do?*, also co-authored with her daughter, a short story in the anthology *Jane Austen Made Me Do It*, *The Rucastles' Pawn*, *The Copper Beeches from Violet Turner's POV*, and, of course, there's the Sherlockian novel in the drawer – who doesn't have one? Jane lives on a barrier island at the New Jersey shore.

Geri Schear is a novelist and short story writer. Her work has been published in literary journals in the U.S. and Ireland. Her first novel, *A Biased Judgement: The Diaries of Sherlock Holmes 1897* was released to critical acclaim in 2014. The sequel, *Sherlock Holmes and the Other Woman* was published in 2015, and *Return to Reichenbach* in 2016. She lives in Kells, Ireland.

Roger Silverwood was educated in Gloucestershire before National Service. He later worked in the toy trade and as a copywriter in an advertising agency. Roger went into business with his wife as an antiques dealer before retiring in 1997, and he now leads a fairly happy existence with his wife Mary in the town of Bromersley in South Yorkshire. The Yorkshire author excels in writing crime books and is known for his sensational series featuring the fictional Detective Michael Angel.

Robert V. Stapleton was born and brought up in Leeds, Yorkshire, England, and studied at Durham University. After working in various parts of the country as an Anglican parish priest, he is now retired and lives with his wife in North Yorkshire. As a member of his local writing group, he now has time to develop his other life as a writer of adventure stories. He has recently had a number of short stories published, and he is hoping to have a couple of completed novels published at some time in the future.

S. Subramanian is a retired professor of Economics from Chennai, India. Apart from a small book titled *Economic Offences: A Compendium of Crimes in Prose and Verse* (Oxford University Press Delhi, 2012), his Holmes pastiches are the only serious things he has written. His other work runs largely to whimsical stuff on fuzzy logic and social measurement, on which he writes with much precision and little understanding, being an economist. He is otherwise mainly harmless, as his wife and daughter might concede with a little persuasion.

Gareth Tilley is a writer whose works include several scripts for Imagination Theatre's *The Further Adventures of Sherlock Holmes*. One of these was included in *Imagination Theatre's Sherlock Holmes*, where the contributor royalties benefit the Stepping Stones School at Undershaw, one of Sir Arthur Conan Doyle's former homes.

Thomas A. (Tom) Turley has been "hooked on Holmes" since finishing *The Hound of the Baskervilles* at about the age of twelve. However, his interest in Sherlockian pastiches didn't take off until he wrote one. *Sherlock Holmes and the Adventure of the Tainted Canister* (2014) is available as an e-book and an audiobook from MX Publishing. It will also soon appear in *The Art of Sherlock Holmes – USA Edition 1*. In 2017, two of Tom's stories, "A Scandal in Serbia" and "A Ghost from Christmas Past" were published in Parts VI and VII of this anthology. "Ghost" was also included in *The Art of Sherlock Holmes – West Palm Beach Edition*. Meanwhile, Tom is finishing a collection of historical pastiches entitled *Sherlock Holmes and the Crowned Heads of Europe*. The first story, "Sherlock Holmes and the Case of the Dying Emperor" (2018) is available from MX Publishing as a separate e-book. Set in the brief reign of Emperor Frederick III (1888), it inaugurates Sherlock Holmes's espionage campaign against the German Empire, which ended only in August 1914 with "His Last Bow". When completed, *Sherlock Holmes and the Crowned Heads of Europe* will also include "A Scandal in Serbia" and two additional historical tales. Although he has a Ph.D. in British history, Tom spent most of his professional career as an archivist with the State of Alabama. He and his wife Paula (an aspiring science fiction novelist) live in Montgomery, Alabama. Interested readers may contact Tom through MX Publishing or his Goodreads author's page.

Charles Veley has loved Sherlock Holmes since boyhood. As a father, he read the entire Canon to his then-ten-year-old daughter at evening story time. Now, this very same daughter, grown up to become acclaimed historical novelist Anna Elliott, has worked with him to develop new adventures in the *Sherlock Holmes and Lucy James Mystery Series*. Charles is also a fan of Gilbert and Sullivan, and wrote *The Pirates of Finance*, a new musical in the G&S tradition that won an award at the New York Musical Theatre Festival in 2013. Other than the Sherlock and Lucy series, all of the books on his Amazon Author Page were written when he was a full-time author during the late Seventies and early Eighties. He currently works for United Technologies Corporation, where his main focus is on creating sustainability and value for the company's large real estate development projects. Learn more about the Sherlock and Lucy series at *www.sherlockandlucy.com*

Matthew White is an up-and-coming author from Richmond, Virginia in the USA. He has been a passionate devotee of Sherlock Holmes since childhood. He can be reached at *matthewwhite.writer@gmail.com.*

The MX Book of New Sherlock Holmes Stories
Edited by David Marcum
(MX Publishing, 2015-   )

"This is the finest volume of Sherlockian fiction I have ever read, and I have read, literally, thousands." – Philip K. Jones

"Beyond Impressive . . . This is a splendid venture for a great cause!
– Roger Johnson, Editor, *The Sherlock Holmes Journal,*
The Sherlock Holmes Society of London

Part I: 1881-1889
Part II: 1890-1895
Part III: 1896-1929
Part IV: 2016 Annual
Part V: Christmas Adventures
Part VI: 2017 Annual
Part VII: Eliminate the Impossible (1880-1891)
Part VIII – Eliminate the Impossible (1892-1905)
Part IX – 2018 Annual (1879-1895)
Part X – 2018 Annual (1896-1916)
Part XI – Some Untold Cases (1880-1891)
Part XII – Some Untold Cases (1894-1902)
Part XIII – 2019 Annual (1881-1890)
Part XIV – 2019 Annual (1891-1897)
Part XV – 2019 Annual (1898-1917)
Part XVI – Whatever Remains . . . Must be the Truth (1881-1890)
Part XVII – Whatever Remains . . . Must be the Truth (1891-1898)
Part XVIII – Whatever Remains . . . Must be the Truth (1898-1925)

In Preparation
Part XIX – 2020 Annual

. . . and more to come!

The MX Book of New Sherlock Holmes Stories
Edited by David Marcum
(MX Publishing, 2015-)

<u>*Publishers Weekly* says:</u>

Part VI: *The traditional pastiche is alive and well . . . .*

Part VII: *Sherlockians eager for faithful-to-the-canon plots
and characters will be delighted.*

Part VIII: *The imagination of the contributors in coming up with variations on the
volume's theme is matched by their ingenious resolutions.*

Part IX: *The 18 stories . . . will satisfy fans of Conan Doyle's originals. Sherlockians will
rejoice that more volumes are on the way.*

Part X: *. . . new Sherlock Holmes adventures of consistently high quality.*

Part XI: *. . . an essential volume for Sherlock Holmes fans.*

Part XII: *. . . continues to amaze with the number of high-quality pastiches . . .*

Part XIII: *. . . Amazingly, Marcum has found 22 superb pastiches . . . This is more catnip
for fans of stories faithful to Conan Doyle's original*

Part XIV: *. . . this standout anthology of 21 short stories written in the spirit of Conan
Doyle's originals.*

Part XV: *Stories pitting Sherlock Holmes against seemingly supernatural phenomena
highlight Marcum's 15th anthology of superior short pastiches.*

The MX Book of New Sherlock Holmes Stories
Edited by David Marcum
(MX Publishing, 2015-   )

MX Publishing

MX Publishing is the world's largest specialist Sherlock Holmes publisher, with several hundred titles and over a hundred authors creating the latest in Sherlock Holmes fiction and non-fiction.

www.mxpublishing.com